A Higher Standard

A NOVEL

E. F. DODD

For Pa, Granddaddy, and Daddy.

You set the standard and made sure I never settled for less.

chapter one

GIDEON

Wire fencing and wooden posts whipped past me in a blur. Clods of dirt flew up and broke apart against my face, thrown by the hooves of the deranged beast I was currently clinging to for dear life while it rocketed wildly across a field. This was *not* how this morning's land inspection was supposed to go. Why had I listened to the two idiots who'd insisted I view the property from horseback "to get a true feel for it?" I'd envisioned a serene walk-through and idyllic setting while I evaluated the suitability of the land for development. Instead, I was about to be murdered by a two-thousand-pound psycho with four toothpicks for legs. In addition to scrub grass and weeds, my life flashed before my eyes. All the places I'd never go, the things I'd never see, the women I'd yet to sleep with. It was a travesty that I would be taken from the earth in my prime—so young, so virile, so many more orgasms to give.

Suddenly, out of nowhere, a slender arm shot out and grabbed the reins of my marauding mustang. I squeezed my eyes shut as terror took over my body. A firm yet wholly feminine voice commanded, "Whoa!" And, miracle of miracles, the rampaging stallion listened. His thundering hoofbeats slowed incrementally until we'd come to a halt.

"You can open your eyes now, John Wayne," that same voice said, a heavy dollop of sarcasm oozing over the sides of its distinctly flat tone.

I did as I was told. My view of the grass and the skittish horse's stomping hoof confused me momentarily. That wasn't right. At least, it wouldn't have been if I'd been seated properly in the saddle holding the reins. It was, however, precisely the right scenery for a person who'd dropped the reins at the first sign of trouble, wrapped their arms around their steed's neck, and prayed for divine intervention to save them. It was a tad humiliating to learn I was the second kind of person.

Releasing my death grip on my equine tormentor, I pushed myself up and looked to my left to thank my savior, who'd seemingly dropped out of the sky into the pasture to ride to my rescue. Only, there was no one there. Instead of a person, there was a massive coal-black horse, standing there regarding me with contempt. The huge animal was saddled, but the rider was missing. I might have been terrified, but right before clamping my eyes shut, I'd *seen* a human arm. I'd *heard* a woman's voice. Had one of those dirt clods given me some type of brain injury? How could someone appear and disappear so quickly? Was I hallucinating the horse, the sound of her voice? But then why had my maniacal mount come to a stop? Before I could get all the way down the path to concussive head trauma, a woman walked in front of the giant horse.

In tattered jeans and a stained white tank top, she was more street urchin than savior. A filthy ballcap shielded the majority of her face. I watched her run a hand down the foamy neck of my less-than-gallant steed. While I wondered where she'd even come from, she cooed to him in a voice noticeably kinder than the one she'd used on me.

"It's okay, Monty. You're okay, boy." Her Southern accent sugared the words, and the horse responded in kind. He nickered, tossing his head and nuzzling against her.

Vaguely, I recalled being told his name and that he was "gentle as a lamb," which was a blatant lie, obviously. But how in the devil would she know what to call him? Intrigued, I was about to ask when she bent forward and picked up his front foot. Her ministrations caused his big body to shift and, I admit, I emitted a tiny but completely manly shriek. Monty sidestepped, making her drop his foot. She cursed a blue streak but in that same soft voice so as not to spook the horse any more than I already had.

Stepping into him, she pressed her small body against his neck, stroking his mane and making soothing noises. Her new position gave me a view straight down her tank top. Mesmerized, I watched a rivulet of sweat travel between the perfectly shaped valley of her . . .

"Hey, jackass!" Grubby fingers snapped in front of my face, interrupting my ogling of her cleavage. "Eyes up here."

I blinked then refocused on her face. Luminous green eyes glared out at me from beneath the sweat-stained brim of her hat. Several streaks of dirt marred her high cheekbones, and even the thin line her mouth was set in couldn't detract from the plump sensuality of her lips. Standing in front of me, covered in filth and mad as a hornet, was an undeniably attractive woman.

"I beg your pardon," I said, channeling my inner Cary Grant from the Saturdays spent watching AMC with my Nonna. I somehow dismounted without killing myself and extended a hand. "Gideon West, at your service."

She looked at my hand like it could give her leprosy. Her top lip pulled up into a sneer, displaying even white teeth. "What you are, Gideon West, is on my nerves and in my way." With that, she stormed over to her horse and swung easily into the saddle.

"Wait!" I called out, throwing up a hand.

Holding the reins in one hand, she leaned an elbow on the front of her saddle. "Yeah?" she asked, suspicion etched into her posture and dripping like molasses from that one word.

Feeling and likely looking idiotic with my hand raised, I lowered it and rubbed awkwardly at the back of my neck. "I, ah . . . well, that is . . . I didn't catch your name."

"You didn't catch it, Romeo, because I didn't throw it." Nodding to the four-legged death trap now grazing calmly to my right, she added, "Make sure you give him a good rubdown and check his fetlocks for swelling once you get back to the barn."

Given how sore my posterior was at that exact moment, a rubdown sounded great; however, I was less inclined to do the same for the lunatic animal who'd tried to kill me. Plus, I had no clue what a "fetlock" was. Before I could ask, she reined her horse around and cantered away.

Guffaws erupted behind me, and I glanced away from the retreating form of my reluctant rescuer. Luke and Dale Collier, the two brothers tasked with giving me a tour of the hundred acres my development firm was evaluating for acquisition, strolled up beside me wearing matching shit-eating grins. It had been their brilliant idea to show me around on horseback, despite the fact there were multiple ATVs that would've done the job sans emasculation and attempted murder.

"I see you met Everest," Luke said with a chuckle.

"Everest?" I asked.

He nodded. "Yep, Everest Kennedy." Pointing to the fence line about fifty yards in front of us, he said, "That's her land over there. You buy this place—she'll be your neighbor."

A niggle of recognition jingled at the back of my mind.

"Kennedy?" A cold finger of dread scratched between my shoulder blades. "Any relation to the mayor?"

"I'd say so. He's her daddy," Dale supplied helpfully.

"Her father?" I asked, the scratch between by shoulder blades becoming a painful jab of concern.

He nodded. "Yep."

That monosyllabic explanation was a bucket of cold water rinsing away any contemplation of Everest and how well she filled out a tank top. Mayor Jackson Kennedy was the key to my development plan for the acreage upon which we were standing. Without his help to gain approval of what I had in store for the sleepy little burg of Mimosa, North Carolina, the project was dead in the water—a fact I had been thoroughly briefed on by my partners prior to departing Boston two days ago. I had assured them there would be no problems. Watching the retreating form of Everest Kennedy made me wonder whether I'd been a little hasty with my assurances.

chapter two

EVEREST

Sin's long strides devoured the terrain and gave me the distance I needed from whoever the hell Gideon West was. I didn't have to give the big horse much direction. He knew where we were headed: back to the gaping hole in the fence next to Leroy's utility vehicle. He and I had been repairing the damaged section when I'd seen Monty come flying by with reins dangling and some idiot flopping around on his back.

Leroy looked up at the sound of Sin's hoofbeats. "You get the damsel in distress sorted out?" Shading his eyes with a gloved hand, he looked up at me with laughter deepening the wrinkles at the corners of his dark eyes.

Looping Sin's reins around the back gate of the UTV, I shrugged and gave the horse a gentle pat. He nudged my shoulder in return, the affection a far cry from the skittish bag of bones he'd been on arrival as one of our first rescues. "Yeah, we rode to the rescue . . . and managed to put us further behind schedule. Yippee!" I took the snips from Leroy and faced the fence panel.

He took off his straw hat and mopped his dark brow with a bandana. Tucking it back into his pocket, he said, "You know, you have people on staff who can handle fence repair, Evie."

It was a mellow reminder that as the director of Second Chance Farms, I had other responsibilities that required my attention. Like reviewing the grant applications that were sitting on my desk or responding to the emails no doubt building up in my inbox. But, in all honesty, that was the part of the job I liked the least. I'd much rather be out here in the sunshine, sweating and *doing* something. Spending the day at my desk behind stacks of paperwork was about as appealing as the lame attempt Gideon West had made to check me out. Even when it was made with a downward sweep of his luxuriously long ebony lashes and in that crisp, decidedly posh accent. Nope, definitely still lame.

Shaking off thoughts of West and his chiseled jawline and broad shoulders, I answered Leroy. "Terry's off today, and Jackie's exercising the new babies that just came in," I said, looking at the panel rather than meeting his eyes. I measured off the extraneous pieces of wire so the panel would fit and not overlap.

He wasn't fooled by my excuses. One of the downsides of the fact he'd been with me from the beginning. "Uh-huh, and what about Jacob and Jordan?"

I scrambled for a legitimate excuse to not have them handle this repair. "They're . . . mucking out the barn." There, that was perfectly acceptable.

Leroy snorted. "They finished that about an hour or so before you and I came out here, but nice try."

"Leroy," I whined. "Just let me have this morning. I promise I'll be a good little worker bee in the office this afternoon." I held the snips to my head in a strange salute. "Scout's honor."

He adjusted the fence panel between two posts and shook his head. "You're the boss."

I gave him a peck on the cheek. "You really are the best, you know that?"

"Ah, now, quit that mess," he said with an embarrassed grin.

I positioned the snips at the edge of the panel and got to work. Once I'd gotten the edges of the wire trimmed down, Leroy held it while I prepared to hammer the brads home. Holding one metal "U" up to the wire, I drew the hammer back.

"So, who was that on Monty?" Leroy asked when I was mid-swing. The hammer slammed onto my thumb.

"Son of a bitch!" I said and shoved my thumb into my mouth, trying to lessen the pain radiating up my hand.

Leroy dropped the panel to the dirt and reached for my hand. "Good grief, Evie, you all right?"

Reluctantly I pulled my thumb from between my lips and let him examine it. It was red and throbbing, with a dark purple bruise already forming under the nail.

He whistled between his teeth. "You gave that one a good wallop, honey," he said, his brows dipping in concern.

Pulling my hand out of his grasp, I flexed my thumb back and forth. It cooperated, so it wasn't broken, but it was going to hurt like the dickens later that day.

"You need to put some ice on it," Leroy advised.

Shaking my hand out, I resisted. "Nah, it'll be fine. I'll deal with it once we get this hole patched."

"Evie," he chastised.

I picked up the hammer, determined to finish what we'd come out here to do. One task left unfinished would add to the pile of things on our already full plates. Taking the time to nursemaid a bruised thumb wasn't a luxury I could afford. "I promise, Leroy. First thing back at the barn, I'll put some ice on it. Now, the quicker you get that panel back up here, the quicker I'll get to the ice."

I managed to hit the brad and not my thumb when he reiterated his question. "Who was riding Monty?"

The sharp rap I gave the fastener was undeserved. "Some guy with the Collier brothers. They were riding up when I left."

"Some guy?" Leroy pressed.

I shrugged and hammered another brad into the wooden post. "Gideon something or other."

"Gideon West?"

Startled, I looked up at Leroy. "Yeah, how'd you know that?"

He looked worried, which made me worried, because Leroy was never, ever worried. Even when we'd barely had enough money for feed or the farrier's bill, he had the same placid tranquility day in and day out. That resolute demeanor gave him a way with even the most reticent of our rescues. Animals who'd survived unimaginable circumstances warmed quickly to his gentle voice, kind eyes, and easy manner. To see concern about something on his craggy face scared the crap out of me.

"I saw him at your daddy's office yesterday afternoon," he said.

I noted the intentionally vague quality of his answer, along with the way he'd glanced over my shoulder when he said it. The claws of worry sank deeper into my skin.

"Okay. . ." I said, drawing out the syllables and waiting for more.

Leroy rubbed the back of his neck and glanced away again. With a resigned sigh, he said, "He's a developer."

My heart clenched with fear. Reflexively, my fingers curled around the wire. There was only one reason some hoity-toity developer would be hanging around the Collier brothers after visiting my dad.

As one, Leroy and I glanced over at the hundred acres that bordered our property. The Colliers owned it and another tract roughly the same size on the other side of the far tree line. It was land I'd love to have in part for expansion and also to create a buffer zone on that side of the farm. But even though we'd made strides in the last few years, our operation was still lean. All the funding we managed to secure had to go to pay for the staff we had and the horses we helped. I didn't have any real reserves, especially not enough to acquire an additional hundred acres.

Given that the land had been in the Collier family for generations, I figured I had nothing to worry about. There'd been no scuttlebutt about them selling it, and I'd assumed if they were, Aunt Betsy would've told me. She, along with everyone else, knew about my long-term plans for expansion. Except now it seemed they were entertaining offers. I wondered why, as horrifying visions of shopping malls, crowded parking lots, and urban sprawl danced before my eyes.

"A developer," I said, tasting the bitterness of that word on my tongue. *I knew it.* First impressions are rarely wrong, and mine about Gideon had been spot-on. Not only did he feel entitled to eye-grope my boobs, he was also planning on helping himself to the property next door. My stomach roiled at the thought of it. I'd already planned so much for that property and now here he was swooping in to snatch it out from under me. Over my dead body.

"Now, Evie," Leroy said, reading my face, "don't go getting all twisted up about this. We don't know what's going on."

"Right," I agreed aloud, my tone flat. My mind was already spinning with possibilities, none of them good. I knew where I was going as soon as Leroy and I finished up, and it wasn't to sit behind my desk drafting grant proposals.

chapter three

GIDEON

How's small-town life treating you?" The booming voice of Jameson Standard, Jamie to his friends, echoed through the speakers of my rental car. Jamie was the namesake behind our firm, Standard Development.

"It's going well," I said as I navigated around a tractor hauling what had to be four tons of hay. "I met with the mayor yesterday afternoon, and I just finished a property tour." I purposely left out my near-death experience.

"How'd it go with the mayor?" Davidson Brooks, my other partner, chimed in.

I should've known they'd have me on speakerphone. Neither would want to hear anything secondhand, and I imagined them in the conference room of our office on Northern Avenue jockeying for position around the phone, both determined to elicit as much detail from me as possible. Tooling down the two-lane road in small-town North Carolina, passing barns and pastures, I might as well have been on another planet.

"It was fine," I answered.

"Just fine?" Davidson prodded. I could hear the frown in his voice. "We need more than fine, Gids. We need fantastic."

"He's right, brother," Jamie said, his voice serious. "We need him in our corner on this."

The "this" in question was the largest planned development we'd ever set into motion: roughly 450 acres in the small town of Mimosa, North Carolina, a suburb of Charlotte.

Mayor Jackson Kennedy was, according to the research assembled by our team, a hometown boy who'd made good. Born and raised in Mimosa, he'd returned after getting his degree in equine science and management and, just for shits and giggles, an MBA. He'd transformed his family's farm into one of the most successful quarter horse breeding and training programs in the Southeast. He wasn't just respected by his fellow Mimosans—he was downright revered.

"I'm well aware of what we need to get this deal to happen," I said, irritated by the reminder. "I was the one that found Mimosa, after all. *And* the one who agreed to be the one doing all the legwork down here for the next few months."

Neither of them had been clamoring to leave Boston and head south to the small yet charming town for weeks on end. I hadn't been eager to do it myself, although when I'd left behind spitting snow flurries and piles of gray slush only to deplane to temperatures in the sixties with blue skies and wispy white clouds, I began to think maybe I *hadn't* drawn the short straw.

Jamie's contrite exhale whistled through the car. "Sorry, man."

"That accent of yours throwing off the locals? And here I thought it'd work to our advantage," Davidson said, and I could hear his teasing grin.

"They find it perfectly charming, thank you very much," I said, putting an extra crispness in my voice.

Then I remembered the way Everest had snarled at me. So maybe charming was a stretch, but I was certain she'd come around. Most women did. *Something tells me she's not most women,* my gut forewarned, but I ignored it.

"Good to hear," Davidson said. "Seriously, though, how was the meeting with the mayor? And I want to hear more than 'fine.'"

I gave them the rundown of my first meeting with the man who held our future in the palm of his meaty hand. We'd gotten along well, and he'd seemed genuinely interested in our plans for his town. Especially the potential for a spike in property tax revenue that would allow him to implement some overdue improvements. He was, after all, a businessman who realized the importance of a healthy bottom line.

"Did you know he had a daughter?" I asked at the end of my spiel.

"A daughter?" Jamie repeated.

"Yes," I said. "Everest. She owns the property next door to the Colliers."

"To the east or west?" Davidson asked sharply.

"Er . . ." I thought a moment. "The west, I believe. Why?"

"Oh fuck," Jamie said, storm clouds in his tone.

"Oh fuck is right," Davidson said, echoing Jamie's desolation.

My mind raced to understand what the issue was. "Why is that a problem?"

"Remember that horse rescue, Second Choice Farms or whatever?" Davidson asked.

"Second Chance Farms," I corrected. We'd learned of the operation and its home in Mimosa in our initial research. I thought it could be a helpful draw to our development, given the current view of the American public on rescuing abused animals. "What about it?"

"It owns the land to the west of the Colliers," Jamie informed me.

"Okay, so what's the problem?" I asked, still failing to grasp whatever had gotten them so anxious.

"So we've been doing some research into the neighborhood, trying to get a better lay of the land. Guess what happened to the last person who tried to develop property around that place?" Davidson asked.

My stomach cramped into a tight ball of foreboding. "What?"

"It didn't get past the first zoning hearing, man," Jamie said.

"Because?" I asked, already knowing the answer.

"Because Everest Kennedy torpedoed it right out of the water," Davidson said. "That chick is anti-development in general but especially on the property around hers. She doesn't want it used for anything other than holding the earth together."

"How did we not know this before now?" I asked, heat creeping up my neck. I couldn't afford to have Everest view me, or my company, as some kind of Armageddon to her chosen way of life.

"Because the land itself is owned by an LLC—EAK, LLC. Property records don't show the direct affiliation between EAK and Second Chance," Davidson explained, and I heard the creak of his chair as he slumped back into it. "Until you went down there for a site inspection, we didn't know that place was right next door."

"Okay," I said, keeping a tight hold on my temper before it exploded. "Why didn't we know she was the daughter of the mayor?"

"First of all," Jamie said, his own temper flaring, "every third person down there has the last name Kennedy. It's like Smith or Jones anywhere else. And second of all, her dad wasn't the mayor when the last developer came to town, so there was no mention of their relationship."

"He's the biggest business in town," I protested. "How could there not be any mention of it?"

"How the fuck am I supposed to know the answer to that?" Jamie bellowed.

"Let's focus on what we do know and not on casting blame here, okay?" Davidson, ever the mediator, insisted.

I relaxed my hands on the steering wheel, inhaling and exhaling in the slow rhythm I'd learned in yoga. This wasn't going to be a problem. I'd worked too hard and too long to get this project from its infancy to the doorstep of fruition. There was a solution, and I'd find it.

Ahead on the right, I saw the small cottage I'd rented for the month. With its white clapboard sides and wide front porch framed by huge oak trees, it was quaint and picturesque—and a far cry from my sleekly modern and fully automated high-rise condo back home. But it did have two bedrooms, which allowed me to have an office here in town and space for Davidson and Jamie to crash when they flew down.

Turning into the gravel driveway, I asked, "What was it?"

"What was what?" Davidson asked.

"The development," I clarified. "What was the development she didn't want?"

Papers rustled in the background, and I could picture the two of them sorting through files on our large glass conference table.

Jamie spoke first. "It was an industrial park." I could hear the relief in his voice.

"Okay," I said, energized by that bit of news. "That's good. We're obviously doing something completely different. Something that's going to be great for her hometown and that has zero chance of spewing toxic chemicals or creating noise pollution."

"You need to get her on board with this," Davidson said, and I mouthed "duh" at the speakers. "Before she catches wind of anything and bends her dad's ear with the wrong information."

I disconnected my phone from the rental car and jogged up the few steps to my front door. "Well, I met her today, so it shouldn't be too hard to . . ."

Jamie interrupted me. "Wait, you've already met this girl?"

"Yeah, didn't I mention that?" I pushed open the front door and dropped my keys on the small table in the foyer.

"No," Davidson said. His suspicion hung in the air, then he added, "You left that part out."

"Huh," I said, enjoying getting them riled up. I plucked a beer from the fridge and twisted off the cap. I figured I was due after almost being trampled to death.

"What aren't you telling us?" Jamie asked.

That she'd looked at me with undisguised scorn if not outright hostility a few hours ago. The memory of the way her lip curled right before she'd ridden off like some Old West hero almost made me laugh.

Clearing my throat, I lied through my teeth. "Nothing. I met her during the property tour this morning. That's it."

The silence on the line stretched long, which let me know they knew there was more I wasn't saying. Finally, Jamie said, "She's a goddamn smokeshow, isn't she?"

"You're the ones with all the research on her," I deflected.

And no, I didn't think either of my friends would categorize the surly, denim-clad woman I'd met earlier as a smokeshow. She was undeniably attractive, but sullen and grouchy weren't character traits that would have Jamie or Davidson anxious to spend more time in her company. Add to that fact that in the world I lived in, most women wore jeans ripped by designers, not manual labor. The only mud on their faces cost $450 a swipe and was applied by some Swedish woman with a jade roller at a five-star spa. Everest was most definitely *not* someone who was usually on my sexual radar. And yet . . . there was something . . . *intriguing* about her. Beyond the moss green of her eyes and curves those filthy jeans couldn't disguise.

"There's no pictures of her in there, asshole. And don't think I missed you dodging the question," Davidson said, butting into my thoughts.

"Jamie's right, isn't he?" I heard his muttered curse and knew it was followed by both hands shoving through his dark hair then immediately smoothing out the mess. Even frustrated, Davidson was fastidious.

Before he could actually pull his hair out, I said, "She's very . . ." I groped for a word that would satisfy rather than enhance their curiosity. I settled on, "Interesting."

"Interesting?" Davidson repeated, his skepticism coming through loud and clear.

I took several swallows of beer and decided that was the best word to describe Everest at the moment. "Yeah, interesting."

"That better not mean that your dick is interested in this girl, Gids," Jamie threatened, his voice loud and close to the phone. He wasn't yelling—yet. "We've got too much on the line for you to risk it all on some toss-away fling while you're down there. Do not piss off the mayor by trying something with his daughter. This deal is too important."

I bristled at the insinuation I'd let my libido get in the way of business. "You think I don't know that?" I asked, heat searing the words. "I'm down here to get the deal, not hookup with some local."

No matter *how* good her ass looked in those jeans.

Davidson remained unconvinced. "Keep your eyes on the prize and your dick in your pants, Gids. Do. Not. Fuck. This. Up."

I shoved down my anger, knowing if I got pissed, it would just add fuel to the fire. "Oh, ye of little faith," I said lightly. "I've got everything under control."

chapter four

EVEREST

The screen door creaked in protest when I opened it to knock on Betsy Collier's back door. I ran a nervous hand down my ponytail, smoothing out the tangles as best I could. Through the small panes of glass set in the wood, I could see Betsy walking toward me. I gave a little wave, and she was smiling when she opened the door.

"Everest, what a nice surprise," she said and stood back. "C'mon in."

"Hey, Aunt Betsy. Thanks," I said, wiping my boots on the welcome mat and walking past her into the living room. "Sorry to come by without calling," I said.

Betsy waved off my apology. "Since when has my honorary niece needed to call before stopping by?" She headed further into her house. "I just made a fresh thing of tea. Would you like any?"

Stepping inside, I felt the familiar squeeze of my heart that happened every time I'd come over since Mama passed away. The ache had dulled, but it was still there. Being in her best friend's house without her was hard, but I swallowed down the memories and pushed my lips into a smile.

"Uh, sure, thanks," I said, now wishing I'd planned a little better before charging over here. My thumb throbbed under the gauze Leroy had insisted on, and I rubbed it absently.

Betsy reappeared in the living room with two tall glasses of iced tea. She nodded at the sofa. "Please, have a seat." She settled in the armchair next to the couch.

I accepted a glass from her and did as I was told, sinking down into the floral cushion. After taking a sip, I set my glass on a coaster. "Betsy, I wanted to talk to you about—"

"Let me guess," she interrupted, a knowing twinkle in her bright blue eyes. "You're here to pepper me with questions about Gideon West."

I gaped dumbly at her for a second then recovered. "Well, yeah, but how did you—"

Her smile widened and she shook her head. "You know Luke and Dale gossip more than any woman in town. They couldn't wait to get back here and tell me how you rode to the rescue this morning. I cannot imagine what got into Monty to take off like that."

Worry had my chest tightening, and I resisted the need to rub my sternum. I needed to steer the conversation away from his lack of horsemanship and over into what the hell they were thinking in selling to him. "Right, well, it is hard to fathom. But, Betsy, I'm more interested in why Luke and Dale were showing him around in the first place. I hadn't heard you all were even thinking about selling."

The light in her eyes dimmed a little, and her smile faltered. "Well, we weren't until recently."

I scooted forward, resting my elbows on my knees. "What changed?"

She touched her hair, tucking a few wayward strands of her bob behind her ears. "You know this land has been in our family since . . . well, it seems like since forever. And we all just assumed it always would be. But then . . . we got a letter from Standard Development." Betsy rose and walked behind her chair to an old sideboard. Pulling open the center drawer, she retrieved an envelope and handed it to me.

Worry morphed to dread when I saw the gold "S" emblem and Boston address in the top left corner. I took it and slid out the letter, unfolding it to read. When I got to the price per acre, my eyeballs resembled a *Tom & Jerry* episode, bugging to the point they may have actually touched the paper. I glanced over at Betsy, and she nodded with a small lift of her shoulders.

"There was no way we weren't going to at least *listen* to what they had to say if that was the number they tossed out before they'd even been down here."

My throat was tight, and I forced a swallow. "Right, but . . ."

Betsy shook her head. "Believe me, I know, Everest. It's hard to think about selling land that's been owned by a Collier since the memory of man runneth not to the contrary. But that amount of money . . ." She paused and ran a finger along the piping of the arm of her chair, looking down at her lap. With a sigh, she brought her eyes back to mine. "That amount of money can take care of not just Luke and Dale but their kids. And, if they manage it right, their kids' kids. My holding on the past shouldn't hurt my children's futures, Everest."

How could I argue with that? She was right, of course, and I couldn't blame her for thinking about her family's future. I swallowed roughly, choking down my vision for the property and doing my best not to begrudge their windfall. "Absolutely, Betsy. I completely understand your thinking."

Her face softened, and she reached out to squeeze my knee. "I know you want that land for your farm, Evie. I'd much rather sell it to you than Standard, but . . ."

Betsy didn't need to finish the sentence, because I knew what followed the "but." Second Chance Farms was a fledgling operation, in existence a mere five years and dependent upon donations to stay afloat. To say we lacked the funds to compete with the price Standard was offering might have been the understatement of the century. Even absent their offer, I'd been years away from being able to come up with less than half of what the Colliers would receive if this sale went through. I couldn't blame them for being wooed by that many zeroes.

I patted her hand and leaned back against the sofa cushions. "I know that," I said, trying to erase the guilty shadows in her normally bright eyes. "And I really do understand. I promise."

Betsy smiled a little wider. "And who knows? Maybe they'll change their minds and look elsewhere."

"Maybe," I said, without much conviction. She and I both knew that was a pipe dream. The Collier land was pristine and untouched—rolling hills interspersed with swaths of hardwoods. It was a developer's dream parcel, so the idea that Standard might just walk away from it was laughable.

"You know," she said, a sly grin on her face. "You do know someone who could give you the inside scoop on all this. I have it on pretty good authority that he's rather fond of you too."

For a split second, Gideon's face popped in my head. I bobbled my glass of tea and looked over at Betsy.

She looked at me curiously. "Your daddy hasn't resigned from his position as mayor in the last twenty-four hours, has he?"

"Right, my dad," I said, just a tad too loudly. Clearing my throat, I went on in a normal voice, "No, he's still the man of the people, just like always."

Thankfully, Betsy let my weirdness go without comment. "If I were you, I'd pop over and ask him about it."

Guilt-laden hope took flight with her advice. This was a huge opportunity for the Colliers, and I was a grade A jackass for hoping it fell through. But maybe . . . maybe there could be something worked out where we'd all benefit. If anyone would have an idea how to make that happen, it would be my dad.

"Everest," chirped Miss Angeline, my dad's secretary, "how lovely to see you. I didn't know you were coming by today."

"Spur-of-the-moment decision," I said, dropping a kiss to her cheek. "Is he in?"

"He is, honey. Go on in," she said and returned to the document on her screen. She'd been my dad's secretary since he'd come back to town thirty years ago. He claimed he couldn't run Kennedy Acres without her. I'd yet to hear her deny it.

Pushing open the door to his office, I took a second to study the man himself before he knew I was there. At sixty-two, Jackson Kennedy remained a handsome man. His dark hair was peppered with silvery strands, and his green eyes were surrounded by the lines of a life well lived. Broad-shouldered, with the hands of a working man, he'd never looked entirely comfortable behind a desk. He'd much rather be out with his horses, checking the fences or talking to his barn manager about the latest crop of yearlings. He was a man made for open spaces and blue skies. My unwillingness to let my butt grow more accustomed to an office chair than a saddle was hereditary.

Today, he was scanning through a thick binder, reading glasses perched on the tip of his nose. He frowned at something and penciled a note in the margin, muttering to himself.

"Hey, Daddy," I said, and his head popped up.

Putting aside whatever he'd been reading, he pushed himself out of his chair and came around the desk, arms wide and eyes smiling. "Hey, there, sweetheart. What brings you by to see your old man today?"

I hugged him, inhaling the familiar scent of wood shavings and Old Spice. I perched on the edge of his desk and pointed at the binder. "Whatcha reading?"

"Some preliminary studies on a project that's coming before the zoning board. Early-stage stuff," he said.

"Wouldn't have anything to do with the Colliers thinking about selling their land, would it?" I pried shamelessly.

He arched a brow and folded his arms, amusement warming his face. "And what would you know about that?"

"I saw Betsy earlier. She let me know about this outfit from Boston that's approached them about selling. Plus, I *may* have run into one of their . . . representatives with the Collier brothers this morning."

I leaned over to peek at the notebook. He nudged it out of view.

Dad took in my dusty jeans and worn boots. Before going to Betsy's, I'd changed my tank top into something that wasn't streaked with dirt and sweat but didn't waste time with the rest.

"From the looks of things," he said, "you rushed right over to ask me about it."

I held up my hands in a what-can-you-do gesture. "Couldn't help it. If something's going on with that property, I need to know about it so I can determine how it will impact Second Chance. That's no surprise to you."

He squeezed my arms briefly and sat back down, dropping his glasses onto his desk. "I know, Evie. But, before you get your hackles up, let me assure you this is not another industrial park." At the look on my face, he added, "Nor is it another debacle like they had up in Weaver, so don't even start with that."

The tension in my gut wound tighter. "How can you be so sure of that?"

"Because I'm not an idiot," he said calmly. "I think you know by now it's not so easy to pull the wool over my eyes. I'm not blinded by some glossy proposal and the promise of an increase in revenues. I've looked at their plans and think they've got some progressive ideas that will be good for our little town. We'll need to make some tweaks here and there, but on the whole, it's a solid presentation with none of the loopholes council experienced with that snake over in Weaver."

The vice around my lower intestine continued its compression as his look turned contemplative.

I knew that look. It was the same one he got when he was considering his run for mayor or which stud to use for the spring foaling season. That look told me he was giving serious consideration to whatever Gideon Fancy Pants West was planning.

My stomach felt like it was being pulled through a garbage disposal. Selfishly, I asked, "But will it be good for Second Chance too?"

"You do know that I have more than a single constituent to answer to, don't you?" he joked.

"Yeah, but you only have one daughter," I said and regretted the churlish comment when I saw the hurt on his face. "You know I didn't mean that," I said, resting a hand on his shoulder.

Dad's eyes softened, and he took my hand. "I know. I also recall mentioning to that only daughter about a year and a half ago that I'd be happy to provide funding for her to—"

I didn't let him finish. "You did, and I appreciated it then, just like now—although I could do without the 'I told you so' vibe. But you also know why I couldn't let you do that."

Getting started in the horse business as Jack Kennedy's little girl had been hard enough but would've been ten times worse if I'd taken the money he'd offered to help me expand the operation. I couldn't backtrack on that now. Second Chance was my responsibility, and even if Daddy could match the offer from Standard—which I doubted—I couldn't accept it. I'd worked too hard to be taken seriously, and I knew how folks would view my accepting help from my father.

His lips pulled down at the corners, and he glanced out his office window. Huffing out a breath, he ran a hand through his hair. "I know exactly why. Because you've got too much of your old man in your personality, and it means you're stubborn as a damn ox."

"Takes one to know one," I said, and he laughed, patting me on my knee.

"I guess so. I still haven't forgiven you for poaching Leroy from me."

I grinned. "Who wouldn't choose to be the barn manager at a struggling charity rescue over being named head trainer at Kennedy Acres? I mean, c'mon. Who needs a steady, reliable paycheck when you can be stressed over how the farrier bill will be paid each month? The perks are truly endless."

The truth of it was, Leroy had been a godsend. His experience and patience had gotten us through our infancy and given our fledgling operation some gravitas I wouldn't have been able to provide at age thirty-one. Having Leroy as second-in-command gave credence to my abilities as executive director. His faith in me meant something to people in the horse world and helped push me out of the broad shadow of Kennedy Acres.

Daddy's eyes narrowed. "Things that tight these days?"

I rolled my eyes and hopped off his desk. "How many different ways do I need to say 'no thank you' before you understand I'm not taking your money? It's a rescue, Dad. Fully dependent on donations, so yeah, we aren't exactly flush with cash. But we're *fine*."

"If you need donations, why can't I make one?" His expression had turned downright mulish.

I kept my voice level but firm. "Donations are perfectly fine, Daddy. Hop on our website and sponsor one of the new foals that came in. Or, better yet, go ahead and get your tickets for the July Jubilee. You and I both know, though, that what you're talking about isn't a donation. It's a handout to your daughter, and that's not going to work. *Ever*."

His sigh could've pushed sailboats to the South of France. "Fine, fine," he relented. With a wry shake of his head, he smiled up at me. "You know how proud I am of you, right? Even when you're being a stubborn pain in my ass?"

"I'll take that for the compliment it was intended to be," I said, warmed by his praise. "Thanks, Dad."

His eyes softened, and he took my hand in his. "Your passion for what you do reminds me so much of your mother."

I swallowed past the lump in my throat and squeezed his palm. "She was a force, that's for sure."

"Even the cancer couldn't dim that," he agreed.

When she got sick my junior year of high school, it had knocked both our worlds out of orbit. A little over a year later, I lost my mom, and he lost the love of his life, different pains but equally devastating. It had taken both of us years to come to grips with her death. Even after all this time, there were still days when I expected to walk into his office and find her there on a midmorning visit. Moira Kennedy had been a once-in-a-lifetime woman, and her absence left a hole in the lives of all those who'd known her.

Once it was clear the prognosis wasn't good, she'd left strict instructions that there was to be a party after the funeral and that anyone who felt they would cry for any longer than five minutes should please excuse themselves so as not to dampen the mood. Stories and sharing memories were encouraged but only if they brought a laugh instead of tears. Moira had picked the venue, organized the menu, and managed every detail with a party planner.

"I'm sorry," the planner had asked at the initial meeting. "You want me to plan your *what?*"

"My wake," Moira said, thoroughly unbothered by the woman's eyebrows shooting up to her hairline. "One of the only perks I've found about being diagnosed with terminal cancer," her mother continued, "is that it gives me the time to plan one last shindig before I go."

"Mama!" I said, shifting with embarrassment.

Moira arched a brow. "What?"

"You're not supposed to joke about . . . you know."

"What? Cancer? It's not a swear word, Evie. You can say it out loud in public. And who said anything about joking? I'm perfectly serious. Thus far, other than the extremely cute nurse at the oncology clinic, getting to plan my exit is the only good thing I've discovered about this whole experience." Moira glanced across the planner's desk and lowered her voice. "Honestly," she deadpanned, "I give cancer a one-star review. Absolutely *do not* recommend."

As with everything else, Moira Kennedy got her way . . . and her party.

The desk phone bleated, drawing both of us from our memories, and Miss Angeline's voice filled the silence, "Jack? I've got a Gideon West out here to see you. He doesn't have an appointment. Should I send him back?"

My gaze whipped from the phone to my dad and then back, as though it were a coiled rattler. My feet twitched in my boots, and for a second, I contemplated ducking out the back door. Only . . . there wasn't one. "What's he doing here?"

Entertained by my overreaction, my dad chuckled. "You heard Angeline. He doesn't have an appointment, so I'm not sure why he's dropped by." He paged Angeline back. "That's fine. Send him on in."

I sidestepped around the desk to face the door when it opened, ignoring my sweaty palms and praying the angry heat climbing up my chest didn't show in bright splotches.

In pressed dark slacks and a starched button up with no tie, Gideon West was the epitome of the consummate, casual professional. Unlike my own scuffed footwear, I could see my reflection in the shine of his shoes. His dark brown hair was still damp from a shower, curling slightly at his temples. Polished perfection, in stark contrast to my dingy denim. He held several cardboard tubes under his arm and wore a dazzlingly white smile.

"Mr. Mayor," he said cheerily as he entered the room.

His accent tickled my ears and coasted down my spine in a cultured caress. I willed my ovaries to go completely deaf and not be tantalized by the lyrical quality of his voice. Now was *not* the time for my lady parts to go rogue.

"I hope you don't mind my . . ." He trailed off, and his smile faltered when he spotted me glowering by the window. "Oh, I'm sorry. I didn't know you were already with someone. I can come back . . ."

Dad waved away his concern. "No need for that, Mr. West."

"Gideon, please," West entreated, upping the wattage on his smile back to blinding.

"All right, Gideon," my dad acquiesced. "This is my daughter, Everest." His gaze implored me to be civil, and since he was my dad *and* the mayor, I'd do my best.

Placing his bundles in the guest chair across from the desk, Gideon turned to me. "We met earlier today. However, I didn't get the pleasure of your name, Ms. Kennedy." His voice was so smooth and refined, I could see how he could charm his way around anything. Or at least try. The soles of his shoes clacked against the wood floor as he walked over to me. Extending a hand, he said, "Gideon West."

I took it grudgingly, but when his fingers closed around my hand, a warm tingle zinged up my arm. His palm was soft and broad and his grip firm. Up close, his eyes were almost indigo, dotted with flecks of navy. Little crinkles formed at their corners when he smiled.

No! Resist! Resist the enemy at all costs! Shields up! Battle stations! With my hand in his, I said, "Everest Kennedy."

"What can I do for you, Gideon?" My dad's voice broke in, and I jerked my hand back.

Gideon's eyes stayed on me for a moment, then he turned away. "I wanted to drop off some larger renderings for your review, Mayor," he said. Spying the thick tome on the desk, he added, "The same drawings are in that proposal, but I wanted you to have some full-sized ones. I think they will give you a better feel for what we'd like to put together here in Mimosa."

"Thank you," my dad said.

Gideon looked back at the open binder. "I see you've been reviewing things," he said, his smile turning hopeful.

"I have," Daddy answered without elaborating.

I stifled a laugh. He'd taught me to play poker, and there was *no one* with a better poker face. The man had zero tells, so if this guy thought he was going to get Daddy to give any more than the bare minimum detail, he was sorely mistaken.

"Ah, well, I'll leave you to it then," Gideon said, unphased. To me, he said, "Lovely to see you again, Ms. Kennedy. I hope I'll see more of you while I'm in town."

Again, I felt the crackle of energy between us but ignored it. "I think you can count on that, Mr. West. I have a vested interest in finding out exactly what it is you have planned."

His smile widened, but the light in his eyes looked calculating instead of humorous. "I look forward to it, Ms. Kennedy. I'm an open book and available to answer any questions you may have. And, please, call me Gideon."

I didn't acknowledge, much less reciprocate, his invitation to use his first name. There was no reason for any sort of familiarity between the two of us. He was, until proven otherwise, the enemy. Sinfully hot, but then so was the devil, and I wasn't keen on being on a first-name basis with him either.

The door closed behind him, and my dad didn't waste any time. Steepling his fingers beneath his chin, he looked at me with an arched brow and a half-smile.

"What?" I asked, even though I knew very well what that look meant.

"Wanna tell me what that was all about?" he asked.

"I don't know what you mean," I said, crossing my arms. It was a tell—I knew it even as I did it but couldn't help it. I needed to barricade myself until I had the full lay of the land.

"Evie, you need to keep an open mind about things."

"I have an open mind!" I dropped my arms to emphasize how open I could be.

He laughed and stood to wrap an arm around my shoulders. "Sadly, I think you really believe that." He squeezed me close, and I looped an arm around his waist, letting him guide me to the door. Before he opened it, he lifted my chin with a knuckle. His look was serious. "Do you honestly think I'd do something that would hurt you or this town?"

I flushed guiltily. "No, of course not. It's just that . . ."

"It's just what?"

What if what's good for the town and good for me are two totally different things? I thought but didn't say. "I don't trust him," I said. It was true but not my real concern.

"You trust your dear old dad, though, right?" he asked.

"You know I do," I said.

"Well, then, you've got nothing to worry about, do you?"

"I guess not."

"Your confidence is staggering," he deadpanned. "I should elevate you to my campaign manager."

"Sorry," I said. "I know you'll make the right choice."

"That's my girl," he said and kissed my temple.

We said our goodbyes, and I waved to Miss Angeline.

A cold feeling of unease slithered up my spine as I exited into the spring sunshine. Sure, I trusted my dad. How could I not? He'd been my rock since Mom passed, and he had always been in my corner, supporting my every move.

But Gideon West was another story. I didn't trust that smooth-talking, charm-school phony any farther than I could throw him. He was out for profit, nothing more. I just had to make sure my dad, and everyone else, didn't fall for what I was certain were empty promises spilling like warm honey from Gideon's perfectly symmetrical lips.

chapter five

GIDEON

Lurking in the alleyway next to her father's office, I waited for Everest to appear. I wasn't sure how long she'd be, but I'd committed to hanging around for at least a few minutes to see whether I could catch her. What I was going to do if I did, I had no idea. But it rankled me that she thought of me as lower than pond scum. The look on her face when I'd walked in was one of utter revulsion. It wasn't one I was used to receiving, especially from a woman, and I wanted to change that. Purely for business reasons. She was the mayor's daughter and, even before that, held enough pull in this town to torpedo the last developer that came through. I *needed* to get on her good side, and that was why I was skulking about like some sort of stalker. My loitering had nothing to do with the weird pulse of energy I'd felt when we shook hands. No, this was about securing the deal, not the girl.

Fate rewarded my efforts when she pushed open the glass doors a few minutes later and walked quickly down the sidewalk in the opposite direction of my hiding spot. A glossy tail of red hair threaded out the back of her cap. How I missed that earlier was beyond me. I hustled to reach her before she made it to her car. When I was a few feet behind her, I called out, "Ms. Kennedy!"

The slight stiffening of her shoulders was the only sign she'd heard me. Her stride never slowed, and she didn't look back. Determined little minx. I double-timed my steps and came to stand in front of her. She had no choice but to stop if she didn't want to plow into me.

"I thought that was you," I said jovially.

She dodged around me without speaking or looking directly at me, but I fell into step beside her. "You know, you're besmirching the legend of Southern hospitality with this treatment of me, Ms. Kennedy." That got me a sidelong glance from under the bill of her cap but no verbal response.

I tried again. "If we're going to be neighbors, you might at least . . ."

That did the trick. She whirled to face me, hands on hips. "We are *not* going to be neighbors," she hissed out.

I had her attention. "Oh, but I thought you owned the land next to the Colliers," I said, furrowing my brow in feigned confusion.

"I do." Her reply was more of a growl, like a cornered animal warning it was about to lunge.

"Ah, well, you see my partners and I are buying that acreage from the Colliers." I leaned in as though spilling a secret. "Which makes us, in a sense, neighbors."

Everest recoiled with a nasty smile. "Not if I have anything to say about it."

Reflexively, I reached out and took her elbow. The same thrumming current from our earlier handshake raced up my arm with the contact, similar to the longing pull you felt when holding magnets apart. Admittedly spooked by it, I released my grip, the feel of her lingering on my fingertips.

I tucked my hands in my pockets to keep from touching her again. "Have I done something to offend you?" I asked.

Crossing her arms, she wiped at her elbow like she was trying to erase the memory of my hand on her arm. "Your very presence offends me," she said, eyes narrowed to slits.

I felt the sting of her words like the ice pellets they were. We'd stopped underneath one of the many trees lining the street. Sunlight filtered through the leafy branches and cast dappled shadows over her face.

"You don't even know me," I said, which earned me an eye roll of epic proportion.

"I know your type." She took a step forward—which, given our height difference, meant she had to crane her head back to look at me.

This close to her, I could see the smattering of freckles marching over her cheeks and down the bridge of her nose. I tamped down the urge to count them. *Remember what you're doing here, Gids.*

"Oh?" I said, my pleasant tone contrasting jarringly with her sneer. "And what type is that?"

"Developers," she spat out. She might as well have said "neo-Nazi skinheads" for all the vitriol coating the word. "Ever since the sprawl of Charlotte started, people just like you have come down here from your fancy high-rise offices somewhere up north, because places like Mimosa are 'a great opportunity' or have 'untapped potential'."

Her fingers hooked into air quotes then dropped back to her hips. Her lips curled in scorn as she continued. "Then, you cook up all these plans to try and change it from a small town with its own unique people and charm into another link in the chain of suburbs surrounding big cities. You plan these housing projects that aren't marketed to the citizens of this town but to city dwellers looking for a nightly escape from their concrete jungles. You gobble up land and dissect it into minuscule lots."

Her hands made grabbing motions in the air between us. "Rectangle after rectangle with cheap, shoddy identical houses on each one. Fields turn into parking lots and farmer's markets to minimalls. You take something beautiful and make it a monotonous river of asphalt."

The surge of anger wasn't unexpected, since this woman had just denigrated my entire career. She'd relegated my carefully constructed, beautifully planned developments into nothing more than fields of bland tract housing and strip retail centers. Her anger also seemed rooted in something much deeper than run-of-the-mill opposition to development. It felt more . . . personal.

But regardless of what made her launch into her tirade, I had to admit—albeit grudgingly—she was at least partially right. She'd hit the nail on the head as far as what we were doing in Mimosa. Charlotte, unlike Boston, was surrounded by expansive rural areas with the untapped potential she'd mentioned. I'd homed in on Mimosa because it was an ideal bedroom community for those who wanted to escape the hustle and bustle of the city but remain close to work. It was perfect, and I was certain people would flock to our little paradise. All we had to do was build it.

Collecting myself, I stepped forward. Moving into her space was a show of dominance, but I tempered it by keeping my voice passive. "You know, you're making an awful lot of assumptions about what I want to do here in Mimosa. Are you always so quick to judge without having all the facts?"

Undaunted by my power move, Everest didn't back away. If anything, she stood taller, her shoulders slanting farther back and hands curled into fists at her sides. Her chest heaved with indignation and, drawn as I was to its rise and fall, I didn't give into the temptation of a glance. She'd already caught me staring at her boobs once, and I wasn't going to give her the satisfaction of a second time.

She leaned in closer, pinning me with a skeptical glare. "Are you saying you don't want to develop the Colliers' land?"

I shook my head, holding her gaze. "No, I'm absolutely going to develop it." She opened her mouth to pounce on my admission, but I held up a hand. "But not into—what did you call them?—minimalls or parking lots. I have a vision, Ms. Kennedy."

Everest snorted. "Your vision is my nightmare."

"How can you be so sure?" I challenged her. "Oh, right, you 'know my type,'" I said, my turn to hook my fingers into air quotes around her words.

Unable to resist, I shifted forward, inching further into her personal space. The tips of her boots met the toes of my wingtips. She held her ground, brows pinched and lips thinned. Her hands flexed and opened at her sides, as though she were restraining herself from throttling me while preparing to verbally eviscerate me and my plans. Irritation made the color rise in her cheeks and her catlike eyes glow.

Leaning down so we were eye to eye, I said, "Trust me, Everest Kennedy, you've never known a man like me before. But before I'm done"—I dropped my voice, letting a little gravel seep into my tone—"you're going to want to."

The innuendo in my words didn't escape her. Or me for that matter. What the fuck was I doing? Her jaw slackened, and her lips parted on a shocked inhale. The flutter of her pulse at her throat became an undulating throb, its rhythm slightly hypnotic. It made me want to do astronomically stupid things, like trace that little spot with my tongue.

Jesus, man, get a hold of yourself! But I couldn't step backward, couldn't retreat away from the undeniable pull toward her.

Everest's lips moved, forming shapes but not words. The air sizzled with possibility as we stared at each other, frissons of energy pinging between us like dozens of tiny lightning bolts. The busy street faded into the background, and I lost myself in pools of green framed by sooty eyelashes.

"Evie?" A voice penetrated the fog encircling us.

Everest blinked, and the moment was broken. She took a huge step back and looked away, a telltale flush creeping out from the neckline of her tank top. A diminutive brunette stood behind her, holding a sullen-looking white . . . was that a rat or a dog? It growled in irritation, confirming it was canine rather than rodent.

"Hey, Cammie," Everest said, touching a hand to her cap. Her fingers curled around the bill, curving it further downward and hiding her eyes from mine.

The interloper's gray eyes looked at me then flicked back to Everest. She made no effort to hide her interest, her lips crooked upward into a crafty grin. "Am I . . . interrupting something?"

"No!" Everest said, a bit too loudly. Clearing her throat, she said in a quieter voice, "Mr. West and I are finished."

Oh, sweetheart, I thought, *we haven't yet truly started.* To Cammie, I said, "Gideon West."

She took my proffered hand with her free one, somewhat skeptically. "Cammie Givens. How do you know Evie?"

"He doesn't," Everest said before I could answer. "He came to meet with my dad as I was leaving his office."

Theatrically, I grabbed my chest. "Everest," I said in mock horror, "have you forgotten our interlude this morning so quickly? Did it mean that little to you?"

Everest's head jerked up, and green eyes flashed angrily at me from under her hat.

Cammie's silver ones sparkled curiously. "What's he talking about, Evie?"

Fisting her hands, Everest said, "Nothing, Cammie." Her voice was tight and strained, as though she'd had to push the words out of her.

I'd never seen a person be angry with their whole body, but that was the only way to describe Everest. Her entire frame was coiled tightly, like a snake about to strike. A sliver of coal in her palm would've created a diamond, her fists were so tightly clenched. Even her *hair* looked pissed.

I elected to poke the bear. I leaned toward Cammie but avoided the ferocious dog-rodent in her arms. In a low voice, I said, "It was, quite simply, one of the more memorable mornings of my entire life." Shooting a wicked grin at Everest, I continued, "But, apparently, it was something she does all the time."

If we'd been in a cartoon, steam would've billowed from her ears and the top of her head would've shot into the sky. She was livid. I knew it was stupid to aggravate her for the simple fun of it. *No matter how oddly satisfying it was.* There was too much riding on this project for me to get on her bad side. Everest Kennedy had the ear, and the heart, of the most influential man in town, who could crush all my plans with a flick of his finger. I had no business in doing anything but my best to ingratiate myself to her. Instead, I was lobbing thinly veiled sexual innuendos like hand grenades. I needed to shut up and walk away. To stop talking to, much less antagonizing, her. And yet, there I was, shooting her my cockiest grin and begging for trouble. Jamie and Davidson were going to kill me.

Cammie's head swiveled back and forth as if she were at the finals of Wimbledon. Her gaze, and the dog's, settled on Everest. "Spill it, Evie."

Still glaring at me, Everest said, "I met Mr. West this morning when he was touring the back part of the Colliers' property. It seems he's interested in developing it. That's why he came to see my dad this morning."

"Oh, Everest did much more than meet me this morning," I corrected slyly. "She saved my life."

"Say what now?" Cammie asked. Even the dog perked up at this bit of news, one of its ears cocking in my direction.

Everest huffed, using her boot to try and bore a hole in the sidewalk. "It wasn't anything that dramatic. He did something to spook Monty, and I had to help him out."

"Monty?" Cammie repeated in disbelief. "I've seen that horse ignore fireworks." She pinned me with a steely gaze, which her dog seemed to mimic. "What did you do?"

Well, this had gone south quickly. "I didn't *do* anything," I said. "That horse tried to kill me of his own volition."

Two pairs of female eyeballs regarded me balefully. Three if the dog was a girl.

I could handle this. I'd been in boardrooms and backrooms filled with cutthroat businessmen and left with signed deals and handshakes. These two should be a cakewalk in comparison. The trickle of sweat that worked its way down my spine belied my confidence.

"He did!" I said, fists clenched. Aware that I was one foot stomp away from looking like a toddler about to throw a tantrum, I forced my body to relax. "I assure you ladies, *Monty*, not I, was the aggressor."

The women exchanged a look that let me know they were absolutely siding with Monty. *Stupid horse*, I thought. Then immediately reversed my opinion of the beast because without him, I wouldn't have hurtled into the path of Everest Kennedy. And no matter how infuriatingly insulting she was, I had to admire the way she unabashedly stood behind her beliefs. Her certainty in her convictions was alluring separate and apart from the flush it put into her cheeks. The woman was a force to be reckoned with, and I found myself invigorated by the challenge she presented.

"Anyway," Cammie said slowly, "I'm glad I ran into you, Evie. Wyatt and I are going to head over to Stumbles tonight around eight or so. Wanna come?"

"I don't know," Everest hedged, but Cammie wasn't having it.

"Oh, please," she said, shifting the dog to her other arm. "You don't have other plans, so why not come out with your best friend and her boyfriend to hear a little music, have a couple beers, and"—she clutched imaginary pearls—"horror of horrors, *have a little fun.*"

"I have fun," Everest argued.

"I mean fun that doesn't involve horseflesh of any kind," Cammie said. She grabbed Everest's hand. "C'mon, Evie, don't make me beg." She made her eyes wide and batted her lashes at Everest, jutting out her bottom lip into a pitiful pout.

Everest laughed, and the musical sound of it surprised me. Not that I'd expected her to bray like a donkey, but the innately feminine quality of it was as much of a shock as the immediate desire I had to hear it more often.

"Fine," Everest relented. "I do *love* being the third wheel."

Cammie jumped up and down in excitement, making the tiny dog's ears waggle.

Everest locked a hand around her arm. "I'll come for a little while," she amended.

Cammie giggled. "I'll take what I can get." She glanced over at me then back to Everest. I watched the wheels turn in her mind and mischief light up her grin. "You should come too," she said to me.

I'd been watching their exchange with interest, intrigued by what it said about Everest. Cammie's invitation made things even more interesting.

Smiling, I said, "Well, I—"

"No, he shouldn't," Everest interrupted sharply.

"Now, Evie," Cammie said, eyes wide and innocent, "if he comes, you won't be the third wheel anymore, will you?" Not letting Everest answer, Cammie turned to me. "Stumbles isn't much more than a little hole-in-the-wall, but the beer's cold and the band's lively."

"Sounds good to me," I said, making Everest frown even harder.

Cammie's grin reappeared. "Perfect. Everest can tell you where it is. I'll see y'all later," she said, waving jauntily with the hand not holding the dog.

Everest stared mutely after her.

I seized the opportunity. "So Stumbles sounds like a pretty good ti—"

Whirling around to face me, Everest poked me in the chest. "You're not going."

Putting on my deal-closing—in bedrooms and boardrooms alike—smile, I said, "Now, *Evie*, what kind of guy would I be if I didn't accept Cammie's gracious invitation?"

Everest blanched at my use of her nickname. To be honest, I wasn't a huge fan of it myself. It conjured images of little girls in pigtails, which didn't jive with the Valkyrie who'd ridden to my rescue hours ago.

"I'll tell her something came up," Everest said.

I risked my life for the second time that day and slid an arm around her. She fit perfectly, her shoulder notching easily under my arm. The now familiar buzz radiated through me when I touched her. This time, however, it could have been the waves of rage flowing off her at my forwardness. Fueling the fire, I chucked her under the chin. "That's nice of you, but I couldn't ask you to do that for me. We barely know each other."

Her fury could've powered one of the smaller Central American countries. She jabbed me in the ribs and, deciding I'd cheated death enough times in a span of hours, I dropped my arm.

"So," I said, "should I pick you up or meet you at the bar?"

"Pick. Me. Up?" Everest enunciated each word, lining each one with more disgust than the last.

She shook her head so violently a few red strands came loose from their ballcap prison to float around her face. Her glare should've set me on fire, but I kept my easygoing smile in place—serving only to make her madder.

"You aren't picking me up, nor are you meeting me there, because *you*"—she poked me in the chest again—"aren't going."

"Meet you there it is," I said. Touching two fingers to my forehead in salute, I left her fuming on the sidewalk. Tonight was going to be so much fun.

chapter six

EVEREST

Tonight was going to suck giant goat balls. I flopped down onto my bed with a frustrated groan. If Cammie hadn't been my best friend since first grade, I would've tracked her down and removed her spleen through her nose after the stunt she pulled today. I'd seen the gleam in her eye when she came up to me and . . . *him*. And, okay, sure, things had gotten a little heated between him and me but *only* because he was the true embodiment of evil as I knew it—a developer. Someone who didn't see the beauty of land in its purest state. Who couldn't see rolling hills dotted with old oak trees without carving them up into minuscule lots with cracker-box houses or parking lots with some hulking concrete building in the center. Oh, they saw green all right, just not that of lush pastures. No, where I saw the symphony of nature in the way the wind rippled through a verdant field, they saw dollar signs ready for harvest. It disgusted me. Ergo, *they* disgusted me.

And Gideon West, with his suave certainty and movie star smile, was the embodiment of those money-hungry cretins. *You've never known a man like me.* His words from earlier in that silkily strange accent of his glided through my brain, making me shiver involuntarily.

"Gah!" I shoved myself off the bed and wrenched open my closet door. The standard fare of jeans, tank tops, and suits greeted my eyes. Not that I expected there to be anything different, because those had been the two uniforms I'd worn for the past several years—barn attire and donor-wooing attire.

My fingers drifted down the stack of tank tops more thoughtfully than usual. Where was the one I'd bought most recently, as in six months ago when Cammie had insisted we go shopping? Digging through the folded shirts, I found the fitted black top and tossed it onto the bed, followed by a clean pair of jeans. The outfit was basic . . . no, it was boring. The out-of-the-blue thought startled me. How long had it been since I'd actually *looked* at what I was wearing? And why the hell was I doing it now? Again, Gideon popped in my head, and I mentally shut the door in his smug face. *Nope, not a chance.*

Music and laughter rolled over me when I pushed open the door of Stumbles. It was a small place, nothing more than a smattering of tables in front of a tiny stage, with a bar to the right. Self-consciously, I tugged at the hemline of my tank. Scanning the faces of the patrons, I saw Cammie and Wyatt at a table for four near the front of the room. Cammie waved when she saw me by the door, and I headed their way.

Before I'd taken two steps, a hand landed on the small of my back. "Ms. Kennedy," Gideon said in his posh accent. "Fancy seeing you here."

Dressed in jeans and a well-worn Rolling Stones T-shirt, he didn't look out of place in our local watering hole. I'd expected him to show up in something much trendier, like persimmon-colored skinny jeans with weird pointy shoes and a too-tight V-neck topped by every douchebag's go-to accessory, the unnecessary sport coat. I had to admit he looked good in the soft cotton, with his dark hair casually mussed and the barest five-o'clock shadow decorating his jaw.

The heat from his hand seared through the light cotton of my shirt like a branding iron. It wouldn't surprise me to find his fingerprints stamped on my skin. A personalized Gideon West tramp stamp, just what I needed.

Remember, I cautioned myself, *you know who and what this guy is.*

"Mr. West," I said evenly. I quickened my pace, but with his long legs, he easily kept up. His hand remained just above my lumbar, not touching me, but hovering as though tethered to my spine by an invisible cord. It was an oddly solicitous gesture, which irritated me because it chafed with my perception of him as a mouth-breathing troglodyte. I didn't want him to think I'd noticed or was bothered by it, so I resisted the urge to sprint over to the table, settling instead for channeling thoughts of leprosy to his appendages. *All* of them.

After what seemed like an eternity, we reached the table where Cammie and Wyatt sat. Wyatt half rose from his seat. His eyes went first to Gideon, whose presence elicited a raised brow, then to me, then Cammie. To her, he asked, "What did you not tell me?"

She gave him an innocent smile. "Nothing, I promise," she said.

"Right," he said with a wry shake of his head. He held out a hand to Gideon. "Wyatt Jackson."

Gideon clasped his hand. "Gideon West."

After a bit of male posturing, Wyatt reclaimed his seat next to Cammie. Gideon pulled out the chair on her other side and stood back, waiting for me to sit. Wyatt's other brow arched, but he didn't say anything.

Again, irritation at Gideon's unexpected chivalry flared within me. He wasn't staying in the box I'd constructed for him. He *needed* to be the asshole I knew he was so I could keep him in that category. His veering outside that made things confusing and weird. But if I didn't sit in the proffered chair, then *I* was the asshole.

Glumly, I sat down, and Gideon sat next to me, resting his arm on the back of my chair. Again, not touching me, lounging just close enough that I could feel the ping of energy generated by his proximity.

I couldn't afford to be sucked into his surface charm and polished manners, because there was no way it ran deeper than his epidermis. Despite his claim to the contrary, I *did* know his type. As my dad would say, all hat and no cattle. Once you peeled back that superficial fancy facade, there was nothing but dead air and hollow promises. And that's all the sizzle between us was too. Purely a shallow, physical response to a sinfully attractive man who knew how to wield his looks like a finely honed blade.

Never one to ignore the elephant in the room, Wyatt asked, "Wanna tell me what I'm missing here?"

He and Cammie had been together for almost two years, since their meet cute at the clerk of court's office. Cammie worked in the civil division, and when Wyatt showed up to file some paperwork related to his job as a deputy sheriff, he left with his requisite number of copies and her phone number.

"Your girlfriend was kind enough to take pity on the new guy in town and invited me to join you tonight," Gideon said.

"Uh-huh," Wyatt said, unconvinced. His brown eyes focused on Gideon's hand on the back of my chair. "How do you know Evie? You in the horse rescue business too?"

Gideon laughed. "No, but that *is* how I met Everest." The hand resting on my chair moved to cup my shoulder in a half hug.

Unprepared, I tilted sideways, my shoulder fitting snugly under his arm. That close to him, I could smell the faint leathery spice of his cologne. The refined scent probably cost a zillion dollars an ounce—and was worth it because it made me dizzy in a wholly good way. I needed either to switch seats or learn how to breathe through my skin like a frog.

Turning my head to avoid OD'ing on Eau de Gideon, I spoke up, "He's interested in buying the Colliers' property for some kind of development." I put an extra bit of stink on the word "development" and wriggled out from under his hand, scooting my chair a discrete distance to avoid any further contact.

Wyatt's brow wrinkled then his eyes lit with humor. "Wait a second," he said, "are you the guy Evie had to chase down on horseback?"

Gideon's salesman's smile dimmed a bit. "Yes, I'm afraid I am that guy. Had it not been for Everest's timely intervention, I'm not sure where I would've ended up."

Wyatt cracked up. "Oh, man," he wheezed out in between whoops of laughter. "I wish I could've seen that." He wiped the corners of his eyes, still chuckling. "What'd you do to Monty, man?"

"Why does everyone assume *I* did something?" Gideon asked, affronted. "That horse took off like a rocket with no warning whatsoever! It had nothing to do with me."

"Honey, you don't get it," Cammie explained. "Monty has been used for everything from children's birthday parties to Fourth of July parades and all things in between. He is the most easygoing horse you'll ever find. He has two speeds: slow and stop."

"Well, I can assure you," Gideon said, slapping the table for emphasis, "that horse has multiple speeds, including hyperdrive, which I experienced today."

"Huh," Wyatt said noncommittally. "Well, I suppose anything's possible. Where the hell are you from, man? That accent is . . . definitely not from around here."

"I'm from Boston," Gideon answered.

"Go Sox," Cammie said with a giggle. She cocked her head, "But you don't sound like anyone from Boston I've ever heard."

"The only people you've heard from Boston would be in the movies, babe," Wyatt said with a laugh. To Gideon, he added, "This one loves to watch anything with Affleck, the deeper his accent the better."

Gideon laughed. "Well, I'm from Back Bay, not Charlestown or Southie, so that's the main reason I sound nothing like that. The other is that my dad is British, so my accent is a little less . . ."

"Sexy?" I offered. My attempted insult failed spectacularly.

Gideon leaned in, gifting me with another delicious whiff of his cologne. "The fact that the first word you'd use to describe my voice is 'sexy' is the best thing I've heard all day."

"That's not what I said!" I could feel heat rising in my chest and spreading up my neck. Soon, my face would resemble an overripe tomato. *Freaking great.*

"Sure, it is," he said, annoyingly cool and relaxed.

"No. It isn't," I said, ignoring the flush climbing its way across my skin. "I said your accent *wasn't* sexy like Ben Affleck's in *The Town*."

He shook his head, refusing to concede. "Nope, what you said was my accent wasn't *as* sexy. Huge difference, namely that you find my voice at least somewhat sexy." Indigo eyes danced with laughter. "Warms my heart to know you think that, Everest. I can assure you the feeling is entirely mutual."

"Oh, yeah," Cammie said, pleased with herself. "I was absolutely right about inviting you out tonight, Giddy-Up."

Gideon grinned. "Giddy-Up?"

Wyatt clued in immediately on the nickname. "Yeah, seems only fitting since you're the only person who's ever been able to make Monty move at anything more than a leisurely stroll."

Continuing in the running theme of the evening, Gideon surprised me. I figured some hotshot, big city guy like him would be miffed at being nicknamed by the locals.

Instead, he grinned widely at Wyatt. "Well, I guess I'm officially a Mimosan now that I have a nickname." He looked absolutely thrilled.

"Guess so," Wyatt said. "As the newest member of our little community, you've got the honor of getting the next round." He touched Cammie's knee. "Your usual, babe?"

She nodded. "Please."

"What about you, Evie?" Wyatt asked.

"Whatever pilsner is on draft is fine, thanks," I said.

Gideon pushed his chair back to join Wyatt. Before he left the table, he winked at me. "Try not to miss me too much."

"I'll struggle through," I said, scratching the side of my nose with my middle finger. He laughed and followed Wyatt to the bar, attracting the attention of several female patrons along the way. Apparently, I wasn't the only one who noticed how good he looked in worn denim.

Once they were out of earshot, Cammie grabbed my arm. "I'm seeing some *serious* sparks between the two of you."

I pulled away from her. "Don't be ridiculous. What you're seeing is abject loathing on my part and calculated baiting on his."

She narrowed her eyes at me and leaned in closer. "That's bullshit. I just saw you *sniff* him, for goodness' sake! That isn't loathing, Evie, honey—that's *lusting*. And I gotta say"—she snuck a glance over her shoulder to the bar—"I *totally* get it." Her eyes focused back on me. "And it's about damn time. You've been a hermit with your horses for too long, girl. Hell, I'm pretty sure the last date you went on we still had an eleven o'clock curfew!"

"I'm too busy to date," I said. "Plus, you know how it is. Mimosa is so small. I already know everyone *and* the 'cute brother/cousin/nephew' they want to set me up with." I nodded toward Wyatt. "You're just lucky he moved here for work when he did. Otherwise, you'd have ended up with Clint Forsnather."

Her eye roll was paralyzing. "Please, I would *not* have ended up with him. Do you honestly think I'd set my kids up to be called 'Foreskin' like he was growing up?" She bumped my shoulder. "And anyway, we aren't talking about me. We're talking about you. It's not like you have some broken heart you're nursing and that's the reason you refuse to date. You'd have to have put yourself out there once to have a broken heart."

I started to argue, but she held up a hand. "Stop, Evie. Just stop. *No one*, not even the president of the United States, is as busy as you claim to be. I know you love what you do, and I know a big part of that is because you know your mom would've loved it too. But what she absolutely wouldn't love is you hiding yourself away and not having any life separate from what you do. Your horses might need you but so does the rest of the world. You need more than what you've got right now, Evie." She glanced toward the bar. "And that guy right over there looks like a prime candidate to show you a little of what you've been missing."

I looked over to the two men waiting on our drinks. Gideon's height and broad shoulders made him easy to spot. He leaned against the bar; his head tilted toward Wyatt with an affable smile on his face. He gave every appearance of lazy relaxation, but closer inspection revealed it as something different. Gideon wasn't relaxing, I realized. He was lying in wait like a leopard in a tree, surveying his surroundings before pouncing down on unsuspecting prey. No matter his casual posture and easy grin, his eyes gave him away. They swept the bar with a practiced gaze, never lighting on anyone person or thing but taking inventory all the while. Noting what he could about his fellow patrons and no doubt filing it away to use later.

When they swept back to our table, the crash of his gaze into mine was as jarring as a physical slap. I could feel the way he looked at me, the sensation of those blue eyes like fingers on my skin. Gideon West was a *very* attractive man. As in thigh-clenchingly sexy.

Turning away before I offered myself as a sacrificial lamb to the jungle cat in man form, I said, "I could never be interested in someone who . . ."

"Someone who what?" she asked, irritation making her nose wrinkle. "Someone who is smoking hot and obviously into you? Oh no, how could you possibly have any interest in someone like that!"

"Cammie, you know what I'm talking about."

"You know what they say about people who assume, girl. And that is exactly what you're doing." She leaned forward, wagging a finger at me with a frown. "You don't have any idea what he's got planned for that property. You don't even know if he has *anything* planned for it. You're just assuming the worst without any evidence."

"I've got plenty of past experience that tells me I'm *right* to assume the worst when it comes to someone out to bring development to Mimosa. As to what he has planned, no one pays that much for property to let it sit there and hold the earth together. Plus, he admitted to me today he wants to develop it."

Her frown deepened, illustrating her dismay with my rebuttal. But she wasn't giving up yet. "Then find out what he what he wants to develop it into. Don't automatically assume it's something horrible. There are a lot of ways property can be used other than concrete plants and tanning salons. Why do you *always* think about what could go wrong instead of the possibility this could be a good thing?"

I didn't have a great answer for her, other than my gut told me to be wary where Gideon was concerned. It was currently fighting with my ovaries, who regarded Gideon like a desert vagabond would view an oasis. Their dry spell was similar in size to the Sahara, though, so I couldn't exactly blame them for wanting to dive right in.

"Even if you're right and I'm wrong about him, it doesn't matter, Cammie," I said. "He's only going to be here a few weeks." Truthfully, I wasn't sure how long Gideon would be in town. Or at least commuting between Mimosa and Boston. I figured he'd hang around at least until he got his approvals, which would take several weeks, a few months on the outside.

"Even better!" Cammie said, her grin stretching to Cheshire cat proportions. "You're the one who always says they have no time for a relationship, so why start one? He's hot and here, so have a fling with him. Nothing serious, nothing long-term, just a little fun. Which we both know you need, despite how loudly you deny it. I mean, seriously, girl, I can think of worse ways to spend the next few weeks than with a guy whose ass looks that good in jeans."

I stole a peek at the ass in question, and Cammie was right, it did look *really* good in the faded denim. I bit my lip, weighing my options. Great ass or not, I couldn't dismiss completely the uneasy feeling I had about whatever Gideon was planning. There was no way for me to just shuck off my innate suspicion of anyone with a shiny smile, deep pockets, and lofty promises. But Cammie was right. I shouldn't just assume things. I needed to gather facts first.

An idea began to form in my mind, taking shape slowly at first then focusing in vivid detail. "Maybe you're right," I said, leaning back in my chair.

Cammie's gaze came back to mine. "Of course I am." She saw my smile and frowned in response. "Wait a second. I know that look. That look means you're planning something, but I can't tell if it's good or bad."

I spread my hands wide. "What? I'm agreeing with you. What's wrong with that?"

"What's wrong is that self-satisfied little smirk on your face. That means you've got something cooking in that big brain of yours. Don't bother denying it."

"I'm simply taking the advice of my closest friend and considering the idea of a fling. It *has* been a while, as you so kindly pointed out."

"Uh-huh," Cammie said, unconvinced. "Why don't I believe you?"

"I'm just taking your advice, I swear," I said, making a cross over my heart.

I *was* going to take Cammie's advice—or at least a bastardized version of it. Getting to know Gideon could also mean getting the inside scoop on what he had planned. There was a reason for the saying "Keep your friends close and your enemies closer." Only time would tell whether Gideon was the evil, money-hungry troll I'd made him out to be. Which meant the more time I spent with him, the sooner I could confirm that and run him the hell out of town. And on the offhand chance I was wrong, and he was the one developer out of a hundred who wasn't motivated solely by money, well . . . there *were* worse things than spending some no-strings-attached quality time with a guy who looked like the one currently carrying my beer.

chapter seven

GIDEON

I hadn't been sure what to expect when I'd shown up at Stumbles. I'd seen Everest twice that day, each time in the same worn, faded jeans and ballcap. So I wasn't prepared for the unruly mass of red hair that brushed the middle of her back. Waiting on our drinks, I watched her run her fingers through it and was hit by the desire to bury my hands in it and pull her in for a kiss.

Sweet Christ, did I need to rein it in—no pun intended. Except, as I crossed back to our table, cold beers in hand, I wanted to give into the desire to get to know Everest and find out what lay beneath that prickly exterior she wore like a shield. She intrigued me and not just by the way she filled out a tank top. Although that was not to be discounted by any means.

There was something different about this girl who was seemingly immune to bullshit and inherently suspicious of someone well-versed in it. Namely me. She was blunt to the point of bruising and had no patience with anyone she saw as either wasting her time or impeding her work. Work to which she was stubbornly, almost single-mindedly dedicated, given her exchange with Cammie earlier. Everest Kennedy, in her jeans and cotton tank top, was what my Nonna would've called a woman with gumption.

"Your tankard of the house's finest ale, milady," I said when I presented her with the frosty pint.

She took it from me and sipped then asked, "That whole Jon Snow, *Game of Thrones* thing actually work for you up in Boston?"

"Everest, if you want to see my dragon, all you have to do is ask," I said amiably, taking a drink of my own beer.

Her lips curved into a smile. Propping her elbows on the table, she leaned toward me. "Am I supposed to be turned on by the thought of your dick being covered in scales and plagued by a burning sensation? Cause, I gotta be honest, it's really not doing it for me."

My nose burned as I snorted beer through my nostrils and gagged. Tears sprung to my eyes, and I coughed raggedly, struggling to pull air into my lungs all while wiping snot from my face.

Everest jumped from her chair and pounded me, a little too enthusiastically, on the back.

Cammie pressed some napkins into my hand, which I took gratefully and used to mop first my face and then the table.

"Are you okay?" Everest asked, begrudgingly alarmed.

"I'm fine," I croaked then collapsed into another round of hacking coughs. I thought my lungs would be hurled across the table at any minute.

Everest snatched a glass of water from a neighboring table. "Here, drink this," she ordered. I hesitated, and she scolded me. "Gideon, it's a fresh glass of water. It doesn't have cooties, I promise."

Properly chastised, I accepted the glass and took several swallows. "Thank you," I said, my voice scratchy and raw.

Satisfied I wasn't going to choke to death, Everest sat back down. She smirked at me. "Just because I didn't buy into your whole 'my cock is a mythical beast' schtick didn't mean you had to try and breathe fire to prove a point."

My laugh was strangled but genuine. "I've always been an overachiever."

"I'm sure," she said wryly.

"You good, man?" Wyatt asked. I nodded, taking another sip of water to soothe my ravaged throat. "Want a fresh beer?"

"Sure, thanks," I said appreciatively. He headed back to the bar, leaving me alone with the two women. "You know," I said, "a lesser man would be completely humiliated by the fact that in one day, you've seen me flailing about on the back of a horse *and* shoot beer out of my nose."

"Am I supposed to infer you are not a lesser man?" Everest asked.

"I'm a prime specimen," I said, waggling my eyebrows. "If I weren't, the beer shower would've landed on you and not the table. But for my lightning quick reflexes, you'd be soaked right now."

She laughed and shook her head. "You're so full of shit."

"But oh so entertaining," I said.

Wyatt returned with my beer, right as the band switched to a slow song.

Cammie grabbed his wrist. "Babe, I love this song."

He gave a good-natured harrumph. "My truck's speakers and I are well aware, sweetheart." Holding out his other hand, he said, "Let's go." Happily, she linked her fingers with his and followed him to the small dance floor in front of the stage.

"They seem smitten," I said.

Everest watched Wyatt pull Cammie into his arms and sway to the love song. "That's a good word for it," she agreed.

"What about you?" I asked, truly interested in the answer. "No handsome cowboy waiting in the wings to pummel me senseless for making time with his girl?" The churning sensation in my gut took me by surprise. My getting acid reflux over the thought of Everest being with someone else made zero sense for multiple reasons, not the least of which was my two partners would have my balls in a vise for starting anything with her.

Her smile wasn't sad but more apathetic. "No. I don't have much time to date."

"Oh, why is that?"

She lifted one shoulder in a small shrug. "My work keeps me pretty busy."

"Everest, don't tell me you're an all-work-and-no-play kind of girl. That's no way to live your life," I teased.

Green eyes sized me up. "Yeah, I can tell that's a lifestyle to which *you* would never become accustomed. You seem to have a different tux for each day of the . . ." Her voice trailed off and her cheeks flushed a pretty pink as she avoided looking at me.

Her words sank in. *A different tux for each day of the week.* She hadn't seen me in a tux, which meant . . .

"Why Everest Kennedy," I said, bumping her shoulder with mine. "Have you googled me? I'm flattered!"

The flush deepened, and she became mesmerized by a water mark on the table in front of her.

"Which one was your favorite?"

Her eyes came up to meet mine, questions brimming in their green depths. "My favorite?"

I nodded, enjoying the fact she'd looked me up. It signaled a level of interest on her part I hadn't been certain was present. Of course, it was probably motivated more by a quest to get the dirt on my development than any real interest in me, but I'd take it. "Yes. Do you prefer the Tom Ford or the Armani? Maybe the Hugo Boss?"

Those green eyes widened, and the corner of her lips twitched. "You actually own multiple tuxedos?"

"Guilty," I said unabashedly. "I tend to live life to as full an extent as possible. Why toil on this mortal coil if you can't have a little fun too?"

"There's more important things in life than having fun," she said.

"Name one," I challenged her.

"Saving lives," she said evenly.

"Okay, fine, be noble. See if I care," I said with a laugh. Her lips quirked, but she didn't laugh. "Seriously, though, it *is* possible to have a life outside work without your work suddenly falling to pieces. Balance is important, Everest."

"You don't understand," she said somewhat dismissively.

"Try me."

For a moment, I didn't think she was going to answer, but then she blew out a long breath and said, "Second Chance is more than my career—it's a calling. Something I've been drawn to do since I was a kid. It's what motivates my every passing thought or decision. Some horses come to Second Chance having endured unimaginable cruelty, while others are the victims of neglect, whether it's intentional or a result of circumstances outside the control of the owner. They're bruised, broken, and sometimes almost starved out of existence." She shook her head but then smiled. "But if I work hard enough for them, all of them blossom into their true selves while under my care. I know what I can make happen for them if I stay dedicated to it."

Taking a sip of her drink, she continued, "Which leaves little to no time for a personal life. Rescue isn't exactly conducive to romance." Green eyes met mine. "But it's so completely worth it."

Passion for what she did vibrated off her like sound waves from a tuning fork. She practically hummed with it. I was very familiar with the feeling, given it was the same one I always experienced when we started a new acquisition or broke ground on a new development.

"Believe it or not, I do understand in a way," I said, making her mouth twist into a doubtful frown. "No, I really do. The promise of a new future for your wards is what drives you, right?"

She nodded slowly, as though sensing a trap. "Well, yeah, at the heart of it."

"Future possibilities motivate me, too, Everest."

She snorted in response. "Yeah, the possibility of future income."

"Are you saying you *don't* look forward to infusions of cash made by your donors?"

"Those are for the horses, not to line my own pockets. There's a big difference."

"Maybe so," I conceded. "But, despite what you seem to think, I don't do what I do solely for the money. I do it because I find it invigorating. Everything from selecting a site to designing the layout and seeing the first shovel of dirt turned over. There's nothing as exciting as taking a project from idea to reality." I sipped my beer. "But it's also a tad overwhelming at times trying to juggle deadlines, financing . . . temperamental locals who want to run you out of town." That got me a small grin.

"Which is why," I continued, "it's important to take a step back every once in a while. Burnout is a real thing that you should be wary of. If you're as important to your horses as you say you are, they'll be a lot worse off if you go off the rails because you never took a break."

I felt the vibration of my phone in my back pocket. Pulling it out, I saw Davidson's name on the screen. Did the guy have ESP? I debated not answering but knew he'd just keep calling if I didn't. Pointing to the phone, I said, "Excuse me for a second," and left the table.

"Hang on," I said to Davidson as I hurried through the tables to the front door. As it closed behind me, sealing off the noise from inside, I said, "Sorry about that."

"Where are you?" Davidson asked.

"Local watering hole. What did you need?"

"You there with anyone in particular?"

"Just a few locals," I hedged. "Did you need something, or did you just miss the dulcet tones of my voice?" I heard the rustling of papers in the background. "Are you still at the office?" It was after nine on a Friday night.

"Nah," he said distractedly. "I'm at home. Sorting though some of the stuff for the meeting on Monday." A group of possible investors was coming to the office to hear a pitch on what we had planned for Mimosa. Not that we needed a cash infusion, but if they ponied up, we could use it to pad the coffers to help with anything unexpected.

"Well, I hope you're at least doing it with a nice glass of scotch."

"It's at the ready, trust me. I wanted to touch base with you, see if you were planning to come back up, or if Jamie and I need to handle things."

"Need me to hold your hand, Davey Boy?"

A dry chuckle came through the phone. "I think we can muddle through without you, Your Highness. But if you are planning to make an appearance, I'd like to get together Sunday night to brainstorm and get us all on the same page for the pitch."

I considered it but knew there was no need for me to fly back. He and Jamie could handle this meeting without me. It was an initial meet and greet—or dog and pony show. If things progressed, I'd need to be there for some of the follow-up meetings to provide additional details on schedules and the like. But there was nothing earthshattering I had to contribute on the first go-round. My time would be better spent here, getting a handle on the local politics and putting out feelers to gauge the general thoughts of the populace about new developments, both business and residential. And *hopefully* sway the currently dark thoughts of one certain redheaded resident a little more in our favor.

"I think you boys can handle this one without me. If I need to join by phone, I'm happy to. I doubt you'll miss me though."

The shuffling of papers stopped, and Davidson mumbled under his breath.

"I didn't quite catch that," I said.

His concern was audible when he spoke. "Tell me you were listening earlier."

"Listening to what?" I asked, even though I knew damn well what he was referring to.

"Don't play dumb with me, man," Davidson said, his voice tired. I imagined he was rubbing a hand over his brow and giving the phone his trademark scowl. "You know I'm talking about Everest Kennedy."

"What about her?"

"She's much more than a piece of ass," Davidson said, and my temper flared.

"I never said she was anything of the sort," I growled.

"You never do," Davidson continued, missing the anger in my voice. "You've worked your way through the female population of Boston, from the North End to Dorchester. None of whom have ever lasted longer than a few months and the majority of whom aren't your biggest fans. We cannot afford for this girl to become another casualty of your cavalier sex life. Find some other townie to screw and leave her alone."

My grip tightened on the phone, my skin suddenly hot and tight. "Don't call her that," I bit out.

"Call her what?" Davidson asked, perplexed.

"She's much more than just some 'townie,'" I said, letting the anger I felt rising in my chest seep into my tone.

There was a pause, then Davidson spoke slowly, "Gids, is there something you need to tell me?"

The door to Stumbles opened and Everest appeared in the parking lot. She didn't notice me while she rummaged in her bag for what I assumed were her car keys. Finding them, she walked swiftly toward the side of the lot.

"Gideon?" Davidson asked, since I hadn't answered his question.

"I've got to go," I said and hung up on him, forestalling any analysis at my insta-rage over his referring to Everest as just another townie shag. Gravel crunched under my feet as I hurried after her. My phone buzzed, and I clicked it off. I knew it was Davidson calling back, and I didn't give a shit.

Not wanting to scare her, I slowed to a walk once I was within a few feet of her. "Everest, wait a second."

Startled, she whirled around, clutching her keys to her chest. Seeing it was me, she relaxed a bit. "Jesus, West, you scared me."

I held out my hands in a nonthreatening manner. "Sorry, sorry. I didn't mean to startle you."

"It's okay," she said. Her phone chimed, and she checked it. Glancing at the screen, she grimaced and turned away.

"Leaving so soon?" I asked, falling in step with her.

She wiggled the phone. "Duty calls."

"Are you a doctor too?" I joked, but she didn't laugh.

"In a manner of speaking," she said and unlocked a small pickup truck to our left.

"Oh, come on now, love. You must give me more than that," I said.

A garnet brow curved upward as she regarded me over the hood of the truck. "Love?"

I shrugged. "A figure of speech. Blame my dad." I leaned against the truck. "What's got you rushing away in the middle of the night like Cinderella in cowboy boots?"

Everest opened the driver's side door. "It's not even nine thirty," she said.

"Not an answer to my question."

"One of my horses is colicking," she said, as if that was a clear explanation for what necessitated her departure. At my blank look, she clarified, "She's sick, Gideon. I have to go."

"I'll ride along," I said and opened the passenger door.

"What? No!" she said, flustered.

Her denial was too late. I was already buckled in and waiting on her to start the truck. "I thought we were in a hurry," I said with a grin.

chapter eight

EVEREST

I had to be in the *Twilight Zone*. That was the only possible reason for my speeding back to the farm with Gideon West in my passenger seat. Wheedling information out of him at Stumbles over a pint was one thing—except somehow, we'd ended up talking mainly about me—but this was something else entirely. I wasn't prepared for having him hop into my truck as though it were the most natural thing to do. I definitely wasn't prepared to be immersed into the scent of his cologne and the lights of passing cars reflecting off his chiseled profile. I could deal with only one crisis at a time though.

I pushed the speed dial for Leroy's number. He answered on the second ring.

"Leroy, how is she?" I asked, gnawing anxiously on a cuticle.

His calm baritone filled the car. "She's up and walking, like I told you she was fifteen minutes ago. Doc Barnes is on his way." Leroy paused then asked, "Are you in your truck?" I didn't answer, and he muttered what sounded like a curse under his breath. "Everest, I told you not to come back over here," he said. "It's a mild case of colic."

"I know," I said, unable to stop a sheepish wince.

"Then why are you on your way over here right now?" he asked, his exasperation coming through loud and clear on the speakers of the truck.

"Because . . . you might need me," I said, knowing how lame it sounded.

"I've been in the horse business for thirty years, Everest. I think I can handle a case of colic."

"I know that! I do! I just . . ." I trailed off.

And I did. Leroy was more than qualified to handle 95 percent of anything that could befall one of the horses at Second Chance. He did not in any way, shape, or form need me there to handle this situation. But I couldn't help the pull I felt to be there when anything happened. To be the person there to hear directly from the vet, or farrier, or whomever what the plan was.

"You just can't let go," Leroy said, but his words didn't have any sting. "You need to get a life, Evie. A life *outside* the four walls of this barn and beyond the driveway of this farm."

"You're on speaker," I blurted out before he could lament my woeful social life any more than he already had in front of Gideon. Even in the darkness, I could see his smirk at Leroy's words.

"Well, I assumed as much, since you're driving," he said.

"I'm, um, not alone." Cue a blush that stole up my neck and tinged my cheeks. Thank God Gideon couldn't see it. At least, I hoped he couldn't.

I could hear Leroy's smile through the speakers. "Is that right? Who's with you? I know it's not Cammie, 'cause she would've already said hello."

God, I did not want to tell him who was next to me, wearing a shit-eating grin. I'd have done almost anything to keep from admitting Gideon was in the passenger seat. But I didn't have a good way to dodge his question, and I knew he'd keep asking until I caved. "Gideon West," I said, cringing a little.

There was a pause, then Leroy said pleasantly, "Well, then, I reckon we'll see the two of you here shortly."

Gideon was quiet for a few minutes before he said, "It's tough handing over the reins, so to speak, isn't it?"

I braked for a left turn, glancing over at him as I slowed down. I braced for the lecture about my needing to get a life, but it didn't come. He didn't seem judgmental but simply curious.

Letting my guard down a fraction, I huffed out a breath. "Yeah, it is."

"I was the same way when we first started Standard," he said wistfully. Another peek over at him revealed a faraway look in his eyes, as though he were remembering a different time in his life.

"Standard?" I asked, even though I already knew that was the name of his company.

"Standard Development," he answered. "It's the name of the firm I formed with my two partners about ten years ago. Back then, I was as bad at delegating as you appear to be at Second Chance. Had to have my hand on the tiller of all things. Drove a lot of people crazy."

This was a side of the devilish playboy that I hadn't expected. "I can't say that is an easy image to conjure up."

"What do you mean?" he asked.

"You don't exude the essence of a micromanager," I said. "You seem like more of the big-picture guy. The one they send in to sell the deal on the front end while someone else is in the backroom crunching out the numbers you spout over drinks at the yacht club."

Gideon's laugh was deep and filled the small cab of my truck. "God, Everest, you really don't think much of me, do you?"

I shrugged. "I don't really know you."

"Well," he said, and I caught a glimmer of his smile in the headlights of a passing car, "I guess we'll need to change that, won't we? I can't have you judging me as a superficial schmoozer until you get to know me a little better."

"I don't think I need to dig much beneath the surface to know all I need to about you," I said honestly.

"Ouch," he replied, rubbing his chest.

"Sorry," I said, not meaning it.

"I don't believe you are," he said, but his voice didn't sound bothered. If anything, he sounded amused by my comment. "Believe it or not, Everest, I'm more than the pretty face sent in to close a deal. I'm also the one working hard on the numbers behind the scenes. Thankfully, it didn't take me long to realize that I wasn't going to last long enough, or be that successful, if I didn't learn how to delegate some things."

"Well, it's a little harder to delegate when lives hang in the balance," I said defensively.

Gideon gave me a long look. "I thought Leroy said whatever this colic thing is was a mild case."

"He did," I admitted.

"Is he in the habit of lying to you?"

"What?" I asked, appalled at the suggestion. "Of course not."

"Then there aren't really lives at stake tonight, are there?" he asked, adroitly maneuvering me into his trap.

Flabbergasted at the ease with which he'd turned the tables on me, I almost missed the turn into the farm. I slammed on the brakes at the last minute, and we screeched into the driveway. Gravel slung from my back tires as the truck sought purchase, the deep tread digging into the soft soil beneath the rocks. I winced. Leroy was going to be pissed at the mess I'd made of the entrance.

Beside me, Gideon had grabbed what Cammie had affectionately dubbed the "oh shit" handle above the passenger side window. His white-knuckled grip let me know he was not a fan of my driving. Served him right for being so high and mighty and above it all. I hid a smile and drove on back to the barn.

Doc Barnes's beat-up old work truck was parked in front of the wide double doors. I pulled in next to it and killed the engine. Gideon dropped his hand to open his door, but I put a hand on his arm. He was on my turf, so he needed to understand not to interfere or hold me up. "If you're coming in," I said seriously, "you need to keep out of the way. This isn't a field trip."

He nodded somberly. "Understood."

Message delivered, I pushed open my door and hustled into the barn. I didn't wait to see whether he followed.

The main barn was a big building, with a wide center aisle flanked by spacious stalls on either side. It was bisected down the middle by another hallway leading to the paddock on one side and the wash stall and tack room on the other. That was where Leroy was walking Savvy, a palomino with an elegant head and big brown eyes. She was a recent rescue we'd picked up from a soldier's family. Her owner hadn't come back from overseas, and his parents didn't want the constant reminder of the son they'd lost. We were happy to step in and help. It was rare that we got in a horse who'd obviously been loved and cared for and only needed us to find her an equally good home.

Savvy saw me approaching and let out a plaintive whinny. I let her give my hand a good sniff then stroked her soft muzzle. Her velvety lips twitched under my hand. "Hey there, sugar," I crooned.

"Doc's gonna run a nasal tube," Leroy said, stroking Savvy's cheek.

I nodded, checking her over for obvious signs of distress. She was doing pretty well, other than a few well-timed swipes at her belly with a back hoof.

Leroy looked over my shoulder. "Wanna introduce me to your friend?"

"Huh?" I asked, preoccupied with Savvy.

Gideon cleared his throat from behind me. "Gideon West," he said to Leroy. "I'd shake your hand, but it looks like you're a little busy right now."

Leroy inclined his head in Gideon's direction. "Leroy Watkins. You like the Stones?"

Glancing down at his T-shirt as if he'd forgotten what he was wearing, Gideon smiled, "Yeah, man."

"Favorite song?" Leroy asked.

Gideon thought a moment then looked at me. His smile was devious. "'You Can't Always Get What You Want.'"

Leroy's laugh was soft so as not to spook Savvy. "All right then," he said. I ignored them both.

Doc Barnes joined us, carrying a long length of plastic tubing and a bucket. He was a short, wiry man with thinning blond hair and a weathered face earned by spending years outside taking care of animals. His horn-rimmed glasses framed kind dark eyes.

"Evie," he said genially. "I didn't expect to see you here tonight. Thought Leroy and I were going to handle this one ourselves."

"I told her we had it under control," Leroy said grumpily.

Doc held up the tubing. "Well, we can always use another set of hands. Let's get to it."

Leroy held Savvy's halter on one side while I stood next to him, holding a pail of water. Doc prepped the tubing then looked at me. "You ready?"

At my nod, he approached Savvy, speaking softly to her. "Easy now, girl." Savvy's eyes rolled a bit at the sight of the tube, but she held still. "That's a good girl," Doc said gently. He placed a hand on Savvy's nose, hooking his fingers into the nostril and working them slowly from side to side. Then he took one end of the plastic tube and inserted it into her nostril. Savvy's head tossed a bit, but Leroy quieted her.

"Oh God," said Gideon from somewhere out of my line of sight. He'd obeyed my instructions and seemed to be staying out of the way.

Doc continued feeding the tube up Savvy's nose little by little. Once he'd gotten it far enough, he blew into the tube to help it slide into her stomach. Reaching behind him, he grabbed a small pump from the bucket of water I held. Attaching the nozzle to the end of the tubing protruding from Savvy's snout, he started pumping water into the tubing to make sure it made it all the way into the stomach.

I heard Gideon step closer but kept my attention on Savvy.

"What is going on?" he asked in amazement.

Without missing a beat, Doc said, "Savvy here's got a little bellyache."

He stopped pumping and removed the nozzle, aiming the end of the tube toward an empty bucket on the ground. But he was looking at Savvy rather than the bucket. The rubber tube hit the rim of the bucket and bounced to the outside of it. Too late, I noticed Gideon standing next to the bucket. Brown liquid shot down the tube, making it jerk against the side of the bucket—and dump a portion of Savvy's stomach contents onto Gideon's jeans and sneakers. Sour feed, dirty water, and half-digested particles of hay spewed out over his shoes.

Doc grabbed the tube and jammed it into the bucket, but the damage was already done.

To Gideon's credit, he didn't do anything that could've scared Savvy. There was no shout of disgust or sudden leap to the side out of harm's way. He stared down at his ruined sneakers for a second then looked up to me. "Well," he said stoically, "you did tell me to stay out of the way."

A hysterical giggle worked its way up my throat, and I clamped my lips shut to keep it from escaping. To my right, Leroy's shoulders shook with repressed laughter, and I was pretty sure even Doc hid a grin as he pumped another round of water through Savvy's digestive system. The sight of Gideon covered in regurgitated slime from the knees down was hysterical, but I didn't want to add insult to injury when he'd been such a good sport about it.

I managed a nod and an apologetic smile. "Uh, you might want to wait over there"—I lifted my chin in the direction of Sin's stall a few doors down—"until we're finished here."

"Right," Gideon said and squelched down the corridor.

"He took that pretty well," Leroy whispered to me.

I shook my head and refused to make eye contact. "Don't start. I'm barely keeping it together as it is, and if we talk about what just happened, I'm liable to let out a laugh that would make a hyena cover its ears."

"Mm-hmm," Leroy said, and I knew he was as close as I was to doubling over with laughter.

A few more rounds of water through Savvy's stomach, and the water ran clear. Doc gave her some of his secret colic elixir that I suspected was made up mainly of mineral oil and told me to call him in a few days if she were still presenting symptoms.

"I'll let you and Leroy finish up here so I can, uh, well . . ." I hooked a thumb toward where Gideon stood, keeping a safe distance from Sin's head poking out of his stall.

A small snort of laughter escaped Leroy's lips, and I gave him a warning look. "Sorry," he said, his lips still twitching. "Doc and I got this, Evie. Go tend to the wounded."

chapter nine

GIDEON

Days like today were supposed to happen to poor saps who didn't have the world on a string. On any other day, I was the one who made it through a footlong chili dog in a white suit unscathed. Yet somehow, here in Mimosa, *I* had become the guy who, in a span of less than twelve hours, had been thoroughly emasculated by a runaway horse, shot beer out of his nose in public, and was now covered from the knees down in a different horse's nose vomit. Those three things were bad enough on their own. The added fact that all three happened in front of the same beguiling woman now walking gingerly toward me left my ego bruised and bloody. The giant black horse in the stall next to where I stood whinnied quietly at Everest's approach. I thought he was the same horse from earlier in the day but couldn't be sure.

Her hand stroked down his broad nose, and she murmured an unintelligible greeting to him. He nuzzled into her touch, and I was oddly jealous of the animal. Ridiculous, yes, but it didn't make the stab of envy any less real. With a final scratch of his head, Everest stepped around him to join me on the other side of the stall door.

Tucking her hands in the back pockets of her jeans, she nibbled worriedly on her bottom lip. Twinkling green eyes peered up at me through thick lashes, and it hit me. She wasn't biting her lip with concern for my well-being. She was doing it to keep from laughing—*at me.*

"You'd really kick a guy while he's down?" I asked, frowning sternly.

The laugh that tumbled from her lips was loud and unchecked. She clapped a hand over her mouth to keep it in, but all it did was muffle the sound of her amusement. The black horse tossed his head at the noise with a loud whicker, almost as though he were joining in the hilarity of my current state. With one final chuffle, he retreated into his stall. I wanted to crawl in there with him but held my ground.

Tears formed at the corners of Everest's eyes as she fought to regain control of herself. "I'm sorry." She gasped, a hand at her stomach and the other fanning her face. "I know it's terrible of me to laugh. I do . . . I just can't help it."

Watching her dissolve into another fit of laughter, I felt my own lips form a smile. A glance down at my destroyed sneakers had the first peal of laughter tickling my throat. I tried to cough to dislodge it, but a rough chuckle erupted instead. Once I'd unleashed it, there was no way to jam it back down. I joined Everest in her giggle fest, until both of us were fighting for breath, snorting with laughter, and dashing away tears.

A blanket was folded onto a sawhorse against the wall next to me, and I sank down on to it. I drew in a big breath and let it out in a rush. Scraping a hand through my hair, I leaned back against the wall. "I'm not used to being the butt of the joke," I confessed.

Everest joined me on the makeshift seat. "You understand how, after today, it is difficult for me to believe that."

"Don't make me start laughing again," I said.

She grinned and nudged my shoulder with hers. "Sorry. Go on."

"In my element, most women consider me to be quite dashing. A modern-day Cary Grant, if you will."

"Today you've been a little more *Bringing Up Baby* than *To Catch a Thief*."

Fireworks exploded in my brain at her naming what were easily two of my favorite old movies. *To Catch a Thief* was an easy one. Most people had seen the elegantly complex film that had Grace Kelly seducing Cary Grant. But the screwball comedy of *Bringing Up Baby* that paired Grant with Hepburn—and a leopard—wasn't as widely known.

Using her index finger, Everest pushed on my chin to close my mouth from where it had fallen open. "Don't look so shocked, Boston," she said saucily. "Moving pictures *have* made their way south." She leaned in, as if imparting covert knowledge. "Happened right after we got running water and indoor toilets."

"No, no!" I said, rushing to clear up her misunderstanding. "I'm just surprised you've seen *those* movies."

Her arch look let me know I'd only made things worse. "Golly gee, Mistah," she said in an over-the-top Southern accent. "What should I be watchin'? *Dumb and Dumber*?"

"Also a great film," I quipped then backtracked quickly in the face of her glare. "You have to admit it's weird that you know those movies. You're what, twenty-six, twenty-seven? That's like you knowing Paul Newman from *The Sting* instead of his salad dressings."

That earned me a laugh. "I'm thirty-one, smooth talker," she said. "And anyone could tell you that *The Sting*, while good, is no match for Newman and Redford in *Butch Cassidy and the Sundance Kid*."

"Who are you and how have you tapped into my cinematic rolodex?"

"Who says rolodex, old-timer?" she teased, and I much preferred her teasing grin to her glare.

With a shrug, she admitted, "My mom loved to watch old movies, especially any with a dashing leading man."

"Enter Cary Grant," I said, and she nodded.

"Yeah, she loved him. Something about the way he talked, I think. All crisp and polished." Everest shot me a sidelong glance and blushed prettily.

"She sounds like a woman of obvious good taste in everything."

With another laugh, the sound of which I already enjoyed entirely too much, she asked, "Are you ever at a loss for words?"

"Only the first time I saw you." The words were out before I could think about it, but that didn't make it any less true. Sure, I'd been almost slain by an equine executioner, which would render most people unable to speak. But the appearance of Everest, in her element and furious with the interruption I'd caused . . . words had failed me. At least briefly.

With an eye roll for the ages, Everest pushed off the sawhorse. "On that note, I'll take you back to Stumbles."

What she didn't seem to grasp was that it wasn't a line. Just the truth. The woman had an uncanny ability to leave me speechless, and it had started with her riding to the rescue. She didn't wait for me to follow.

I caught up with her at the door to the barn, not ready for our time together end. I blurted out, "Have dinner with me tomorrow night."

The invitation sounded pathetically desperate even to my own ears. Not to mention it was something I had no business asking. Dinner with Everest *wasn't* on the menu. And yet, I couldn't help but ask. If her appearance earlier that day had piqued my interest, spending more time with her had served only to fan the flame of it. Hearing her talk about her work then seeing her in action made me want to know more about this woman. Separate and apart from her reason for being so opposed to my chosen profession.

Red hair whipped over her shoulder when she spun to look at me, wide-eyed and open-mouthed. "What?" she asked, as though I'd just asked her to dine on cod liver and tongue.

I lounged against the doorframe, going for cool and collected. "Have dinner with me tomorrow night," I said again, hoping that time it came off more like an invitation and less of a plea.

Her brows came together, putting two lines of confusion between them. She tilted her head, shooting me a slanted look. "Why?" she asked, and I laughed at the perplexed look on her face.

"Because you enjoy my company."

Her lips pursed like she'd bitten into a lemon.

"Okay," I said, trying a different tack. "How about because I enjoy *your* company?"

"I'm busy," she said as a nonanswer.

"Doing what?" The answering pause and shift in eye contact meant she *was* busy—busy searching for something that would let her dodge the invitation. "Let me save us both the embarrassment of you scrambling for an excuse and make a proposition to you."

Her brow furrowed deeper, and she crossed her arms over her chest. "You're propositioning me?"

"Not that kind of proposition." I wiggled my eyebrows. "Although if you're offering . . ." Her eyes narrowed into hard, green shards. "Okay, not offering, got it. The proposition I have for you, Everest, is that you let me help you out with your disturbing lack of a social life. Prove to you that you can step away occasionally and your charitable empire will not crumble around you." It would also offer me the chance to understand her almost violent opposition to development. And find a way to work around it. That was what I needed to focus on, dammit.

"My social life isn't lacking," she said testily.

"I beg your pardon, but I've heard today from two people that it most certainly is. Two people, I think, who are very close to you and care a lot about you. Both of whom seem to believe you need to get out more." I laid an arm around her shoulders and pulled her next to me. A position that felt extremely natural. "While I'm here in Mimosa, I'd like to help you with that."

Everest stiffened and pushed against my side. Reluctantly, I let her go. She recrossed her arms, regarding me cagily but with a decent modicum of interest. "So your solution to my friends' misguided concerns is to what? Offer to date me?"

"What I'm offering, Everest, is that while I'm in town, I can show you a bit of life on the other side. You said yourself that I have a very different way of looking at life than you do. I'm somewhat of an expert on how to experience life yet still run a successful business. I've got balance, and I'm willing to teach you how get that in your own life." I watched her think it over. "No pressure, no strings, and, hey, it won't be forever because I'll be going back to Boston. Look at it this way—at a minimum, it should get Leroy and Cammie to cut you some slack. What's the worst that could happen?"

Her eyes dropped to my muck-covered sneakers, and she smirked.

"*Again*, this is *not* a normal day in the life of Gideon West." I defended myself.

Everest wrinkled her nose. "*If* I agree to this, you're not going to refer to yourself in the third person, are you?"

I saluted her. "You have my word." I could see she was weakening, so I played my trump card. "Plus, you can keep your eye on the big bad developer and make sure he's not going to ply town council with booze and convince them to turn Mimosa into a concrete wonderland with asphalt and rebar as far as the eye can see before he skips town with a wicked cackle of glee."

Everest was going to cave, I knew it. All I had to do was wait.

She exhaled a long breath and closed her eyes. Dropping her head back, she said to the sky, "I'm going to regret this."

Victory was mine. "So . . . that's a yes, then?" I prodded, needing her to say it.

"I guess so," she said with all the enthusiasm of a woman headed to the gallows.

chapter ten

EVEREST

I needed to work on playing coy. That much was clear from the way I'd almost botched things last night when Gideon asked me out. I winced when I thought about how I'd responded to Gideon's invitation. I'd come off more hard-ass than hard-to-get, which wasn't going to work for my plan to wheedle information out of him.

But his invitation seemed so sincere, even a little out of the blue, to me *and* him based on the way he'd paled a little after asking. The sincerity of it, and the bumbling way he'd asked it, had me more focused on Cammie's original suggestion—a spring fling—than figuring out his real plans for Mimosa. Which was dangerous and made me doubt I had the skills to pull off any sort of romantic espionage. I needed to concentrate on the main goal, information, and not get distracted by how forlornly adorable he'd looked standing next to Sin the night before.

So what was the perfect outfit to disarm a man into giving you all the information you were looking for? I mentally buzzed through my options as I pulled into my driveway. I was running late—what else was new?—because Sundance, a paint with a cracked hoof, had thrown his shoe. The damage to his hoof meant he couldn't go a night without a shoe, which meant an emergency visit from the blacksmith. Leroy and Jacob assured me they could handle it, but I couldn't leave before confirming Sundance had been reshod without further injury. My neurotic inability to relinquish control over anything cost me an hour, and there was no way I could make it to Gideon's on time.

I dialed Cammie on the way back to my bedroom before my head exploded.

"Hey, girl," she answered.

"I need your help," I said, desperation creeping into my voice.

"Who do I need to kill?" she asked.

"You do know your boyfriend is a deputy sheriff, right?"

"Which is reason number one hundred forty-three thousand and six that I would absolutely get away with murder."

She was probably right, but that wasn't helpful in the moment. "You really need to lay off the true crime stuff, Cam. But anyway, I don't need that kind of help," I said, throwing open the doors of my closet.

"Forgive me, but you so rarely ask for any kind of help, I automatically assumed the worst. What do you need?"

"Fashion advice," I said, and she squealed.

"My expertise! What's the occasion?" She was giddy with excitement.

"Dinner," I said, perusing the limited options hanging sadly in front of me.

"Dinner?" Cammie asked, interest piqued. "With whom?"

Eyeing a shapeless black top, pilled worse than furniture from the 1970s, I reluctantly said, "Gideon."

"I knew there was a spark!" she crowed. She was probably doing some embarrassing little happy dance on the other end of the line.

"It's just dinner." I cast aside the hideous top, wondering why I even had it and when, if ever, I'd worn it.

Cammie wasn't deterred by my explanation. "Dinner with a man that looks at you the way Gideon does is absolutely a date. Why am I just hearing about this now? When did this transpire?"

"Don't get your panties twisted," I said as I continued to burrow through my closet. "He called me this morning." There was no need to entice her into further hysterics with the admission he'd asked last night and only called this morning to give me a time.

"How does he have your number? And why didn't you tell him you had plans? It's Saturday night, for Pete's sake!" The questions came in rapid-fire.

I snorted. "Well, you and Leroy made it crystal clear that my social calendar is *wide* open these days, so that wasn't an option."

"Leroy? When the hell did he talk to Gideon?" she asked.

Crap. So much for keeping her in the dark about Gideon coming with me. "Last night."

"Last night, huh?" she asked, on the trail of nonexistent scandal. "How did he talk to Leroy last night? I thought you had some horse emergency that couldn't wait."

"Gideon was in the truck when I called Leroy on the way to the stables." I pulled out and discarded a faded navy T-shirt dress. Its neckline was so wrinkled, it practically looked smocked. It was growing increasingly obvious that my wardrobe choices were limited. There weren't any cute dresses, colored skinny jeans, or other trendy outfits. Perusing my meager selection of clothing confirmed I needed to go shopping for things other than horse feed.

"He went with you to check on Savvy?" I could hear her swooning through the phone. If she'd seen what Savvy had deposited on Gideon's shoes, she wouldn't have found it quite so romantic.

"Yeah, he did." My anxiety was picking up the longer it took to find something—read, *anything*—to wear tonight. "Look, Cammie, we can hash through all that later. Right now, I need you to tell me what the hell to wear."

She was silent for a beat then said, "Well, it depends."

"On what?" I asked impatiently, almost as frustrated with her as I was my closet.

"On whether you want the chance at a second date."

"I have no idea what that even means," I said.

Cammie heaved a long-suffering sigh. "You're truly hopeless. You know that?"

"Why else would I be calling you when I'm supposed to be at his house in"—I checked my phone—"thirty minutes?" An edge of panic crept into my voice.

"Why didn't you say so instead of jabbering on?" she asked.

She'd been doing the majority of the talking, but I kept that to myself. Better to bite my tongue than the hand that was feeding me fashion tips. "Sorry," I said. "But what should I wear?"

"Well, he's already seen you in jeans and a tank, since that's what you wear every day," she mused.

I tried not to take that as an insult. I shouldn't, because it was the truth, but it still stung a bit. I definitely needed to go shopping. Somehow, I'd wedge in the time for that.

"You've got that little green dress, right? The one you wore to Mama's sixtieth?"

I knew the dress she was talking about. It was short and flirty with a fitted bodice. "Don't you think it's a little dressy for dinner at his house?"

"Nah," she assured me. "It's perfect. Brings out your eyes and accentuates those long stems of yours. You want to get a second date . . ."

"Cammie, we have no clue if he'll even be here long enough for that," I reminded her. "This is one night, one dinner." *During which I need to glean as much information as humanly possible about his plans here.*

"Whatever," she said. "It's not like he's fleeing town on a red-eye later. But even if he were, if you wear that dress, he'll be thinking about you on the plane."

I found it in the back of my closet while she was talking. Tucking the phone against my shoulder, I held it in front of me. It was a knit jersey material, so being shoved into the inner reaches of my closet hadn't resulted in any wrinkles that the steam from the shower wouldn't take out. The color did do wonders for my eyes, as well as highlight my skin tone and flatter my wild mess of hair. Ugh, my hair.

I must've made a disgusted noise, because Cammie asked, "What's wrong? Does it have a rip in it or something?"

"No," I said glumly. "I just looked at my hair."

"Your hair is glorious," she said.

"It looks like two birds tried to make a nest in it then changed their mind halfway through and rats moved into the remnants."

"That's certainly descriptive," she said with a giggle. "I'm sure it's nowhere near as bad as you're making it out to be."

I tamped down a wild curl, only to have it spring back up twice as frizzy. "Right."

"All you need to do is pull part of it up into a messy bun. Guys love that, because it makes them think about taking it down."

"That assumes I have enough bobby pins laying around to get even two strands twisted together and pinned up," I said, peeling out of my clothes and turning on the shower. It also assumed I wanted to think about Gideon thinking about running his hands through my hair. Which I did not. Nope, the thought of those long fingers of his threading their way through my hair, brushing against my scalp and giving the lightest little tug . . . never entered my mind a single solitary time.

She laughed. "Why do you think I said *messy* bun?"

"Har, har," I said. "I'm getting in the shower now. Thanks for the help with the dress."

"Go get 'em tiger," she said and hung up.

I was fifteen minutes late to Gideon's, which I counted as a win since it meant I got ready in less than half an hour. I'd kept my makeup simple, mainly because I didn't have the time, or skillset, to do it any other way. After a few haphazard attempts, I'd tamed a portion of my curls into Cammie's recommended messy bun. Giselle I was not, but in the green dress and wedge heels, I'd give myself a solid 7.5 out of 10. Perfect amount of hot to cajole information from a suspect.

When he'd given me the address that morning, I hadn't put it together that he was renting Ms. Viola's cottage. I was much more of a landmark than street number kind of girl, so 442 Cotswold Avenue didn't mean much to me. But if he'd said the cute little cottage four houses down from the library, I would've known right where he was staying.

I walked up the stone pathway and three stairs to the small front porch. Running shoes sat next to the welcome mat in front of the screen door. The inner front door was open, and notes of jazz drifted out past the screen into the early spring evening. When I pushed the doorbell, I heard it chime inside, followed shortly by Gideon's cheerful "Come in!"

Smoothing a hand down my dress, I pulled open the screen and stepped inside. The small foyer opened to a large living room. From the kitchen at the back of the house, Gideon, along with the smell of something delicious, emerged with a smile. Barefoot in jeans and a faded gray T-shirt with a shamrock in the center, he looked good enough to be the main course.

I gave myself a mental slap. *Focus on the main goal—information, not finding out what's under that T-shirt!* But when he headed my way, parts of me that had been long dormant woke up and stretched, smacking their lips in appreciation of the way his shoulders and chest filled out the T-shirt. *Down, girl.*

Wiping his hands on a towel, he looked me up and down. "Wow," he said appreciatively.

I couldn't hide the flush that stained my cheeks. Gesturing at his casual attire, I said, "I feel a bit overdressed."

"Nonsense," he said with a definitive shake of his head. He flipped the towel onto his shoulder and held out his hand, waggling his fingers at me. Uncertainly, I placed my hand in his. "Now, let's have a proper look at you," he said and spun me in a circle. My dress flared out, floating around my legs. Gideon let out an approving whistle, and I had to laugh.

"You're ridiculous," I said, but the carefree gesture helped me relax. A little too much, as it turned out. My ankle wobbled in my wedge heel, and I pitched forward.

Gideon pulled me to him, placing a hand at my waist to steady me. "Whoa, there. You okay?"

This close, he invaded all my senses. His fingers pressing into my back, that heady cologne tickling my nostrils, and the warmth of his eyes drawing me in. I could hear the slow intake of his breath as he gazed down at me. Fleetingly, I thought the only thing missing was the taste of him.

"Everest?" Gideon's voice snapped me out of my cologne-induced trance. Blue eyes stared down at me with concern. "Are you all right?"

Hastily but carefully, I stepped back. "Yes, sorry, I'm fine. Just a little klutzy." I averted my gaze from his and chewed my bottom lip.

Gideon's eyes zeroed in on my mouth. "That's one of your tells, Everest." His thumb brushed the underside of my lip. Although his touch had been featherlight, the weight of it lingered on my skin.

My dry throat struggled to force out any sort of response. "Huh?" *Super eloquent,* I thought.

"You chew on your lip when you're nervous," he said, eyes staying on my mouth for a split second before meeting my gaze. If his touch had carried some weight, that look had been positively overburdened with the promise of . . . *Nope, nope, nope. Not going there*, I chided myself.

"Good thing I'm not here to play poker then," I said, barely recognizing the throaty voice that came out of my mouth. I had to get myself under control. Five minutes into the evening and with the smallest touch and barest glance, he'd ignited all the estrogen in my body and stoked it into a four-alarm hormonal house fire. Sex appeal oozed from his every pore. Not that the man had visible pores, for God's sake. He was like the after picture for microdermabrasion.

"How old are you?" I asked without thinking.

The corner of his mouth pulled up into an amused half-grin. "I'm thirty-eight. Why?"

"You've got amazing skin," I said and wanted to kick myself. What kind of social nitwit had I turned into? I needed to make a point to get around more people than horses.

The half-grin morphed into a whole, complete with dimples. How had I failed to notice those before?

"My aesthetician will be thrilled to hear you say that."

"*You* have an aesthetician?" I asked incredulously.

"Of course," he said. "Doesn't everyone?"

I couldn't tell whether he was kidding or not. I thought of my dad seated in a spa with cucumbers on his eyes while someone rubbed green goop on his face. The image was ludicrous.

"No," I said, with an emphatic shake of my head. "Everyone does *not* have an aesthetician."

"Pity," he said and gestured to a small table set for dinner for two in front of the bay window. "Have a seat. Dinner's almost ready. Can I get you a glass of wine?"

"Sure," I said, finding it easier to do simple things like breathe when there was more distance between us. Pulling in one such breath, I watched Gideon head back into the kitchen. I was familiar enough with the layout of the house to know that the two bedrooms were down the back hall on the other side of the house. As was a bathroom, which was the perfect way to excuse myself and snoop for a few minutes without him suspecting anything.

"Mind if I use your powder room first?" I asked, plastering on an innocent smile. Which was wasted, because Gideon was singularly fixated on the various pots bubbling on the stove.

"Not at all," he called over his shoulder and then turned halfway to look at me. "Do you know where it is?"

"Sure do!" I said, a little too brightly. *Dial it down, girl.* "Be right back."

I hustled down the far hallway. I knew the main bedroom was at the back, with the guest bedroom to the right across from the half-bath. Deciding to check in the guest bedroom first, I was rewarded when the door opened silently to reveal a makeshift office. I knew I didn't have much time, so I did a quick scan of the room.

A few thin files were piled neatly on the dresser Gideon was apparently using as a desk. Other larger files were spaced evenly across the bed along the far wall. There was no way I could look through all of those in the less than five minutes I had to poke around. My eyes landed on a binder with a thick black coil down one side resting on the corner of the dresser. I'd seen that before. It was identical to the one Gideon had given my father.

With a hurried glance back at the door, I flipped the binder open to the title page: *Mimosa Grove Design Study and Development Plan.* Jackpot! Before I could turn more than a few pages, I heard a voice behind me.

"Find what you're looking for?"

I froze, each of my vertebra seeming to click into place at his question and a cold trickle of sweat forming between my shoulder blades. Forcing a smile to my lips, I faced Gideon. I expected anger or irritation, but instead, he looked . . . amused? Yes, that wry twist to his lips and the gleam in his eyes was definitely fueled by humor, not anger. He lounged against the doorframe, arms loosely crossed over his chest.

"Well, I . . ." My hand was still resting on the binder, and I jerked it back then regretted the obviously guilty gesture.

Gideon came into the room. "Don't stop on my account." Coming to stand next to me, he picked up the binder and handed it to me. When I didn't take it, he laughed. "Everest, please take it." He pressed the heavy book against my chest and, one at a time, wrapped my arms over it.

My fingers curled around the edges of it as my face flamed. "Gideon, I . . ."

He smiled at me. "You didn't have to snoop for it, you know."

My eyes flew to his in surprise. "What?"

His shrug was easy and relaxed. "If you'd wanted to see the development plan, all you had to do was ask me for it. I would've given you a copy." Blue eyes delved into mine, no longer lit by humor, but solemn and earnest. "I'm not going to hide anything from you or anyone else. That's not how I do business. You can ask me anything you like about what we've got planned, and unless there's some sort of financial confidentiality issue, I'll give you the answer. And if it's something I can't answer or don't know, I'll find out and tell you."

My fingers ruffled the pages of the notebook and I chewed on my lip, which made him laugh. Immediately, I released it from between my teeth. "That simple, huh?" I asked.

Gideon nodded. "That simple."

It was hard not to believe him, given the way he looked at me. It wasn't beseeching, or imploring. It was just . . . *honest.*

"Just one thing though," Gideon said, making my heart rattle in my chest. He leaned closer, still serious, and asked, "Do you mind if we eat before the inquisition starts?" Pulling back, he patted his stomach and grinned. "I'm *starving*!"

Now it was my turn to laugh. "Can't have you passing out from low blood sugar in the middle of questioning. Lead the way," I said and stepped aside so he could.

His lips twitched. "You know only an idiot would leave first after they found you plundering their office."

"I'd hardly call opening one tiny little notebook 'plundering,'" I countered. But even I knew not to push my luck any further. Gideon could've been pissed and rightly so. I needed to take the get out of jail free card he'd offered and get out of his office.

When we reached the table, he pulled out my chair for me, and I obediently sat. I placed the binder next to my place setting.

Gideon put a glass of red wine next to my plate. "I should've asked—do you prefer red or white?"

I was more interested in the book than the wine but answered his question. "Red's fine."

He noticed my gaze stray again to the binder and laughed. "Go ahead and read it."

I looked up at him. "No, no, it's fine." I took a sip of the wine. It was a cab, and it was delicious. "This is good," I said, tilting my glass at him.

"Thank you. It's from Aonair, a small winery on Howell Mountain in Napa that I found a few years ago. The guy who runs it is a friend of mine now. He's a genius at blending flavors and grapes. A true wizard." From his place at the stove, Gideon pointed a wooden spoon at the binder. "Go on. You know you want to."

He was right. I flipped open the cover and skimmed through pages until I came to what looked like a layout of at least a portion of what he wanted to build. There were large lots and winding roads with cutesy names like Champagne Circle and Prosecco Parkway. Turning more pages, I saw lists of restrictions and requirements. No lot could be less than five acres and no house could be smaller than three thousand square feet. Okay, so this wasn't your average tract home development. But I wasn't sold on it yet.

"What do you think?"

I jumped in my seat. Gideon had come up behind me, and I'd been so engrossed in reviewing the plans, I hadn't noticed.

"It's . . . big," I said, turning another page.

"Big?" he asked. "Normally, when a woman says that it's music to my ears, but in this one instance, I find that word severely lacking." He slumped dejectedly into the chair next to me. "But seriously, you do see now that I'm not trying to make Mimosa into a tract home paradise, right?"

I shut the binder and picked up my glass, taking my time with a swallow of wine then setting the glass down on the table. I looked into his blue eyes sparkling with undisguised hope and blew out a breath.

"Gideon, I don't think you understand the issue here." *That your plans eviscerate my own*, I thought, but didn't say aloud. It didn't take a genius to know Gideon West wouldn't hold up his promise to be an open book if he saw me as a competitor for something he wanted. Which meant I should keep my own desire for the Colliers' property to myself. At least for now.

His eyes dimmed a bit, and his smile lost a portion of its luster, but didn't drop completely. He glanced at the binder on the table in front of me. "I don't know," he said slowly. "I thought you wanted to see the plans we had . . . which are in there." Gideon nudged the booklet. "As in right in front of you. How does that not eliminate any 'issue' you have?"

"What you've outlined in there"—now it was my turn to poke at the book—"is a whole new town that seems like it will take the place of the one that's here now."

"Everest, that's not at all . . ." He stopped when I raised a hand.

"The truth of the matter, Gideon, is that you don't know what happens to the places where you come in and put in your fancy new shops and restaurants for all the newly transplanted people who've moved onto Prosecco Parkway in their brand-new houses. You don't know, because once these places are developed, you're gone." I pointed to myself. "Whereas I, on the other hand, will still be here wondering what happened to Mimosa."

"What happened to it?" Gideon's smile dropped. "What do you mean? It's not like I'm going to obliterate your hometown. It will still be here, just a little different."

I shook my head. "No, Gideon, it won't. I know that for a fact."

"Oh really?" Irritation crept into his voice as he moved back into the kitchen. "And how is that?"

"Because I've seen it in person."

He stopped halfway to the stove and turned to look at me. "You've seen the decimation of Mimosa in person?" With a derisive snort, he turned back. "Where? In a crystal ball?"

Anger licked up my spine and my hands fisted at my sides as I rose to my feet. "This was a mistake."

I hadn't gone two steps before Gideon was in front of me. He held his hands out, much like you would to convince an animal not to attack. "Everest, wait, please." One hand raked nervously through his hair. Gone was the salesman's smile and confident swagger. He looked . . . unsettled.

"I'm sorry, okay? Your . . . reticence just took me a little off guard, and I overreacted. That's all."

"So my telling you yesterday that your vision was straight out of my nightmares didn't clue you in I was a tough sell?"

His laugh was a little brittle and only showcased one dimple, but some of the earlier twinkle came back into his eyes. "No, you certainly didn't promise to do anything but hate everything I had planned. I just thought . . ." He trailed off and looked around as though the answer were hiding somewhere in the tiny cottage.

"That luring me here with the scent of basil and oregano and the promise of dinner eaten somewhere other than my desk and *not* out of a can would—what? Convince me you're a great guy and I should give you a break?"

"I asked you to dinner, *Everest*, because I wanted to have dinner with you." The rough emphasis on my name spiraled through me, teasing along my nerves in a way that made me suppress a shiver. "I'd hoped we could get to know each other a little better and, sure, it would be great if you no longer thought I was some sort of ogre here to pillage your town." His smile turned impish. "And maybe, just maybe, I was overly confident in my PowerPoint skills and their ability to win you over."

I couldn't help but laugh. "It *was* pretty impressive all bound like that and on such nice paper."

Gideon nodded. "How could you not be awed by the font alone?" He stepped over to the chair I'd vacated. "What do you say we press rewind on the evening and start again on the getting to know each other part? Can we do that?"

"Are you asking for a détente in the development wars?"

With a grin, he pulled my chair out and unfolded a white napkin, waving it in my direction. "I come in peace, Everest."

chapter eleven

GIDEON

I'd hoped by showing Everest the vision I'd put on paper, very glossy and expensive paper, she'd see I wasn't her adversary or the brute she'd made me out to be. Sure, I had big plans for her little town, but they were *good* plans. Everything I wanted to do would be good for Mimosa. It would bring in revenue for local businesses. It would create *more* local businesses and possibly lure a few larger but still tasteful chain stores, which would all help fuel the local economy. This was a good thing, not Armageddon.

Her reaction to the binder told me I had quite a way to go before she saw that. Which was fine. I could get her on my side. It would just take a little more effort on my part. And if the byproduct of that was our spending more time together, I was more than okay with that. I flapped the napkin at her again. "I'm actually waving a white flag here, Everest."

The corner of her mouth curled upward, and she came back to the table. Picking up her wineglass, she looked at me over the rim. "Why do you call me by my full name?"

Interesting segue, but I could roll with it. "Instead of 'Evie,' you mean?"
She nodded. "Well, you've never asked me to call you by a nickname."

Looking pensive, she said, "I've never *asked* anyone to call me that. They just do."

"Started when you were a kid?" I guessed.

"Yeah."

A timer dinged, and I headed to check the food. "Can I be honest with you?" I asked.

Her lips thinned. "Meaning you haven't been up to this point?"

I stirred the sauce and tasted it. The perfect blend of spices melted on my tongue. "You shouldn't read something into *everything* I say."

She said nothing, so I continued. "I only asked because you may not like what I'm going to say."

When she watched me like a green-eyed sphinx, I bit the bullet and said, "I would never call you 'Evie' even if you asked me to. I'm sure it was fine when you were five years old with pigtails and overalls running amok on your father's farm. But 'Evie' doesn't fit the badass who rode to my rescue. *That* woman was Everest, not Evie."

I'd had to stop myself from drooling over her when she'd come through the door. In her green dress and partially upswept hair, she was gorgeous. The little skirt of her dress teased around her long, toned legs. The slight dip in the bodice gave me a glimpse of cleavage that only made me want to see more. I'd dated women wrapped in couture and made up like starlets, but none had the same effect on me as Everest did that night.

Not wanting to scare her off by getting too deep, I dialed things back to flirty. "Although, if you do bring back the pigtails, I could work with that," I said.

She laughed, and I enjoyed the sound.

"Settle down, pervert," she reprimanded then asked, "Can I help you do anything?"

"I've got it," I assured her, and she took her seat.

I plated up two servings of pasta and sauce, slid a slice of crusty garlic bread onto each plate, and carried them to the table. Depositing hers on the placemat in front of her, I returned to the kitchen for the freshly grated parmesan and bottle of wine.

"This smells amazing," she said and spooned a healthy dose of cheese onto her pasta. Her eyes closed and she hummed with pleasure at her first bite. "Good Lord," Everest said around a mouthful of food, "where did you learn to cook like this?"

"My grandmother on my mother's side was Italian," I replied, twirling pasta around my fork. "She made Sunday dinner every week. I paid attention."

"Aren't you a melting pot of cultures," she said.

While we ate, I learned more about Everest. After she graduated college, she'd worked briefly for her father but then struck out in a slightly different direction by starting Second Chance Farms. Leroy was her second-in-command, and she had a ragtag crew of loyal folks working there. It wasn't a large operation, but I could tell by the way she talked about it she was extremely proud of what they'd put together. And she should be. She'd accomplished a lot in her thirty-one years.

"What made you choose the rescue business over working for your dad?"

"I don't look at Second Chance as a business," she corrected, swiping a crust of bread through the remaining sauce on her plate. "It's more of a calling than a career."

"Oh, trust me, I only burned my shoes from last night, not the memories of our discussion at Stumbles. What I want to know is how you found this 'calling.'"

She pushed her plate away and sighed. "The horse world isn't all blankets of roses and mint juleps," she said, her eyes dimming. "There's a darker side to it that most people don't see every day."

"What do you mean?" I asked and held the bottle over her glass in silent question. At her nod, I refilled it and topped off my own as well.

"Thanks," she said. "What I mean is that while there aren't stray horses in the same way there are stray cats and dogs, it doesn't mean every horse spends each night in a warm stall with plenty of food and water. Horses are a substantial, long-term investment, which you'd think would be obvious to everyone when they acquire over a thousand pounds of living, breathing animal. But a lot of people don't understand what they are getting into."

Everest picked up her glass by the stem, twisting it this way and that. She looked over at me, and her eyes were tired and sad. I had an overwhelming need to reach for her, at least take her hand in mine, but that was way over the line for dinner with a friend, so I stayed where I was and waited for her to continue.

"I'm being generous to humankind," she said, and I heard the undercurrent of anger in her words. "The truth is people are just plain awful to animals a lot of the time, whether it's dogs, cats, horses, or whatever little creature is unlucky enough to get picked by the wrong owner. Some people don't see a horse as anything other than property and treat them accordingly. I've seen some pretty disgusting displays of what humans are capable of." She gave me a weak smile. "I'll spare you those gory details, but suffice it to say there's a reason I'd rather spend time with animals than people."

This had certainly turned maudlin. I wanted to erase the darkness that haunted her eyes but didn't know how. More than anything, I wanted to track down the bastard who'd put it there and deliver a good thrashing.

After a sip of wine, she said, "But you asked how I discovered it, not for the dirty underbelly of an occasionally beautiful business. And that's an easy question to answer. My mom."

"The Cary Grant fan?"

Everest nodded. "It's sort of how my parents met. My dad was at a horse sale when he was a freshman in college. It was a reputable place with well-respected sellers and well-vetted buyers. Which made what happened that much more appalling, I guess." Her eyes focused on the far wall, and she toyed with her placemat.

"Mama was there too. She was down at the stables to talk to one of the sellers about a few of their colts. She said that when she rounded a corner . . ." Everest paused and swallowed hard. She took a sip of wine then continued. "When she rounded a corner, she heard the most terrified and desperate sound in her life coming from a small paddock where a few horse trailers had been parked."

I could see tears pooling in her eyes, and this time I did reach for her, covering her hand with mine.

"Mama said she knew something wasn't right. That nothing, not man nor beast, would make a noise like that unless something was very wrong. She hurried on over to find out what was going on. When she got past the trailers, she saw it. A horse didn't want to load into one of the trailers. From fifty feet away, she could see the whites of his eyes rolling and the foamy sweat of fear on his shoulders. The poor thing was scared to death and trembling. According to Mama," Everest said with a weak smile, "the man holding his lead was straight of out central casting for poor white trash. He wasn't making any effort to calm the horse or reassure him."

Everest's eyes turned flat and hard. "He'd taken the lead rope and was flogging the horse with the end of it. He hit him again and again, cussing the entire time and trying to jerk the horse forward. Mama swore she could feel each crack of that heavy lead against her own skin." Her laugh was rigid and harsh.

My own skin prickled because I knew where this was going and it scared the bejesus out of me. But I had to ask. "What did she do?"

"She claims she did what anyone else would have."

"Which was?"

"Hopped the fence and tried to deescalate the situation," she said with deceptive simplicity.

"How?" I asked, not falling for her blasé explanation.

She laughed. "You have to understand something about my mother. She's who the phrase 'If you see something, say something' was invented for. Anytime she saw anything she deemed unjust, you better believe she was going to speak up about it. To whomever she saw fit. Including this pot-bellied, chain-smoking redneck who was twice her size."

"She sounds a lot like someone else I know who isn't afraid to tell someone precisely what they think," I said, making her smile.

"Comparing me to Mama is one of the best compliments you can give me."

When our eyes met and held, everything paused. For the space of several breaths, I lost myself in the honest grace of her. It wasn't a practiced elegance or a glossy perfection. It was . . . an authentic acceptance of herself, flaws and all. Everest was so comfortable with who she was, it radiated from her. The woman glowed with it, and it was the sexiest thing I'd ever seen.

Everest cleared her throat, and the needle hit the record again, making the world around us restart.

I sat back a little, running my hands down my jeans in what even I knew was a nervous twitch. "So . . . what did she do?"

Laughing, she twisted her curls into a haphazard knot at the back of her head and then released it. It unfurled in shimmering coppery ripples down her back, and I wanted to know what it felt like to have my hands in it. "Her version is that she took the lead away from the guy and explained to him that wasn't the way to treat any animal."

"And he just handed it over, simple as that?" I knew that wasn't what had happened.

"What do you think?"

"I'm guessing no."

Her lips twitched, and she picked up her wineglass, swirling the liquid. "She stomped on his foot, which made him drop the lead. Then she grabbed it and smacked him across the face with it."

"She did what?" I was floored, both by what she'd just described and the sudden, unexpected jolt that ran through me. All I could see in my head was Everest taking on some belligerent asshole armed with nothing more than a length of nylon. The idea of it rattled me in a strange way, stirring up some long dormant urge to . . . what? Protect her? That idea was somewhat ludicrous, given that I'd just met the woman. But it was there, nonetheless.

Unaware of my inner turmoil, Everest sipped her wine and nodded. "Oh, yeah. Right across the face. Bam!"

I pushed out the breath I hadn't realized I was holding and made my hand relax on the table. "Something tells me that wasn't the end of things though."

She laughed, shaking her head. "Not by a long shot. The guy rallied, and pretty soon they were toe-to-toe and nose-to-nose. I mean really going at it. Fingers pointing, shouting—the whole nine yards."

"Not a pretty scene," I said.

"Nope," Everest agreed.

"So, what happened?" I was still confused as to how this was the start of her parents' romance. Thus far, it seemed more of a "how my mom got arrested for assault" story.

"Well, as you might imagine, they were making quite a racket. And the poor horse wasn't exactly dozing either. My dad was in the closest paddock and overheard the ruckus. He came over to see what the fuss was all about and walked up on them. By the time he got there, Mama was trying to calm the horse down, while Mr. Body Odor International kept screaming his head off at her."

"I don't imagine that went over well with your dad."

Everest's eyes glinted, and she gave me a sly half smile. "What you have to realize, Gideon, is that there is no one in the world as good at analyzing a situation as my dad." I could hear the pride in her voice as she talked about her father. "It's almost freaky how quickly he can read a room or a person and know instantly how to react."

Good to know, I thought. Inwardly, I winced with shame at how quickly the sleazy idea to use her parents' backstory to help a business deal popped into my head. My pragmatic side bristled a bit, because, after all, that was why I'd invited Everest to dinner, right? To help the deal, not to get the girl. I was here to do a job and couldn't afford to lose sight of that.

I cleared my throat. "Doesn't seem like a tough situation to read though. Angry animal abuser yelling at pretty lady soothing scared horse."

"True," Everest admitted but then wiggled her finger at me. "Let me guess. You would've roared in there, fists flying to defend her honor."

Again, I imagined Everest as the lady in question, and my fist clenched involuntarily.

She noticed and smirked at me. "I'll take that as a yes. That's the difference between the two of you, Caveman. My dad didn't just read the redneck. He read *my mom.* The way she'd inserted herself between the guy and the horse. According to him, she was plastered against the poor thing, using her body as a shield. She was trembling almost as hard as the horse was, but hers was more of a vibrating anger than fear. Daddy knew the most important thing to her was getting that horse out of harm's way, not pummeling the guy to feel like a macho savior."

"Save the horse, get the girl," I said.

"Bingo," she replied, pointing at me with a smile.

I was fully invested in this story now, deal or no deal. I really wanted to know what happened. I leaned forward in my seat, resting my forearms on the table. "So . . . what did he do?"

Equally caught up in the retelling, Everest shifted in her chair, excitement making her move to the edge of her seat. Her hand curled around the edge of the table, our arms nearly touching. "He just walked up in between them, easy as you please, and says, 'This your horse, mister?' Totally ignores my mom and puts his *whole* focus on the guy."

While she spoke, her other hand arced through the air in emphasis. Her eyes were bright and wide, her cheeks flushed as her hand moved animatedly. She used her entire body to tell a story.

"Guy puffs up like a rooster strutting through a barnyard. Says hell yeah, it's his horse to do with as he pleases. Daddy dials up the charisma then, gives him a full Kennedy grin, and says, 'Then I guess you're the one I talk to about buying it.'" Everest grinned at my shocked expression. "I imagine the guy's face looked a lot like yours does right now. But disgusting slob or not, he wasn't going to turn down cold, hard cash. Daddy gave him two hundred more than he paid for the horse at auction. He pockets the money, points at my mom, and says, 'Guess she's your problem now.' Daddy looks at her, winks, and says, 'I sure hope so.'"

I was floored. "He bought a horse to meet your mom? That's an *epic* level of game."

She lifted a shoulder in a careless shrug. "That's just my dad." Her nonchalance didn't fool me. I could hear the love in her voice—for both her parents. "He always said it was the best investment he ever made. His one sure thing."

"Your mom must be one amazing woman."

Everest's eyes clouded, and her smile wobbled. "She was."

My stomach bottomed out at her use of the past tense. I'd inadvertently stepped in something but had no tactful way of backing out of it. "Was?"

She nodded. "She passed away when I was in high school. Breast cancer."

I put a hand over hers, giving it a gentle squeeze. "Everest, I'm so sorry."

"It's okay. I mean, it's not. But it's gotten . . . easier. Having Second Chance has really helped. It's like . . ." Her voice trailed off, and she looked over my shoulder, staring at something only she could see. "It's like she's still with me. Each new horse we bring in that's a hollowed-out husk of what they should be, she's the reason I know we can bring the life back into their eyes. With every milestone they reach or surpass while at Second Chance, until one day they're back to being this vibrant, beautiful animal, I know she's there every step of the way."

"No wonder you love the place so much."

Her eyes came back to mine. Little gold fissures wove through the green of her irises. I was keenly aware of how close she was to me, the ridge of her knuckles under my palm, the brush of her knee against mine. I saw the moment she realized it too. The slight flare of her nostrils and lift of her lashes telegraphed her surprise at our gravitating toward one another while she talked.

When she tugged her hand from under mine, I wanted to clutch it tighter, pull her closer. Tuck her head under my chin and hold her against me, succumb completely to the all-consuming need to kiss her. Sample those bow-shaped lips and taste on her tongue the wine she'd been drinking.

But instead, I let her draw back and away, distancing herself. Which was precisely what *I* needed to do as well. This dinner was designed to answer her questions and get her to see Standard as something other than the enemy. It was *not* for the purpose of seduction, and I'd do well to remember that.

Her hand went to her forehead with a nervous flutter, only to halt at her hairline, her haphazard bun keeping her from pushing her fingers through her riotous mass of hair. Blushing, she let her hand fall to her lap, where she twisted her fingers together.

She risked a look at me, eyes guarded. "Not exactly a quick answer to your question. Bet you're sorry you asked, huh?"

"Not at all," I said, sitting back in my chair and giving her additional space. "I want to know about you, Everest. The good . . . the bad . . ."

"What about the ugly?"

I gave her a long look. "There could never be anything ugly about you." *Stop it, you twit!* But I couldn't. I couldn't look at the dynamic woman in front of me and have her believe there could ever be anything about her that wouldn't fascinate me.

"You haven't seen me when I get up in the morning," she said then blushed even deeper.

"Is that an invitation?" I asked with a wolfish grin, trying to restore the easy camaraderie from a few minutes ago. Everest had opened up to me in a way she hadn't expected, and I didn't want her to see that as a mistake. *Dial it down, you imbecile! She's not for you!*

"You're terrible," she said but laughed.

That laugh that was my final undoing. Everest had a great laugh. It wasn't a demure little titter but an honest-to-God outburst of amusement. The sound of it tickled my ears and made me want to hear it again and again. I could berate myself all I wanted. Tell myself this dinner had a singular purpose, but that was all crap.

In the span of two days and a single dinner, I'd become hooked on this girl. I didn't just want to get Everest comfortable with Standard and its plans for Mimosa Grove. I wanted her to be comfortable with *me*. I knew it was wholly reckless and a tremendously stupid idea. The litany of reasons I should pull back and leave her alone was endless. I knew all that, but selfishly, I didn't care.

chapter twelve

EVEREST

C'mon, you stubborn piece of junk," I muttered through gritted teeth. Readjusting my grip on the wrench, I took a deep breath and pushed hard to the right. My muscles ached and my wrist shook, but I felt the nut loosen a bit and danced a small mental jig. Bracing my wrist with my other hand, I levered the wrench again. It turned sharply, and my hand slammed into the side of the mower deck.

"Mother of fudge!" I dropped the wrench to clutch my bruised knuckles. Thankfully, instead of landing on my nose, it clattered harmlessly onto the concrete next to my head. Why I'd thought it was a good idea to change the blades on the mower myself escaped me in that moment. Wedged under the hulking orange contraption between two jack stands, I questioned my life choices. My hand throbbed, and I knew I'd have one more bruise to add to the collection of nicks, scrapes, and scars I'd received over the years.

I picked up the wrench and, carefully this time, worked to loosen the nut. The blade shimmied a bit, and I knew the blade bolt was almost ready to drop. Just a few more turns, and I'd have it . . .

"Everest?" Gideon's voice came from above, scaring the crap out of me. My focus on the mower had been so singular, I hadn't heard him approaching. With a yelp, I dropped the wrench again, only this time, it bounced solidly off my cheekbone instead of the floor.

"Ouch!" I cried and mistakenly reached to cover my face, which put my forearm in contact with the not-so-dull edge of the mower blade. "Shit!" I said as the metal sliced into my skin.

"Jesus Christ," Gideon said from somewhere to my left. "Are you all right?" His voice held a tinge of panic.

Bleeding and humiliated, I wanted to stay in my cramped little spot until he went away. A glance down between my feet revealed the hem of his sharply creased slacks and shiny dress shoes pacing rapidly back and forth in front of the mower. He did not appear to have any intention of leaving. I could either live the rest of my days flat on my back with blades of doom hovering inches from my face, or I could roll my mechanic's creeper out from under the lawn mower and see him. Leroy would have to use the mower later in the week, so option one was a no go.

Flattening the soles of my boots to the floor, I bent my knees and rolled out into the sunlight streaming in through the large bay door to the equipment shed. Squinting in the sudden brightness, I glanced up. Gideon stood above me, silhouetted by the sun. Even his dark outline was sexy. All broad shoulders and manly angles. Maybe that wrench had given me a concussion, I thought.

He crouched down next to me, hands on his knees and eyes alight with worry as they scanned over me. "You're bleeding!"

I touched my tender cheekbone, but my hand came away dry. Thank God for small favors. I checked my forearm next and saw a long scratch below my elbow. Blood oozed slowly from the deeper end. Oozing was better than gushing. It meant I didn't need stitches. Shifting to one side, I dug an old, reasonably clean bandana out of my back pocket and held it against my arm.

Gingerly, Gideon put a hand on my elbow. "Let me help you up."

"I've got it," I said testily, but his grip remained firm on my arm as I rose to my feet. His broad fingers spanned out like a brace, the warmth of his palm seeping into my skin. I stepped away from him before I caught a whiff of his cologne.

"What are you doing?" he asked in bewilderment.

I laughed and gestured to the creeper in front of the mower, sitting in an arc of various tools. "What does it look like I'm doing?"

He looked from me to the lawnmower then back again, brow furrowed and blue eyes cloudy with confusion. Broad shoulders lifted in a hapless shrug. "I honestly have zero idea."

Smiling hurt, and I winced, touching my cheek gingerly to determine the damage.

"Are you sure you're all right?" Gideon asked, taking my elbow once again and peering into my face.

"I'm fine," I said, ignoring the heat of his touch. "I'm changing the blades on the lawnmower. At least, I was until you snuck up on me and almost made me lose an eye."

"I didn't sneak," he said, insulted by the accusation. "I came looking for you, and Leroy told me you were out here. It can hardly be called 'sneaking' when I called your name. Several times, as a matter of fact."

I blew out a breath and turned toward the old fridge in the far corner. His hand fell from my arm. "I need to get some ice for my face. What are you doing here?"

His shoes slapped against the concrete behind me. "Lovely to see you again, too, Everest." I didn't miss the hint of teasing in his voice.

My shoulders hitched guiltily. I had no reason to be rude to him. It wasn't his fault I'd hit myself in the face and scraped my arm. At least, not really. He hadn't startled me on purpose.

"Sorry," I said contritely. "I need to brush up on my social skills, I guess. What brings you by today, Gideon?"

He came up beside me as I reached into the small freezer and took out an ice pack someone left behind. I was about to put it against my cheek, when he held out a white linen handkerchief monogramed in royal blue with the initials GHW.

"Use this," he offered, shaking out the clean white cloth.

"I can't," I said, holding up the grease-stained hand not pressing a rag to my arm. "It'll get filthy."

His eyes flickered, and he took the ice pack from me. "Nothing wrong with getting a little dirty," he said, wrapping the linen around the ice pack and putting it in my hand.

The man was a master of the double entendre, with his refined accent coating the words in sex appeal. Heat shot through me, and it had nothing to do with the lack of air-conditioning and everything to do with the way Gideon was looking at me.

"Thanks," I said and put the ice to my cheek. Of course, his handkerchief smelled delicious and felt even better. "I'll wash it and give it back to you." I knew I looked ridiculous, with a ratty bandana pressed to my forearm and his fine linen against my cheek. A study in contradiction, much like the two of us.

"Don't you have someone who can do that for you?" he asked.

"What? My laundry?" I asked, puzzled. I checked my arm. The ooze had stopped, so I tucked the bandana back in my pocket, making a mental note to do laundry.

He chuckled. "No, Everest. Your lawnmower maintenance. Don't you have people who work for you that can handle that sort of thing?"

I blushed. "Well, yeah, but I . . ."

Understanding dawned. "Ah, this is one of the many examples of your failure to delegate. I see." I wanted to chuck the ice pack at his smug face, but he kept talking. "You don't need me, or Leroy, to tell you that the more of these little tasks you give to others, the more time you'll have to dedicate to your real focus—saving horses." His eyebrows wiggled. "But then you wouldn't be able to hide away here in the barn and avoid having a social life."

Throwing the ice pack at him was becoming more and more appealing as he activated both of his stupid dimples with a knowing smile.

"I'm not hiding! I had dinner with you last night, didn't I?"

"A single dinner does not a social life make," he said, sounding like some weird proverb.

I shifted the ice pack on my cheek and changed the subject. "What *are* you doing here, Gideon?"

He adjusted the already straight cuffs of his shirt, his head tilting sideways, eyes sliding away from mine to roam over the shelves lining the walls. He looked . . . awkwardly nervous. Interesting.

"Gideon?" I prompted.

His eyes dropped to study the shiny tips of his shoes. "I, uh, well, I wanted to . . ." He cleared his throat, "That is . . . I wanted to see if Savvy was all right today." He dragged his eyes up to meet mine, and his smile had turned bashful, as if embarrassed to admit he was worried about the little palomino.

He could've said he was here to find the aliens that stole his luggage, and I wouldn't have been more surprised. I wasn't used to people surprising me, but Gideon seemed to be making a habit of it. In my experience, a person was exactly who they appeared to be at first glance. I'd pegged Gideon as a moneygrubbing carpetbagger; however, in the brief time I'd known him, he'd shown himself to be anything but. And now, he was here not for me but for one of my horses. To see for himself if she were okay.

The thought made my heart trip over its own feet, narrowly avoiding a pratfall into a full swoon. Technically, it had a head start, since I'd been trying all morning not to think about how much fun I'd had at dinner last night. About how good he'd looked in that T-shirt or how the rich sound of his laugh resonated into my bones. And especially not the moment after I'd told him about my mom. That moment when time slowed to a languid crawl and the world around me faded away until the only thing left was Gideon and his devastatingly dimpled smile.

None of which was a good thing, because assuming he was the one honest real estate developer in the history of time, there was no way I could fall for this guy. I couldn't afford the distraction of developing this type of connection with him. His development, if it went through, would essentially torpedo my opportunity for expansion. Which meant I needed to go back to the drawing board on that. Which meant I needed to ramp up looking for sources of funding. Which would pull time away from the actual work of rescue. There simply were not enough hours in the day for me to fritter any away on something other than Second Chance. Romance and all its distractions were completely off the table.

So I'd refused to think about how good it had felt when he put his hand on mine or the sexy way his eyes twinkled. And I certainly didn't go to bed fantasizing about the shape of his mouth or what it would feel like to have that mouth brush over mine.

But now, oh God, *now*, he'd broken out the kryptonite. This man. This gorgeous, sexy man had come by to make sure a horse who'd essentially regurgitated swamp water onto him was doing okay. Yep, that one shyly uttered sentence was like a nuclear bomb to my defenses designed specifically to keep Gideon at arms' length. That small kindness pushed me into unfamiliar territory—the vast and mostly unexplored land of romantic opportunity. After all, it would only be temporary. Things between us had a predetermined end date because long distance would be impossible. Short-term, no-strings *might* work, but there was absolutely no way I could commit to anything beyond that. Assuming Gideon was actually interested in me and not just a good-hearted guy who was sweet on a little blonde horse.

"Everest?" Gideon broke into my thoughts, waving a hand in front of me. "You sure you're okay?"

I blinked back to reality and found him looking at me, concern palpable in the dip of his brows and worried line of his mouth. "No, no. I'm good. Savvy's doing fine. You wanna see her?"

One corner of his mouth tipped up into the beginning of a grin. "That depends. Has she had any water today?"

I laughed. "Yes but not through her nose. C'mon, I'll walk you over."

chapter thirteen

GIDEON

Everest Kennedy was . . . hell, I wasn't sure what she was, other than a wholly magnetic force pulling me in to experience more of her. Even though the longer I spent in her company, the worse it seemed to be for my ego—a wholly new and not altogether comfortable experience. Normally, I felt in command of any situation, whether it was walking into a boardroom with an impeccable suit or slapping on a hardhat and barking orders at a construction site. *I* was capable, confident, and in control. But today, walking beside Everest, I felt as outmatched as Ichabod Crane facing down the Headless Horseman. Or in this case, the Jack-of-All-Trades Horse*woman*.

The only thing I knew about lawnmowers was that the landscaping crews we hired used them to cut beautiful lines across the sod we paid other people to lay. Growing up in the city, I'd never even had to use one. We'd lived in apartments or townhomes, not houses with yards that required any maintenance. Hell, the majority of houses in Boston had yards the size of postage stamps. The behemoth contraption Everest had been tinkering with was larger than the entirety of the green space most of the people I knew owned.

The woman could do it all, as far as I could tell. She was a regular Rosie the Riveter. On the one hand, it was sexy as fuck, especially the way she looked in those little cotton tanks she wore. It was enough to drive a man to drink, the way they hugged her curves and showcased her taut abdomen. And somehow, they were always a little dirty, which made it that much hotter.

On the other hand, she wasn't some vapid pinup posing braless with a wrench and a strategically torn T-shirt. The woman *knew* how to fix things. And not just a fence. But huge machines that could dismember human beings. She hadn't batted an eye at the deep cut on her arm or the bruise that already started to bloom on her cheekbone. It was slightly terrifying and insanely intimidating. And let's not forget the whole horse intubation thing. Everest roared by independent doing one hundred and eighty while masterfully shifting into fourth gear and steering with her knees.

I was a schoolboy with a crush on the coolest tomboy in class. A crush I couldn't act on, because of the myriad of things that could go wrong if I did. All the ways this could blow up in my face kept me up until well into the evening after she had left. And what was the first thing on my mind when I woke up? Everest. What had I done at the first opportunity? Come to find Everest. Because foolish or not, I couldn't help myself. Couldn't stop myself from wanting to be around her. It was a craving I had to satisfy. Which brought me here, strolling along beside her on the gravel path.

"I appreciate you coming to check on Savvy," Everest said as we made our way to the barn.

"What can I say? Once a woman vomits on me, I'm hers forever."

She huffed out a laugh. "Good to know."

"Seriously though," I said. "I did want to make sure she was okay." And I really did. I'd found myself thinking about the little blonde horse that morning. Which was kind of weird. Not that I didn't like animals. I did. I fawned over cute little puppy memes like anyone else. But before Everest, I'd never given much thought to horses.

The ice pack hid most of her smile, but I still saw the curve of her mouth. "That means a lot, Gideon."

Her words packed the same zing I'd experienced when Mary Beth Masterson told me I was cute in sixth grade. My chest puffed out, and I stood a little taller.

We walked into the barn, and she led me down the long center aisle. Leroy must've heard our footsteps, because he poked his head out of a stall about halfway down. He took one look at Everest and came jogging toward us.

"What happened to your face?" he asked with a worried frown.

Everest tried to wave him off. "It's fine, Leroy. I dropped a wrench."

"On your face?"

"It was my fault," I said.

Crossing his arms over his chest, Leroy trained hard eyes on me. "I'm waiting, boy." The steel in his voice could've supported the Bunker Hill Bridge.

Should've thought that one through a little better. "I startled her while she was working on the lawnmower. That's why she dropped the wrench." My explanation tumbled out in a rush. What was it about these people and this place that was constantly throwing me off my game?

Leroy relaxed a little then scolded Everest. "What were you doing working on that thing anyway?" He took her chin in his hand and tilted it up to the light. "Hmph, now our executive director looks like she got into a bar fight."

"You should see the other guy." Everest tried to joke, but it fell flat.

Leroy scrubbed his hands over the back of his head, frustration obvious on his face. "Dammit, Everest, you don't have to do everything around here. You've run yourself ragged over these past few years. It's got to stop. You need to trust the rest of us to do our part."

Everest toed the earthen floor, embarrassed. "I do trust you, Leroy. You know that."

His face softened for a moment. "I know you trust me, but you also need to trust the other folks you've hired. You gave them jobs so they could do them. Not so you could do their work and yours too." He handed the ice pack back to her. "Keep this on your cheek, girl. Maybe you won't look like you went a few rounds with Tyson."

"Thanks, Leroy," Everest said.

He tutted his disapproval, but I could tell it was mainly for show. To me, he said, "What brings you around, Mick?"

The nickname threw me for a second until I remembered the Rolling Stones T-shirt I'd worn the other night. "I just came by to check on my girl."

Leroy's eyes darkened and he frowned a little. "Say what, now?"

"Savvy!" I said quickly. "I came by to see if Savvy recovered from her, uh, tummy ache." *Tummy ache? What are you five years old?*

Leroy's thick, dark brows winged up in surprise. "Did you now?" he asked, rubbing his chin. "Well, then," he said, sweeping a hand in front of him, "don't let me keep you. She's in that stall there." He indicated one about two doors down from where we stood.

The stall had a split door, with the top half open and secured against the barn wall. Cautiously, I walked up and looked inside. Savvy stood in the center of the stall, dozing a bit. I didn't want to scare her, so I said quietly, "Hey there, girl."

Big brown eyes opened, and her head turned at the sound of my voice. She whickered delicately and ambled over to stick her head out into the hall.

"You can give her this," Everest said from behind me. I glanced back and saw a cylindrical nugget in the palm of her hand. "It's a peppermint treat," she said.

Taking it from her, I reached forward to hand it to Savvy, but Everest stopped me. "Unless you want to lose a finger, hold it out in the flat of your palm."

Following her advice, I opened my hand flat with the small treat resting in the center. Savvy's velvety lips worked overtime as she gobbled it from my hand. She crunched happily for a moment then snuffled against my chest, looking for more.

Everest laughed and scratched the white star on Savvy's forehead. "Easy, little piggy. We've got to get you back well before you go snarfing down too many treats."

Disappointed, Savvy snorted and tossed her head. I stroked her soft muzzle. "Sorry, girl, but I don't make the rules around here." She lipped my hand a little, still hopeful. When that got her nothing, she retreated into her stall.

"She seems to be doing okay," I said to Everest.

She smiled. "Yeah, it was only a mild case, so she was on the mend pretty quickly."

"That's good."

Everest moved the makeshift ice pack, and I got a good look at the initial dark stain of the bruise. I felt like a complete cad. "Are you sure you're alright?"

"What?" Everest asked, her brow wrinkling. Then, she remembered the reason for the ice pack. "Oh, this? Yeah, I'm fine. Trust me, bumps and bruises come with the territory," she said lightly, extending her arms in front her. Scratches, small cuts, and an assortment of bruises, all in various stages of healing, decorated her slender forearms. It impressed and irritated me all at once.

"Let me make it up to you," I said.

Lowering her hands, she gave me a slow once-over, taking in my slacks and button up shirt. "You're not really dressed to muck out stalls, so I'm not sure how you can." Her green eyes shone with mischief.

"There are things besides manual labor," I insisted.

"What did you have in mind?" she asked.

In that moment, looking down at her bruised and makeup-free face, so relaxed and in her element, I would've given her anything she wanted. Including shoveling horseshit in my custom-tailored pants. But I wasn't sure whether she wanted anything I had to offer. I decided to start simple. "How do you take your coffee?"

"My coffee?" Her eyebrows winged upward, and she laughed.

I nodded. "Yep. The least I can do is get you your favorite caffeinated beverage."

"Gideon, I'm sure you've got more important things to do than fetch me coffee."

"Not unless it's getting you lunch too," I replied. "In fact, that's a much better plan. What would you like?"

Tucking a hand in the back pocket of her jeans, she rocked back on her heels, studying me over the top of the ice pack against her cheek. "You're something else, Gideon."

"In a good way, I hope," I said.

"So do I," she said, her smile small but hopeful. "So do I."

chapter fourteen

EVEREST

I had things I needed to be doing. Things that didn't include pulling into the driveway of Gideon's rental cottage bright and early the following Saturday morning. I *should* be in my office editing the final draft of a grant proposal that I'd put off all week long in favor of working around the barn. I *could* have been reviewing the latest round of volunteer applications or finalizing the feed order for next week.

Instead of any of the litany of tasks I could or should be handling that morning, I was steering my truck into the neatly kept drive of Ms. Viola's house. Pulling under the large oak tree to the left of the house, I parked but stayed in the cab of my truck. Nervous energy ricocheted through me like live wires writhing under my skin. Gideon's refusal to fit into the pigeonhole I'd made for him was confusing to the point of irritation.

No, that wasn't it. It wasn't *his* actions that made me twitchy. It was me. Or rather my rapidly growing hope that he was different. This morning would be the true test. I knew he'd know about my objection to the industrial development that had tried to come to Mimosa a few years ago. He'd thought that by showing me his binder of pretty new residences and tidy commercial districts, he'd assuage any concerns I had. Because he didn't understand my real concern. But he would after this morning. And his reaction to it would be the key to . . . to what?

Try as I might want to—and I had, *all week long*—I could no longer deny at this point there was more at stake than either my own desire for the property next door or what Gideon planned to do here in Mimosa. I was interested in *him*. Which meant that I *wanted*, no not wanted, *needed* him to have the right reaction to the impromptu field trip I had planned for today. And, if he did . . . if he did, then what? Was I really going to embark on some spring fling with the guy? Even with Cammie's encouragement to cut loose and have a little fun with him, the idea of a fling felt . . . off, somehow. But what other choice did I have? Gideon was going back to Boston, whether it was three weeks or three months from now. There was zero long-term potential here. That thought sat like a rock in my gut.

A knock on my window made me jump in the seat, clutching a hand to my chest. I'd been so lost in my jumble of thoughts, I hadn't seen Gideon approaching.

"Everest?" The window muffled his voice, but I could still hear his surprise at finding me parked in his yard.

The window whirred down. "Hi," I said a little sheepishly.

Gideon cocked his head to the side, giving me a curious half-smile. "What brings you by this morning?"

Wasn't that the question of the hour? "Well, I, uh . . ." I fumbled to explain what in the hell I was doing there. "I wanted to show you something."

The half-smile spread into a full grin. "Oh? If I'd known you were coming, I would've made sure I was dressed and ready. As it is, I'm afraid I'm a little . . ." He ran a hand through his hair. "Disheveled."

The hand that raked through his short hair was connected to a muscular arm. An arm that was not covered by any sleeve. That arm joined a similarly naked shoulder, which stretched into an equally bare chest. An extremely broad, toned chest with just the barest dusting of light brown hair. Tracking down, my eyes followed the defined ridges of his abdomen to the low-slung waistband of his athletic pants. A light sheen of sweat made his body glisten in the early morning sunshine. Cradled in the crook of his arm was a . . . rolled-up mat?

"I'm afraid I just finished my morning asana."

I blinked, refocusing on his face and wholly unsure of how long I'd been ogling him. "I'm sorry. You finished your what?"

He jiggled the mat at his waist. "Asana." At my still blank look, he added, "Yoga."

"Yoga?"

"What?" Gideon replied. "You can't imagine me in downward dog or cobra pose?"

I could imagine Gideon in multiple poses; however, none involved yoga. *Kama Sutra*, maybe, but not yoga. "Not exactly," I responded.

"Well, you should join me one morning. It's excellent to loosen the hips."

The absolute last thing I needed was for my hips to feel any looser around Gideon.

His dimples winked on with an easy smile. "I try to practice regularly. Keeps my brain from getting too cluttered and . . ." He smoothed a hand down his stomach. "It's not so bad for the waistline either."

Somehow, I'd gone from looking at his face to staring at where his hand rested right at the top of his waistband. I wasn't sure how that had happened, nor was I sure how to redirect my gaze away from the small bead of sweat currently making its way down the narrow line leading to his belly button. I knew I should. That I shouldn't track that drop of moisture the way a cat tracked a mouse. And yet my eyes locked onto it like a homing beacon, tracing its path until it disappeared beneath his hand.

My swallow was audible when I dragged my eyes back up the expanse of his chest to meet his laughing blue ones. The twinkle in them was unmistakable, as was the fact it was there because of the way I'd just drooled over him like a twelve-year-old looking at pictures of boy bands on Instagram.

"Everest?"

"Yeah?"

His dimples deepened as his grin stretched wider. The fingers of his free hand curved around the bottom of the window frame, pressing into the worn leather of the door. "You said you wanted to show me something?"

I shook my head to dispel the thoughts of those fingers pressing into my skin. "Yes, right, I did. I mean, I do. But I can see"—I gestured weakly at his bare torso—"that you're busy, so I'll just let you. . ."

"Everest," Gideon said, his voice warm. "Give me ten minutes to shower and change, okay? Then I'm all yours."

All mine. . . nope, no, no ma'am, uh-uh. "Oh, okay," I said, the words sounding a little strangled.

He withdrew his hand from the door and stepped back, angling his chin toward the small house behind him. "You're welcome to wait in the living room if you want."

"Sure," I said, fumbling for the door handle. Gideon was quicker, though, pulling the door open from his side. Nerves made my legs a little rubbery, but I did manage to extricate myself from the cab of the truck and not face-plant next to him.

We passed the short walk to the porch in silence, albeit not uncomfortable. Once I was in the living room and turned down his offer of something to drink, he disappeared down the hall. I heard the shower cut on.

I shoved from my mind all thoughts of Gideon pushing those low-slung pants to the floor and stepping into the shower. Okay, so maybe "shelved" is a better word than "shoved," but the point is I didn't dwell on them for longer than two *maybe* three minutes tops.

True to his word, Gideon reemerged ten minutes later with hair still damp from his shower, fastening his watch. Finding me seated on the couch, he said, "I guess I should be glad I didn't find you sorting through my rubbish bin."

I blushed and stood up, suddenly unsure of where to put my hands. "Yeah, well, it would've served you right for leaving me unsupervised after last time."

Grabbing his keys from a dish on the table in the entryway, he laughed. "I told you, Everest. I'm an open book. Anything you want to know, just ask. No need to dig through spilled coffee grounds and old banana peels looking for answers."

He pulled open the door. "But according to your somewhat uncertain explanation as to what brought you by this morning, *you're* the one with something to tell *me*." He gestured for me to go ahead of him. "Let's get this show on the road, shall we?"

GIDEON

Everest's appearance at my house that morning had been an unexpected but very welcome surprise. I tried my best not to stare at her profile as she steered the truck through downtown Mimosa and onto the highway leading west. It was more difficult than you might imagine. Dressed in what I was coming to recognize as her standard uniform of tank top, jeans, and scuffed boots, she wore no makeup, and her hair was drawn into a haphazard ponytail. Sunlight streaming in from the windshield highlighted her freckles and made her look much younger. So did the way she chewed her bottom lip.

"So," I said, breaking the silence, "do I get a hint about where we are going? I didn't notice a shovel and tarp in the back. Is it safe to assume you're not taking me into the wild to murder me and dispose of my body?"

She smiled and spared me a glance. "Not yet anyway."

"Ah, so the jury's still out, huh? Good to know."

Her laugh loosened up her posture, and she relaxed into the driver's seat, her hands dropping to the bottom of the steering wheel. Without looking at me, she said, "I wanted to buy the Collier property to expand Second Chance."

That news roiled my gut a little but wasn't a complete surprise. It made sense, given her dedication to the rescue, that she would want the ability to expand the operation. I also knew that there was no way she could compete with the price per acre we'd offered the Colliers. "Everest, I—"

She shook her head. "That's not what this morning is about, Gideon. I just wanted to be up-front with you about it. Your development, if it goes forward, will throw a wrench in the works for me and what I want to do with Second Chance." The glance she shot me wasn't angry though. It was more . . . understanding. "But I'm trying to look at the big picture for Mimosa, not just myself. Because that's the most important thing. This town means something to me, and I won't stand idly by and watch anything bad happen to it."

Her frustration at losing out on the property was understandable, but that didn't seem to be the real reason for her resistance, and her irrational insistence that my plans for Mimosa were somehow "bad" rankled me. Developments I constructed made places more prosperous. They brought in tax dollars and other revenue that could then be invested back into the community. There was nothing *bad* about what I had planned. Hell, there was certainly nothing bad in it for the Colliers, based on the price we'd offered.

"Everest," I said, trying to keep my voice even and calm. "I'm at a loss as to why you think Standard coming down and developing a portion of Mimosa is somehow going to end badly for you or anyone else in this town. I don't think you've thought through—"

"Really think mansplaining what I have or haven't thought about is the best way to go here, Mr. West?" Her eyebrow arched like a cocked weapon, and I had the good sense to wince.

"That's not what I was doing, I promise. I was just—"

"Now you're mansplaining how you weren't mansplaining?" I heard the laughter in her tone, so I knew she wasn't that angry with me.

Not enjoying the taste of my own foot in my mouth, I put up my hands. "I'm done. Please, continue."

"I'm not saying that there are no good aspects of what you've shown Standard wants to do here in Mimosa." She flicked a glance at me then settled her eyes back on the road. "On the surface, at least."

I bit back the multiple retorts that threatened to leap out of my mouth. If I wanted Everest to hear my perspective, I owed her the same courtesy. Even if it meant permanent teeth marks on my tongue.

"I can't put blind faith in what's on the surface though," she continued. Her hands tightened and released around the wheel, as though she were feeling her way through this conversation. "I have to delve deeper and make sure there's some substance beneath the shiny pictures you're painting that's going to provide a good foundation for what you've got planned."

"Who's the mayor of this town, you or you dad?" I quipped. "Isn't project review more in his job description than yours?"

Her smile was fleeting. "This is about more than project review, Gideon. This is about the preservation of a place that cannot be replicated. It's not just my hometown. It's ingrained in my identity . . . practically a helix of my DNA. Changing it into some glossy developer brochure means changing a part of myself. Deleting a chunk of my life. And I don't want that. Mimosa is unique. The people here are unique, and they have a deep and genuine affection for each other." She paused, wrinkling her nose. "For the most part, at least."

At my quizzical look, she said, "There's assholes everywhere, Gideon. Surely, I don't need to tell you that."

I laughed and shook my head. "What makes you so convinced that what we want to do is going to change Mimosa?"

Everest didn't answer but activated her turn signal. My attention went from her profile to out the windshield. We had come to a very attractive, well-maintained development. Multistory brick buildings housed what I identified as commercial below and residential spaces above. Semi-mature trees were planted, and there was a large green space that had what I assumed was a walking trail snaking through it. Storefronts were bright and colorful, as were the open-air patios attached to the restaurants interspersed throughout the area. People milled around, popping in and out of stores and generally enjoying the early spring day.

"What am I looking at?" I asked, taking in the sight of a young mother wrangling two younger kids while piloting a stroller.

"Weaver Village," she said, disgust dripping off her words. Everest didn't park, just continued piloting us around the large, bustling area.

"Oh-kay," I said, drawing out the word to emphasize my confusion. "Mind lady-splaining to me what we're doing here?"

That earned me a laugh, and she turned the wheel, directing her truck out the back entrance. "You'll see," she said, pulling back onto the main road. I didn't break the silence that descended in the cab of her truck as she exited the four-lane highway and merged onto a smaller two-lane road.

Within minutes, we were driving down a cracked asphalt lane marred by deep potholes and a chipped double yellow line. The edges of the road crumbled into high weeds growing out of brittle red soil. In front of us, I saw the outline of what I assumed was a downtown. Only it looked more like a ghost town out of an outdated western than something you would see in this day and age.

Everest slowed down as we passed the first rundown building. The glass storefront was partially boarded over, and graffiti streaked across the plywood half of the front door. The truck bumped down the road, passing buildings each more dilapidated than the last. As she navigated around a ruptured portion of pavement, I couldn't stay silent any longer.

"I'm no longer so certain you have not driven me to the middle of nowhere to murder me and steal my organs to fund the expansion of Second Chance."

Everest smiled tightly. "No need to be scared," she said. "I just wanted you to understand the reason for my skepticism about development."

I snorted, peering out at the dismal landscape around us. "Seems to me this place could benefit from a little development."

"Development created this place," she said, and my gaze shot to her. She looked back at me with a knowing smirk, waiting for me to ask the question.

"All right, I'll bite. What on earth are you talking about?"

"This is downtown Weaver," Everest said. "At least, it used to be before the people who developed Weaver Village essentially killed it." She parked her truck in one of the multiple empty spaces. Killing the engine, she curled into the corner of her seat, angling her legs out from beneath the steering column so she was facing me.

"The company behind Weaver Village initially approached Weaver about opening a shopping center closer to downtown. Town leadership resisted because their preference was to have the developers to take certain buildings that had been without tenants for some time and rehab those buildings to incorporate them into the development. That way, the town would get some much-needed revitalization, and the developer could still open its trendy new coffee shops and boutiques."

"I'm guessing that's not what happened," I said, starting to grasp the true purpose of this little field trip.

"That's putting it mildly," Everest said. "Rather than entertain the mutually beneficial proposal made by the folks here in Weaver, the developer approached a local farmer who owned a substantial amount of acreage just outside town limits and offered him a ridiculous price per acre." Her eyebrow quirked at me while one corner of her lips tugged upward. "Sound familiar?"

My neck felt hot, and my stomach cramped a little, but I didn't look away. Everest glanced out the window and continued. "The developer convinced the powers that be to relocate the exit that had been planned for Weaver to a few miles north, effectively siphoning traffic away from downtown Weaver and depositing it squarely at the entrance to Weaver Village. Didn't take long for the stranglehold to work and choke the life right out of downtown."

"Surely, you don't think that's what—"

Green eyes watched me carefully. "Why shouldn't I, Gideon? What assurances do I have that your plan for Mimosa won't gut it the same as Weaver Village gutted Weaver? Nothing you've shown me so far is any different. Your plan is new construction, start to finish, which my dad and the rest of council seem fine with, and maybe they're right. Maybe your plan won't be the death of Mimosa, but I can't shake the feeling I have that there's a better way to ensure that doesn't happen."

Glancing away, Everest ran a hand lightly over the steering wheel, chewing on her lower lip. I struggled to keep silent, sensing she was weighing what to say next. I was rewarded when she looked back at me and continued. "What about *existing* downtown Mimosa? *Your* plan is to use our fancy new four-lane highway to lure folks out of Charlotte, *past* downtown, and over into your shiny new mini-metropolis. You claim it will bring people *to* Mimosa, but from what I've seen, those people will pass *through* town while also passing *by* existing business to get to your overpriced lattes and vegan kombucha or whatever other overly indulgent trend of the moment is in style."

Everest took a breath and looked at me, her eyes dark with worry. "In short, what I've seen is *very* good for Standard, and again, my dad seems to think it will be a boon for Mimosa. But I've seen what happened in Weaver, and I just want you to see it too. So, you understand why, regardless of what council thinks, *I* want to know what your plans are going to do for the people who've lived here their whole lives, Gideon. People who've grown up here, raised families here, and make their livelihood here? Are we going to wake up one day and be faced with this?" She swept an arm out to take in the boarded up and rundown buildings lining the street.

"Obviously, I can't . . ." My voice trailed off because what I'd been about to say was so trite and perfunctory that I knew it would do nothing to sway Everest to my side. Hell, her little speech had *me* questioning what we had planned. Because the truth of the matter was, she had a point. A *good* point.

I'd targeted Mimosa because of its accessibility to larger cities *and* the wide swaths of vacant farmland that would allow us to construct our development from whole cloth. At no point had I considered implementing any existing part of the town into my plans. It was quicker, cheaper, and simpler to start fresh with new buildings.

The only thought I'd given the citizens of Mimosa was how thankful they should be to Standard for the influx of cash that would flow not just from Standard but from the new businesses and new residents that would flock to the town. There'd been no consideration of how their actual lives would be affected by what Standard had planned, good or bad. It simply hadn't been on my radar. I'd been engrossed by the project, not the people.

Clearing my throat, I started again. "Everest, I . . . well, hell, I don't know what to say." *Where had that truth nugget come from?*

She laughed. "First time for everything, I guess."

I couldn't stop my answering smile. "You make a good presentation, Ms. Kennedy. No wonder you've got donors lining up to contribute to your operation." *An operation you're in the process of hampering with your plans*, trilled an annoying voice in my head. I shoved aside the guilt, deciding I could worry about that later.

"I don't know about that, Gideon," she demurred with a shake of her head. "I just wanted to level with you the way you have with me. You showed me your plans, held nothing back." Her eyes narrowed in suspicion. "Allegedly."

I put a hand over my heart. "As God is my witness—"

"No need to get biblical," she said with a smile. "My point is, you've been open and honest with your plans, which I appreciate. I figured I should at least reciprocate by showing you the heart of my concerns. Sure, I'm frustrated that Standard buying the Collier property means I've got to rethink how to expand Second Chance. But that's not my main worry. Mimosa is my home, Gideon, and the people who live in it are important to me. If what you have planned is really going to be good for them and my town, then I've got to shelve my own desires and get behind it. Even if I'm not completely thrilled with the idea of having thousands of new neighbors for my farm. But I won't let you turn Mimosa into the next Weaver. Even if I have to fight my dad and the rest of the council to do it." Her smile turned into a wry grin. "I can be pretty convincing when necessary."

I wanted to take her hand in mine, to squeeze it reassuringly and promise her I'd never do anything to hurt her or her town. It was a ridiculous thought. I barely knew her, and that was a dangerous and unkeepable promise to make. Especially by me and especially while we sat in the desolate wasteland created by a development so similar to what I had in mind. There were no guarantees in life, and I was smart enough not to make Everest one. No matter how badly I wanted to in the moment.

"Everest, I've been nothing but honest with you, and that won't change going forward. I can also say with certainty that neither Standard nor I have any intention of making Mimosa into a ghost town."

"I hope that remains true, Gideon," she said, reaching to turn the key in the ignition.

As she drove us away from the sad remnants of Weaver, I did too.

chapter fifteen

EVEREST

The Friday after showing Gideon around Weaver, I pushed open the door of Mean Muggin' and was greeted by the heavenly scent of coffee and freshly baked breads. Elektra Robinson, owner, barista, and all-around wonderful person, was behind the counter. Some days, I was sure she had to be a human-octopus hybrid with the way she seemed to have multiple hands to pull the various levers and create the delicious, caffeinated concoctions that made her café so popular. This particular morning, her blue hair was woven into intricate braids that highlighted the sharp angles of her cheekbones and upward tilt of her almond-shaped eyes. Long dangly earrings swung from her earlobes as she whirred around faster than her espresso machine. She looked a lot like a punk rock Siamese cat, only with more attitude.

She noticed me walk in as she was finishing up an order. Her mocha brown eyes—appropriate, given her chosen profession—lit up with her wide smile. "Everest! Haven't seen you this week." Her hands were already moving toward a mug. "Your usual?"

"Hey, Elektra," I said and nodded. "Yep, the usual."

"Coming right up," she promised and set to work on my banana-nut chai latte.

Don't knock it until you've tried it.

"Ponies been keeping you busy?" she asked as she steamed the milk.

"Yeah, we've been pretty swamped lately."

Her eyes danced, and she said, "Rumor on the street is that's not the only thing occupying your time these days."

My cheeks went pink, and she delighted in my discomfort. "Yep, from what I've heard, there's a certain dashingly handsome developer who's been wining and dining my favorite redhead."

"I've been to dinner with him once," I said, trying my best to dispel the gossip. I knew it was futile, but I had to try.

"Technically, you've been to drinks and dinner, *and* he's come in here to get you coffee at least twice." Elektra's meticulously groomed brows arched suggestively. "And a little birdie told me your truck was at his house last Saturday morning . . ."

I should've known she'd have the entire timeline of my interactions with Gideon since I'd met him a few weeks ago. In Mimosa, you didn't go to the salon for gossip. You came to Mean Muggin'. That was mainly due to the fact Roberta Hazelton, Elektra's grandmother, and her bridge club had their coffee here every morning. Those ladies had their arthritic fingers on the pulse of the town and their noses in each resident's business. If it happened within fifteen miles of the town limits, CNN had nothing on Mrs. Hazelton as far as breaking news went.

Glancing over my shoulder, I saw she'd commandeered the table in the front window for herself and the rest of her octogenarian news crew. Not that Mrs. Hazelton had to do much to snag the table. The whole town knew it was "her table" and not to sit there unless invited. She caught me looking and waved her hand in the air, the large diamond on her finger winking in the early morning light. Dearly departed Mr. Hazelton's family had invested in more than one blue chip stock back in the early 1950s, which explained the rock on her hand and her ability to invest in Elektra's coffee shop.

"Everest, darling!" she trilled. "Do come over here."

"You've been summoned by the queen," Elektra said quietly, handing me my coffee with a little giggle.

No one refused Mrs. Hazelton, so I drummed up the courage to withstand the inquisition and headed to her table. Bending down, I dusted my lips against her papery cheek. The scent of Oscar de la Renta perfume wafted up to greet me.

"Mrs. Hazelton, you're looking well," I said.

She patted my hand. "Thank you, dear." Even at eighty-four, her glacier blue eyes were sharp while she studied me. "I hear you've been spending time with that young man who's renting Viola's cottage for the summer."

Straight for the jugular, I thought. Shifting on my feet, I debated how little I could reveal without offending her. "Gideon? Yes, I've shown him around a bit. I don't know that I'd go so far as to say we've been 'spending time' together."

Daintily, she lifted her coffee to her lips and took a small sip. "What would you say about it, then?"

Multiple pairs of wizened eyes focused on me, eager to hear the news straight from the horsewoman's mouth. *Walked right into that one.*

What would I say about Gideon? There wasn't much to say at this point, as I'd hardly seen him since Saturday other than when he'd dropped off a coffee with a flash of dimples and a promise to catch up soon. I certainly wasn't going to regale Mrs. Hazelton with the way my stomach had dipped into a freefall at his smile—or my disappointment that "soon" had yet to happen.

I sipped my drink, seeking solace in the spice of the chai mixed with the nutty banana flavor. Elektra was truly a magician. I let the caffeine seep into my system, debating what type of reply would keep follow-up questions to a minimum.

"Well, I—"

"Mrs. Hazelton!" a familiar baritone said from behind me. "Aren't you looking divine this fine morning."

Gideon appeared at my side, dapper as ever in charcoal pants and a baby blue polo shirt. The way the soft cotton fabric stretched across his broad shoulders didn't escape my—or any other female in the room's—notice. He leaned down to kiss Mrs. Hazelton's cheek, and she tittered coquettishly.

Wait, they knew *each other? When had that happened?* I glanced back and forth between them in disbelief.

"Gideon," she said, a light flush staining her porcelain cheeks. "You're kind to flatter an old crone like me."

He reared back, aghast. "Mrs. Hazelton, that's blasphemous. You are an unrivaled vision of loveliness each time I see you." That dazzling blue gaze turned to take in the rest of the ladies seated at the table. "As is the rest of your court. Ladies," he said, sketching a deep bow that left them giggling like middle schoolers.

"Go on with you," Mrs. Hazleton chided, but she was clearly pleased with the attention.

"Why, what do you think brought me in this morning, other than seeing this passel of gorgeous ladies having their morning coffee? And to try and tempt you once more into joining me for my morning yoga. Sun salutations are the best way to start a day."

Had I entered some alternate dimension? What was happening? How in the world did Gideon know Mrs. Hazelton?

Mrs. Hazelton peered up at me then back at Gideon. "Oh, I think I have a pretty good idea of what brought you in this morning."

My confusion morphed into embarrassment as I felt the curious eyeballs of every customer in the place taking in this little scene like it was a matinee showing. My skin crawled, and I tried to duck out. "Mrs. Hazleton, ladies, a pleasure to see you this morning, but I've got to get over to the farm."

"What a coincidence," Gideon said cheerily. "I'm headed in that direction myself. Let me give you a lift."

"That's not necessary," I said, backing away. "My truck's right outside. Thank you though."

"Ah, well then, I'll walk you out," he persisted.

"You haven't even gotten your cof—"

"Gideon," Elektra sang out, "your order's up."

Blue eyes glowed down at me. "Perfect timing." He stepped back, to allow me to go first. "After you," he said.

My smile was stiff as I said my goodbyes to Mrs. Hazelton and her crew.

Gideon took his leave much more gallantly, sprinkling compliments like powdered sugar over the table of elderly ladies until they were practically swooning. But he was fast enough to make sure he was there to open the door for me, so we stepped together into the spring sunshine.

We walked a few steps before I said, "You do know you just threw enough grist into the rumor mill to keep it churning for days."

He chuckled and winked at me. "I think we both know it's been grinding about us since our evening at Stumbles. But how could they not? As I understand things from . . . well, everyone in town, it's been quite some time since Everest Kennedy let her hair down and had a little fun in life. It's only natural that when that fun involves a devastatingly handsome man from out of town, it's going to set their tongues wagging."

I shot him a look. "How do you already know Mrs. Hazelton?"

"My dear," Gideon said reproachfully, "if there's one thing I've learned over the years, it's that the best way to get a foothold in town is to make yourself accessible to the local gang of busybodies. Once they've had their chance to rake you over the coals, they're your best PR team. You're no longer an outsider if you've been indoctrinated into the fold." He winked at me again. "Plus, *someone* did suggest that I take a little time to get to know Mimosa and make sure my plans were the best thing for it. Who am I to ignore such sage advice?"

I tried not to get too hopeful at his words. It was hard to reconcile Gideon with my prior experiences with real estate developers. His tactics were in stark contrast to the snakes who'd ruined Weaver. They certainly had taken zero interest in the community.

"Careful, or Mrs. Hazelton will have you filling out a membership for the country club. Of course, that way your tuxedos wouldn't need to go in mothballs for the duration of your stay here."

Gideon's lips quirked, but his eyes grew thoughtful for a moment. After a blink, though, they were back to their normal teasing glint. "No question here. Mrs. Hazelton requires the Tom Ford. The Armani has too much of a European cut. She'd turn me out on my ear."

I couldn't hide my smile but downplayed it with a shake of my head. He genuinely seemed to enjoy Mrs. Hazelton and her band of nosy nellies. Sure, it was beneficial to his cause, but his flirtatious banter also shone a playful spotlight on them that had been dark for decades.

"You don't approve of my methods," Gideon said.

"No, it's not that." I actually thought his tactics were smart *and* pretty freaking adorable. I pictured him cozying up to and thrilling little old ladies up and down the eastern seaboard.

"Then what?" he asked.

"I guess I'm still trying to figure you out," I admitted. *You mean figure out what to do about wanting to jump his bones,* my subconscious helpfully—and bitchily—pointed out.

"Figure me out? Why, Everest, as I've said ad nauseam at this point, I'm an open book. As easy to figure out as two plus two," he said.

"Except with you, it keeps adding up to something other than four," I said.

We'd reached my truck, and I grabbed the handle. Before I could tug it open, his hand slid over mine, sending those pesky bolts of energy up my arm. His palm was warm and smooth over my knuckles, and his chest pressed against my shoulder blades. The desire to lean back into him was potent.

"Allow me," he said and wrapped long fingers over mine and around the handle. When the door opened, he moved his hand to the top of the doorframe, holding it open for me.

I slid behind the wheel. "Thank you."

"Any time, Everest," he said.

Before I could shut the door, he asked, "What are you doing later?"

"Well, I—"

His phone rang and he pulled it out. After a quick look at the screen, he declined the call and dropped the phone back into his pocket.

"Sorry about that," he said. "Where was I? Oh yes, how do you feel about Italian for dinner?"

"I don't think—"

The shrill ring of his cell phone interrupted me again. Gideon grumbled under his breath and took the phone out once more. This time, he accepted the call but held it against his chest. "One second, Everest."

He turned around, standing squarely in the space between the door and the body of my truck, so I could do nothing but sit in the driver's seat. Well, nothing but sit there and sneak peeks at his toned backside. Downward dog, indeed. I heard enough snippets of his short conversation to know it wasn't what he wanted to hear.

When he turned back to me, irritation was written in the bulge of his jaw and the stiffness of his posture. Rubbing the back of his neck, he said, "Looks like I'll need a rain check on dinner."

"I don't think I agreed to *have* dinner with you," I said.

Dimples appeared with his smile. "You would've."

I started my truck. "I guess we'll never know, since you've now got other plans."

He draped an arm over the roof and leaned down into the truck, looking up at me with regret in his blue eyes. "I have to head back to Boston for a few days."

An unnerving sense of disappointment bloomed in my chest, which was crazy since I *knew* he'd be going back to Boston. Not just today but permanently at some point in the near future. Hiding my discomfort with both his absence and my reaction to it, I slapped on a smile. "Have a good trip."

"I'll text you once I know when I'll be back. I shouldn't be gone longer than a few days."

"You don't report to me, Gideon," I insisted but couldn't completely quash the flittering of my heart at the concept.

Rising back to standing, he grinned down at me. "Nonsense. I made you a promise to draw you out of your self-imposed isolation and show you how to live a little. It would be bush league of me to renege on our deal so quickly."

With a tug of my hair, he added, "You're not getting off the hook that easily, Everest." Shutting my door with a jaunty salute, he headed off down the sidewalk, leaving me staring after him and watching the twin benefits of sun salutations tucked into a pair of designer slacks.

chapter sixteen

GIDEON

I'm sorry. You want to do *what*?" Jamie glared across the conference room table at me.

Uncowed, I met his stare head-on. "Which part did you not follow, Jamie? I thought I was clear." I gestured to the roughed-out sketches and plans scattered over the center of the table.

I could almost hear the click of his hair-trigger temper as his brows drew into a severe "V," his mouth going white at the corners. "No, you were perfectly *clear*, Gids. What I'm trying to understand is why you're talking about sacking tens of thousands of dollars of plans, not to mention the delay in the schedule, in favor of some half-baked idea you cooked up in a week!"

"Let's all take a step back here," Davidson chimed in. He rose from his seat next to Jamie and crossed to the windows, hands clasped behind his back while he looked down at the harbor. "This project has been in the works for several months now, Gideon. We all had a hand in putting these plans together, all agreed on what this project was going to look like and *where* it would be constructed." Glancing back at me with a wry smile. "Surely, you can understand how this . . . pivot in direction is hitting Jamie and me out of the blue. After all, last we talked, you said things were going swimmingly down there and we shouldn't worry."

"There's still no reason to worry," I said, doing my best to keep the edge out of my voice. "After spending some time in Mimosa, I realized there might be a new, better direction to go with the commercial side of the development."

Jamie's eyes narrowed. "Spending time in Mimosa or spending time with one local in particular?"

I didn't flinch, at least not outwardly, at the accusation. "I'm not sure I follow what you're saying, Jameson."

He rose, palms flattened on the table in front of him. "Then let me spell it out for you, Gideon. I think you've gotten your head turned by some hot piece of local ass and it's affecting your judgment."

Anger—quick, hot, and dangerous—flared within me. "I'll caution you to tread carefully," I said, ice seeping into my tone.

Jamie rocked back with a sharp bark of laughter. "Jesus Christ, Gideon, you wanna fuck a townie, be my guest. Hell, go down there and bang the whole goddamn garden club for all I care. But for fuck's sake, don't let your dick make business decisions! The plan we had is solid, bankable, and proven. There's no reason to deviate now, especially not when we're about to close the fucking deal!"

"Jamie," Davidson cautioned, but there was no stopping him once he got on a roll.

"We told you," Jamie continued. "We *told* you to stay away from Everest Kennedy." His laugh was tight and humorless. "But you just couldn't do that, could you?" Scrubbing a hand down his face, he went on. "I must admit, though, this is a wrinkle I didn't see coming. My main concern was that you'd screw her and then the deal would get screwed. I never thought you'd get your dick wet and decide to fuck us too."

If he didn't shut up, I was going to murder him right there in our bright, sunny conference room in front of all our staff. "I'll tell you one more time, Jameson. Watch your fucking mouth."

He sneered at me. "Or what? What exactly are you going to do to me that's worse than costing me months of delay and God knows how much money?"

I rose from my seat, tugging the cuffs of my shirt below those of my suit jacket. Davidson tensed as I rounded the end of the table toward Jamie. Jamie, of course, simply turned to face me with self-assured arrogance, confident I wouldn't beat him to a pulp. That confidence was sorely misplaced. He realized it in the final seconds before I'd grabbed him by his lapels and shoved him against the floor-to-ceiling windows. Shock registered in his eyes as his back hit glass.

"We've been friends a long time, Jamie," I said, punctuating my statement with a small shove. "But don't mistake longevity for permanence. You've overstepped here, my friend, and would be wise to retreat while you are still able."

Jamie's eyes went wide with confusion. "Gids, what the fuck? All this over some—"

Another shove made the window behind him shudder. "Don't," I said, my voice low and flat.

Davidson appeared at my side, hand on my bicep. "Can we not act like frat bros on a Friday night in front of the staff, please?" When I didn't immediately release Jamie, he gave my arm a firm squeeze. "Gideon," his voice was quiet but assertive.

I let go of Jamie and stepped backward, my hands flexing with the need to throttle the life out of him. He smoothed down his jacket and rolled his shoulders, still looking at me as though I'd gone a little mad.

Which, given the red haze that had descended over my vision, was entirely possible. I needed to regain control.

Turning my back on them, I walked to the opposite window and stared out. It was a beautiful day, and the water was smooth, boats barely bobbing in their moorings. "I'm not sleeping with Everest," I said to the window. *Not yet,* said the annoying little voice in my head that also liked to catalog all the times I'd *thought* about sleeping with Everest.

At Jamie's disbelieving snort, I turned to look at both of them. "It's the truth," I said. "I know the ramifications for the project if Everest and I were to get together. We all do. We can't afford to have her dad recuse himself at this stage of the negotiations with the town, especially if we make the changes I'm suggesting. His support for the project is too important to risk having him step back for conflict of interest reasons. We don't need the council getting antsy about our motivations for the change—or any other reasons. Which means that I haven't slept with Everest, nor do I intend to." *Liar.* God, that inner voice was a complete dick. He was right, but fuck, did he have to be so superior about it?

Jamie tilted his head in contemplation, as though he couldn't understand the concept of being swayed by something other than sex. "You're serious," he said. It was a statement, not a question, but I nodded nonetheless.

"Then what—" Jamie started, but Davidson cut him off.

"We'll get to the recusal issue later, since it's apparently not yet an issue." I caught the "not yet" but kept my mouth shut. Davidson pointed at the sketches and photographs on the table. "But these came from her, didn't they?"

"In a manner of speaking, yeah," I said.

After Everest had shown me Weaver Village and what used to be downtown Weaver, I hadn't been able to let go of the concerns she'd outlined. She'd shown me actual proof of what she feared would happen.

I couldn't just ignore it and soldier on without giving serious thought to whether she was right—and if she were, whether I could live with it. I'd spent the intervening week doing my own research into other options. Starting with what was available in Mimosa. As it turned out, there was *a lot* available.

Davidson resumed his seat at the table and waited until Jamie and I had done the same. Steepling his fingers, he relaxed back in his chair. "Why?"

"Why what?" I asked.

"Why are you taking suggestions from a woman you haven't even known a month? Suggestions which, I might add, would result in a large-scale revamp of what we'd planned to do in Mimosa." There was no judgment in his question. He simply wanted to know the answer.

I couldn't translate into words the feeling I'd gotten listening to Everest or seeing Weaver. Even if I could, "feelings" had no place in this discussion. Jamie and Davidson wanted reasons supported by data they could research and prove. My not wanting to be the death knell of a community would not suffice.

"Because they're good suggestions," I said. Davidson raised a brow, waiting for more. Sighing, I rested my elbows on the table and outlined the other reason I was advocating this change. The reason that had me excited in a way I had never been about a project before. "What we planned was good but unoriginal. Just one more eat-work-play development of which there are thousands all over the East Coast."

"There are thousands of those developments because they work," Jamie said, but the quick flare of his temper had been banked, and his shoulders had relaxed. He might still be irritated, but he was at least willing to listen. "Just like this one would work."

"Don't we want to build something better than that? Something that doesn't just 'work'? Something that . . ." I hesitated, searching for the words that would capture my enthusiasm for this plan. "Something that stands out. Really sets us apart. This change might shrink the size of what we'd planned, but it elevates the level of the development. This, if it works out, could be *the* unique jewel in the portfolio. Something that puts Standard head and shoulders above the competition."

I spread out the photos I'd taken of downtown Mimosa over the last week. "Look at this architecture," I said. "It's unique in ways we can't build anymore. At least not within a budget. But restoring it, rehabbing it, and repurposing it? *That* is something we can do. Something *different*."

Davidson slid a few of the photos closer then picked them up to look through them. His brow creased in thought as he stared at the buildings. "What's the construction date on these?"

Latching onto his interest, I leaned forward. "Some of them predate the Civil War, but the majority are 1890s to early 1920s."

Jamie leaned in, anger forgotten as quickly as it appeared. "What's their condition?"

"For their age? Excellent. For rehabbing? I'd say good with a small percentage of fair to not great."

Davidson and Jamie exchanged a look then pulled the rest of the photos toward them, slowly flipping through them.

I tried not to let their interest get my hopes up, but it was difficult. I'd become invested in this new direction. After speaking with Everest and seeing the shell of Weaver, I'd questioned our whole approach in Mimosa. Did we need the commercial element to be constructed on the same site as the residential? Did we need all the new homes to be built there? Or was there some other option that would give us a more distinctive product while keeping the character of Mimosa as intact as possible? The character that would make people want to move there, work there, visit there. The character I'd not just experienced but wholly enjoyed during my brief time in town.

These had been the thoughts rambling about in my head as I'd walked down the main thoroughfare, past open shops as well as spaces marked with "Available Now." One such space had a bright blue door set into charmingly crumbling brick with wide bay windows looking into an empty yet clean interior. For a moment, I envisioned a bustling office within that space, with stylish period pieces in the lobby and a wide, masculine desk in the room with the bay window. The person seated at the desk looked remarkably like me, which gave me a start. Staring into that window and the possibility the empty space held, an idea hit with staggering intensity. Why build new space when there were better spaces already constructed?

Renovation and rehab were all the rage now, especially in the demographic we wanted to attract. Most of them would shave off their immaculately coiffed facial hair for first dibs on a building with exposed brick. Especially if that brick were original to the building. The more I thought about it, the better it sounded. The better it would sound to Everest. This would be one PowerPoint she'd be unable to resist. Not that her opinion was the most important, but it did rank highly—a thought I wasn't certain what to do about, so I'd shoved it away and concentrated on getting as much information about available, existing buildings in downtown Mimosa as I could within the week. I had to convince Jamie and Davidson this was a solid idea, which was the purpose of that morning's meeting.

Davidson looked up first, passing the stack of photos to Jamie. His face was impassive but open. I took that as a good sign. "This is an interesting direction," he said noncommittally. One corner of his lips hooked up in a not quite smile. "A direction I wish we'd thought of before securing the architectural renderings and site analysis for a completely different area, but interesting just the same."

Jamie glanced at Davidson then me. He sighed then shook his head with a half smile. "I wish I could say you're both crazy . . . but I can't.

Regardless of where this idea came from, it's a good one. Late in the game but good."

Relief settled over me, and I smiled. "Glad you think so. I'll head back down to Mimosa and start the real due diligence on all these locations. See if we can really make a go of this thing."

"Before you skip back off to the airport, Gids," Davidson said, his tone deceptively light, "let's circle back to that issue of recusal, shall we?"

Fuck. "Sure," I said. "What else is there to discuss?"

"How about all of it?" Davidson asked.

I fought to keep my face and voice impassive. "All of what?"

Davidson adjusted his tie and sighed. "I'd rather you do me the courtesy of not trying to bullshit me, Gids, but if you want me to do this via cross-examination, that's fine too."

"Always gotta find a way to mention you went to law school, huh?" I asked, trying for humor, but Davidson wasn't biting.

"Everest Kennedy is the mayor's daughter. The mayor cannot vote in the self-interest of either himself or a family member, nor can he vote on a project in which he or said family member has an interest. In the event Everest Kennedy—again, *the mayor's daughter*—were to strike up a relationship with a developer presenting his plans for approval to council, then it follows that Everest Kennedy has a personal interest in that development. Which means, does it not, that the mayor would not be allowed to participate in any discussion, and more importantly, any *vote* related to that project in which his daughter's boyfriend has an interest?"

"I'm not Everest's boyfriend," I said, hating the word and the way it juvenilized things.

"Then what precisely are you, Gids?" Davidson asked. "And let me take it one step further. Is whatever you are, or whatever you want to be with this girl, worth losing the most important voting member of council at a point in time where you're essentially changing the scope of the project?"

"Everest and I are friends," I said.

Davidson smiled tightly. "No, Gids, you and I are friends. You and Jamie are friends. You and Everest are most certainly more than friends. Just because you haven't acted on it doesn't mean you don't want to or you're not going to."

"You don't even know her, so I don't think you're in a position to—"

"I know you," Davidson interrupted. "And because I know you, I know when you're interested in someone. And *not* as a friend. You want something with this girl, Gids. What we all need to know is whether what you want with her is worth the risk you're taking, for all of us, if you act on it."

Jamie chimed in before I could respond. "This is something you need to think about, man. We know if Mayor Kennedy votes in our favor, this is a done deal. The rest of the council will fall in line. If he recuses himself, there goes our guarantee. Is Everest enough of a sure thing to justify that?"

A few hours later, I sank onto a barstool, loosened my tie, and signaled the bartender for a drink. After the meeting with Jamie and Davidson, I'd gotten pulled into a zoning crisis on one of our projects at the Cape. The day had been absolutely rugged, and all I wanted was a stiff drink, after which I planned to crash facedown into my bed and sleep for the twelve hours between now and my flight back to North Carolina.

The bartender brought my bourbon, and after a grateful swig, I swiveled on my stool to survey the crowd. It was a little after nine on a Saturday night, and the lounge area of the small bar was already crowded. Women dressed in sleek, body-hugging dresses with skyscraper heels, while men were dressed similarly to me in dress shirts and slacks. Everyone buffed

and polished to perfection, preening and posturing amongst themselves—
the elite version of the urban jungle.

Unexpected melancholy crept over me at how detached and impersonal everything seemed. There was a sense of anonymity, even among
all these people. I was an island unto myself among a sea of well-dressed
strangers. It was a far cry from the jean-clad familiarity I'd seen at Stumbles
or well-intentioned meddling at Mean Muggin'. People here stuck to
their little groups and didn't meander over to ask how someone's grandmother was doing or whether a promotion had come through. Instead
of welcoming smiles and slaps on the back, there were calculated conversations using body language of a whole other variety. I'd been coming
here for years and never noticed the transactional undercurrents swirling
in the interactions of the patrons around me. Probably because I'd been
content to let them carry me along, dallying a night or two in the shallower eddies, only to flow smoothly downstream to the next encounter
without a backward glance.

"Gideon?"

I surfaced from my existential musings. Standing to my left in a fitted
white sheath dress and nude stilettos was Amanda Alcott. If I'd had my
wits about me, I would've seen her coming and exited stage left. Amanda,
or Mandy as she was known to those of us who'd been stupid enough
to end up in bed with her, and I had "dated" briefly earlier in the year.

I hadn't seen her since we'd parted in early February. She was a beautiful woman, with long blonde hair and killer legs. But there was something
vacant in her smile. As through it weren't a smile at all. Her lips curved
into the requisite shape and her perfectly straight teeth shone unnaturally white against her deep red lipstick. For all intents and purposes, it
was worthy of a toothpaste ad, all bright and glossy. But that's all it was.
An ad. It wasn't there because she was genuinely happy to see me. It was
there, because she was pushing a product—herself.

Surreptitiously, I leaned back on my stool, putting a little distance between us. "Amanda," I said with cordial formality. "Lovely to see you."

She stepped closer and rested her hand on my forearm, notes of an expensive perfume drifting toward me. "Amanda? Gideon, I think you of all people know to call me Mandy." Wide blue eyes, rimmed by long lashes, batted flirtatiously at me. One more step and her breasts grazed my bicep. "You're looking well," she said, her eyes wandering slowly over my body, lingering pointedly at certain areas.

"Thank you," I said. "As always, you look beautiful."

Lifting her martini glass, she drained the remaining liquid. Her tongue slid artfully over her bottom lip, as much to draw the male gaze as to get the last drop. The crowded lounge provided the perfect excuse for her to squeeze next to me and set the empty glass on the beveled bar top. I could feel the swell of her breasts against my shoulder as she angled her body to line up with mine. It was a deft move, one designed to entice me into her practiced web of seduction. One I would most likely have fallen for less than a month ago. But tonight, it simply made me want to head for the door. Alone.

With a move that would've made Channing Tatum jealous, I spun off my stool and extracted myself from the mantrap she'd cunningly set. I tilted my glass at the now vacant stool. "Please, take my seat. I was just heading out."

"But I thought we could catch up." She pouted prettily, her fingers sliding down my forearm.

Putting my half-full glass next to her empty one, I gave her my best letdown smile. "Another time, perhaps. I've had a bear of a day, I'm afraid." I wedged a fifty between our glasses. "But have your next drink on me."

Without giving her a chance to make a second run at getting me to stay, I shouldered my way through the throng of people and into the cool evening air. The sounds of the night in Boston hit my ears in an immediate onslaught. Cabbies honked, traffic whooshed by, and various conversations spilled from the outdoor patios of restaurants lining the street. People were shaking off the eternally long winter and grabbing the warmer spring temperature with both hands. It was a busy night, and the city thrummed with a vibrant energy.

This was the pace I was used to, the one that kept my blood pumping and my synapses firing with brilliant ideas. It was disconcerting to suddenly miss the chirping of crickets and slow spring evenings spent with a cold beer on the porch of my rental in Mimosa.

Strolling toward my condo, weaving through the crowd, my thoughts drifted to Everest and what she might be doing. Without me there to show her the finer points of relaxation, she was probably still at work, grinding away. That wouldn't do. I slipped my phone out of my inside jacket pocket and swiped screens until I pulled up her number, but I hesitated before making the call.

I hadn't been able to answer Davidson and Jamie earlier about whether taking a chance on something with Everest was worth gambling with council's vote on the project. Because, in all honesty, I didn't know. I didn't know whether Everest would be receptive to any sort of relationship. I could tell she was attracted to me, but she'd also made it very clear work was her main focus and she had little inclination to allow anything else to intrude.

But there'd been moments, like the one at dinner, or when she'd taken my handkerchief, or just looked at me that I felt . . . something. Something deeper than lust, stronger than desire, and more urgent than the current burning need I had to know what she tasted like. Whatever that was, it crackled between us like lightning in a summer storm, and I wanted more of it. But did she? Would she be open to exploring what I thought was brewing between us? Only one way to find out. I hit "call."

Sidestepping a street vendor, I listened to the phone ring repeatedly. I was mapping out a scolding voicemail in my mind when she answered.

"Hello?"

"Should I be insulted that you don't have my name saved in your phone?"

"Gideon?"

"Who else would be calling you from Boston?"

"A telemarketer."

"So you don't have my number saved."

There was a pause. "I didn't say that."

I smiled in triumph but said, "Then why did you sound surprised it was me?"

She huffed irritably. "Probably because I wasn't expecting to hear from you."

"I called to make sure you weren't still working," I said. "Where are you?"

This time, the pause went on longer before she dodged the question. "Where are you?"

"I just left a bar, and now I'm headed home. Your turn."

"I'm heading home myself." I heard papers shuffling in the background and knew she was at work.

"From where?"

"Why does it matter?" She continued to evade answering me.

"Because, Everest," I answered as though she were a two-year-old, "if you're still at work this late, I'm going to be very disappointed in you."

"What are you going to do, punish me?"

This time, the silence on the line was thick and heavy. Several illicit scenarios buzzed through my mind and straight to my groin. Jamie and Davidson's earlier warnings helped to shove those aside, and I cleared my throat right as she blurted, "I didn't mean that the way it sounded."

I swallowed my chuckle at the embarrassment in her voice. "Yes, well, it sounded very . . . intriguing."

She groaned in humiliation then said, "Can we just forget the last forty-five seconds?"

"Only if you admit that you were toiling away at your desk until I called and now you're guiltily slinking down to your truck to drive home, already planning to be back at work bright and early tomorrow."

"I'm not slinking, guiltily or otherwise," she muttered. "But what about you? Nine thirty is awfully early in the evening for a man-about-town like you to be heading home. Not enough ladies around for you to chat up?"

"Darling, your Boston accent is positively awful," I said and couldn't hold back a laugh at her terrible impression. "Honestly, I'm beat from the past few days, and I didn't have it in me to participate in inane babble with anyone about anything. One drink was all it took for me to decide I had better booze and more comfortable seating at my own home."

"Leaving dozens of broken hearts in your wake, I'm sure," she said.

I thought about the disappointment on Amanda's face at my hasty exit and couldn't bring myself to give two shits. Changing the subject, I said, "I plan to cash in that rain check when I get back tomorrow."

"That implies we'd actually made plans. I don't remember agreeing to have dinner with you," she persisted, but I could hear the smile in her voice.

"Our dining together was a foregone conclusion," I said, and her laughter broke free. It brought what I knew was a goofy smile to my face. "I'll pick you up at six."

"Sounds like I don't have a choice," she said.

"We all have choices, Everest," I said. "I'm just helping you make the right ones."

"And you're the right choice?"

"Sweetheart, I'm the best one you'll ever make."

chapter seventeen

GIDEON

At 5:55 the following evening, my fingers tapped against the steering wheel in restless anticipation as I turned my rental car into Everest's driveway. I was twitchy with energy and had been since waking up that morning. Like a high schooler with a crush, I'd been counting the minutes until I would see Everest. It was rather pathetic, but since no one knew what I was doing, my humiliation was at a minimum.

I parked next to her truck and almost skipped up the three stairs to her front porch. Her little bungalow was neat and tidy, with spring flowers starting to spill out of the baskets hanging from the eaves on the porch. A welcome mat with intertwined horseshoes lay in front of the screen door. I pulled it open to knock, but the inner door opened before my knuckles hit the wood.

A frazzled, jean-clad Everest was on the other side rummaging through her purse and muttering to herself. Her long red hair was pulled through an overwhelmed elastic tie into a messy ponytail. "Aha!" she cried triumphantly and hoisted her keys from her purse.

"I'm not familiar with whatever game this is," I said, "but it appears as though you've won."

The keys she'd been so excited to find clattered to the floor in a noisy tinkle as she yelped in surprise. "Gideon! What are you doing here?"

I retrieved her keys from the porch floor and handed them to her. "I'm here to take you to dinner," I said.

"Dinner?" she asked, her brow wrinkling in confusion.

"Yes, Everest. It's the meal that typically follows lunch in a given day. I think you're familiar with it, since we've shared at least one together." I sized up her scuffed boots poking from beneath worn jeans, topped by a half-buttoned flannel over a T-shirt. I knew she was a more casual girl but was reasonably sure this wouldn't be an outfit she'd wear to dinner.

"I take it you weren't rushing to the door to greet me because you were so excited I'm back in town," I said.

She closed her eyes and tilted her head back against the door. "Crap," she said softly. Opening them, she looked at me regretfully. "I'm afraid *I'll* need a rain check on dinner," she said and stepped onto the porch, pulling the door shut firmly behind her.

"Hot date?" I asked teasingly, even though the thought of that made my stomach knot.

"Hardly," she said as she headed down the steps. I followed behind her.

"I got a call from Wyatt. They just had an abuse and neglect case get reported and wanted to know if I had space for a mama and baby. I'm headed over to the barn to hook up the trailer and head out." She was halfway down the walk when she said, "Sorry about dinner."

"No need to be sorry," I replied, perversely relieved that she was going to rescue some poor, pitiful animal instead of seeing another man. Sure, it made me an insensitive, self-centered asshole, but I couldn't help it. "I'm happy to come with you and help."

Everest looked back at me with an appreciative but disbelieving grin. "I don't know if that's a good idea, Gideon."

I looked down at my slacks and button-up, which I'd paired with my favorite Prada loafers. "Trust me," I said. "This outfit is more durable than it looks." It wasn't, not in the slightest, but I wasn't going to let that stop me from seeing her tonight.

"Like the last one you wore?" she asked.

The jeans and sneakers from my last encounter with her workplace had been thrown into the trash as soon as I'd gotten home that night. "Exactly like that," I said.

She hesitated a moment longer but then gave in with a shrug. "Hop in," she said but stopped with her hand on the driver's side door. Turning around slowly, she looked at me. Her expression was patient but also cautious. "Gideon, you should know situations like this are more than messy. There's more involved than possibly ruining your fancy shoes or high-priced wardrobe. The sadness of these rescues can break your heart. I don't want you to be unprepared for this. I appreciate your offer—really, I do. But I also won't think less of you if you stay behind."

I rounded the hood of her truck, determined to prove I was up to the challenge. "How could I possibly turn down that delightful invitation?"

Four hours later, I was filthy, sweaty, and in further awe of Everest Kennedy. It wasn't that I didn't know people who cared about animals or other worthy causes. I did. I'd gone to galas where people spent thousands of dollars to save some endangered species or the other. I had given money to local shelters back in Boston and toyed with the idea of getting a rescue pup. And it wasn't like my heartstrings were immune to the sad-eyed dogs on the television with Sarah McLachlan singing mournfully in the background.

But never in my entire life had I experienced anything like what I'd just done with Everest. I looked over at her from the passenger seat of the larger truck she used to haul a horse trailer. She drove with one hand on the wheel, the other resting lightly on the window frame as the cool night air blew through the cab of the truck. She was as dirty, if not more so, than I was, having been knocked face first into the muck by a terrified horse. Her flannel was torn in two places, and a streak of mud decorated her right cheekbone. She should've been exhausted and ready to drop, but instead, an energized serenity shone like a halo around her. I could see it in the small smile that hovered on her lips and warmed her eyes.

Those gorgeous eyes flicked over to me when she felt my stare. "What?" she asked.

I didn't know how to tell her how amazing I thought she was. "I think you've got a little something . . ." I pointed to my own cheek.

She tugged down her visor and checked the mirror. "A little something, huh?" she said with a laugh as she scrubbed at the mud on her face. "More like I look like I went for one of those fancy mudpacks you probably get."

"Don't knock it until you've tried it," I said.

Everest glanced down at my clothes. "Sorry about ruining another designer outfit," she said.

I didn't even try to deny it. Thankfully, Wyatt had been there when we pulled up and loaned me a pair of boots to spare my Pradas. But the rest of my ensemble couldn't be saved by the best dry cleaner on the planet. "No big deal," I said.

"I'll make it up to you," she promised.

"You will, huh?" I asked.

She nodded and grinned. "Sure. Once I get these two bedded down and calm, I'll take you to dinner at the closest drive-through."

The "two" she referred to were an emaciated lady horse and her baby. When we'd pulled down the rutted lane that led to a ramshackle building behind a rotten fence topped with rusted barbed wire, I thought we must have made a wrong turn somewhere. It couldn't be possible for anything to live in that. Everest's mouth had been set in a grim line when she parked the truck next to Wyatt's patrol car. Before we got out, I saw a tiny little horse face peek out from the structure, its wide, frightened eyes partially covered by matted bangs. Dread pooled in my stomach when I realized that had to be the baby horse Wyatt had called Everest about.

It only got worse when the mama horse appeared from the gloom behind the baby. She was so thin, her forehead looked concave and her cheeks sunken. I didn't see how she could move—her chest was so withered and narrow. The saddest part were her eyes though. It was like someone had drained the hope right out of them. I'd never experienced simultaneous anger and despair before, but looking at that poor, wretched creature, I felt like I were being strangled by both.

Everest, on the other hand, was cool and collected as she conferred with Wyatt. She retrieved some type of collar thing and some other tiny little macramé-looking thing, along with a leash from the back seat. I watched, transfixed, as she slogged her way through the muck toward the two horses. Needing to get closer, I scrambled down out of the truck and over to Wyatt.

"Hey, man," he said, taking in my attire. "Let me guess. This wasn't what you had planned for tonight."

"Not exactly," I said.

He grinned. "What size shoe do you wear?"

"Ten and a half. Why?"

"Because you're in luck," he answered and reached into the back of his squad car to grab a pair of galoshes. "Those," he said and pointed to my loafers, "aren't gonna last out here."

Once I was properly shod, he and I walked over to the fence to watch Everest.

Her gait was slow and measured, and I could barely hear her mumbling softly to the two horses. She didn't hurry or rush, so it felt like an eternity before she reached the door. Stretching out a hand, she held it under the larger horse's nose. The horse's nostrils flickered slightly, but there was no other sign of interest. Just a placid acceptance that broke my heart. The baby had disappeared at Everest's initial approach.

I tensed, gripping the weathered wood of the fence.

Wyatt gave me a casual glance. "You do know she's done this before, right?"

Forcing myself to relax even though my heart was in my throat, I said, "Sure, of course."

"Then why do you look like you're gonna puke?"

I pulled my eyes from where Everest was gently stroking the horse's face and looked at Wyatt.

He smirked and shook his head. "I thought so."

"I'm sorry," I said. "You thought what?"

"Everest is pretty blind about matters that don't involve horses," he said. "It's one of the things that makes her so good at what she does. Me, on the other hand"—he propped a foot on the lowest rung of the fence—"I've got to be a little more observant. Comes with the badge, I suppose. You, my friend, are ass over teakettle about Everest."

"Excuse me?" I asked. "I'm what?"

"You've got it bad, brother. Can't blame you. Everest is pretty awesome, and I'm not saying that because she's my girl's best friend. It's just the honest truth."

"Everest and I are friends," I said, repeating the semi-lie I'd told Jamie and Davidson.

"Right," said Wyatt, his drawl making it clear he would sooner believe almost anything else. "That's cool, man. And so long as you do right by her, it always will be. But . . . if you don't . . ." He gave me a long, cool stare that went on a beat or two past comfortable. Then he smiled and clapped me on the shoulder. "I don't think we need to get into that, do we? Since y'all are just friends and all."

"Right," I said, suddenly fearing banjo music and a long ride down a desolate road. "Nothing to worry about."

"Glad to hear it," he said.

The two of us looked back to Everest, who had clipped a leash onto the collar-like thing she'd put around the horse's face and was trying to coax her forward. Even in her weakened state, the horse balked a little before stumbling out. Her sides could've been used in an anatomy class to illustrate the location of each rib and hip bone. I couldn't tell whether her coat was dark brown or she was covered in mud. Twigs were knotted in her mane, and her tail was a disheveled mass. It was beyond tragic.

Everest led her in a slow march toward us. I met her eyes, and the sadness in them almost brought me to my knees. Before I even realized what I was doing, I had the gate open and was walking toward her. Mud sucked at the bottoms of my borrowed boots, which kept my steps slow.

"Hey there, Gideon," Everest said in a soft, even voice. "Meet Ruby."

"Hi, Ruby," I said, making sure my tone stayed low and even. I glanced over Everest's shoulder. "What about the baby?"

Everest kept up her steady trek toward the gate. "I'm hoping Lil' Bit won't be too far behind his mama," she said.

As if on cue, the tiny little snout I'd seen earlier poked out, followed by a smoky gray head with a white star in the center. A reedy whinny bleated out, making Ruby stop in her tracks and pull against the lead in Everest's hand. Her answering neigh was sharp and a lot stronger than I expected. Evidence that maternal instinct trumped starvation.

"Wyatt," Everest called quietly. "Back the trailer around, will you? We'll drop the ramp right here at the gate."

Wyatt wasted no time in following Everest's orders and had the trailer in position with lightning speed.

"Gideon, I need you to open the gate and let down the ramp. Can you do that?"

"Sure," I said and hurried to do my part. The creak of the ramp had Ruby doing a little high step in retreat, but Everest held her ground, uttering soothing noises to calm the horse.

"What else can I do?" I asked, returning to stand in front of Ruby.

The next few seconds unfolded in slow motion. That is, after a little gray blur came darting up to the other side of Ruby. Sensing a threat to her baby, Ruby tossed her head and rocked onto her wobbly back legs. Her nose caught me squarely in the chest and completely off guard, sending me sprawling backward. There was no way to brace myself or get my footing in the sludge we were standing in, so I went down like a tree. Terrified of being trampled, I rolled to the side, which only served to further cover me in grime.

Everest managed to keep hold of Ruby but was sliding around herself. The end of the lead dragged through the mud and swung back up to slap Everest in the face. But still, she held on, and somehow her voice never rose above a peaceful murmur as she talked to Ruby. I shoved myself up to my hands and knees and then rose like *Swamp Thing*, cautiously keeping my distance from Ruby.

"Come stand on this side," Everest directed me. "Wyatt, get on the other. I just need you two to keep her going straight." I did as I was told, and so did Wyatt.

In the interim, Everest switched the short lead for a longer one, which she wound through the bars on one of the trailer windows. Using that like a hoist, or a pulley, she started pulling Ruby closer and closer to the trailer. Finally, her front hooves were on the ramp, which she didn't like at all, and she tried to bail toward Wyatt. He reacted quickly and stepped closer, spreading his arms wide. Ruby skittered away and higher up the ramp. Everest swiftly took up the slack on the lead, giving Ruby no choice but to clamber up the last few feet into the trailer. Everest dropped the rope and shut the small gate behind Ruby.

Everest put her hands on her knees and drew in a few breaths, shoving back strands of hair that had escaped her ponytail. "One down," she said with a triumphant grin. She peeled out of her flannel and hung it on the side of the trailer. "One to go."

Wyatt and I looked over at the tiny gray foal scampering back and forth, whinnying its head off for its mother.

"Take your positions, boys," Everest instructed, and Wyatt and I once again faced each other at the base of the trailer ramp.

"What are you going to do?" I asked.

"You ever see *Rocky*, Gideon?" she asked.

"Uh, yeah. Why?"

"Remember the chicken chasing scene?"

"Who doesn't?" I asked, thoroughly confused.

"Well, that's sort of what's about to happen," she explained as she headed toward the frightened baby.

For the next fifteen minutes, the two of them juked, jived, and dodged around each other. Everest was relentless, even when she ended up sprawled face down in the mud after an ill-timed lunge. I don't know how it happened, but somehow, she got behind the little horse and shepherded it between Wyatt and me. There was nowhere other than the open bay of the trailer for it to go. It sidestepped and whinnied and tossed its little head.

"C'mon, baby," Everest cajoled from behind it. "Mama's already in there. Don't you want to join her?"

The little gray cocked its head, like it actually understood her. Then Ruby gave a low whicker, and that was it. Baby hooves clattered up the ramp and into the trailer, where it stood quivering. Everest hurried to close the bay, and then together we shut the ramp and slumped back against it.

Everest dragged a hand over her forehead. "Not a bad day's work, is it?" she'd asked me.

Standing there, dripping sweat and covered in dirt and who knew what else, she looked positively radiant. The situation we'd happened upon was dark and dismal and would have had most people spiraling into a three-day bender at the thought of what the two scrawny animals had gone through prior to our arrival. But instead of dragging her down, it seemed to invigorate her.

She rolled forward onto her toes and rubbed her hands together. "C'mon, Boston, let's get these two back to the farm."

I'd just opened the passenger door of the truck when a jacked-up pickup roared down the rutted lane and skidded to a stop behind Wyatt's patrol car. A bear of a man emerged from the driver's seat and lumbered toward us.

"Just what in the Sam Hill do you people think you're doin'?" he asked, beady eyes squinting out at us from the fleshy folds of his cheeks.

Everest closed her door and walked to the front of her truck. I flanked her, unease walking up my spine with heavily booted feet. Watching the guy's angry churning gait, the story she'd told about her mother standing up to a similar bully flashed through my mind. There was no way in hell I was going to let her get within an arm's length of him. Shifting slightly, I tried to position myself between her and the newcomer. She noticed and shot me a glare that would've scalded milk, stepping around me to face him head-on.

Wyatt beat us both to the punch and approached the man. "Sir, I'm Sergeant Jackson with the Colson County Sheriff's Department. We received a call about two horses in distress and are here responding to that call. Are you Earl Nance, the owner of this property?"

Hitching his jeans up, the man responded, "Yeah, that's me. And I want to know who in the hell called you."

"That matter is not up for discussion, sir," Wyatt responded calmly. He pulled a folded piece of paper from his hip pocket. "This is an order requiring these horses be surrendered into the care of Second Chance Farms until their condition can be evaluated by a licensed veterinarian and a court can rule on their final placement."

Bushy brows drew down when Nance looked over at Everest, taking in the farm's logo on the door of her truck. "Second Chance Farms? That's your place?"

"It is," she responded coolly.

He crossed his arms, ignoring the paper in Wyatt's outstretched hand. "You're Jack Kennedy's girl, aren't you?"

"I am," Everest said, her voice still pleasantly calm.

With a snort, Nance said, "I knew your mama before she passed. I see you're just as uppity as she was."

Everest's smile was knife-sharp and just as deadly. "Everyone looks uppity to a pig wallowing in its own slop, Mr. Nance."

Nance's face turned florid. "What did you just say to me, girl?" He started to move toward Everest.

I tensed, but once again Wyatt intervened.

"You don't want to do that, sir," Wyatt said, grabbing Nance's arm. "Things don't have to get any worse than they already are. You need to get back into your truck and let Ms. Kennedy take these horses out of here."

"The hell I will," Nance bellowed, trying to sidestep around Wyatt.

Before I realized what was happening, Everest pushed off the front of the truck and headed into the fray. Swearing, I followed, unsure of how to intervene without simultaneously offending her independence and further riling up Nance, who already looked like he was going apoplectic.

Uncertainty aside, she'd have to get over any slight to her female pride if it looked like Nance could actually hurt her. Independent or not, I'd haul her out of there on my shoulder if I had to.

"Did I speak too quickly for your feeble brain to follow?" Everest taunted from behind Wyatt. "Let me slow it down for you then. You, sir, are a disgusting excuse for a human being who deserves to spend the rest of his miserable life trapped in a cell that looks a lot like this hellhole you call a barn." Her hand went to her back pocket, and her fingers curled around something I hadn't even seen her grab.

"Not helping, Everest," Wyatt muttered, doing his best to remain in between Everest and the object of her vitriol.

I tried to intervene. "Now, there's really no need for this to get out of hand here, is there? I'm sure there's some arrangement we can come to that will be mutually beneficial for everyone, including the horses."

Everest glanced over at me, her hand tightening on whatever she had in her pocket. She frowned uncertainly but said nothing.

I took that as a sign to keep going. "Mr. . . . Nance, is it? You seem like a reasonable fellow, a man who's business minded. Why don't you and I turn this into a transaction? You name your price, and I'll gladly pay—"

"Don't," Everest said, her voice hard as steel. "Don't you even think about finishing that sentence and offering to pay this pustule one fuck-ing dime."

Keeping my eyes on the aforementioned human abscess still trying to get to Everest, I said, "Discretion is the better part of valor, Everest."

"Look around you, Gideon," she said, keeping her eyes trained on Nance. "And tell me this is a fight I can avoid. That you honestly believe I'd rather have you pay this toad than force him to face charges."

"If it means getting you out of harm's way . . ."

Everest swung her gaze to me, green eyes blazing with emotion. "Ruby and her baby are the ones in harm's way, Gideon. Not me. The question is whether you're going to help me make sure *he's* the one who pays for what he did."

Reality crashed into me with devastating force. Protecting the horses, not Everest, was the point of today. My offer to pay Nance would only rob Everest of seeing justice done. It went against everything she wanted. *Save the horse, get the girl.*

I looked at Nance. "Sorry, offer's off the table. I hope you rot."

"You little bitch," he roared as he broke free of Wyatt's hold and headed straight for Everest.

My stomach dropped because I was still a step behind her and there was no way, absent a diving tackle, I could reach her before he did. But, as with everything else, Everest was prepared. When Nance lunged, meaty hands aiming to throttle her, she drew out a short black rod and flicked her wrist, extending a tactical baton to its full two-foot length. Dodging nimbly to her left, she caught Nance's ankle as he charged past her and, with a quick jerk of her wrist, sent him sprawling face-first into the dirt.

Nance yowled in pain and humiliation, cupping his bleeding nose. "You saw that, Deputy! She assaulted me."

Wyatt stood over him and shook his head. "All I saw, Mr. Nance, was you trip and fall." He looked at me. "Is that what you saw, Mr. West?"

Slowly, I unclenched my fists as my heart resumed beating. "Actually," I said, "what I saw was this . . . *person* try and assault Ms. Kennedy before he fell on his face."

"Good point, Mr. West," Wyatt said, rocking back on his heels. He reached down and hauled Nance to his feet, an impressive accomplishment given the other man's size. "Seems like I've got a few charges to add to a growing list that starts with animal cruelty."

While Nance spouted off various obscenities, Wyatt spun him away from us and cuffed his hands while shooting Everest a wink. She responded with a grin and a quick bow that made me want to both kiss her and strangle her. "Ms. Kennedy, I think it's best if you get going," Wyatt said, with a barely disguised chuckle in his voice.

"Yes sir, Sergeant," she said sweetly and headed to her truck.

In a quieter tone to me, Wyatt added, "Make sure she gets rid of that baton."

And now, seated next to her in the truck cab, I grappled with my newfound understanding of just how dedicated she was to her cause. She would've stayed out there all night if that was what it took to get the job done and get the two horses out of harm's way. Hell, she probably would've wrestled Nance to the ground with her bare hands. What she did gave her life purpose, and it bled through onto everything else.

Everest didn't micromanage because she couldn't let go of things. She did it because she couldn't *not* make sure everything was right. To her, every decision and every task mattered just as much as the next one, because together they all impacted the animals she fought so hard to save. Guilt at standing in the way of any part of it by buying the property next door tugged at my insides. I could tell myself that was business and wholly separate from whatever was growing between us, but that was total bullshit. I needed to figure out how to make it right.

"You're staring again," she said with a half grin.

All I could think was, how could I not stare at this beautiful woman who honored her late mother by making it her life's work to rescue the perishing? And taking on the world to do it. It would've been easier to ignore the Mona Lisa than it was to take my eyes off Everest.

I was so screwed.

chapter eighteen

EVEREST

Gideon West at the Black and White Ball escorting Ms. Amanda Alcott. The caption of the picture blared out at me from the screen of my computer as though it were in 3-D. Of course, the picture itself was worse. Ms. Amanda Alcott was at least seven feet tall, three-quarters of which was leg, and the rest was all boobs and perfect teeth. Okay, maybe there was a tiny portion left over for her immaculately styled blonde hair, but there was zero room for flaws. I knew that because I'd spent the last half hour zooming in and out of the photo looking for them. Yes, it was petty. Did I care? No, not at all.

My desk chair creaked loudly as I sank back into it, the sound almost as despondent as I now felt. Hand on the mouse, I clicked back to the main page of photos, torturing myself with more images of a tuxedo-clad Gideon and Ms. Amanda Alcott. To be fair, there were a slew of other tall, willowy blondes featured in the photos. Each one glamorous and expertly made up with a smile that would give the tooth fairy a lady boner. It was glaringly apparent that Gideon had zero problems finding beautiful women to squire around town to the various social events he attended.

Of which there were legion. At least, based on my saved internet search. The one I'd had bookmarked since the day I met him. Gideon West was not, it appeared, a man interested in spending an evening on the couch with takeout pizza and a streaming service. He was a man who went to *balls*, for God's sake. Honest to God balls, like a secret prince in some holiday rom-com.

I glanced down at my dusty jeans and work boots. There was a noticeable coffee stain on my tank top and . . . when had that hole gotten there? I had never been red carpet ready at any point in my life. I lived in functional clothes—jeans, cotton shirts, and work boots. The few suits I owned came out only on special occasions, and none of them had plunging necklines or mid-thigh slits. My heels weren't that high and came only in black and nude. I wasn't like the exotic hothouse flowers who decorated Gideon's arm in the photos on my screen. I was, at best, a sturdy geranium, or on a really good day, a jaunty little petunia. How could I compete with the women he was used to? More importantly, did I really want to engage in that type of competition for something that had a limited shelf life? It would be a mistake to start something with him. Wouldn't it? Assuming, that is, if he even wanted to. The man was a consummate flirt, so maybe I'd read a little too much into things.

"You know, maybe I was wrong. Maybe Mrs. Hazelton *would* prefer me in the Armani," Gideon said from over my shoulder.

"Gah!" I hastily jabbed at the mouse, my movements ineffective because my brain had totally forgotten how to minimize a window. It was akin to when a steamy part in the romance audiobook you're listening to automatically starts playing when you start your car. Only you're not alone—you're with your dad. And the narrator won't shut up about the hero's rigid length and his lady love's throbbing core. Somehow, you hit every single button within reach to make it stop instead of just turning down the volume.

Rather than minimize, I'd somehow blown up the last picture of Gideon to a size that allowed me to see he *did* in fact have pores. *Crap, crap, crap!*

His low laugh sounded at my ear, and his hand came over mine, warm and wide. With a single click, he managed to make his giant face disappear from the screen. Mortified, I refused to look at him until he spun my chair around.

In dark navy suit pants and matching jacket over a crisp white shirt, he looked like a menswear model. I marveled at the lack of mud on his impeccable outfit. He was the only person I knew who could come to the stables in the middle of a spring storm and remain pristine. It was one of life's sexier mysteries.

"Good morning, Everest," he said, a smile playing at the corners of his mouth. "Miss me that much, did you?"

"I wasn't . . . I mean, I was. . ." Yeah, there was no way to explain what I was doing. He knew it, and much worse, he knew I knew it too. With no defense, I went on the offensive. "What are you doing here?"

The smile broke free. "Your cordial greetings get sweeter every time I see you." He glanced over my head at my computer. "Although I guess you've already seen me several times in several settings."

Humiliation washed over me in a red wave. "Can you just pretend you didn't see that?"

"Can I? Certainly. Will I? Not a chance, I'm afraid. It was too good for my ego."

I groaned and hid my face in my hands.

Gideon laughed and tugged them down. "Considering you've seen me at quite possibly my worst multiple times since we've met, I don't think you have anything to be embarrassed about. You were probably just confirming that I can in fact walk around in the world without chaos befalling me."

I smiled up at him. "You do seem to be down a few designer pieces since arriving in town. I haven't seen you for a few days. I was starting to wonder if the loss of that last pair of slacks was the straw the broke the camel's back."

He waved the idea away. "It takes more than a few couture casualties to deter me, Everest."

"I'll keep that in mind next time someone calls off and I need help mucking the stables. Seriously, though, what brings you by this rainy afternoon?"

"Trying to tempt the big boss into playing hooky with me," Gideon said with a boyish grin. The dimples alone had me considering it.

I glanced at my watch—a quarter till five. "What'd you have in mind?" I asked, combing through my mental to-do list. "I could probably duck out of here a little early today if you wanted to grab dinner or something." I hoped I didn't sound too pathetically eager.

From his inside jacket pocket, he withdrew a key ring and jangled it gently. "Dinner sounds lovely, but I've got a stop to make first."

"What sort of stop?"

"Ah, ah, ah, it's a surprise."

He rounded the corner of my desk and propped one perfectly shaped ass cheek on it. His long legs invaded the small space. "What do you say? Up for a little adventure?"

Intrigued, I spun back around and shut down my computer. "Lead the way."

"This is the adventure?" I asked, looking through the rain-coated windshield of Gideon's rental car at the old Wallace Building. The "Available Now" sign that had hung in the large double glass doors on the ground floor since forever was still there. Although it looked like the dust had been cleaned off and . . . were there lights on inside?

"It is indeed," Gideon said, pushing open his car door and snapping open an umbrella. "Don't move," he said. Before I could respond, he'd dashed around the front of the car and was at my door, opening it and shielding the space with the umbrella.

"Thanks," I said, stepping out and under its protective expanse. Gideon wrapped an arm around me, and we hustled over to the door. Deftly, he plucked from his pocket the keys he'd jangled at me earlier and inserted one of them into the lock. It turned easily, and he pushed the door open for me to go in first.

Once inside, the sound of the rain lessened to a quiet thrumming. Gideon shook the rain from the umbrella then propped it by the door. "Well," he said, spreading out his hands and turning in a small circle, "what do you think?"

His excitement was palpable, but I was at a loss. "Um, what do I think about what?"

"This!" he said, flapping his hands up and down.

I glanced around again, thinking maybe I'd missed something. All I saw was the unchanged interior of the old lobby. It was a cool old building. Brown paper had been put over the flooring to reduce the damage, but in the spots where it had torn, I could see the intricate marble inlay peeking through. Plaster ceilings arced high above us, and the chandelier, although dusty, was still impressive. I looked apologetically over at Gideon. "Sorry, I've got nothing. What is it I'm supposed to be looking at?"

He huffed his disappointment at my obliviousness and grabbed my hand, pulling me to the stairway. "C'mon," he said, his large hand engulfing mine.

I didn't have time to dwell on how much I liked that, because I had to scramble to keep up with his long-legged strides. We passed the ancient elevator cage and started up the wide staircase. Once we'd made it up to the third level, Gideon made a quick right and pushed open a doorway to reveal a long hallway. The old wood creaked under our feet as he propelled me down to a door. Flinging it open, he ushered me inside.

It was a wide-open space, with massive arched windows lining one wall. Wide wooden plank flooring ran the length of the room, and the ceiling was pressed tin. Even with the rain outside, light filtered in and illuminated the space. I could feel Gideon waiting for me to say something, vibrating with anticipation for my reaction to . . . whatever he thought he was showing me.

I faced him. "I'm pretty sure it would be easier for you to tell me what I'm supposed to be excited about here. It's becoming blatantly obvious I'm not in tune with whatever is making you so wired."

His smile dimmed but not by much. "You were right, Everest."

"Words I love hearing but still not cluing me in here."

Again, he extended his arms and turned in a small circle. "Why build something new when this is available for restoration?"

Surprise rippled through me, followed by an unexpected warmth radiating out from my chest and unfurling through my body. I needed clarification before I got too excited though. "What do you mean?"

Gideon stopped spinning and tucked his hands into his pants pockets, looking almost bashful. "What you said over in Weaver resonated with me, Everest. Mimosa is more than just its proximity to Charlotte and available acreage. It's got a real history here. A history my partners and I would be fools to overlook."

He walked to the window and waved a hand to get me to join him. I did, standing next to him and looking out. Gideon pointed to the buildings across the street. "You're standing in the center of what I hope will be Standard's new commercial district here in Mimosa. With the Wallace Building as the flagship of it." Glancing down at me, his smile was wide, excitement etched into his expression. "You opened my eyes to a whole new challenge, Everest. *This* is going to be something exceptional. It's going to push Standard to a new level—open up an entirely new avenue for us. And"—his voice lowered as he turned to face me completely—"I've got you to thank for it."

I flushed with pleasure at the compliment. "Well, I don't know that I can take all the credit. All I did was make some thinly veiled threats. You were the one who's apparently spent the past few weeks researching every available building in Mimosa."

Gideon reached out and took my hand in his, brushing a thumb over my knuckles. "You were the impetus for this, Everest. No matter what anyone else thought, you kept pushing, because you knew there was something more we could do here. Something better. You pushed me to think outside the box and get creative in ways I haven't done in years. Without you, renovation of downtown would never have occurred to me. You're an eye-opening kind of woman."

My heart stuttered, and my skin heated at his touch, a whole new kind of warmth spreading through me. "Is that so?"

He nodded, his eyes never leaving mine. "You are quite the unexpected surprise, Everest."

"Isn't unexpected inherent in the word surprise?" I asked, my voice coming out in a soft exhale.

His answering laugh was a low rumble in the empty space. "Are you ever without a comeback?"

Memories of being struck mute by his shirtless appearance two weeks ago flitted through my mind. "There have been occasions when words failed me," I admitted.

Gideon laughed again, bringing his other hand to my waist, fingers spreading wide over my jean clad hip. I could feel the heat of his touch through the denim, and my breath caught. The gentle pressure of his fingers urged me closer until there was but a hint of space between us.

"Sometimes there are situations that call more for action than words," he said, lowering his head. "Wouldn't you agree?"

I licked my lips, and his eyes tracked the movement of my tongue, going a darkly dangerous shade of blue. I felt myself being pulled into their depths, losing myself in the inky indigo.

He edged closer, tilting my chin up, and my eyes drifted closed. "Everest?" We were so close, his breath whispered against my lips.

"Mm-hmm?" I said without opening my eyes.

"Look at me, sweetheart," he said, his voice low and wicked.

I did as he asked and saw my own want reflected back at me.

"I don't know if this is the wisest course of action, but I find myself not caring. In fact"—his hand at my waist shifted until it pressed at the small of my back, removing the last few inches of separation and pressing my body to his—"these last weeks, I found myself thinking of little else but you."

"Uh-huh," I said lamely.

He brushed the hair away from my forehead, and the *zing!* of his touch sizzled from my scalp all the way to my toes, scorching everything in between. He was so close, all I had to do was push onto my toes and our lips would meet. Humor lit his eyes when he said, "Until I stumbled across your internet sleuthing, I wasn't sure if I'd occupied your thoughts even half as much."

I frowned and pinched his side. "What were you saying about words being overrated sometimes?"

Gideon laughed. "I'm simply trying to tell you what a relief it was to arrive and see my face on that computer screen. It meant I wasn't crazy to be thinking of you. Of what your lips might taste like. Of how your delectable body would feel next to mine. Of what you might look like wearing nothing but that sexy half-smile you seem to favor. That, ill-advised as it may be, I wasn't alone in the way my body ached for yours."

Holy shit. Maybe words weren't overrated, especially when they were super sexy words spoken by this man.

"Am I alone, Everest?" he asked, lips hovering a millimeter from mine. "Or can I assume you're with me in what might not be the best idea?"

chapter nineteen

GIDEON

Those gorgeous green eyes practically glowed with heat as she gazed up at me. The air around us sizzled with longing, and I burned with the need to kiss her. To taste her. To press her up against the window and fucking ravage her. But before I could do anything, I had to hear she was right there with me. Because this was more than ill-advised. It was, as both Jamie and Davidson had told me, inherently stupid.

Spending time with her was one thing. Pushing her to have a little more fun in life was fine. Making her see there was no reason she couldn't be dedicated to her job *and* have a social life was also fine, admirable even. But what I wanted to do to her right then was anything but a good idea. My time here in Mimosa had an end date, which meant anything between us would as well. But I didn't care. I'd take whatever I could get from her and enjoy it while it lasted. If it were a fling, so be it. If it were more, even better. I was going into this with my eyes wide open that the ending could be an immolation of the highest order, the flames of which could destroy everything. Even that wasn't enough to stop me.

Everest pulled her bottom lip between her teeth, and I stifled a groan. "This would be . . . temporary, right?" she asked, her hand skimming underneath my suit jacket and teasing over my side.

"If that's what you want," I said.

There was a pause, long and weighty, then she said, "It's what I can give."

"Then that's what I'll have," I said, even as my gut twisted at the prospect of a time when I didn't have her.

She smiled, sliding her other hand over my chest to curl around the nape of my neck. "You could always open an office down here. I know a guy who I think is looking to flip some office space." Her fingers pressed lightly against my neck, pulling me toward her.

I laughed, savoring her touch. "I'm sure you could talk him into anything, so I'll keep that in mind. But if I can't make the move . . ."

"Then let's make the most of what we've got," she said and rose on her toes to press her lips to mine. I groaned at the contact and felt her smile beneath my lips. I took advantage of the parting of her lips and deepened the kiss, licking into her mouth. Everest gave a little hum at the back of her throat that shot straight to my dick.

I slid both hands down her back and around the curve of her ass, lifting her up. She came willingly, wrapping both legs around my waist and her arms around my shoulders. Her head tilted and her tongue tangled with mine, her eagerness shooting sparks down my spine. The hum in her throat became a growl, and she nipped at my lip.

"Fuck me," I rasped, squeezing a handful of her ass. "You do know this ass has been on my mind since the day I met you."

"Is that so?" she asked then bit my earlobe. "And why is that?"

"You're kidding, right?" I asked as I kissed up her neck, sucking on the tender skin just behind her ear. "You are aware of what you look like riding a horse, aren't you? Especially from *behind?*" I punctuated the last word with another generous squeeze.

Her legs contracted, grinding her pelvis against me. Sweet Christ, I wanted her.

"Well aware," Everest said, fingernails digging into my scalp as she came back for another searing kiss. Breaking away and letting me chase after her lips, she added, "I'm also well aware that was weeks ago. What took you so long to get your hands on it?"

"As we just discussed," I said, making my way to the far wall and pressing her into it, "*this* is a patently flawed idea. One I've done my best to resist. Add to that the fact you loathed me on sight, and I think I got my hands on your ass in record time."

She leaned her head back to look at me, fingers raking through my hair. "Wanna know a secret?"

I grinned at her. "Always."

Angling back toward me, she whispered the words against my lips, "You should've tried sooner."

With a growl, I kissed her hard and desperate, letting each and every one of the days that made up the weeks of wanting her show in the way I plundered her mouth. It was a taking, and she was willing. Lips, tongue, and teeth collided in a frenzy of want until we were both forced to come up for a full breath, panting and wild-eyed.

"Jesus Christ," Everest said with a gasp.

"Right back at you," I said, moving in for another kiss. Her ass started to vibrate beneath my fingers. She jolted in my arms, breaking away. "Can't say even I've gotten that response from a woman before," I joked.

She rolled her eyes at me and wiggled against my grip. "I need to get that."

"Isn't that why I'm here? To show you not every phone call is an emergency and there are times when you *really don't* have to answer the phone?"

In response, Everest pushed at my shoulders, and I reluctantly let her slide to her feet, taking pride in the slight wobble of her knees when her feet hit the floor. Sliding her phone out of her back pocket, she checked the screen then answered.

"Hey, Leroy, what's wrong?" I heard a muffled response, then Everest said, "No, I don't always assume something is wrong. But you rarely call after hours *unless* something is wrong. So . . . what's wrong?"

Her brows knit together as she listened, her head falling back against the wall and her eyes closing. "How many?" Another pause, then, "No, it's fine. Tell them we'll find room for them somehow. I'm sure I can lean on my dad to spare a few stalls if absolutely necessary. I'll call him on my way over."

She hung up and looked at me, somewhat apologetically but with the same fire in her eyes I'd seen the night I'd accompanied her on the neglect call. "Duty calls. Sorry, but I have to cut this short."

"Not a problem," I replied. *At least not one a cold, cold shower wouldn't fix.* "I can go with you, if you like."

Everest smiled then rolled up onto her toes to kiss my cheek. "That's sweet, Gideon, but I cannot afford to replace the suit you're wearing. And I don't have time to wait. Can you just take me back to Second Chance, please?"

Two weeks. Two. Fucking. Weeks. It had been two weeks since I'd kissed Everest and, apart from a few stolen moments in the tack room outside Savvy's stall, we'd had zero opportunities to continue what we'd started in the Wallace Building. Between my having to fly back for an emergency with a project in Providence and her having to step in with a hoarding case, we hadn't even had a chance to *discuss* what had happened, much less anything else. Like the parameters of whatever this thing was between us. This electric, vibrant thing that I knew she felt as much as I did. Because there was no use denying its existence. I couldn't lock it down, shut it out, or refute it. It was there each time I drew in a breath. Stuck in my chest like a burr that latched onto every part of my heart.

I needed to get her alone, away from her work, my work, and everything in between. Regardless of whether this was a fling or, as the idea my mind toyed with between the hours of two and four in the morning, something more . . . if we didn't get some time to ourselves with limited interruption, it would die on the vine before it had any chance to grow.

Which was why I arrived at her office that Friday afternoon in early April with a mission. A mission I'd spent the last week putting together. She didn't notice me at first, so I took advantage of the opportunity to study her. A woman so often in motion, it was rare to catch a glimpse of her sitting still. Her hair was in its trademark messy ponytail with what looked like two pencils haphazardly stuck into it at odd angles. Squinting at her computer screen, she wrinkled her nose and huffed then spun to retrieve a file from the precarious stack on her desk. Mid-turn, she spotted me leaning on the doorframe of her office.

"Gideon," she said, a bright smile spreading across her face. The pleasure in finding me there was evident in her voice, and it spread over my skin like sunshine.

"Afternoon, Boss Lady," I said then winced inwardly at the cheesy phrase.

She laughed and sat back, the springs in her ancient chair protesting the movement. "What brings you by today?" Her smile faltered, and she shifted the stack of files on her desk, scanning the half-covered calendar on her desk blotter. "We didn't have plans that I somehow forgot about, did we?"

It was my turn to laugh. "No, but I'm hoping to change that."

"Oh?" she said, curiosity plain on her face. "Do tell."

Pushing off the doorjamb, I made my way to her desk, taking care not to dislodge any of the stacks of papers. If she had a filing system, it was apparent to her and her alone. I withdrew an envelope from the inner pocket of my suit jacket and dropped it on the closest pile.

Her head tilted quizzically as she reached for the envelope. "What's this?" she asked even as her finger slid beneath the flap to open it.

"Plans," I said simply, watching her face as she extracted a folded sheet of paper.

Scanning it quickly, her face fell. She looked back to me. "You're going back to Boston this weekend? You were just there last week."

Coming around the corner of her desk, I plucked the paper from her fingers and flattened it out with my palm on the sole empty space on her desk. "Read it again, Everest," I instructed.

Frowning, she leaned closer, and I caught the smell of her shampoo. That clean scent that conjured steamy images of her in the shower. Biting back a groan, I waited as she read.

Slowly, Everest straightened, and then her head swiveled to me. "*We're* going to Boston?"

I tried to gauge her expression, to see if underneath the surprise was excitement or happiness or any emotion other than pure horror. Her eyes had flown wide, and her lips parted slightly. "Well," I said, drawing out the word, "that was the plan. However, you being paralyzed by the shock of it is making me rethink things."

"No!" she said, the word quick and sharp. Running her hands up and down her jeans, she licked her lips then continued. "I mean . . . no, you don't need to reconsider anything. At least, that is, not because I don't *want* to go. I do. I absolutely do . . . It's just that I'm not sure I can." Weakly, she gestured to the literal piles of work surrounding her. "I've got so much to do here, and I don't know if I can—"

"Everest," I said, cutting her off.

She blinked. "Yeah?"

"Is there anything in"—I waved a hand over the stacks on her desk—"any of this that can't wait until Monday?" Her mouth opened with a ready response, and I held up a hand. She closed it. "Don't answer until you've really considered my question. There are no horses in dire need residing in any of these paper files, are there? No knot-kneed little foals with giant, pitiful eyes that need you to ride to the rescue in the next seventy-two hours?"

Her lips twitched, and she shook her head. "No, there aren't."

"If I had to guess," I said, surveying the files, "these are adoption applications, grant agreements, and general paperwork that can all keep until Monday morning." I leaned a hip on her desk, careful not to dislodge anything. "Am I close?"

Everest leaned forward, resting her hand on my knee. Her touch was as electric as ever, sending jolts of heated sparks rocketing through me. "You are," she admitted.

"Which means there's nothing within these four walls to keep you from getting on a plane with me."

Her fingers fanned out, thumb stroking just inside my knee, making it difficult to concentrate on anything other than her touch. "But what about all that needs to be done in the barn?"

This was where things could get a little dicey. "I may have already discussed with Leroy my plan to whisk you away for the weekend."

Red brows shot to her hairline, and her fingers curled around my leg. "You did what?"

I put my hand over hers, stroking her knuckles. This was the clincher. She'd either be pissed I'd interfered or—I mentally crossed my fingers—grateful for my foresight.

"Everest, while I may have made it my mission to get you to loosen up and live a little, I am aware that you aren't in a position to be truly spontaneous. There's too much at stake here to skip away into the sunset without a little planning. I knew you wouldn't . . . *couldn't* leave if you weren't comfortable that all your equine wards would be taken care of in your absence. So . . . I broached the topic with Leroy, and he's arranged everything to let you have a weekend away."

"He has?"

I couldn't glean much from those two words, so I nodded and forged ahead. "According to him, he's 'more than capable' of running the barn in your absence and that 'it was about damn time' you trusted him to do it."

Her face flushed and she chewed her lip, glancing back at her computer screen then at the cluttered top of her desk. Finally, she looked at me, and I saw the warring emotions in her eyes—guilt, excitement, worry. She wanted to go but was holding herself back because she wasn't convinced she should.

I took her hands in mine. "Everest, if this is too much, feel free to tell me. I don't want you to do anything you're not ready for." Even as the words pained me to say, because I *needed* this weekend with her, I knew it had to be her decision. Otherwise, even if she came, I'd have half of her at best. With the majority of her still mentally in Mimosa.

Everest rose slowly from her chair and moved into the space between my knees, releasing my hands and letting hers trail up my arms to rest lightly at my shoulders. Her scent surrounded me, heady and intoxicating. I swallowed and she grinned, enjoying the effect her proximity had on me.

"Just one question," she said.

I rested my hands at her hips. "What's that?"

"How quickly can we get to the airport?"

As it turned out, *very quickly* was the answer to her question. Mere hours later, Everest and I were seated next to each other in first class. Dressed in soft gray leggings and an oversized T-shirt, she looked more like a graduate student than the head of a charity. We were somewhere over Philadelphia and maybe twenty minutes from descending into Logan International Airport.

Everest tickled my side. "What's got you looking so serious?"

I wasn't going to tell her I'd been wracking my brain over the best way to break it to Davidson and Jamie that I now knew the answer to whether I was willing to take a chance on things with Everest. It might not last, and it might end in disaster, but I couldn't resist the pull I felt for her any longer. Grinning, I shoved my concerns about my partners from my mind, concentrating on the excited sparkle in her eyes. "Just planning how to spend our first night in the city," I said with a suggestive brow waggle.

She wasn't fooled. "Somehow, I doubt choosing between lobstah places has you frowning that deeply. Maybe you're trying to remember where you pahked ya' cahr." Her soft Southern drawl smoothed the edges of her attempt to speak Southie.

I tweaked her nose. "You're somewhat adorable, you know that?"

She grimaced. "Just how every grown woman longs to be described."

I moved closer, letting my lips touch the shell of her ear. She shivered and I smiled. I'd gotten her on a plane and almost to my home turf. Time to ramp things up. "What if I told you I've spent the entire flight thinking about that small strip of skin you flashed when you put your carry-on in the overhead bin? And how much I'd like to trace it with my tongue. Is that more to your liking, Ms. Kennedy?"

Everest's ears turned pink, and her breath caught. When she tilted her head to look at me, our lips were within inches of one another. I could count the flecks of gold in her wide green eyes. Her tongue darted out to wet her lips, and the sight of it shot straight to my groin.

"Well, Mr. West," she said quietly, "a true gentlemen would've been more concerned with helping me stow my bag than licking various parts of my anatomy."

Touché, I thought but didn't concede just yet. "I guess I better confess, Ms. Kennedy, that *I* am no gentleman."

Holding her ground, she smiled. "I'm starting to pick up on that, Mr. West."

I leaned in, and her eyes went hazy while her lips parted in anticipation. I ached to kiss her, and I could see she wanted me to. At the last second before our mouths connected, I turned, letting my cheek graze hers. Once again, I spoke into her ear. "But please don't think there are only *parts* of your anatomy that interest me. I'm fully committed to memorizing every inch of your beautiful body before this weekend is over." I pressed a soft kiss on the tender skin right behind her ear, savoring the satiny feel of her flesh. After going weeks without her, she was going to be lucky if I let her out of bed all weekend. Her shaky breath and the way she curved into my touch told me she was probably okay with that plan.

I sat back, and she looked at me, eyes clouded with desire. Propping an elbow on the armrest between us, Everest let her hand drop casually to my upper thigh. Her thumb rubbed small circles over the fabric of my trousers.

The delicate graze of her small fingers had all the blood in my body headed south. I silently recited every sports stat I could think of to combat my growing arousal. It did no good, so I switched to what was normally a guaranteed erection deflection—the memory of catching my grandmother and her latest boy toy *inflagrante delicto* at a family reunion ten years ago. Don't ask. Trust me—it's a visual you don't want and I never deploy unless absolutely necessary.

It was working, at least until she dipped her shoulder and flashed me a modest peek at her cleavage. Pretty white teeth nibbled on her lower lip, and the image of Nonna in red lingerie faded into the ether. Everest was so close, I felt it when she laughed.

"Two can play at your teasing game, Mr. West," she said.

When I shifted with a grunt, she withdrew her hand from my leg and settled back into her seat. I missed its warmth and her closeness. "Just remember, sweetheart," I cautioned her, "payback can be a bitch."

Her smile widened. "Oh, I'm counting on it, honey."

How had my life seemed even close to full before I met this woman? I wondered. My male anatomy had its own question, namely, why I had waited this long to get her alone. If things were up to him, we'd spend the last ten minutes of this flight contorted and sweaty in the tiny bathroom.

The captain announced our descent, and Everest glanced over at me. "What's on the agenda for this weekend?"

My eyes traveled down the length of her and then back up slowly. I opened my mouth, but she covered it with her hand.

"Please," she said, "don't give me another line about how you want to spend the next forty-eight hours ravaging my body or whatever. Give me a real answer."

"What if that was the real answer?" I asked, my question muffled by her palm.

She rolled her eyes with a huff and dropped her hand. "C'mon, I'm serious."

"Well, assuming I let you escape my bedroom for longer than fifteen-minute increments," I said, "I'd planned to show you my town. We'll dine in the North End, rummage through all the tchotchkes at Faneuil Hall, have drinks on Newbury Street, then for the big finish take you on the swan boats in the Public Garden. My plan is essentially to have you fall as hard for Boston as I have for Mimosa."

Her grin was gentle when she asked, "You do know I've been here before, right?"

Shit, shit, shit, how had I not asked her that? I thought but recovered quickly. "That actually works perfectly."

One eyebrow quirked up, smile widening. "It does?"

I nodded and took her hand in mine. "That way, we can dispense with all the touristy stuff and spend the entirety of the weekend naked in my condo, sending out sporadically for food and water to keep up our strength."

"Man," she said, laughing, "once you turn on this side of things, you go full speed, don't you?"

"I cannot have the woman of my dreams think for even a moment I do not find her to be the most desirable female on the planet. Forgive me if it's too much."

Everest held her thumb and forefinger a small distance apart. "Maybe dial it down a little, okay?"

"Consider it dialed," I said, enjoying the feel of her hand in mine.

She looked down at our entwined fingers then back to my face. "I can't remember the last trip I took that had nothing to do with horses or fundraising." In response to her appreciative smile, my chest swelled with pride for being the one to put it there. "All kidding and innuendos aside, this was really nice of you, Gideon."

"I know I said I'd dial it down, so you have to know this is merely a disclaimer, not another tawdry come on, but my motives were not altogether altruistic," I said.

"I gathered that from the first six times you mentioned wanting to see me naked," she replied. Her green eyes glimmered. "And honestly, if you hadn't done something soon, I was planning to show up at your house wearing nothing but a trench coat and a smile."

The idea of opening my door to a nearly naked naughty Everest short-circuited my brain. My dick seized its chance to take control. "Remember how I said we'd get dinner after we landed?"

"Yeah?" Everest said, bewildered.

"We're ordering in."

chapter twenty

EVEREST

I waited for the guilt to set in the way it usually did when I was away from Second Chance. The feeling that I was shirking some greater responsibility by taking a few days off. That there was no way some imminent crisis wouldn't arise in my absence. But it didn't. There was no tense moment on the plane, when I normally thought of all the thousand little things that needed my attention. My gut wasn't in knots worrying about all the weekend tasks that normally arose, nor was there that telltale tension in my shoulders as I debated whether to cut my trip short.

None of that was present, and it was all thanks to the man in the driver's seat next to me. He'd somehow navigated through all my standard objections to taking a trip and whisked me away before I could secondguess myself. And thanks to his enlisting Leroy in his scheme, I felt *almost* relaxed about it. Cammie had been right about Gideon, it seemed. He was the perfect passing distraction at the right time. My own little spring break of sorts, which now included a jaunt to one of my favorite cities.

I'd always loved coming to Boston. Somehow, Daddy was a Red Sox fan. I have no idea how he was able to sidestep the attachment to the

Atlanta Braves that so many North Carolinians had, but he did. He was devastated when the Sox traded Mookie to the Dodgers.

His love of the team meant we'd been to several games at Fenway over the years. Even if you don't like baseball, if you've never been to a game there, you're crazy if you don't put it on your bucket list. There's nothing quite like downing a Fenway Frank with a giant beer while listening to some of the most creative heckling you'll ever hear in your life.

But Fenway was nowhere to be seen as Gideon and I sailed through the Ted Williams Tunnel under Boston Harbor. His car, a sleek black BMW M5, floated over the road. I didn't know much about luxury cars, since I'd never had the need for one, but I knew this car was expensive with a capital "E." And while I wasn't that into cars, I was very into the way Gideon drove. Like anything he did, he operated the powerful machine with relaxed confidence. Snug in my supple leather seat, I watched him navigate traffic. Since when had putting on a turn signal been that sexy?

We emerged into the sunlight, and Gideon took a right, leading us back toward the harbor. At the next left, he pointed in the opposite direction. "My office is back there." Before I could turn to look, he'd already made another right and a quick left. In front of us was a large, curved rectangle of glass, maybe nine stories tall. Balconies jutted out like haphazardly pushed-out drawers between large expanses of windows. The building arced out into the harbor, and I knew every room would have a spectacular view of it and a part of the city skyline.

Gideon pulled up under the covered portico, past a line of cars, and over to a separate small podium. The uniformed man behind it sprinted to open my door. "Welcome to the Anthony, miss."

I took his offered hand and let him help me out of the car. "Thank you," I said, somewhat overwhelmed by the sheer opulence of the place.

With a little bow to me, he hurried around the car to Gideon. "Welcome back, Mr. West."

"Thank you, Benny. It's good to be home," Gideon said and handed him a folded-up bill.

"Thank you, sir," Benny said with an appreciative smile. "Will you be needing the car again tonight?"

The look Gideon shot me should've burned the clothes right off my body. "Not if I can help it, Benny. Thank you. Can you have someone send the luggage up?"

"Certainly, sir. Have a good evening."

"You do the same," Gideon said and walked around the trunk to my side. His hand came to the small of my back like he'd been doing it for years. "Shall we?" he asked.

I let him guide me through the huge glass doors into the expansive lobby. Abstract art hung suspended above us, and a wall of glass showcased the harbor. Gideon didn't spare it a glance as he headed straight to a bank of elevators. Waving a small plastic square in front of an almost invisible electronic pad, he then typed in "P4," and I heard a soft chime.

"This is some place you've got here," I said, taking in the exotic wood flooring and marble counters in the lobby. Fresh flowers were everywhere, the smell of their blossoms permeating the space.

Gideon looked around, as though seeing the lavish lobby for the first time. He gave me a sly grin. "Keeps the rain off my head, at least."

I had to smile at his attempt to downplay our extravagant surroundings. The elevator doors opened silently, and he held out his hand for me to go first. There were no buttons on any of the mirrored walls, but there was another sleek touchpad. Gideon reached out and typed in a sequence.

"Mr. West, how may I assist you this evening?" asked a disembodied female voice, making me jump in surprise.

"Good evening, Melany," Gideon said. "I'll need dinner for two sent up in an hour or so."

This was like something out of a movie. Anxiety spiked within me as it began to dawn on me that Gideon West wasn't some guy from Boston who'd headed south looking for an opportunity. The life I'd stepped into minutes ago had been crafted by a man who'd already capitalized on multiple opportunities that provided an *extremely* wealthy lifestyle. My palms started to sweat as the elevator began its upward climb.

"Certainly, sir," said Melany. "Anything in particular?"

Gideon looked over at me, and I shrugged, not trusting myself to speak. "Have the chef surprise us, please," he said.

"He'll be thrilled, sir," Melany said.

"Well, surprise us *within reason*," Gideon supplemented.

Melany's laugh tinkled out of the speakers. "Absolutely, sir."

Before I could ask him about the Alexa in the elevator, the doors whooshed open onto a posh hallway. A single door stood in front of us. Gideon used the same plastic card to open it. Again, he signaled for me to go ahead of him.

Gideon lifted a hand to the touchscreen on the inside wall by the door. It illuminated, and he tapped a few buttons. A whirring sound came from farther within the space. Shades rose on the floor to ceiling windows that encircled the living area, revealing, as expected, a panoramic view of Boston Harbor. Lights came on then adjusted to a welcoming glow. Somehow, I'd walked onto the set of *Billions* without my knowledge.

A gourmet kitchen with stainless steel appliances and granite counters gleamed in front of me, separated from a dining area by a modern-looking bar lined with four stools. A behemoth teak table surrounded by eight chairs sat before a massive sliding glass door. A steel and wood staircase rose behind the table. The corner of a fireplace in what I assumed was the living room was just visible beyond the stairs. A hallway to my right with a door on either side probably led to guest rooms. I wondered whether Gideon's room was upstairs.

"Welcome to my humble abode," Gideon said, heading into the kitchen and opening the refrigerator.

The little house he was renting in Mimosa could've fit within the first floor, with enough room left over for most of my house too. For all I knew, the stairs led to a second level that was even larger. Now, it's not like I grew up deprived or anything. Daddy made sure our lives had always been comfortable, and for the most part, if there were something I wanted, he made sure I got it. But this . . . this unabashed display of luxury was a whole new level I'd never experienced. Gideon was *loaded*.

If I'd harbored even an inkling that what was happening between Gideon and me could ever be anything more than temporary, walking into this palace obliterated that. It hammered home the reality that his whole life was here, not in Mimosa. And from the looks of things, it was a damn nice life. Certainly not something most people would choose to leave behind in favor of a sleepy little town where there were no elevator butleresses or private chefs willing to whip something up for you on a moment's notice. And for what? A girl whose fashion sense extended only to the newest line of Ariat boots? I would be a fool to think anything we could have together would ever be able to compete with what Gideon already had at his disposal.

"Everest," Gideon said, breaking into my wayward thoughts. He held two bottles of water.

I'd been staring out the window without really seeing the view.

"Are you all right?" he asked. "You look a little pale."

"I'm fine," I said and walked into the kitchen, trying to shove down the regret that clawed at me. It had been a mistake to come here. We should've confined whatever was going on between us to Mimosa. That way, when it ended, I wouldn't have a frame of reference for what he was coming back to. I wouldn't be able to picture him lounging on his designer sofa with one of his seven-feet-tall blondes feeding him grapes or something equally bile-inducing.

Gideon gave me a long look from across the island and set the waters down. "Want to tell me what's going through that overactive imagination of yours?"

Trying to not let my inner monologue ruin the weekend, I said, "This place is a few steps above Ms. Viola's house back in Mimosa. It must feel good to be back in civilization." Okay, so yeah, that was a little passive-aggressive, but so what?

Blue eyes narrowed on me, and Gideon crossed his arms. "Civilization?" he asked. "I've found Mimosa to be quite civilized in my time there."

"Well, yeah, but compared to this place, you must feel like you've been roughing it for the past few weeks." My laugh was shrill and forced.

"Everest, if you've got something to say, why don't you just say it?" When I kept silent, he spread his hands wide. "Hit me with it, sweetheart. Because this whole saying something without saying it is a little trite, don't you think?"

"Spoken like the self-righteous, pompous ass who'd want to live in a place like this," I retorted and instantly regretted it. There was no reason for me to snap at Gideon. He'd never come close to self-righteous or pompous. My outburst had nothing to do with him and everything to do with me being uncomfortable and out of my depth standing in what had to be a multimillion-dollar condo. Gideon took the brunt of my self-consciousness right on the chin.

"Is there something wrong with my condo?" he asked calmly and rounded the corner of the island to stand in front of me.

I fingered the edge of the counter, because I couldn't look at him. Now I was embarrassed and insecure. What kind of a person insults someone four minutes after walking in their door? I was a complete ass. I sighed. "There's nothing wrong with your condo. What I've seen of it is beautiful."

"What's going on, Everest?" he asked softly. "Just tell me."

I looked up at him and saw the genuine worry in his eyes. "It's just that . . . I'm trying to wrap my head around how the guy who seems so comfortable in Mimosa lives in a place like this." My hand swept out to take in the elegant furniture and dazzling view. "I mean, you've got this whole futuristic private elevator with your own personal Alexa who's apparently sending up a gourmet meal from 'the chef.' This condo is huge and modern and probably worth multiple millions! And yet, when I met you, you're living in a two-bedroom house that's the size of your walk-in closet in this place. That doesn't add up."

He took my hands in his. "I can assure you, Everest, whether I'm laying my head on Ms. Viola's down-filled pillows underneath the lovely patchwork quilt she made, or on the ergonomic bamboo ones here and snuggling under my linen duvet, I'm the same guy. I'll let you in on a little secret." Leaning in, he whispered, "It doesn't usually go well when you start out by telling a girl that you're obscenely wealthy. Tends to make you seem like a douche. And I started pretty far in the hole with you anyway. I wasn't going to dig it any deeper."

I laughed but said, "I'm serious, Gideon."

"So am I, Everest," he said earnestly, squeezing and releasing my fingers. "The guy you've gotten to know is the same guy who lives here." He thumbed a vein in the granite. "That's why I invited you, Everest. I wanted you to see that. Whether I'm down in Mimosa with you or up here—"

"Living life in the lap of luxury," I interrupted.

Gideon shook his head with a grin. "I was going to say burning the midnight oil on a project. But either way, the point doesn't change. I'm the same man in both places, Everest. I want you to know all sides of me, just like I want to see all sides of you."

"I can promise you I don't have any hidden mansions back in Mimosa," I said, trying to lighten the mood.

"Oh well, then we'll just have to call this whole thing off. I've got to call the airline to change your ticket now," he teased, and I slapped his stomach. "Ouch!" he cried and covered his abdomen.

"Stop being such a baby," I said, and he stuck his lip out in an exaggerated pout. "Want me to kiss it and make it better?"

When his eyes darkened and a wicked smile curved his sensuous mouth, my stomach dropped to my toes. Gideon advanced on me, backing me up against the countertop. His big hands landed on either side of my waist, holding me in place. Having him touch me so possessively was a new and altogether exciting experience. His fingers pressed into my ribs as he zeroed in on my mouth.

This was it, I thought, my heart beating wildly. I'd finally have his mouth on mine. I was starved for it. Desperate to feel the slide of his lips over mine. I tilted my head back and he bent his forward. My eyes drifted closed, and my lips parted, anticipating the sealing of his mouth to mine. But there was no press or brush or any sort of touching of lips.

Instead, his breath tickled my ear as he said quietly, "I'll hold you to that. But first, let me give you the tour."

He stepped back, and I swallowed a frustrated groan. If this man didn't kiss me soon, I was going to go insane and tackle him to the ground. The self-satisfied look on his face told me he knew what he was doing to me. Gloating was a mistake. He wanted to play tease? Well, game freaking *on*.

I closed the small distance between us, letting my hand trail down his chest and come to rest at the waistband of his slacks. His pupils dilated and he swallowed roughly, his body telling me he was as affected by me as I was by him. My fingers hooked through a beltloop, tugging him even closer. Lifting onto my toes, my lips brushed his ear, and he stiffened slightly. "Then let's get this show on the road," I cooed, punctuating my request by nipping his earlobe.

I dropped back down onto my heels and rubbed my hands together, excitement replacing my earlier bout of insecurity. "I can't wait to see the rest of your place."

A rough grunt came from deep inside Gideon as he stood stock still, the rise and fall of his chest the only thing making him appear lifelike. Well, that and the heat in his eyes as he looked down at me. *Gotcha!*

"Gideon?" I asked innocently.

Breaking out of his statue impersonation, he rubbed a hand over his jaw and cleared his throat. "Right this way," he said, his voice raw. Turning on his heel, he led me into the dining area.

I suppressed a wicked cackle of glee and followed obediently behind him.

chapter twenty—one

GIDEON

I was in grave danger of my most favorite appendage cracking in two as I watched Everest bend over for what had to be the four thousandth time. Her leggings were hermetically sealed to her ass, so I could see every flex or jiggle when she moved. No visible panty line, though, which created a series of images in my mind that would remain for some time to come. Somehow, during the entire time I'd been showing her my condo, she'd managed to be in front of me, either bending over, reaching up, or moving her body in some specific way that highlighted its curves and planes. She'd looked under the dining table to admire the pedestal legs. She'd raised up on tiptoe, her shirt following suit, to examine the hardware on the uppermost cabinet in the kitchen even though that same hardware was on the cabinets right at eye level. When she'd bent at the waist against the side of my mattress to get a closer look at some fucking throw pillow my designer had picked out, the sight of that perfect ass in the air just ripe for the taking almost brought me to my knees.

By the time she scampered ahead of me up the stairs to the rooftop terrace, simply walking had become painful. I'd been hard the entire time, and the impish little grin on her face told me she knew what she was playing at. Well, it was time to give her a taste of her own medicine. I grabbed the roof access door handle before she could and pressed the front my body against her back.

"Let me get that door for you," I said, resting my other hand on her hip. The slight pressure of my palm angled her pelvis back against me, and I shifted my hips forward. My dick jumped in response to her proximity, straining against my zipper. Her sharp inhale and the accompanying tremor that ran down her spine told me she'd felt, and liked, the hardness of my cock against her backside. I held us in place for the smallest of moments, enjoying her closeness, then pulled open the door and stepped back.

"After you," I said, releasing her hip. Everest's steps stalled for a second before she recovered and walked out onto the roof. It was my turn for an impish grin. Her antics might have taken me right to edge of my sexual sanity, but she wasn't far behind me.

The expansive vista from the roof helped drag us both back from the brink. "Oh my God, Gideon," Everest exclaimed. "This is gorgeous!" Below us, the waters of the harbor glowed pink and red with the setting sun. Boats of all kinds bobbed gently in the marinas with the rhythm of the tide. The skyline of downtown Boston curved around behind us. The view from up here was one of the main reasons I'd bought the place. It was spectacular.

Everest hurried over to the rail and looked out. The breeze caught her hair and blew it around her face in a copper halo. Annoyed, she raked her hands through the red curls and twisted them, holding the makeshift knot in place at the nape of her neck. She looked beautiful in the fading light, and when she turned to look back at me, I was drawn into her orbit.

I settled my hands on the railing on either side of her and breathed deeply. I could smell the salty tang of the air mingled with the fresh scent I would forever associate with Everest. I wasn't sure whether it was perfume, shampoo, or what, but I wanted to buy it by the gallon. She leaned back against me, and my hands fell to her waist, encircling her in my arms. It felt so natural to hold her, so right.

This close to her, I could practically feel the contented sigh that escaped her lips. "How do you ever leave this place?" she asked dreamily.

"It's tough," I acknowledged. I stroked a thumb over her ribs. "Although these days, it's not as difficult."

"Is that right?" she asked, angling her head back to look at me.

A sharp gust blew a stray lock of hair into her eyes, and I brushed it back, my fingers lingering on the curve of her cheek. The rosy evening light painted her fair skin an angelic hue. As usual, she wasn't wearing much makeup, so I could count the freckles along the bridge of her nose.

"Yeah," I said, stroking her cheek.

Her throat bobbed with her swallow. "Why is that?"

I smiled down at her, moving my hand so my fingers curled around the base of her skull. Her hair was soft to the touch. "I think you know why, Everest."

Slowly, she spun fully in my arms, her small hands dropping from her hair to slide up my biceps and come to rest against my chest. "Doesn't mean I don't want to hear you say it, Gideon."

I brought my other hand up to cup her face. "Because these days, I don't want to be where you aren't, Everest."

"Good answer," she said quietly, with a sexy little smile as her hair fanned out on the breeze.

Her tongue darted out to moisten her lips, and I dipped my head. She lifted her chin, those gorgeous eyes drifting closed. Dark lashes swept over her cheeks as she rose up on her toes, lips pursed and waiting for my kiss.

Inches apart from each other, our breath melded together, and my nose brushed hers. Her hair blew around us, tickling my face. I was seconds away from tasting her again, sampling the lips that had lived in my mind for weeks. I could feel my pulse in every part of my body, surging with excitement at finally getting to kiss her once more. I was surrounded by the freshness of her, from her subtle scent to the silkiness of her hair beneath my fingers and the soft curves of her body against mine. I knew she could feel my heartbeat speed up beneath her hand on my chest. I lowered my head the last few centimeters . . .

The sound of an air raid siren blared through the tranquil twilight air. Gulls screeched loudly as they vacated their perch below us. Their squawks mingled with Everest's startled cry as she stumbled away from me.

"What is that?" she shouted, covering her ears.

With a heavy and disappointed exhale, I pulled my phone from my pocket. The siren got louder without the fabric of my trousers operating as a muffler. Quickly, I stabbed a few buttons, silencing the screaming alarm. A few more clicks accessed the camera at my front door. The grinning faces of Davidson and Jamie stared annoyingly back at me. Great, just great.

I scrubbed a hand down my face in irritation. "It appears we have some unexpected guests."

"Who? An invading army?" Everest lowered her hands from where they'd guarded her hearing. "What the hell was that?"

"It's my door alarm," I said, waggling the phone in explanation.

"Is there a reason it's set at a thousand decibels?"

"Because my two best friends are a couple of bastards who consistently find ways to screw with me," I said grimly. Once Davidson figured out how to hack into the systems at my condo and monkey with the controls, his pranks ran the gamut—from making the lights flash on and off to a Barry White song, the shades open at 5:00 am on a Saturday, or, as we'd just heard, changing the chime on my door camera to something ear splitting. I was going to throttle him, but first I had to figure a way out of this debacle.

"Does this mean you need to summon Alexa and have dinner changed from two to four?" The sarcasm in Everest's voice ladled over her question like Sunday gravy.

"No," I said firmly. "They are not horning in on tonight."

Everest chuckled and leaned back against the railing. "You mean any more than they just did?"

My phone chirped at a normal volume this time. I answered it, putting a gruff edge to my voice. "Yeah?"

"Hey, man," Davidson said. "You going to let us in or what?"

"What are you doing here?"

"Your assistant mentioned you were flying up this weekend. We wanted to check in, see how things are going down in Mimosa," Davidson said. He paused, then said, "Why? Is someone with you?"

"Yes," I said without elaborating further.

Silence stretched over the line then Davidson said, "Let us up, Gideon."

From her place at the railing, Everest watched me intently. I knew she was trying to decipher everything she could from my side of the conversation. I could almost feel her ears straining toward me.

"I think this is something that we should wait to discuss—"

"Gideon," Davidson interrupted. "Open the fucking door."

I closed my eyes and dropped my head back in defeat, so I didn't see Everest's approach. Deftly, she plucked the phone from my hand, which made my stomach settle somewhere around my ankles. Before I could stop her, she'd put the phone to her ear.

"Hello, this is Everest Kennedy. With whom am I speaking?"

Her question must have been met with silence, because she pulled the phone away from her ear to check and see if the call had dropped. Given my minimal attendance to Mass in the past, oh, twenty years or so, it was no surprise my prayer for that to be the case went unanswered.

Putting the phone back to her ear, Everest said, "Hello?"

Either Davidson or Jamie must have found their voice and said something, because Everest's eyes flicked over to me. "I see," she said, her expression inscrutable. My gut twisted, wrapping itself around my anxiety. What were they saying to her?

"Well," she said, "I guess you should come on up and find out." She handed the phone to me. "Looks like we're going to have company." Her voice told me nothing, nor did the placid smile she gave me.

I took the phone from her. "Still there?" I asked into the receiver.

"Oh, you better believe we're still here," said Davidson. "And we're *not* leaving, so you might as well buzz us in."

Resigned to my fate, I disconnected the call and opened the app to unlock the front door. I looked at Everest. "I'm going to go downstairs to meet them. Do you want to . . ."

She waved an arm to the stairs. "Lead the way." Nerves kinked my stomach and knotted my shoulders as we walked down the stairs, but I did my best to hide it. What had they said to her? Was she pissed? Had our weekend just been torpedoed by my two idiotic best friends, or rather, by my piss-poor handling of this situation?

Davidson, Jamie, and our luggage stood next to the kitchen island. The bellman must have brought it in without buzzing, which made him much less of an asshole than either of my two friends. I made a mental note to send down a large tip in the morning.

"Gids," Jamie said pleasantly. "Good to see you, man." He came over wearing a smile, but his eyes brimmed with questions.

"Jamie," I said, and we exchanged bro-hugs.

Davidson looked past us to Everest. "You must be Ms. Kennedy," he said, coolly assessing her.

Undaunted, Everest walked over and extended a hand. "I'm afraid you have me at a disadvantage. You know who I am, but I don't know who's who." She flipped her gaze to me. "Although I think I have a pretty good idea."

Davidson took her hand in his. "Davidson Brooks," he said. Nodding toward Jamie, he added, "That's Jameson Standard, but most people call him Jamie."

"Ms. Kennedy," Jamie said.

Everest waved a hand. "Y'all aren't meeting Jackie O, so the 'Ms. Kennedy' isn't necessary. Please, call me Everest." She took in their tailored suits and monogramed dress shirts. "I feel a little underdressed for this party."

"Nonsense," I said, trying to set her at ease, even though she didn't look bothered in the least.

"Says the man in Italian loafers," she said teasingly. To my friends she said, "You boys won't mind if I go freshen up, will you?"

"By all means," Davidson said. "But it's not necessary on our account, really."

Turning to me, she asked, "Guest room?"

Guest room? The images of how I'd hoped this weekend would go shattered into a million tiny little shards I planned to use to murder Davidson and Jamie. Keeping my best poker face, I said, "Let me show you." I grabbed her bag and led her back toward the door, pointing out the hallway to the left. "Each of those doors lead to a guest room." I leaned in closer to her. "But the hallway to the right is the master."

Her response was a demure smile and a decisive turn toward the guest rooms.

Well, fuck. Once the door clicked shut behind her, I rejoined my friends.

Davidson had helped himself to a bourbon. Sipping the deep amber liquid, he looked at me, challenge evident in the set of his jaw. "Seems like you've figured out a few things since we last spoke, Gids. Why don't you fill us in?"

chapter twenty—two

EVEREST

What am I missing here? I wondered after the door to the guest room shut behind me. Gideon's reaction to seeing his friends at his door had been bizarre. He'd gone ashen, anxiety replacing the earlier laughter in his eyes. The change in his expression hadn't lasted long, but it *had* been there. And the nervous energy rolling off him as we'd come downstairs was so potent that I'd almost smelled it in the air around us like a sparking, open wire.

What did he have to be nervous about? Me? But why? Davidson had been fine, if a bit stiff, on the phone. He hadn't seemed too surprised by my presence, either, which didn't jive with Gideon's odd reaction. If they knew about me, then what was the big deal about them showing up with me here? Maybe he was embarrassed for some reason? But about what? The whole scenario seemed off, like a puzzle with missing pieces. I couldn't see the picture that was trying to take shape.

I gnawed on my thumbnail while I considered the implications. My reflection looked back at me from the mirror over the dresser, and I cringed. My well-worn T-shirt and leggings and wind-ravaged hair were more than a bit underdressed. I tossed my suitcase onto the bed and thanked the gods of fashion for a friend like Cammie. When I'd called in a frenzy to tell her Gideon wanted to whisk me away for a weekend in Boston, she'd marshaled every ounce of her fashion sense, and a large portion of her closet, to help me pack.

I pulled out a chocolate-brown sheath dress with a thin belt. Faux alligator pumps with killer heels completed the outfit, even though the sight of them made me wince a bit. Falling on my face wasn't completely out of the question, but I knew they were a necessary part of the impression I wanted to make. These boys might have met "country comes to town," but by God, that wasn't going to be who reemerged into the living room. Within twenty minutes, I'd changed, slapped on mascara and lipstick, and tamed as many of my flyaways into submission as I could. A final spritz of perfume and I was ready to get to the bottom of things.

The plush runner of carpet muted my footsteps when I emerged into the hallway. Male voices reached my ears, and I decided to take advantage of the fact they thought I was still primping and eavesdrop. Stealing down the short hall, I hovered just out of sight and listened.

"As much as I enjoy being right, Gids," Davidson was saying, "I would've appreciated at least a heads-up that you'd made a decision. I think we're owed that much from you on a topic that impacts all of us, not just you."

Well, that certainly couldn't be me. How could I have any impact on two men I'd never met?

"I'd like a little insight on that one, too, man," Jameson said.

I heard Gideon release a deep growl-like sigh. "Look," he said, his voice resigned, "it's not like I meant for anything to happen with Everest. Believe me, it wasn't in my plans either."

Huh? So, this *was* about me? The puzzle still wasn't coming together, so I held my tongue and my position in the shadows, waiting to see what else he had to say on the matter.

Gideon went on. "I probably knew the answer when you asked me about it the first time, but I just wasn't ready to admit it. And, yeah, maybe I should've told you before now. I can't escape that fact, and I'm sorry. But I'm telling you now. You asked if taking a chance with her was worth the risk, and I'm telling you I think it is."

What in the hell is he talking about? What risk?

Jameson piped up. "Look, man, are you sure about this? I mean *really* sure about it? Because we've got a lot riding on this for you to go into this without being one hundred percent certain getting into this chick's panties is more important than . . ."

A startled shout and resounding crash brought me out of hiding to see what had happened. Rounding the corner, I saw Gideon standing over Jameson with clenched fists and a stormy scowl. Jameson was sprawled out on the floor holding his jaw. An overturned end table was next to him. Davidson grabbed Gideon's arm and backed him away. None of them had noticed me entering the room.

Shrugging off Davidson, Gideon stabbed a finger down at Jameson, his eyes murderous. "I told you before to tread lightly, Jamie, but you just wouldn't listen." Anger rippled off his rigid shoulders, as visible as the heat wafting over a Mimosan sidewalk in July. His fists clenched and released as though he still wanted to pound Jameson to dust. The set of his jaw was so tight, I worried he'd crack a molar. When he glanced up and saw me in the mouth of the hallway, embarrassment quickly replaced the rage on his face.

He moved toward me then froze. "Everest, I . . ." he said and stopped, but his eyes sent a clear plea—*Don't go.*

My uncertainty over the root cause of the fight paled in comparison to the exhilaration of having a guy throw his best pal into a table to avenge what he perceived as a slight to my honor. Was what Jameson had said really that bad in the grand scheme of insults? Not based on my experience, but still, as someone who'd spent the last few years grappling with the ingrained prejudices aimed at women in the horse world, it was surprisingly satisfying for Gideon to topple Jameson over that table. A man who'd take on his best friend to defend me was not someone I was going to let slip through my fingers. Even if it were only for a short time, I was carpe-ing the hell out of this diem.

Like metal to a magnet, I went to him. Even in heels, I was still several inches shorter. Expressive blue eyes widened when I wrapped my arms around his neck and drew his mouth down to mine. I felt his surprise in the rigid set of his lips, but they quickly softened to receive my kiss.

Gideon's mouth was warm and firm as it moved over mine. He pulled me closer, those strong arms coming around my waist to hold me against him. The kiss was slow and deliberate. It was our way of confirming without words what was brewing between us. Had we been alone, my lips would have opened to welcome the slide of his tongue. The thought of it almost made me whimper with disappointment. But, alas, we had an audience, so the tantalizing preview would have to suffice. For now.

When we broke the kiss, Gideon rested his forehead against mine. "How much did you hear?" he asked quietly.

"Enough," I answered, so only he could hear me.

Davidson cleared his throat, and both Gideon and I looked over at him. He and Jameson had the good sense to look ashamed and apologetic over what had happened.

Davidson spoke first. "Ms. Kennedy . . . Everest, I think we've gotten off on the wrong foot here, and for that, I apologize."

Jameson stepped forward. "Davidson's right, as usual. I was an asshole and—"

"Also as usual," Gideon grumbled under his breath.

"I deserve that," Jameson said contritely. "Look, Everest, I don't know what you heard, but I . . ."

"You what?" I asked evenly. "You don't often go around discussing the minimal impact some 'chick' and her panties, or lack thereof, should have on one of your business deals? Somehow, I find that hard to believe."

Jameson's neck flushed, the red stain spreading up to his ears. "Well, this is embarrassing," he said.

"Which part?" I asked, unwilling to let him off the hook. "That you talked about my panties or that I caught you doing it?"

He tugged at his collar and looked at me with a hangdog expression. "Both?"

"Well, then," I said, stepping away from Gideon. "Maybe this should be a lesson on how you should speak about women, regardless of whether you think there are any around to overhear. Because, let me clue you in, *Jamie*, most of the time there's at least one of us around to hear every sexist or misogynistic thing you say. And you can bet your ass we'll remember it."

To his credit, he didn't bark back at me or try to evade responsibility for being a complete tool. He simply nodded, said, "Noted," and righted the end table.

Davidson regarded me like some type of lab specimen he couldn't quite classify. His face was impassive, but those deep brown eyes were pensive. I must have passed his inspection, though, because his face relaxed into a genuine version of the smile he'd given me when we met. It was amazing what that did for his features. Don't get me wrong—the guy was classically good-looking, but he had an aloof quality that didn't do much for his appeal. When his smile reached his eyes, though, it was like looking at a completely different person. As though a plaster cast had cracked open to reveal the real man beneath.

He chuckled and shook his head. "Everest, while we haven't had the most auspicious of beginnings, if you're willing to overlook the last ten minutes or so, you could turn into a very positive influence on me and my rightfully chastised colleague." He turned toward the wet bar. "Can I fix you a drink?"

It was my turn to assess Gideon's two friends. With Davidson's dark, brooding good looks and Jamie's blond, golden-boy aesthetic, I had no doubt they'd wreaked havoc on the single ladies of Boston. Throw Gideon into the mix and I was sure there were more broken hearts bobbing in the harbor than cast-off crates of tea. I was also reasonably certain very few women, if any, had ever dressed any of them down the way I'd just done. But they were Gideon's closest friends, so I was willing to at least examine the extended olive branch.

"Sure," I said. "I'll have a bourbon with just a tad of ice."

"Coming right up," Davidson said, turning to grab a bottle of Angel's Envy.

"Oh, and Davidson?" I said sweetly.

He turned back to me, brows raised.

"Forgiveness might be possible, but I don't overlook anything."

He nodded, his smile more subdued now. "Understood. A characteristic we have in common." I recognized the warning for what it was and filed it away.

Gideon's hand came to the small of my back. "Would you respect me less if I told you how incredibly turned on I got watching you tell off the assclown twins?"

I patted his cheek. "Only if you fail to act on it later."

Jameson approached the two of us with a contrite expression. "Listen, man, I'm . . ."

Gideon stepped around me to clasp a hand on Jameson's shoulder. "I know, Jamie." He extended his other hand, and Jameson took it with a smile. They did the standard man side hug, let's-make-sure-our-dicks-don't-touch thing, and peace was restored.

Davidson handed me my drink and tapped his against it. "Cheers," he said.

"Cheers," I responded and took a sip.

Gideon asked, "Where's my drink?"

"It's your house, Gids," Davidson said with a smirk. "I think you know where the booze is."

"So, Everest," Jameson said tentatively, "what made you decide to give our boy here a chance?"

I tapped a finger to my lips in a pretense of deep thought. "Hmm, well, the first thing that caught my attention had to be the way he rode a horse." A clank sounded from the wet bar, where Gideon bobbled his glass. The look he shot me was laced with equal parts panic and warning, which I ignored with a smile.

Davidson looked between Gideon and me, a calculating gleam in his eyes. "How he rode a horse? Gids, I didn't know you were an equestrian."

"It's not like you know everything about me," Gideon dodged defensively, his look now more pleading than anything else.

I ignored that too.

"Pretty sure I'd know if you rode horses," Davidson said.

The doorbell chimed in a much more sedate, musical tone than the screaming siren from earlier. Gideon put his drink down so fast, half of it sloshed onto the counter. "That must be dinner!" He practically tripped over himself in his haste to answer the door.

"I've seen starving men move more slowly at the prospect of food," Jameson said.

Gideon threw the door open hard enough to rattle the hinges.

The kid standing on the other side jumped back and emitted a little squeak.

"Come in, come in," Gideon said effusively, welcoming the waiter with a broad smile and too eager hand gestures.

"*He's* definitely scarred for life," Davidson murmured, and I held in a giggle. He sidled closer to me and said, "I'm guessing there's a very interesting story, since I'm reasonably certain Gids hasn't been on a horse since a pony at his fifth birthday party."

"You could say that," I said impassively, sipping my drink and watching Gideon continue his dance of avoidance and terrify the poor guy who'd brought our food.

"You could say more," Davidson said, his eyes also on Gideon.

"I could indeed," I replied.

Davidson grinned. "I'll find out eventually," he said, "about *everything.*"

I shrugged amiably, not letting his veiled promise rattle me. "Maybe so."

"Already keeping his secrets," Davidson said, and I clocked the grudging admiration in his tone. "I like it."

After a handsome tip, the poor waiter escaped into the hallway. Once the door closed behind him, Gideon wasted no time in ushering his friends out. He took the glass from Davidson's hand and picked up Jameson's from the side table, dumping both into the sink at the wet bar.

"Hey, I wasn't finished!" Jameson whined.

"Such hospitality," Davidson said, a sardonic twist to his lips. "You let me have two whole swallows."

Single-minded in his mission to throw them out, Gideon ignored their complaints. "I really hate you can't stay for dinner, but I only ordered enough for two. So, if you don't mind seeing yourselves out, Everest and I are ready to eat."

His two friends exchanged an amused look. Holding out his hand, Jameson was the first to say goodbye. "Everest, a pleasure meeting you."

"Jameson," I said mildly.

"Please," he said, folding his other hand on top of our joined ones, "call me Jamie."

I simply smiled, not ready to be pals quite yet. Residual anger at his callous remark had its own bass beat in my mind.

When he released my hand, Davidson took it in his. "Everest," he said, eyes still assessing me, "I look forward to getting to know you." His words were pleasant enough, but I could hear the promise behind them. Davidson wasn't letting this go, because he still harbored a concern that I was bad for business.

"Likewise," I said with a smile, refusing to let him get to me anymore than their unexpected appearance on Gideon's doorstep already had. This weekend was for us, not them. And I was going to enjoy it.

chapter twenty—three

GIDEON

Wow," Everest said, wiping her mouth with a napkin. She patted her stomach and slouched back into her seat. "I should've kept on the leggings."

"You certainly could've. There was no need for you to change clothes," I said. But she did look amazing in her dress and heels. It was a marked difference from her uniform of jeans and boots. But she could've come out in a potato sack held up with twine and I'd still have salivated over her.

Her answering smile was frosty. "I wasn't taking on the two of them without all available armor, heels included."

I didn't like Everest thinking she had to do battle with my two friends, but I couldn't blame her. Their initial reception hadn't been an open-armed welcome. I could've murdered Jamie for what he said, but on the positive side, she'd seen my reaction to it. The resulting kiss she'd planted on me told me she put the two of us solidly on the same side.

"I'm sorry about them showing up out of the blue," I said. "And I'm sorry for the way they reacted to meeting you at first. But I promise they're good guys. Just a little . . ."

Everest put her napkin over her plate and leaned forward on her elbows. "Please, Gideon. This isn't the first time I've dealt with entitled trust-fund brats, and I'm sure it won't be the last. Let's skip the whole 'boys will be boys' speech, okay? Plus," she said with a smirk, "you're the one who punched one of them, not me."

She leaned forward and fixed me with those emerald eyes. "What I'm more interested in is what they were upset about. Why are they so invested in what happens between us?"

"Because they know the sway your dad holds over council, and they don't want to lose that."

Her brow wrinkled in confusion. "But so far, my dad's been on board with your plans, and I can't imagine that changing with your new downtown district. If anything, he should like that even more. So why would they be worried about my dad?"

"His support for the project is exactly *why* they're concerned, I'm afraid."

"Gideon, you're not making any sense. If he's supportive, what's the problem?"

"Because if we're together, he can't be supportive. He'll have to recuse himself from any discussions or votes because of his personal interest."

"What personal interest?"

I covered her hand with mine. "You're the personal interest, Everest. Or rather, your relationship with me. It wouldn't be proper for him to vote on anything where there would be a perceived benefit to me as a result of my relationship with you. It's standard fare on any project involving governmental approvals. No one associated with the development can have ties to a member of the board, and if they do, that board member has to recuse themselves from any vote or discussion."

Her mouth fell open, and she slumped into her chair. "But I thought you needed my dad to make this happen."

I shrugged. "Sure, it would've been easier to have him leading the charge in support. In the meetings we've had, he's been pretty vocal about how he thinks this will benefit Mimosa. But it's not like we can't get it done without him. It just might take a little more work on my part. A little more schmoozing of the other board members and a larger dog and pony show, but it's no big deal."

That was an understatement, if not an outright lie. Jack Kennedy ducking out of the discussion would likely raise lots of questions from the other board members. Because he'd give a reason for his recusal—Everest—and, unfair as it was, could make the rest of the board suspicious of me and my intentions. Was I with Everest just to further the deal? Had I pursued her just to eliminate any problems with acquisition of the Collier property? Was I using her to get what I wanted?

But there was no way I was going to voice any of this to Everest. She'd balk at the thought of being the topic of town gossip any more than she already was and go back to hiding behind her work, leaving me out in the cold. I had no choice but to downplay the impact of the mayor's recusal. I could make it work, with Mimosa *and* Everest. I was certain of it. I just needed the opportunity to try.

Everest regarded me with skepticism etched in the downturn of her lips and dip of her brows. "But why would you give that up for something we've already agreed is going to end. Why would you do that?"

I ignored the sting of her words, because I wasn't ready to give up on the possibility that I could get her to see things between us could be more than short term. That we could find a way to make things work long distance that wouldn't interfere with her work with Second Chance. Still, she wasn't there with me, so I needed to tread lightly. "Everest, I knew as soon as we got involved it would mean your dad would have to step aside in any discussions about the project. That's what Jamie and Davidson were talking about, because they could tell

I was interested in you and they were concerned about how it would impact Mimosa Grove."

Bewilderment took the place of skepticism as she drew in a sharp breath, the fingers of her free hand pressed into her collarbone. With wide eyes, she struggled to ask, "But why would you . . . I mean, wouldn't it be better if I wasn't . . ."

"No," I said, giving her hand a tight squeeze. "Don't even think that, Everest."

"But, Gideon, I . . ."

"Everest," I said, gentling my tone. "Don't. Don't use this to second-guess what we've started." *What we could have,* I wanted to say but didn't want to overwhelm her.

I watched her face, her teeth sinking into her lower lip in that familiar worried chew as she considered what I'd said. My chest was tight, and it was hard to breathe around the lump in my throat as I waited for her to say something.

Finally, she said in a faltering voice, "Gideon, I don't think you've really thought this through. We agreed this was temporary. I can't give you more than that, because I'm not in a position to make that work. Second Chance takes all my time. You've seen how hard it is to just finagle a few days away. I don't have the bandwidth to take on a serious relationship, right now, so I can't—"

"Everest." I interrupted her, doing my best to infuse her name with enough quiet purpose to derail her doubts. Rising from my seat, I came to her side. I gripped the table and put my other hand on the back of her chair, leaning into her space. "You are one of the most enigmatic women I've ever met, and it drives me to distraction. Every time I turn around, there's something about you that sets you apart. You don't care about money, unless it's donations to your charity. You are ridiculously comfortable in your own skin. You don't back down from anything, at least nothing I've ever seen. And, to top it all off, you're one of the most selfless and self-sufficient people I've ever met. Whether it's fixing lawn mowers or saving wayward, wannabe cowboys and the horses they ride on, there's absolutely nothing you can't do. In essence, Everest, darling, there's nothing you need from me, because you have the ability to do everything for yourself." I took a breath then pushed forward before she could speak.

"If I'm honest, at first, I found that terrifying, because what could I offer the woman who could do it all? If I brought nothing you needed to the table, how could we possibly have a relationship? But then, I realized that was what I'd been missing my entire adult life. I'd never had a woman choose to be with me solely because she wanted to. A woman who didn't give a shit about money, or power, or anything else that I had in spades. I figured out that if you chose to give me a chance, it would be because you wanted *me*, not anything I could give you."

I swallowed, trying to figure out how to tell her the way I felt without scaring her back to Mimosa. "I know it seems counterintuitive, but Everest . . . I cannot stress this enough. Losing out on having you, even for a short time, is not something I'm willing to consider. I refuse to spend the remainder of my life knowing that I sacrificed a chance with the most intriguing woman I've ever met in exchange for an easier path to plat approval. I can't pass you up, for however long I can have you, regardless of what else that means for me. It seems"—I grinned down at her—"you've bewitched me."

Her lips twitched. "How am I supposed to do anything but beg you to take me right here on this table after that little speech?"

"All you have to do is ask. No begging would be required," I assured her, dropping a hand to her bare shoulder.

The smile she'd been fighting broke free, and Everest curved her hand around my jaw, her thumb stroking my cheek. "Are you sure, Gideon? *Really* sure this is a good idea? It's not too late to—"

"I'm sure," I said, my thumb brushing the hollow of her throat. The honest truth, one I knew she wasn't ready to hear, was that I'd never been more certain of anything in my entire existence. *She* was worth whatever sacrifice I had to make. I just had to get her to see that.

Her hand dropped from my cheek to my wrist, her touch cool and light. "I trust that you know what you're doing, so I won't ask again. But Gideon—" Her lashes swept down with a throaty laugh. Opening her eyes, she pinned me in place with an iridescent green stare. "I have to warn you that you are wrong about something."

I recoiled as though she'd struck me. "About what?"

Everest dragged the toe of her shoe up the leg of my trousers, stopping right below my crotch. My strangled breath made her grin wickedly. "There is *absolutely* something you have that I need and very, *very* much want."

I shoved her place setting back, making her laugh and grab her wineglass. Wrapping my hands around both her arms, I pulled her to her feet.

"Gideon," she whispered huskily as my chest brushed hers. God, I wanted this woman. My body thrummed with the need to have her, to claim her as my own. Letting my hands trace down her ribcage, I lifted her up and set her on the edge of the table. I couldn't wait to get to my bedroom. I was so desperate for her that things were going to begin right here on the dining room table.

Except her dress had other ideas. The fitted skirt, which so perfectly clung to and highlighted the gorgeous curve of her ass, was not conducive to spontaneous hanky-panky. Standing in front of her, I could barely wedge one knee between hers and, when I did, there was no way that skirt was moving in any direction. For a moment, I debated ripping the seams.

"Don't even think about it," Everest warned after seemingly reading my mind. "Unless you want to explain to Cammie why her dress came back in tatters."

"Right," I said but wouldn't admit defeat. I did what any male whose blood flow to the brain was severely disrupted would do. I leaned down, put my shoulder into her stomach, and hoisted her into a fireman's carry. She shrieked with laughter, still managing to hold on to her wineglass.

"You're insane," she said, and I slapped her bottom. "Gideon, I'm too full! You're going to make me puke!" Everest squealed and wriggled, which served only to quicken my strides to the bedroom. This was much better. Now, I could peel her out of that dress, inch by scrumptious inch, until she lay naked before me.

Reaching the master bedroom, I plucked the glass from her hand and dumped her onto the mattress with a satisfying bounce. Her smile was wanton (and thankfully, not queasy in the least) as she leaned back on her elbows, cocking her knees to the side. Red hair hung around her face in tousled waves, wild from her upside-down journey to the bedroom. I wanted to touch all of her at once. But first, I had to get rid of my own clothes. I slid one cufflink from my sleeve and Everest shifted into a kneeling position.

"Let me," she said and slipped the other silver square from its notch. It hit the nightstand with a plink, and she was back before me. Small fingers worked their way down the front of my dress shirt, nudging buttons from their holes and spreading open my shirt. As she neared the waistband of my trousers, she tugged on my shirttails to release them. When the last button popped free, she pushed the shirt from my shoulders.

"My, my, Gideon," she said, tracing the lines of my fitted tank undershirt. "I definitely didn't picture you wearing something so deliciously simple."

I caught her wrist. "You've thought about what's under my clothes, have you?"

Everest rose higher on her knees, so we were almost eye to eye. With her lips a sigh away from mine, she said, "Only every night for the past few weeks."

With a growl, I closed the distance between us, crushing my mouth over hers. It was a bruising kiss, full of the pent-up desire and other emotions that had raged through me since she'd come riding into my life. Her answering moan allowed my tongue to slip inside and tangle with hers. She tasted like wine and the chocolate we'd had for dessert. I wanted to devour her until there was nothing left. And then start all over again.

My fingers slid beneath the curtain of her hair, hunting for the zipper to the damn dress. The thin tab scraped over my thumb, and my dick almost wept with relief. Tugging it down, down, down until it hit the belt at her waist.

Everest broke our kiss, biting my bottom lip as she pulled away. Slowly, she slipped out one arm, then the other, until she was just holding the front of her dress against her chest. I held in a groan at the sight, and she licked her lips. With one hand, she slipped the thin belt from its buckle and tossed it toward the foot of the bed. Reaching back, she pulled the zipper of her dress the rest of the way down and dropped her other hand from its bodice. The fabric fell away, revealing Everest's perfectly rounded breasts on display in a sheer black bra.

My mouth watered at her nipples, peaked and eager, behind the gauzy fabric. Never looking away from me, she cupped her breasts in her hands, letting her thumbs drag across her skin. My cock went impossibly harder as she shuddered in response to her own touch. Unable to resist any longer, I advanced on her. Pressing my palm on the center of her chest, I pushed her gently.

"Lie back, sweetheart," I said in a gravelly voice.

She complied, letting her legs dangle over the edge of the bed. Her hips lifted as I gripped the hem of her dress and pulled it down until it was a puddle on the floor. I don't think even La Perla would have the audacity to call what Everest had on panties. The tiny triangle was so sheer, the strips of fabric over her hips so thin, that a harsh wind would've simply blown it off her body. Seeing her in nothing but her bra, that tiny scrap of cloth over her center and a pair of stilettos had my blood roaring in my ears then plunging south.

"See something you like, Gideon?" Everest asked, trailing a finger between her breasts.

Unwilling to be the only one coming undone, I grabbed the back of my undershirt and dragged it over my head. Everest's eyes glazed over then sparked with heat as they raked down my chest and the ridges of my abs. Yeah, I might be a few years from forty, but I busted my ass to make sure those years stretched out for as long as possible.

"My, my," she said again and crooked her finger invitingly.

Obeying her command, I moved over her. Looping one arm underneath her shoulders, I slid her farther back onto the bed. She bent one knee, pushing the back of her shoe against the bedspread to take it off. I grabbed her ankle. "Oh no, sweetheart. These stay on."

"These need to come off," she said, tugging at my belt buckle.

"Whatever the lady wants," I said, withdrawing from her hastily to undo my belt and drop my slacks to the floor. Green eyes wandered slowly over my body, bared to her except for a pair of black boxer briefs. I smiled under her perusal and flexed my pecs.

She giggled. "C'mere, lover boy."

I sank back down on the mattress, hovering above her. Her pale skin and copper tresses stood out against the darkness of the comforter. She looked like an offering to the Celtic gods, whoever they were. Lowering to my elbows, I let the full length of my body connect with hers, pressing her deeper into the mattress. Her legs parted, and she hummed in anticipation as she felt the impatience of my cock at her center. Everest bucked her hips, and the heat of her core burned through the thin layers of fabric separating us.

"You're beautiful. You know that?" I asked.

"Sweet talker," she said and guided my lips to hers. Our mouths glided together, tongues stroking, each of us seeking more. More contact, more sensation . . . just more. Her hips writhed under me, teasing my dick until I thought I would come right then.

Needing to regain control, I relinquished her mouth and worked my way down the arch of her throat then kissed along her collarbone. It was my turn to cup Everest's breasts and drag my thumbs over the tight buds of her nipples while she gasped in pleasure. Rolling them between my fingers turned her gasps to moans.

"Gideon," Everest's voice came out in a raspy purr, and I loved the sound of my name on her lips.

Delving beneath the lace of her bra, I pulled first one nipple, then the other between my teeth. I alternated between them, suckling, nibbling, and licking until she was reduced to a panting frenzy of want.

"I need you," she begged, nails dragging over my shoulders.

"I'm right here," I said, kissing the underside of one breast.

She reached between us to cup my raging hard on. "I need you inside me, Gideon," she said, stroking my shaft. I pushed forward into her grip, savoring each pass of her hand along my cock. A groan started at the back of my throat and rumbled free as she gripped me, squeezing and teasing me with the promise of what was to come.

One-handed, I extracted a condom from my nightstand. Tearing open the foil with my teeth, I retreated briefly to shuck off my boxers. I knelt above her, condom at the ready.

Everest took it from my hand. "Let me," she said and rolled it slowly down. Watching her sheathe me was so fucking erotic. When she reached the base, her hands went to her panties.

Mine covered hers. "It's only polite to return the favor," I said and slid her G-string down her legs. Rather than toss it away, I dropped it into the drawer of the nightstand.

"Souvenir?" she asked with a laugh.

"I'll add it to my collection," I teased, and she slapped my chest.

Catching her hand, I pinned it above her head. We were chest to chest, and I could feel the wet heat of her through the condom. My dick pulsed with the urge to slide inside, but I wanted to make sure she was ready.

Reaching down, I teased her slit with one finger. She was slick and hot, letting out a groan at my touch. "Are you ready for me, darling?" I asked, already knowing but wanting her to say it.

Everest wrapped her hand around my dick and notched the head of it at her entrance. Undulating against me, she brought her lips to my ear and bit down on my ear lobe. "So ready, Gideon."

My body shook when I pushed inside her, inch by glorious fucking inch. "Oh God," I said, feeling the initial resistance then welcoming stretch of her body. "You're so tight, Everest. So, fucking tight." For a few breaths, I held still to savor her body's acceptance of mine. Then, slowly, I started to move.

"Oh yes," Everest's voice at my ear was silky and low as her hips angled up to take me deeper. "More, Gideon, please!" Her nails scraped over my skin as her hands ran up and down my back. The warmth of her breath tickled my neck with her sighs of pleasure.

Melting into the intoxicating feel of her, I braced myself on my forearms and took in the sight of her beneath me—eyes bright with desire, cheeks flushed, and lips parted. She was exquisite in her unabashed enjoyment of my body joining with hers. Throaty whimpers and eager noises spilled from her lips, spurring me on, faster and faster. Swiveling my hips with each thrust elicited louder cries of pleasure from Everest, making her fingers curl tighter around my biceps. Her body rolled against mine, the rise and fall of her hips summoning the heady tingle of an impending orgasm, but there was no way I was going before she did.

Pushing her bra up, I massaged one breast, capturing her nipple between my thumb and forefinger. Her eyes shot open, and her hips rocked hard against mine. "Oh, fuck, fuck, *fuck*," she chanted, tossing her head from side to side and biting her bottom lip.

"That's it, baby," I encouraged breathlessly. Her inner walls clamped around me, sealing my shaft in hot, wet luxurious heat—a sure signal I wasn't the only one on the precipice of aching release. I hitched her leg higher on my waist, almost cross-eyed with need but determined to please her first.

"Gideon! Oh yes, Gideon," she said, her fingers feathering over my shoulders.

"I know you're close, baby." I grunted, giving that rosy peak a delicate twist, loving the moan it elicited from her, the way it made her hips jerk primally against me as she chased her satisfaction. "Just let go, let go, Everest."

As her hands tightened their grip, I felt her orgasm take hold and her body unfurl and ripple around me. She cried out unintelligible words, and her hips spasmed against mine, the sting of her nails sharp where she clutched my shoulders, lost to the sensation. Her coming undone was my own undoing. Blood roared in my ears as my heart pounded, and my cock throbbed with relief as I came, thrusting so deeply into her I thought I'd lose myself. Dark spots floated in my vision as Everest clenched around me through the last of her climax. My hips flexed one final time, and I slumped against her chest, thoroughly spent and sated.

Everest's foot, still miraculously clad in her stiletto, drew up the back of my leg and she stroked my hair. "That was . . ." she said languorously and laughed softly instead of finishing her thought.

I didn't have the words to describe what had just happened either. At that point, I questioned whether I had the ability to even speak. I mumbled something against her chest, which was slick with sweat. I felt her laugh beneath my cheek as I contemplated whether it was feasible to spend the rest of my life right there.

She wriggled beneath me, and it dawned on me that I was, quite possibly, crushing the very life out of her. Shifting my weight, I lifted onto my elbows to look at her. Everest smiled up at me, and I could see she was floating along on the same post-orgasmic cloud that I was. Her skin glowed, her lips were swollen from my kisses and her hair was a maelstrom of red curls spread out beneath us.

I dropped a kiss to the center of her chest, tasting the salty tang of her skin. Everest ran her fingers through my hair, linking her hands behind my head and drawing me up her body. I came willingly, and she kissed me lightly on the nose, then on each cheek, and finally, her lips met mine. It was a softer kiss than the barn burners we'd exchanged a few minutes ago, but it let me know she had no regrets.

I didn't want to leave her side, but I also knew I had to deal with the condom. Everest let out a loud wolf whistle when I stood up. I gifted her with a little shimmy of my bare ass, and she applauded. Returning to the bedroom, I found her snuggled beneath the sheets in the center of the bed with *both* pillows propped behind her head.

"So where are you sleeping?" she asked cheekily.

"Saucy little minx, aren't we?" I asked and stalked toward the bed. "Get what you want from a man and then send him out into the cold, dark night?"

Everest was the queen of eye rolls, and she executed a masterful one as she flipped the sheets back and patted the space next to her. "Fine, fine, come on in."

I dove between the sheets, making her squeal as I liberated one of the pillows for myself. Fluffing it to my exacting specifications, I burrowed under the covers next to her. Sliding one arm under her remaining pillow, I draped the other over her waist. My hand spanned along her abdomen, and I scooted up behind her, curving my front against her back. I was delighted to learn she'd shed the bra and was stark naked next to me. I sighed contentedly and nuzzled her neck.

"Comfortable?" she asked drily.

"Very," I answered.

She patted my hand and relaxed back into my embrace. "So am I."

chapter twenty—four

EVEREST

The scent of coffee floated through the air in tempting tendrils, teasing me with the promise of that first hit of glorious caffeine. I'd need it, too, because I had a full day ahead at the stables. There was so much to do that I couldn't just lie around in bed all—*hold on a second.* If I were in my bed, then who in the hell was making the coffee?

My eyes popped open. One look at the shaded floor to ceiling windows and I knew I wasn't in my house, let alone my own bed. Soft sheets rustled around my naked body when I sat up. My nudity brought the memories from last night flooding back in a tidal wave of illicit sensations. I was in Gideon's bedroom. Correction, I was *naked* in Gideon's bedroom, because we'd spent the evening having the most exquisitely satisfying sex of my entire life. I glanced to my left, and the pillow still held the impression of Gideon's head. He hadn't been up long.

Stretching, I luxuriated in the combination of his astronomically high thread count sheets and the scrumptious ache of my body being reawakened after too long without the company of a man. Last night had been . . . well, earth shattering sounded beyond dramatic, but it was the only adjective that sprang to mind. I honestly believed there could've been an earthquake last night and it wouldn't have interrupted the deliciously naughty things Gideon and I had done to each other. The man had stamina, that was for sure.

A low whirring sound accompanied soft streams of morning light as the blinds lowered. The door opened and Gideon appeared, barefoot and clad only in low-slung gray sweatpants (lady porn of the highest order). He carried a tray of coffee with all the trimmings and a plate of scrambled eggs, bacon, and hash browns. My mouth watered, but I didn't know whether it was from the smell of breakfast in bed or the outline of Gideon's impressive . . . well, anyway.

"Ah, you're awake," Gideon said with a panty-melting smile. "I brought you breakfast."

"I see that," I said, tucking the sheet under my arms to save a little modesty.

He placed the tray next to the bed and leaned down for a kiss. I turned my head, covering my mouth. "I need to brush my teeth."

Gideon kissed my cheek then flopped next to me on the bed. "Bathroom's right through there, as you know."

I slid out of bed, doing my best to not to be self-conscious about wandering around naked in front of Gideon in the cold light of day. I needn't have worried though. Before I'd made it two steps, he rolled to the edge of the bed and slapped my ass. "Don't take too long, darling."

I was still smiling at his antics until I looked in the mirror above the sink. *Gah!* My hair was the proverbial rat's nest, and I had a dark smudge of mascara under one eye. That would teach me to do my evening toilette at three in the morning after multiple orgasms. Hurriedly, I scrubbed away the black smear and ran a brush through my unruly locks. A splash of water later, the requisite two-minute scrub with my toothbrush, and I was done.

Gideon's bedroom was a study in masculine style. A king-sized bed took up the majority of one wall. It sat on a thick rug with gray speckled, abstract designs. He had an old steamer trunk as a nightstand, with reading glasses sitting in a dish next to a wrought iron lamp. The far corner held a worn leather club chair and an ottoman, a perfect reading nook. Floor-to-ceiling windows took up the opposite wall. It was painted a warm gray that highlighted the dark herringbone pattern of his comforter.

It was a cozy, well-put-together room, but it all faded into the background once I locked eyes on the man sprawled in the middle of the bed. Gideon West was a mouthwatering feast of maleness. With one hand behind his head and the other resting on his flat stomach, he watched me approach. An appreciative smile stretched his full lips as those blue eyes took in every inch of my body. The hand on his stomach slid south as his sweatpants struggled to contain his excitement at seeing me.

Emboldened by his obvious admiration, I didn't get back under the covers. Instead, I got down on all fours at the foot of the bed and crawled toward him. His eyes gleamed and he sucked his bottom lip between his teeth as I got closer. Reaching his side, I curled next to him, draping one leg over his and resting my head on his shoulder.

His hand came from behind his head to rest on my hip and the other reached up to toy with my breast. "A man could get used to Saturday mornings like this one," he said.

My nipple pebbled under his ministrations, and I arched my back for more. He obliged and used his long fingers to tease and tantalize until my skin was tight and flushed and my breath had been reduced to eager gasps.

"Gideon," I whispered.

"Yes, love?" he asked as he rolled on top of me and took the tortured peak between his lips.

Rays of desire spiraled outward as he bit down gently then used the flat of his tongue to soothe the sting. My hips lifted from the bed of their own volition. Feverishly, I clawed at the waistband of his pants, shoving them down and over his hips.

I felt his laughter against my skin as he moved from one breast to the other to continue his divine assault. Lapping, suckling, nibbling to slowly drive me insane with want. "In a hurry this morning, are we?" he asked then flickered his tongue in a wicked flutter while my toes curled.

A raw sound tore from my lips. With a few lingering looks and masterful touches, the man set my body on fire. In mere minutes, I was aching for him. As taught by the great girl bands of the '90s, I was *not* too proud to beg. "Gideon, please," I whined, palming his cock.

He was no longer in a teasing mood as he hardened and thickened in my hand. "God, Everest," he said harshly. His eyes closed as I wrapped my hand around his shaft and squeezed, letting each finger tighten and release around him, then start again. A breath hissed out from between his clenched teeth, and he put his hand around my wrist.

"Let me just get a condom, sweetheart," he said, tugging gently on my arm.

Before I could even think about it, I said, "I'm on birth control."

He blinked down at me, absorbing the meaning of those words. "Everest, I . . . I'm not asking you for that."

"I know, Gideon. I'm offering." Which was absolutely *not* something you did in a temporary situation, but in that moment, it was all I wanted. To have him within me without anything between us. To *feel* him.

The fire in his blue eyes softened, and he brushed a hand down my cheek. We looked at each other for the space of a few breaths, then he said, "You've nothing to worry about from me. I promise you, I'm good." His reassurance in the moment warmed me, and I never doubted his word.

"I believe you," I said and pushed his pants the rest of the way off.

Trapping my face between his hands, he looked me in the eyes. "Are you sure about this?"

I nodded, feeling overcome with emotion suddenly. "Yes, I'm sure."

Searching my face, he nodded, satisfied I was certain. Then he kissed me slowly, reverently, and thoroughly. It was as though he were pouring his entire being into the kiss, transmitting what he wanted to say but couldn't. When he pulled away, I was breathless.

He hooked my knee over his hip, and his erection pressed against me. I stroked my hands down over his chest and around his lower back. With gentle pressure, I pushed him forward.

Gideon groaned as I slid against him. "Jesus, Everest."

With a tenderness that surprised me, Gideon pushed slowly inside me, eyes on mine the entire time. It was a moment so intimate, I was scared to move, or even breathe, because I didn't want to spoil it. Once I'd taken all of him, he closed his eyes and canted his head back, breathing slowly. The tendons in his neck stood out starkly as he held himself still.

After a moment, he opened his eyes and gazed down at me. "Sweetheart," Gideon said roughly then bent his head to kiss me. His lips were firm but soft, and I opened to him. We kissed deeply as his hips moved against mine. His arms came around my back, and he pulled me closer, as though he wanted no space between us at all. Our bodies rocked together in an ancient rhythm, and I felt myself spiraling higher.

Gideon buried his face in the crook of my neck, his breath hot and heavy by my ear. His thrusts became harder and faster, and I tilted my hips up to bring him deeper, closer. Garbled sounds of male desire fell from his lips as his pace increased.

"Everest, Christ, you feel like heaven," he growled against my neck.

Words escaped me as I was lost in a sea of endless, dizzying sensation and pleasure. The feel of him plunging in and out, dragging heavily against my folds, triggered my orgasm. With a euphoric shout, my hips slammed upward and I spasmed around his cock.

"Fuck, sweetheart," Gideon rasped out, and his hips jerked sporadically as he came with me. My body tingled hedonistically as the warm flames of desire licked over me. Each stroke of his body against mine ignited a new one, until I thought I would be incinerated. I was lost then. No matter what we'd said, our promises that things between us would end once he left, that forever wasn't an option—when he left me, I'd be gutted.

Exhausted, Gideon collapsed against me, his breathing labored. Together, we lay there, neither able nor willing to move from the tangle of limbs atop his bed. Finally, Gideon stirred to life, placing tiny kisses against my throat.

"You know," he said, working his way under my jaw, "you totally ruined my morning plans."

"Is that right?" I asked, forcing normalcy into my tone.

"Mm-hmm," he hummed against my cheek. "I'd made you breakfast and was going to woo you with my superior culinary talents. Little did I know," he said into my ear, "that you just wanted me for my body."

"Ha-ha," I said and half-heartedly pinched his stomach. "You're lucky I'm currently numb from my supernova orgasm. Otherwise, I'd kick your ass."

He snuggled closer and sighed happily. "You do know I'm never letting you leave, right? After that and last night, you are, I'm sad to inform you, stuck with me forever."

His tease of forever stabbed into my heart like an ice pick. A promise of something that could never be. As intoxicating as it was to have this man say he wanted to keep me here forever, the cold, hard truth of it was that couldn't happen. No matter how badly I wanted it to.

Gideon took my chin in his hand. "Hey, where'd you go just now?"

Forcing a smile to my lips, I said, "Just thinking about how cute you're going to look while you make me more eggs. I'll take them scrambled with cheese this time, please." There was no reason to ruin this weekend with talk of what might or might not happen in the coming weeks or months. We were together now, so I'd just roll with that until I couldn't.

Rising up on his elbow, Gideon peered down at me. "Are you sure that's what you were thinking?"

"Well," I said hesitantly, "it might have also crossed my mind there'd be fresh coffee."

He looked at me for a beat longer, so I reached up and tweaked his nose. "Relax, Gideon. I can make my own breakfast if it's going to be that big a deal."

No one can stay serious after having their nose tweaked like a child, and Gideon was no exception. His normal, megawatt smile reappeared. "What kind of scoundrel do you think I am? That's a load of nonsense. No woman of mine is going to make her own breakfast on our weekend of sin." He bounced off the bed and pulled me up with him. "Come on then, let's get you properly fed."

"Uh, Gideon," I said, tugging on his hand.

"Yes, love," he said, looking adorably back at me.

I gestured down my still naked body. "I think we should maybe put on some clothes. Bacon grease hurts."

He looked down at his nude form and, let's face it, so did I. How could I not admire the male perfection before me?

"Right you are." Blue eyes twinkled at me. "Although you could just slip back into those tiny little panties you wore last night . . ."

I rolled my eyes at him. "And have you burn my bacon? I think not."

chapter twenty—five

GIDEON

I adjusted my cufflink then straightened the cuff itself, taking care that a proper amount of white starched sleeve showed under my dinner jacket. Checking my tie in the mirror, I glanced at the clock in the reflection. Seeing the time, I called to Everest.

"Everest, we need to leave soon to make our reservation." *Good grief, I sound positively domestic.* A thought that I would have to *keep* to myself if I didn't want Everest to freak out and run screaming all the way back to Mimosa. She hadn't wavered from her declaration that she wasn't looking for permanence, and I couldn't push her until I'd mapped out a solution to all her objections. I'd gotten her past the recusal issue, but that hadn't been easy, and I needed to bide my time before addressing the larger issue of the future. *Our* future beyond the temporary, tentative relationship that was barely in existence. I hoped our day together had helped my cause in that regard.

After our morning sexcapades, I'd been true to my word and taken her to some of the more popular touristy spots in Boston. To my surprise, and secret delight, she'd never ridden the swan boats. I'd happily paid the paltry eight dollars for two tickets to have Everest cuddled next to me as our guide piloted us, and roughly fifteen other strangers, around the lagoon in the Public Garden. We'd had the obligatory beer at Cheers and noshed our way down Newbury Street. It had been one of the most fun days I'd spent in my city in years.

Tonight, we were dining at a romantic little spot in the North End. It had the requisite starched tablecloths, dripping wax candles, and thick leather-bound menus. The real selling point, though, were the secluded booths that gave you and your date total privacy. Reservations were at a premium, which was why I looked again at the clock on the wall.

"Everest, sweetheart," I cajoled. "We really do need to . . ." Whatever the hell else I was going to say disappeared from my mind when she came into view.

Dressed in a strapless, royal purple jumpsuit with her voluminous curls pinned and twisted on top of her head, she looked like a goddess. The deep purple emphasized her creamy complexion, and she'd done something different with her makeup that made her green eyes appear even larger and more vibrant. A dainty chain of golden circles was cinched around her waist, matching the gold hoops in her ears.

"Close your mouth before you catch a fly, Gideon," she said and sashayed over to kiss my cheek. "I take it from the stupefied expression on your face that you like my outfit."

Her words brought me out of my temporary coma, and I said, "You look . . . different." I shook my head. "I mean, you look . . . wow." Not the most eloquent of compliments, but it got the point across.

"My, my," she said, and I was beginning to love hearing that little catchphrase. "Gideon West at a loss for words. Never thought I'd see the day. Guess I'll have to leave that little YouTuber a five-star rating on her makeup tutorial. Only took me four tries to get it right."

Wrapping my arms around her, I whispered in her ear, "Please pass along my compliments as well. And I seem to recall someone else being a little short on vocabulary earlier this morning. I believe the only words you could bring to mind were 'Oh, Gideon' and 'More, please.'"

She smacked my arm. "Don't be vulgar. It's beneath you." I could hear the lilt in her voice as she reprimanded me.

I bowed over her hand. "Please forgive me, milady."

Everest shook her head at my theatrics. "I take it our chariot awaits? That is why you were bellowing for me to hurry up, right?"

"A gentleman never bellows, darling. He merely speaks strenuously to get his point across. And yes, I believe the car is downstairs."

"Well, I'm ready." She moved to the door, but I caught her hand.

"Just one thing before we go," I said and drew her back into my arms. Dipping my head to where her shoulder met her neck, I took a deep sniff. Her familiar scent made its way into my brain, assuring me that this maven of style before me was the same girl who normally favored tank tops and faded jeans.

"Did you just smell me?" Everest asked.

"Yes, I did," I said, blatantly unashamed.

"You're an odd one, Gideon. But you're dynamite in the sack, so I'll let that slide. Shall we go?"

Heads turned as we made our way through the lobby, and I put a possessive hand at the small of Everest's back. She looked up and smiled at me, slipping her arm around my waist to give me a little squeeze. I loved the way her shoulder notched under mine, like she was made to fit there. I brushed a kiss over her temple.

"What was that for?" she asked.

"I can't really say," I admitted. "Just felt the need to kiss my girl."

"Gideon?"

My stomach curdled at the sound of Mandy's voice. I looked over and saw her striding purposefully toward us from the concierge desk, the clack of her stilettos echoing across the lobby like gunshots. By the look on his face, I guessed she'd been less than pleased with what he'd told her.

Keeping my hand on Everest's waist, I peeled back my lips into a semblance of a friendly smile. "Amanda, what a surprise."

Everest could feel the change in my posture at Mandy's approach. "Friend of yours?" she asked from the corner of her mouth.

Mandy reached us before I could answer. "Gideon," she cooed, "how many times must I tell you to call me Mandy."

When I didn't answer, she frowned. "I heard you were back in town, so I thought I'd come by and we could finish that drink from a few weeks ago." She hadn't so much as glanced at Everest.

Clearing my throat, I said, "Well, I'm afraid that can't happen, since Everest and I are on our way out to dinner." Pulling Everest closer to my side, I made the introduction. "Mandy, this is Everest Kennedy, my girlfriend. Everest, this is Amanda Alcott."

Although I felt her spine stiffen slightly, Everest didn't hesitate at my use of the term girlfriend. Instead, with a polished smile, she extended her hand to Mandy. "It's a pleasure to meet you, Amanda."

Finally, Mandy turned and looked down her nose at Everest then back to me. She ignored Everest's outstretched hand. "Girlfriend? Since when does Gideon West refer to anyone as his girlfriend?" Her tone was no longer friendly or seductive. It was icy, with a tinge of hysteria thrown in for fun.

Everest pulled her hand back, letting it come to rest on my chest. "Well," she said to Mandy, "it *was* a little sudden. It sort of took me off guard too."

Mandy's features pinched into an unflattering sneer. "He certainly didn't mention any girlfriend when he was with me a few weeks ago," she said, her smile practically carnivorous. The implication in her voice sketched a skewed diagram of our last interaction.

I was about to lay into her, but Everest pressed her hand ever so slightly into my chest, and I took the signal to stay quiet. "Well," she said calmly, "that's probably because we weren't together a few weeks ago." Everest leaned toward Mandy, like she was going to share a secret. "But then, I'm guessing neither were the two of you. Now, if you'll excuse us"—she smiled—"we need to get going or we'll miss our reservations. So lovely to have met you, Mandy."

Amanda Alcott was not a woman used to being so easily dismissed, and she stood there flabbergasted as Everest propelled me toward the door. I was in absolute awe at the way she'd easily dispatched the blue-blooded mean girl.

"You know you're amazing, right?" I said as we exited onto the sidewalk.

Everest favored me with a triumphant grin. "Well aware, Gideon. But it's sweet of you to mention it," she said and ducked into the back-seat of the waiting car.

I shoved a few bills into the valet's gloved hand and joined her, sliding across the black leather to put an arm around her. "Everest, I do want to say, what Mandy said about our being together a few weeks ago . . ."

She rested a hand on my thigh, giving it a reassuring pat. "Gideon, don't waste your breath or time explaining something that obviously never happened."

Relief washed through me at her unwavering confidence, but I couldn't stop talking. "I did see her at a bar when I was here. But I promise, the rest of what she implied didn't . . ."

"Gideon," Everest interrupted. "Do you really want to talk about Tall, Blonde, and Boring, or do you want to talk about the whole 'girl-friend' thing? Because I have to tell you, I find that topic *a lot* more interesting." She angled her body, so she could face me and raised a questioning eyebrow.

"Well, I couldn't very well say, 'Oh, hello, Mandy. This is my paramour Everest Kennedy. We haven't discussed any real parameters, or made any promises, but good Lord, you should see this one thing she does with her tongue.' I don't think that would've had the same effect, do you?"

Everest laughed, "That girl might've wanted to join us if you mentioned the tongue thing." She raised a pointed finger at me when I opened my mouth. "Resist temptation and stay on point, West." My mouth snapped closed, and she continued. "Girlfriend might be a bit of an overstatement at this point, but I don't mind saying that I'm not interested in seeing anyone else while we are . . . doing whatever it is we're doing."

She'd given me the perfect opening to broach the topic of permanence, but I couldn't bring myself to take it. This weekend was more about show than tell. I could show her how a trip here didn't tilt her world's axis. That everything she had going on would continue to spin in her brief absence. And if there were a few more trips like this sprinkled throughout the year, the same would be true.

No, it was best to focus on what she'd just willingly offered: monogamy. Which was easy, because the idea of her with another man made my gut clench and my skin itch. Her volunteering that was a baby step in the right direction. I just had to marshal a few thousand more of those, and we'd be all set.

"I think we can agree on that. Besides," I said, my fingers drawing circles along her exposed shoulder, "I thought after this morning, that was a given."

Her derisive snort made me glance up at her. Into an expression that said I might be the dumbest man alive.

"Gideon West, after what just happened with the charming Miss Alcott in there, do you honestly believe it's a good idea to take things as 'a given' between men and women? I'm sure in her eyes, it was a given the two of you would be living your own happily ever after while doing your part to repopulate the WASP demographic of America."

It was my turn to laugh. "Good point. Does this mean I need to slip you a note in study hall asking you to go steady? Oh, maybe I could fold it up in those intricate little designs and have 'Yes,' 'No,' and 'Maybe' boxes."

"You're a riot," she said flatly, but I could see the twinkle in her eyes. "I don't think things need to go that far, but since you brought it up, I think we should be clear on what we really want. Anything else only leads to drama that I don't need in my life."

I had to bite my tongue to keep from blurting out that what I really wanted was to toss aside the ridiculous idea this was anything other than the start of a long-term relationship. Instead, I settled for cuddling her close. "I want you, Everest," I said. "Just you. And I hope you feel the same way."

Her green eyes glowed then clouded, and she frowned. "You mean while you're in town, right?"

Something hot and sharp turned in my chest at her dousing me with the reality of our situation, but I couldn't dodge her question. Ignoring the discomfort beneath my sternum, I smiled down at her. "I'm yours for the duration, Everest." I thought but didn't add, *for however long I can make that last.*

chapter twenty—six

EVEREST

I'd just shoved the last of my shoes into my suitcase when my cell rang. Gideon and I were due at the airport soon, and I needed to make one last trip around the stadium-sized condo to make sure I'd gotten everything. Over the past two days, we'd tested the stability of most of the surfaces of his home, including the sofa on the rooftop deck. Don't knock naughty, naked times out in the open until you've tried them with a man like Gideon. *Life changing.* Trust me.

Concentrating on my sweep of the condo, I didn't even glance at the caller ID before answering.

"Hello?"

"Hey, honey," came my dad's warm voice.

Surprised, I stood up too quickly and cracked my head on a shelf in the closet. "Ouch!"

"Everest?" he said, concerned. "Are you all right?"

Rubbing the top of my dented skull, I said, "Yeah, I'm fine. Just hit my head on a shelf."

"Oh, okay," he said in relief. "What time should I expect you for lunch today?"

Guilt made my chin hit my chest. In the whirlwind of Gideon sweeping me off to Boston, I'd forgotten about our standing Sunday lunch date. Daddy and I always tried to carve out Sundays to spend some time together, and if we couldn't, we gave each other plenty of notice. I swore to myself at my carelessness.

"Um, I don't know if I'm going to make lunch today, Daddy," I said in a small voice.

"Oh? Why's that? A problem at the barn?"

"No, nothing like that. I'm . . . Well, the thing is, I'm not exactly in town today."

"Not in town?" Daddy asked. "Where are you?"

"Boston?"

"Sounds like you're not sure," he said.

"No, I'm sure. I'm in Boston. I came up for the weekend and am flying back in a few hours, so I don't think I'll be home in time for lunch. I'm sorry. I just got caught up in it all and forgot."

There was a long pause, then he asked, "Who are you in Boston with?"

Oh boy, here we go. I rested my head against the cool glass of the bedroom window and stared down at the water. "Gideon."

This time, the pause was so long I wondered if he'd hung up. "Daddy?"

"I'm here," he said gruffly. "You're in Boston with Gideon West."

"Yeah, that's right. It was a last-minute surprise. I barely had time to pack anything," I said breezily.

"I see," he said. "Well, don't let me . . ."

"There you are, darling," Gideon said from behind me as he pulled me back against him. Oblivious to my being on the phone, he kissed my neck and the shell of my ear. "I've been looking all over for you. I have a few creative ideas of how we can end our trip and, surprise, most of them involve you naked and covered in . . ."

I yelped and covered the phone, but it was too late. My dad cleared his throat awkwardly, and I knew he'd heard Gideon. I pointed at the phone and mouthed "my dad," and Gideon went white as a sheet. He slumped down onto the foot of the bed and put his head in his hands with a small groan.

Turning back to the conversation, I said, "Listen, Daddy, about lunch. I—"

"Don't worry about it, sweetheart." The cheery note in his voice was faker than the ID I'd used in high school. "We'll have dinner instead. Here at the house. And bring Gideon. I'll see you at seven. Love you," he said and hung up. I heard the underlying command in his voice. This wasn't an invitation; it was a decree to show up and face the music. Briefly, I wondered whether I could pry the glass out of the window in front of me and simplify things by hurling myself into the harbor.

Phone dangling at my side, I wandered over to the bed and plopped down beside Gideon.

"How bad is it?" he asked morosely, hands still covering his face. "Should I go ahead and choose my funeral suit for when he shoots me? Or for when Davidson strangles me because the mayor just heard me talk about covering his naked daughter in different flavors of ice cream syrup?"

"I don't think you'd gotten to the syrup part yet," I said in a monotone. "But he *absolutely* heard the naked part."

Gideon flung himself backward onto the mattress with arms akimbo. "This is not good. Not good at all. I was going to woo him, too, you know? Knock his socks off with how much of a gentleman I was and the chivalrous way I treated his only daughter. Oh God," he said and covered his face again. "The mayor's only daughter."

I wanted to offer some form of comfort. To tell him that it wasn't as bad as it seemed, but I couldn't. My father now had a very clear picture of how the two of us had spent the weekend. There was no way to ease him into the idea of me and Gideon because, thanks to Gideon's big mouth, the idea of me and Gideon *naked* would be at the forefront of my dad's mind when we showed up later that evening. Which we *had to do.* There was no way we couldn't. We had been summoned to appear and be judged. I only hoped Gideon was wrong and there'd be no issuance of a death warrant.

The flight home was much more somber than the one we'd taken forty-eight hours before. But, to his credit, Gideon tried to be as upbeat as a man could be when facing at a minimum a lengthy interrogation and at the worst—well, I just wouldn't think about that. He held my hand the majority of the flight, occasionally bringing it to his lips for a reassuring kiss. I could tell he was already trying to work through how to spin this in the most positive manner to my dad. I knew he'd turn on his trademark charm, but I wondered how well it would go over.

"It's going to be alright, you know," he said.

"What?"

"This thing with your dad," Gideon clarified. "One way or the other, we'll get it all sorted."

"I admire your confidence," I said. "I just wish I could've broken the news about us a little differently."

"You mean a little less emphasis on naked times?" he asked wryly. "So do I, sweetheart, but we are where we are, and now we have to make the best of it."

I leaned my head on his shoulder. "I'm glad you're coming back with me."

He kissed the top of my head. "I've already told you, Everest, with you is the only place I want to be."

"This is some place," Gideon said as the two of us got out of the car in front of my childhood home fifteen minutes before the appointed hour of doom. He'd insisted on picking me up and driving over. I guess he felt like he had to hold on to as much of his machismo as possible for this meeting, and showing up riding shotgun in my truck wouldn't have helped. I glanced around, trying to see the place from his perspective.

We'd parked in front of the main house, which was a simple white farmhouse with green shutters, bookended by brick chimneys. To get there, we'd wound down the long drive through fenced pastures with horses grazing in the twilight. The barns and outbuildings could be seen in the distance behind the house. To someone seeing it for the first time, it looked like something out of a painting—the quintessential country landscape, complete with Daddy's old hound dog, Rudy, slowly wagging his tail on the front porch.

Gideon smoothed a hand down his shirt and adjusted his cuffs. If lip chewing were my nervous tell, his was tugging at his shirtsleeves.

I took his hand in mine, determined to show a united front. "Ready?"

He smiled and squeezed my hand. "As I'll ever be to face an angry and potentially homicidal father."

Together we climbed the steps to the porch, and I leaned down to scratch behind Rudy's long ears. After three short raps, I pushed open the heavy oak door.

"Hello? Daddy? We're here!" I called.

"In the kitchen," he said, and we followed the sound of his voice down the hall to the kitchen at the back of the house. Dressed in jeans and a dark polo with worn loafers, Daddy was seasoning steaks. I was glad to see there were three filets resting in the Pyrex. At least he'd planned on Gideon surviving long enough to eat. Or maybe it was a last meal for the condemned.

"Hey, Daddy," I said and released Gideon's hand to hug my dad and kiss his cheek.

"Hey, honey," he said and hugged me back. Letting go, he said, "You look pretty. Have a good flight back?"

"Um, yes, it was fine. Daddy, you remember Gideon, don't you?"

"Nice to see you again, sir," Gideon said as he came forward and held out his hand.

Daddy shook it, and I didn't hear bones crunching, although he did hold on a few beats longer than was strictly polite. "Gideon," he said. "Glad you could make it this evening. I'm also happy to see you're wearing clothes."

If I hadn't been so mortified, I would have been able to laugh at Gideon blushing clean to the roots of his hair.

He stammered out an attempt to clear the air. "Yes, well, sir, I'd like to try and explain."

My dad leaned back against the counter and held up a hand. "Gideon, let me ask you something."

"Yes sir?"

"Are you using whatever's happening between you and my daughter to try and get some kind of inside track for your development here?"

"Daddy!" I protested, but he ignored me and kept his eyes on Gideon.

Gideon put an arm around me. "Absolutely not, sir. What I have with Everest has nothing to do with the project I'm working on." His eyes flicked to mine, and he smiled. "Except for, as you know, her remarkable ideas that gave us a whole new avenue to explore."

Daddy nodded. "I've seen the revisions you've made moving most of the commercial development into existing buildings, with additional residential in some of the higher floors. It's a very different vision that will revitalize downtown." He looked at me ruefully. "I'm just sorry I didn't think of it."

Gideon said, "I could say the same, sir. I'm sure you're aware, but it shouldn't go without saying. Your daughter is an amazing woman."

I blushed at his praise, allowing myself a moment to revel in it.

Daddy's eyes moved between us, a hint of a smile playing around his mouth. He looked at Gideon for another few seconds then said, "One final question."

Gideon smiled and said, "Whatever you need, sir."

Rubbing a knuckle up the bridge of his nose, Daddy blew out a long breath. "Do you honestly want to explain what you were talking to Everest about this morning? Or would you rather we all pretend that special few minutes never happened and open a bottle of wine?"

I felt Gideon relax. "Definitely the latter, sir," he said in relief.

"Thank God," Daddy said and finally cracked a smile. "Wine fridge is behind you there. I think you'll be fine with the selection."

While Gideon perused the labels, I gave Daddy another hug. "Thanks for not skinning him," I whispered.

"The night's not over yet," he said with a teasing wink.

Wine was poured, beef was grilled, and potatoes were baked. The three of us had dinner in the small family dining room. Daddy peppered Gideon with questions that ranged from his upbringing in Boston to the other developments he was working on. Conversation was lively and engaging. The two of them hit it off, and it warmed my heart.

As I passed around slices of the peanut butter pie I knew had been made by Miss Angeline, Daddy said, "Well, Gideon, it sounds like you boys know your way around the real estate and housing market pretty well."

Gideon nodded. "I like to think so."

"And," Daddy continued, "I think your project will be a real benefit for us here in Mimosa."

"Thank you, sir," Gideon said, as I squelched the twinge of envy at his plans going ahead while mine for expansion got pushed even further into the future.

I counted it as progress that the feeling had lessened to a twinge and was no longer a gut-wrenching yank of anger. Gideon's project *was* good for Mimosa, and it wasn't like I could do anything with the land next door right now anyway. That was what I needed to focus on. That and coming up with feasible expansion alternatives.

"I just hate that I'll have to recuse myself from any discussions about it," Daddy said, shaking his head.

Guilt made the bite of pie I'd just taken turn to sawdust in my mouth. I watched Gideon happily shoveling creamy filling and graham cracker crust into his mouth as though he hadn't a care in the world. But *I* did. This man, this wonderfully entertaining, hilarious, and by all accounts brilliant man, was sacrificing the support of my father so he could . . . what? Spend the next few weeks, months at the most, with me before everything came to an end? What was the point in making such a sacrifice for a relationship with a predetermined ending?

I managed to choke down a few bites of pie and sips of coffee as Gideon and Daddy continued to chatter away like long lost pals. I barely participated in the conversation, but they were so involved with their new bromance that they hardly noticed. When the plates were cleared and cups rinsed and put in the sink, Gideon and I took our leave. Daddy walked us to the door and gave me a warm hug.

"Thank you for dinner, Mr. Kennedy," Gideon said, holding out his hand again.

"I think we're well past the Mr. Kennedy stage, Gideon. Call me Jack."

"Very well, Jack. Thanks again." They shook hands, and my dad stood on the porch as we made our way back to the car. He waved as Gideon backed the car around and pulled onto the long driveway.

"That went much better than expected," he said, his fingers drumming chipperly against the steering wheel.

"Gideon, I . . ." I wasn't sure how to put into words what I needed to ask him. Even if I could string together a coherent question, I wasn't sure I was ready to hear the answer.

Gideon glanced over at me. "Everest? What's wrong?"

"Gideon, are you sure this is worth it? My dad pretty much just guaranteed he would've supported the new and improved Mimosa Grove. One word from Mimosa's favorite son and the rest of the council would trip over themselves to give you what you want. What if they start to wonder why he's stepping back? What if they think there's something . . . I don't know, untoward with things and get spooked? What if they don't give you the approval? What if—"

"Everest," Gideon said quietly. "I'm flattered by the fact that you're so concerned, but we talked about this in Boston. Plus," he reached over and covered my hands, which were currently twisted into a pretzel in my lap, "this is not my first time. I *do* have a little bit of experience working with councils in the past."

"Right, right," I said. "I know that, but I just don't—"

"I do," he said.

I glanced over at his profile, illuminated by oncoming traffic. "You do what?"

"I do know that I was right that time with you is worth any extra effort I'll have to make to get Mimosa Grove off the ground. You're worth it, Everest. Time with you is worth it."

The breath I took then was dangerous, because it loosened the constricting bands of guilt and allowed Gideon's declaration take root in my heart. The danger was there, because it would be that much harder to let him go. But I couldn't resist it, any more than I'd been able to resist him. Gideon West, with his clever words and equally skilled touch, had seeped into the very fiber of my being. Regardless of what it would mean for me after he left, how much more it would hurt to let him go, I embraced not just what he'd said but the way it resonated so deeply within me.

I could tell myself a thousand times this thing between us was fleeting and ephemeral, but that was a lie. Because I was going to carry Gideon with me the rest of my life. And when he left, there would be a uniquely Gideon-shaped void in my life, unable to be filled by anyone else.

chapter twenty—seven

GIDEON

After surviving dinner with her father, Everest and I fell into a rhythm. A very comfortable, familiar rhythm that I hoped would open her eyes to the fact that she didn't have to choose between work and a relationship. That the two could coexist rather nicely, if she'd give it a chance.

So far, I'd stuck with my "show, don't tell" mantra and resisted every urge I had to tell her how I felt about her. Even if those feelings had grown at an exponential rate. So much so that the pull to see her was so insistent, it was very possible she had, in fact, cast a spell over me. And even when I didn't *see* her, I was thinking of her. Like when I passed by the local hardware store and saw a pair of turquoise muck boots. In an instant, I knew she had to have them.

And the look on her face when she'd read the note aloud after I'd deposited them at her office? Priceless. Her green eyes scanned it quickly and her lips parted into a wide smile, the laugh I'd grown so accustomed to hearing belted free. She turned the note toward me, "Really, Gideon? 'For wading through life, bullshit included.'" Her smile turned sly. "Does that include the lines of bull you toss out daily?"

Pulling her in for a quick kiss, I asked, "Why do you think they're knee-highs?"

Another day, she'd caught me feeding peppermints to Savvy, her soft muzzle twitching across my palm, determined to get every morsel. "Easy, sweetheart. Not too quickly."

At the sound of an amused, non-equine snort, I turned to find Everest leaning against the stall of the black behemoth she'd ridden the first day I met her. I'd learned through my frequent visits to the barn that his name Sin was short for Samson's Sinful Secret, and he'd been one of the first horses she'd rescued. Which explained his undying devotion to her . . . and why he consistently looked at me as though I were something unpleasant he'd discovered at the bottom of his feed bucket.

Pushing off the wall, she'd come toward us. "Busted," she said, smiling widely and giving Savvy a scratch behind the ears.

Leaning closer to Savvy, I whispered, "We've been discovered, love. Guess we'll have to marry now."

A shadow passed over Everest's eyes at my joke but was gone so quickly I halfway thought I'd imagined it. To Savvy, she said, "Lucky girl, but don't get too attached. We've only got Mr. West with us for a short time."

It was a reminder, gentle and teasing, that no matter how I saw things between us, she viewed our time together as limited. Which meant I needed to man up and tell her that things had, at least for me, shifted away from the transitory and were lodged very firmly in the permanent. There was just one problem, I couldn't figure out how to do that. I wanted to, but the timing never felt quite right. It wasn't a topic that you could bring up casually over coffee. "So, Everest, remember how we said this wasn't going to be a thing? That we were going to keep things casual, not make any plans for the future? Yeah, well that doesn't work for me anymore because I cannot seem to think of anything but you and I don't see that changing when I go back to Boston. Anyway, could you pass the sugar?"

No, that was a conversation that had to be planned carefully with the proper amount of thought. It was like any other important negotiation. Planning and preparation were key to success. Which was exactly what I was doing on a mid-May evening after leaving a planning commission meeting. Memorial Day was right around the corner, and I'd been thinking of locations to whisk Everest away for the weekend. Create the perfect backdrop for the conversation. Images of her in a bikini with the clear Caribbean water behind her played through my mind. I'd just gotten to the part where she ran toward me in slow motion when I realized there was someone else in my house.

"Gak!" I screamed, in a very manly way, and brandished my brief-case as a weapon.

"Calm down," Cammie said from her seat on the sofa. "It's just me."

"Right, of course," I said, trying to recover my cool and not collapse from heart failure. "Er . . . " I glanced behind me at the door I'd just unlocked. "How did you get in here?"

"Viola's my aunt. I have a spare key to all her rentals so I can help her out."

"Do you mean break in at will?"

Cammie waved her hand dismissively. "It's not breaking in if you have a key, silly." She patted the cushion next to her. "Come sit for a minute. I want to talk to you."

Curiosity piqued, I set down my briefcase and joined her on the sofa. "To what do I owe the pleasure of this little burgle?"

"I wanted to thank you," she said.

I arched a brow, surprised by her sentiment. "Thank me? For what?"

Her gray eyes searched mine, and she smiled. "For bringing Everest out of her shell. She's been in there for a long time, and no one's been able to coax her out. Until you came along."

While I much preferred my vision of her in a bikini, the idea of Everest as a cute little redheaded turtle made me smile. "She's an amazing woman, Cammie."

"I'm glad to hear you say that," she said, her expressive eyes going a shade darker—like thunderclouds gathering in the distance. "Because I also want to make sure we have an understanding."

The hairs on the back of my neck prickled as though warning me of an impending attack. "Oh, about what?" I asked, intrigued by the whole cloak-and-dagger routine she had going on.

"Everest is my best friend," she said, spinning the silver ring on her middle finger in a nervous twitch. "And I have to look out for her. So, while I'm thrilled she's no longer just sitting behind her desk or cleaning stalls or doing whatever else she can find to save every horse between here and Florida"—her eyes came to mine, steely and unyielding—"I have certain concerns."

"Which are?"

She blew out a breath and looked as uncomfortable as I was starting to feel. "I know Everest is a big girl who can take care of herself, but as her best friend, I'm a little worried about what's going to happen to her when you go back home." Her forehead puckered into a frown.

Hell, there was no way I was going to broach this topic with Everest's best friend before Everest herself. "Well, let me put your mind at ease. Everest and I discussed this weeks ago." *Not a lie and yet still not the full disclosure that belonged only to Everest.*

"As she said when I asked her about it," Cammie said, still frowning. "And I have to admit, it sounds very evolved, very mature. But I'm just trying to understand how exactly that's going to work. Is it really going to be as simple as you leave for Boston when your project is finished? Everest takes you to the airport and waves goodbye, then you each go back to your lives like the intervening months never happened? How does that work in the long run . . . for either of you?"

Before I could answer, a quick rap at the front door was followed by it swinging open.

"Gideon?" Everest called out. "I wanted to stop by and see—" She saw Cammie next to me on the couch. "Oh, hey!" Everest looked between the two of us, brows knitted in confusion as to why Cammie was there.

Quicker on her feet that I was, Cammie rose and said, "I was just dropping off some of Viola's crumb cake for y'all. It's in the refrigerator, Evie. Don't let him hog it all."

Everest laughed and gave her friend a hug on her way out the door. "Thanks, girl. You always did look out for me."

Cammie looked at me over Everest's shoulder. "Always, honey. Always."

Once the door shut behind her friend, Everest dropped into my lap and kissed me, her slender arms winding around my neck. "This is a pleasant surprise. I wasn't expecting to find you here."

Putting Cammie's question—and my own struggle to answer it—out of my mind for the moment, I focused on the beautiful woman in front of me. "My car out front didn't tip you off to my presence?"

She laughed, running a hand casually through my hair. "I *meant* I was surprised to see your car here. Mrs. Hazelton gave me some pictures from the Wallace Building in its heyday." Everest tipped her head back and affected her best genteel Southern accent. "Everest, do be a dear and deliver these to that gentleman of yours." With a grin, she kissed the tip of my nose. "I'd planned to drop them in your mailbox, but when I saw your car, I figured I'd hand deliver them."

"Ah, I guess that means you'll be wanting a tip then," I said, working a hand under her shirt. Her skin was satiny smooth beneath my fingers.

Her grin widening, Everest twisted around on my lap to straddle my hips, putting an arch in her spine. The move let my hand glide higher along her ribcage. "Well," she fluttered her lashes, "it is customary, after all."

"Indeed," I said, feeling my way along the lacy edge of her bra to the back clasp. "Let's see what I have to give you." I undid the clasp and slipped my other hand beneath her shirt, palms cupping her breasts beneath the loosened lace.

Everest's eyes slid closed, and she hummed in pleasure as I kneaded her lush curves. Her lips parted on a shuddering sigh when I tweaked her nipples, pinching and teasing them until she bit her lip and ground her hips against me. I pulled her shirt over her head, and she tossed her bra after it. Lowering my lips to her breasts, I kissed around their curves and down her breastbone.

"Gideon, please," she said, steering my mouth toward her taut nipple.

"Greedy girl," I said and let her guide me where she wanted. Rolling my tongue against the stiff peak earned me a groan from low in her throat—the husky sound almost a purr. Her fingers raked through my hair, pulling on the strands as I licked and nipped my way back and forth between her breasts.

"Gideon," she said, her voice thick with desire. The heady sound of my name on her lips put my heart in overdrive and made me smile against her flesh.

She pulled on the collar of my polo, so I sat back and helped her take it off. Her hands flew to my waist, jerking my belt off and making short work of my button and zipper. With one hand, she pushed me to my back while the other stripped off my pants and boxers. Only once I was naked did she shimmy out of her shorts and panties.

"Come here, beautiful," I said, beckoning her to me.

With half-lidded eyes, she straddled my hips again and dipped slowly down to coat my length with her essence. Her erotic undulation was hypnotizing torture that had my balls tingling and my cock aching to bury itself inside her, but I let her set the pace. Just when I was about to go insane, she took me in hand and sank onto me, both of us groaning as she sheathed me inside her. The sensation of her gliding down over me was simultaneously too much and not enough. The heady slide of her overwhelmed me and made me want even more, to touch every part of her, mark all of her as mine and mine alone.

"Fuck, Everest," I said and reached for her, bringing her down for a kiss. Her lips were soft and pliant as I deepened the kiss, my tongue sweeping inside. She rocked and twisted her hips as I took her mouth, spearing my fingers in her wild mass of curls and keeping her close.

We broke apart on a heavy sigh and she pushed herself up, spreading her thighs wider and planting one foot on the floor. She was completely exposed to me, and I loved it. Enjoying the high of being in control, Everest threw her head back and began to ride me in earnest, hips rolling and bucking as she moved up and down my cock.

"Gideon." She moaned, and again, my name as her cry of pleasure speared deep inside of me, latching on to some yet undiscovered part of me and burrowing deep. The yearning it stirred within me was carnally primal, and my hands curved possessively around her waist, fingers pressing into her flesh, clutching her with an unchecked desperation. I thrust upward, driving deeper inside her, and she tossed her head back, a low moan escaping her.

Her body closed around me, and I pumped harder. When my fingers brushed her clit, her head snapped up and she looked at me with hazy eyes.

"You like that?" I asked as I rubbed the tiny bundle of nerves.

"Do you even have to ask?" she murmured, leaning closer, her breath hot against my cheek. She dropped a hand to the back of the couch, and

I felt the clench of her around me as her orgasm bore down on her. I flicked my thumb faster and savored the sight of her coming apart, her body shaking and incoherent cries falling from her lips. I felt her collapse from the inside out, and when the last of her tremors ceased, I flipped her over and put both her legs over my shoulders. Locking one arm around her thighs, I pummeled into her, fast and hard.

When her eyes started to close, I slapped her thigh. "Eyes on me, baby."

Lust-filled green orbs stared up at me, and I needed to be closer to her. Releasing her legs, I braced myself above her. Her long legs came around my waist, knees digging into my ribcage. I felt the freight train of my release rocketing forward. One, two, three more thrusts, and there it was.

"Oh fuck, oh God, Everest," I said as came deep within her. My arms shook with the effort of holding myself up, so I dropped my head to her chest, sucking in deep gulps of air. Her chest vibrated when she giggled and stroked my hair.

"Fuck," I said again. "You wreck me every time, Everest."

"It's all part of my diabolical plan to weaken your defenses and steal the Collier property out from under you," she said, her nails scratching against my scalp.

Her voice had a teasing air, and her body was relaxed and loose beneath me, so I knew she was kidding. But that didn't stop the stab of guilt at denying her something she wanted. Something I no longer even needed, thanks to her suggestions for the change in the development. That fact made me feel even worse. Given how well my meeting with the planning commission had gone that day, all signs pointed to approval of our shift toward revitalizing downtown. Which meant we no longer needed a good portion of the property beside Second Chance.

But Everest could use it, and I knew she wanted it. No matter how good a sport she'd been about it, I'd seen the other options she'd found for alternate expansion opportunities. We'd reviewed some of them over dinner a few nights ago.

She'd shoved her tablet away in disgust after scrolling through a real estate site. "Ugh, there's just nothing out there that will work for what I want!"

Picking up the discarded electronic, I looked at what had her so disappointed. I'd researched enough available property in my day, so even though I didn't know all her parameters, I knew enough to see she was right. Whether it was location, topography, or some other drawback, nothing on the screen in front of me would work for her future expansion plans.

"I see what you mean," I said, wishing I'd had the foresight she did about downtown and had started there. If I had, maybe she and the Collier family could've worked something out. As it stood now, she was a woman without land, and I had land without a purpose.

"Gideon, are you listening to me?" Everest asked, breaking into my thoughts.

"Sorry, sorry," I said, rubbing my cheek against her breast. "Things got a little distracting for me around here."

She laughed and gave me a gentle shove. "I guess that's only fair since you distracted me from the whole reason I stopped by and now I'm running late to meet the farrier. Which means you've got to get off me and let me get back to work."

Reluctantly, I left the warm embrace of her body and helped her to her feet. As she scrounged around for her discarded clothing, my mind wandered back to the question that was going to plague me until I had an answer. I was in the real estate business, for God's sake; I had to be able to figure out a way to help her find something that would work. I wished I could just give her the damn land, but it wasn't solely mine to give. Standard would have to sign off on it, and we weren't in the habit of just giving things away—

"Jesus Christ, I'm a fucking idiot," I mumbled, making Everest glance up from searching for her bra.

"What?"

Invigorated that I'd finally seen what was in front of me the whole time, I grabbed her in my arms and planted a smacking kiss on her mouth. Pulling back, I grinned down at her like a lunatic.

Her smile was more guarded as she looked at me in concern. "Are you all right?"

"Oh, Everest, I'm *so* much better than all right."

"Then why do you look like Joaquin Phoenix when he played the Joker?"

Difficult as it was, I tried to dial down my excitement and also my apparently deranged facial expression. "Sorry, sorry, I just—" I stopped myself. Because at long last, I'd not only solved how to fix her land problem, I'd also stumbled onto the perfect way to make her see how much I cared about her. That we had a *future*. And I damn sure wasn't going to waste the perfection of this plan by blurting it out to her while naked in my living room. Plus, I still needed to talk to Jamie and Davidson before I did anything.

Smoothing a hand over my face, I kissed the tip of her nose. "Sorry, something just came to me about the project, that's all. A solution to a problem I've been working through for a while."

She patted my cheek, her mouth twisted in a dubious half-smile. "If you say so." A glance at her watch made her flinch. "Gah, I'm going to be so late!"

For once, I was eager for her to go. "Go, go, I'll see you later." One more quick kiss and she was gone. I grabbed my phone before my pants, stabbing at my assistant's contact information. "Alisha, yeah, it's me. I need to get on a flight to Boston tomorrow morning."

chapter twenty—eight

EVEREST

Everest Kennedy out on a school night?" Elektra raised a perfectly manicured brow. Her silver hoop earrings swished against her cheek as she shook her head in exaggerated surprise. "To what do we owe this honor?"

I slid onto the stool next to her and tweaked one of her long braids. "I go out."

"Since *when*?" she said, picking up her beer with a wink at Winston, the newest bartender at Stumbles. With a shy grin in return, he flushed to the roots of his red mohawk and hustled down the bar to help another customer.

"Since a certain ridiculously good-looking real estate mogul started developing things other than property around here," Cammie said as she took the stool on my other side.

Elektra thunked her glass on the bar. "I know that's right."

I huffed out an indignant breath. "I went out before Gideon came here."

Cammie and Elektra exchanged a look that made clear they begged to differ. "Girl, please," Elektra said, taking another sip. "We've invited you to every ladies' night we've had, and you know how many you've shown up to?"

"I do," Cammie said, because apparently I wasn't needed for this conversation. "Just this one."

My neck got hot, and I wondered where the hell Winston was and why he wasn't here to take my order. "Well, you know how hard it is for me to get away fr—"

"No," Cammie said, shaking her head and making her blonde hair fluff around her shoulders, "we know how hard you've *made* it to get away from work. Because you don't delegate anything and can't stand to let someone step in so you get a break." She wiggled her brows at me. "At least, you *used* to."

Elektra giggled. "Yes, pre-Gideon Evie was much more uptight."

"Gee," I said in a flat voice, "how could I have missed these awesome get togethers for so long? This is *so* much fun."

Cammie bumped me with her shoulder. "If you'd been to a girls' night, you'd know the best part is when your friends give you shit about your boyfriend."

"He's not my boyfriend," I said and earned another eye roll. *Where the hell was Winston? Was he actually* making *beer somewhere?*

"Evie, c'mon now," Elektra said. "How is a man you're spending almost every day—"

"And night!" Cammie chimed in.

"Good point," Elektra said. "A man with whom you're spending every day *and* night, who has memorized your coffee order, whisked you away for a romantic weekend, and—the pièce de résistance—convinced you to have a little fun. How is *that* man not your boyfriend?"

"Because he's not . . . because we aren't . . . because he just isn't, okay?"

"That mean he's up for grabs?" Elektra asked. "Because if that's the case, I know at least four or five ladies who would be su—"

"You and your 'ladies' can keep your hands off Gideon, thank you very much," I said.

"Again, I ask, how is a man you're laying claim to not your boyfriend?"

I had an overwhelming urge bang my head against the bar. I blamed Gideon. If he hadn't had to fly back to Boston for some project that needed tweaking, then I wouldn't have agreed to have drinks with these two assholes.

"We're exclusive while he's in town," I said, knowing how stupid that sounded.

"Pfft!" This came from Cammie. "That whole thing doesn't make any sense to me, Everest! I mean, the two of you act like you simply checked each other out of the library for the duration of his stay and it's as simple as returning each other on the due date. I've seen the two of you together, girl, and there is no way it is going to be that simple."

"You were the one that told me to have a fling!"

"Yeah, but the two of you were the ones who cooked up the endgame of it! I never said it couldn't turn into something more. That the present couldn't lead into a future for the two of you."

"And what kind of future would that be?" I asked, unleashing the worry that had made sleep somewhat elusive at around four that morning. "What I do doesn't have a set schedule, Cammie. I can't pick and choose when calls for my help come in, or when one of the horses get sick, or any other number of things. I'm constantly either at work or thinking about work. I don't have time to devote to anything else."

"Everest," Cammie said, "I love you. I really do. But that is a complete load of horseshit that you should be able to smell as you're shoveling it at us."

What I'd like to smell is the scent of a freshly poured beer. "What the hell is that supposed to mean?"

Elektra took over for Cammie. "He's been in town for what, two months, give or take?"

"Yeah, so?" I asked.

She lounged against the bar, one long denim-clad leg crossed over the other. "*So*, in that span of time, name one single time you haven't had time for Gideon."

"Well, I . . ." I floundered for an answer, momentarily stymied by the unexpected difficulty of the task. "I forgot about plans we'd made the night I went to get Ruby and her foal." I couldn't keep the smugness out of my voice. That was a perfect example.

"Errrrnnnhhhh," Cammie made a buzzing sound. "I'm afraid that's not true, Everest."

"Yes, it is! He showed up at my house, and I had to cancel." I was beginning to feel like the net in a tennis match as they volleyed around and over me.

"No, you didn't, you ninny. He went *with* you on the rescue. That's not canceling, that's adapting your plans for someone you care about. Plus, I know you went through a drive-through, so you *still* got dinner." If I'd been smug, Cammie was positively sanctimonious.

"That's . . . He won't . . ." I spluttered my way through a few more words that didn't add up to an argument.

"Mm-hmm," Cammie said. "That's what I thought. Admit it, Evie, in the past two months, that man has shown you that there is more to life than work. And the idea of *that* is what's got you running scared. Because it means you might actually open yourself up to someone, and, Heaven forbid, find real happiness."

"Happiness doesn't last, Cammie," I said. "My parents were happy until . . ." My mouth snapped shut, and I blinked back tears that came out of nowhere. Emotion made my throat constrict, and I sucked in an uneven breath, silenced by the wave of loneliness I felt in that moment. The pain of losing my mother dragged over my heart like broken glass. God, did I miss her.

Elektra reached over to pat my knee, and Cammie's voice was gentler when she said, "What happened to your mother was beyond unfair, Evie. But I guarantee you, your daddy wouldn't trade any of the years he had with her even if he'd known from the beginning they were limited. And she wouldn't want you to keep hiding from your own chance at happiness because you're afraid it won't last."

"I'm not hiding," I said. "I'm being realistic. Long distance is a lot harder than what we have now. Proximity makes this work. Once we don't have that, it's only a matter of time before things fall apart."

"You don't know that, Evie. You *can't* know that because you've never tried."

"I've seen the life he has up there, y'all. It's amazing, and once he's immersed back in it, there's no way he'd choose me over it."

Elektra snorted derisively. "First of all, *you're* pretty amazing yourself, honey. And anyone who sees the way he looks at you can tell you he's well aware of that. Second, who says this is an either-or deal? The man is, by all accounts, Bezos rich. So why can't he keep his place there and still have one here? Why can't he split time between Boston and Mimosa? It's not like we're talking transcontinental. It's barely a two-hour flight."

"I couldn't ask him to do that! We hardly know each other! Who changes their entire life for someone they barely know?"

I wouldn't be the reason Gideon left Boston and the beautiful life he'd built there, even part-time. It was simply too much to ask of him. I wasn't going to give him a reason to resent me, to resent what we'd had, by asking him to give that up for something that could never compare to it.

"No one is saying that his entire life, or yours, has to change right now," Cammie said. "You're jumping to the ultimate endgame when all we're telling you to do is not give up at the starting line. That man is so far gone for you it would make me pea green with envy if I didn't have Wyatt."

"Consider me green," said Elektra.

Cammie laughed then continued. "Why isn't it worth at least giving this thing between the two of you a chance? What are you so scared of?"

"Hey, Evie, Cammie," Winston said, finally appearing and granting me a reprieve. "Sorry for the wait. What can I get you?"

Once we'd ordered and gotten our beers, Cammie continued pushing. "What is it that is keeping you from reaching for what you know you want?"

I took a drink, then another, stalling, because I wasn't sure how to voice what I needed to say. Setting down my glass, I sighed and gave it my best shot. "What if the person I reach for stops reaching back for me? You talk about splitting time between here and there. It's not feasible for me to do that. Second Chance is here, and I can't move it. I've worked too hard to get up and running and can't afford to pull up stakes. Nor do I want to. Mimosa is home."

"Pretty sure what we said is that he could come here," Cammie said.

"And that's exactly the problem. Eventually, he's going to get tired of being the one who has to make the trip, or deal with the last-minute cancellations, or any other number of things. Until the day comes when—"

"You reach out and he doesn't reach back," Elektra said.

"Right," I said.

Cammie said nothing for a moment then asked, "Well, then what are you going to do?"

I had no clue what to do, so I'd worry about it later. "Right now," I said, "Gideon is here, with me, so I'm going to enjoy that instead of ruining it by talking about a future that will find us thousands of miles away from each other."

"I can understand that," Cammie said, and I knew she was holding back on what she wanted to say.

"Go ahead, Cammie," I said. "Let me hear it."

She sighed. "You sure?"

"No, but when has that ever stopped you in the past?"

"True," she conceded. "Well, Evie, I'm wondering if you don't talk about it now, when are you going to? The night before he leaves? Wouldn't it be better for both of you if you knew what the plan was going forward? I mean, not talking about it would make me crazy! It'd be all I could think about."

"It does occupy some rather serious storage space in my mind," I admitted.

"There has to be a plan rattling around in there somewhere too," Elektra said. "There's no way you're taking the ostrich approach with this."

"Ostrich approach?" I asked.

"Yeah, stick your head in the sand and hope all the bad shit just passes you by."

I laughed. "That actually sounds pretty close to what I've come up with so far." Twisting my glass on its coaster, I said, "The crazy thing is that he's gone from someone I never wanted to come into town to the last person I want to see leave it."

"So why let him?" Cammie asked softly.

I sighed. "Say we give long distance a try, even knowing all the obstacles to making it work. The two of us decide to bank on being able to overcome all that. I hear y'all saying all this about splitting time or shuttling back and forth or whatever. But the truth of it is I want more than that. I *don't* want to do long-distance or split or whatever. I want full-time with Gideon. Mimosa is home, so I'm not moving to Boston. And how can I ask him to do something I'm not equally willing to do? How is it fair for me to ask him to move when I absolutely won't?"

"Isn't that his choice to make?" Elektra asked.

"Yeah, but I don't have to force him to make it," I said.

"So, what then?" Cammie asked.

I picked up my beer and took a long swallow. "When he finishes things here and gets on the plane back to Boston that last time, it's going to be easier for me to pull out my own heart than to watch him go. To tell him goodbye and know he's not coming back. To not try and hold on to him just a little longer. It's going to shatter me into a million pieces when he leaves. But I have to let him, because I don't want my greed for something more to ruin what's already been given to me. I don't want to taint our present with a future that will only end bitterly. I want to enjoy having him in my life for as long as I get to, and then when he's gone, I'll mourn the loss of what we had but still cherish the memory of it."

I looked at each of them in turn. "And then, that's when the two of you will pick me up for another ladies' night and let me drown my sorrows back here at Stumbles."

They looped their arms around me into a group hug. "We can do that," Cammie said. "And I promise to not call you a moron for at least the first hour."

chapter twenty—nine

GIDEON

"M r. West?"

I blinked and looked up from the folder in my hands. Across the table from me, Jeanine, the landscape architect with whom I'd been meeting for the past hour, stared at me expectantly. From the tone of her voice, it was obvious she'd said my name more than once. I hadn't heard it or anything else she'd been saying for the past several minutes. My mind was on the next meeting on my schedule.

Jamie and Davidson were each booked into meetings on other projects the morning I got to Boston, so I'd had to settle for a two o'clock. Which meant I could take the meeting I was in, although I should've just stayed far away from the office instead. Because I was completely wasting this poor woman's time.

Clearing my throat, I refocused on Jeanine. "I'm sorry," I said. "I got a little distracted there. Can we revisit the part about revamping the median along Liberty Street? I'm not sure that sketch captures what we want to do there."

An hour—and only one more space-out—later, the meeting wrapped, and I headed back to my office to try to put more flesh on the bare bones of the brainstorm I'd had in Ms. Viola's cottage. I was clear on the bottom line of what I wanted—donate the land we weren't using to Second Chance—but wasn't sure how to get there. Given that the intricacies of things like property swaps, donations, and write-offs that were involved in any of our deals were more Davidson's department, and he was one of the two people I needed to convince of my plan, it made things a little difficult.

"How bad is it?"

I looked up from the plat of the Collier property I'd been redlining to find Davidson in the doorway of my office.

I dropped the red pencil onto my desk and pulled off my readers. "What?"

"You met with the planning commission about the updates to the commercial district in the morning, and then that afternoon you're asking Alisha to get you on the first flight here the next morning and wanting to meet with us ASAP. Something must have gone horribly wrong for you to need to tell us face-to-face. So I'm asking you, how bad is it?"

I'd been so caught up in working through how to broach the donation issue, I'd forgotten to send them my standard update email. "Sorry, no it's nothing like that. The meeting went fine. Everyone is still excited about the new direction we're taking. The planning commission is submitting their recommendations to council, which is looking forward to the renovation presentation from the architects next week."

Davidson's shoulders relaxed slightly, and he smoothed his tie. "Good, good. Glad to hear it." He narrowed his eyes at me. "Then what is so important that you had to meet with us today?"

I gathered up the plats I'd been working on. "Let's take this into the conference room so we can spread out a little. Is Jamie back from Holliston yet?"

Davidson glanced at his watch. "He should be shortly." Stepping back from the doorway, he let me lead the way to the conference room. Jamie stepped off the elevator as we passed it.

"Gids," he said with a smile then glanced down at the rolled-up surveys in my hands. "What's all this?"

"This is what Gideon flew back to discuss," Davidson answered for me as Jamie fell into step next to us.

"The commission wants changes to the plans?" he asked.

"No," I said without elaborating.

Davidson and Jamie exchanged a look around me, but neither said anything. Once in the conference room, I rolled out the various plats I'd marked up while the two of them took seats across the table from me.

They lost no time in leaning forward to peer at my revisions. "Why am I looking at the Collier property?" Jamie asked.

"And why is the boundary line altered?" Davidson asked, rising from his seat to get a better look.

"Remember when we worked with that land bank in Vermont to get a reduction in the tax consequence of an acquisition?" I asked.

Davidson lifted his eyes from the plat to look at me. "Yes," he said slowly. "Donating a portion of the acreage was more beneficial than the tax hit we'd take if we acquired the entire parcel." His eyes narrowed on me, then dropped to the red-hatched line on the plat, then back to me. "Why do you ask, Gids?"

"Well, I think we've got the same opportunity down in Mimosa," I hedged.

Jamie settled back in his chair with a knowing smirk. "Is that so?"

"It is," I said, ignoring his patronizing tone. "We don't need this acreage now that we've shifted a lot of what we want to do to downtown. It makes sense for us to look for a way to minimize the tax impact of—"

"Gids," Davidson interrupted. "Since when have you had any interest in that side of things?"

"Since his girlfriend owns the property next door," Jamie said.

"Don't go there, Jamie," Davidson said before I could respond. "You and I both know Gideon better than that. Even if he is in love with Everest, he wouldn't suggest something like this just because it would benefit her."

"Thanks, man," I said, turning back to the plat. "This could really d—" I looked back at Davidson. "Wait, what did you say?"

Davidson retook his seat, adjusting his suit coat as he did. He arched a brow at me. "I believe I just took up for you putting your fiduciary duty to this company before your love life."

"You said I was in love with Everest."

"And?" Davidson said, cool and collected as ever.

"What do you mean 'and?'" I said, mystified by his low-key delivery.

"Gids," Jamie said, a half-smile curling the corner of his mouth. "C'mon, man." His hands spread wide in front of him. "You almost beat the crap out of me *twice* over this girl. That's not something you do for a girl who's just a fling."

"He's right, you know," Davidson chimed in. "I seem to recall your threatening me with bodily harm right after you met her."

Had I? "I did?" I asked.

"Mm-hmm," Davidson replied. "I believe it was right after I referred to her as a 'townie.' You did not take kindly to that description."

"Huh," I said.

"Huh, indeed," Davidson said.

My brain struggled to catch up to the fact that neither of them were surprised. "Wait, so you two . . ."

"Knew you were falling for this girl and it was only a matter of time before you realized it too?" Jamie asked.

Well, shit.

Davidson laughed. "Poor Gideon, always the last to know."

"Not to sound like an eighth-grade girl or anything," Jamie said, "but what did Everest say when you told her?"

Feeling *exactly* like a pubescent teenage girl, I responded, "I haven't told her yet."

Davidson frowned. "What do you mean you haven't told her yet?"

I pointed to the plats in front of us. "Assuming we can work through the donation of the land to Second Chance, that was going to be part of how I told her."

"Wait," Jamie said, sitting up with a wrinkled brow. "You mean you haven't told her about the donation yet either?"

I shook my head. "No. I wasn't going to broach it with her until we'd worked through the details."

Davidson sighed and shook his head. "Gids, I appreciate you coming to us first, and while I agree that makes business sense, this seems like a big move to make without talking to her about it first. I mean, are you sure she'll be on board with it?"

"How could she not be?" I asked. "She told me herself she wanted this property as a part of her expansion plans. Trust me, Everest will be more than on board—she'll be thrilled."

"Obviously, I don't know Everest as well as you do," Davidson said. "But don't you think she would want to discuss what you're planning to do before it's *fait accompli*? She seems like a woman who wants to be involved on the front end of decisions rather than on the receiving end of a declaration."

"No, no, no," I said, needing to disabuse him of that notion. "It's not like that at all. I need something to show her how serious I am about us having a future. Together. What better way than to give her something she's always wanted?"

"Uh, Gids," Jamie said, studying his cuticles then meeting my eyes. His own were hesitantly skeptical. "Doesn't the word 'together' imply some form of discussion with Everest? It sounds like you've decided what is best for both of you rather than talking to her about what *she* thinks. Which, as I last heard, was that this thing between you wasn't going anywhere beyond your stint in Mimosa."

Davidson nodded in agreement, and both of them looked dubious.

I shook my head, appalled at their lack of vision. "You guys don't get it. Haven't either of you ever watched a romantic comedy? There's always the grand gesture that cements the romance."

"Yes, well," Davidson said, stroking his chin, "not all of us grew up with a grandmother that dictated our taste in movies. However, I do know the need for those gestures is usually because the guy has done something to royally fuck up the relationship and he's groveling his way back into his girl's good graces."

"And, oh yeah," Jamie added, "that's *fiction*, not reality."

How two confirmed bachelors thought they could parcel out advice now that I'd jumped from the *USS Single Man* was beyond me. Plus, they didn't know Everest like I did. She was going to be thrilled at the news.

"Look, I appreciate your concerns, but the two of you aren't exactly the ones I'd go to for relationship advice," I said.

"Oh, and all of a sudden *you're* the expert?" Jamie asked. "Gids, this is the first girl in forev—"

Before we could go round and round again, Davidson jumped in. "For the record, I'm with Jamie on this one. You should talk to her to make sure it isn't like that time at the Sox game when that guy proposed on the jumbotron and his girl said no." The three of us shuddered in commiseration with the poor sap who'd gotten his heart smashed in front of thousands that night.

I shook my head. They were missing the romance of the big two-part reveal. "How could she not be ecstatic over this plan? It's perfect!"

I parked next to Everest's truck, my rental car seemingly piloting itself to Second Chance after leaving the airport. I couldn't wait to give Everest the big news. Which required talking to her. Which first required finding her. She wasn't in her office, of course. If she could find a way out of paperwork, she would. I walked down to the barn and met Leroy as he was walking out.

"Mick!" he said, his wizened, mahogany features spreading into a wide smile as he extended a hand for me to shake.

"I'm never going to lose that nickname, am I?"

"The best ones come from the best stories," Leroy said, a twinkle in his dark eyes. "And *that* story is one for the ages." He glanced down at my dress shoes. "I see you didn't learn your footwear lesson from it though."

Laughing, I said, "Forgive me. My boots are being resoled."

With a chuckle, he asked, "Guessing you're looking for the boss?"

I nodded. "As usual, she's snuck out from behind a desk. Figured I might find her down here somewhere."

"You'd think she was allergic to office work," he said with a rueful fondness for his wayward boss. He jerked a thumb over his shoulder. "She's down in the lower paddock, lunging one of the geldings." With a glance at his watch, he added, "She should be almost through if you want to head down there."

"You do know I have no idea what the majority of those words mean, right?"

His laughter was a quick rasp of sound accompanied by a shake of his head. "Where *did* she find you?" Turning around, he pointed down the hill. "Head down there and look for the circular fence. She'll be standing in the middle of it with a horse on a long lead."

"Got it, thanks," I said and hurried in the direction he'd pointed.

I saw her when I was halfway down the slope and stopped, once again taken in by seeing Everest in her element. As Leroy had said she'd be, she stood in the center of a large ring, her hair in a tousled knot, jeans streaked with what could be any manner of mud or other filth, and a chambray shirt tied at her waist. In one hand was a long lead rope tethered to a massive brown horse with a black mane and tail. The bottom half of each of his legs were black as well, reminiscent of men's dress socks. In Everest's other hand, she held some sort of long, thin pole at the end of which was a small length of nylon string. Rotating in a circle, she flicked the pole along the ground, encouraging the horse to orbit in a slow circle around her.

Long, lithe limbs moved easily and with a careless grace resemblant of a ballet dancer. From this distance, I couldn't hear the words she was murmuring to the horse but could see her lips moving. I'd spent enough time around the barn to know she was uttering soft words of praise, because that horse could bolt and rip her arm off and Everest would still croon to it like a baby. Not wanting to startle either her or the horse, I walked closer, waiting until she saw me to raise a hand in greeting.

When she did see me, her smile was instant, and the sight of it hit me squarely in the chest. Absently, I rubbed the center of my chest while she slowed the horse to a walk then gathered in the long lead. After a few head tosses, he came to her side gentle as a lamb. Together, they walked over to the fence where I stood.

"Hey," she said, her voice warm. "I didn't expect to see you this afternoon. I thought you weren't flying back until tomorrow morning."

"Things wrapped up sooner than expected, so I took an earlier flight." I grinned at her. "You do know it's almost five, right?"

Green eyes rounded in surprise. "Really?"

I pulled my phone from my breast pocket and showed her the screen. "Yep."

"Huh, who knew," she said with a shrug. "Well, I guess this means you can walk us home. Right, Larry?" Everest chucked the horse under the chin.

I looked at the huge animal. "Larry?"

Her lips curled into a wry smile. "His given name is 'Lariats of Fire', which is honestly one of the stupidest things I've ever heard. He's a much more basic, down-to-earth fellow than that."

"Hence, Larry."

"Precisely, my good man," she replied in a terrible English accent.

Together we walked back to the barn, and I stayed out of the way as she groomed Larry and then put him in his stall for the evening. As difficult as it was, I didn't rush her through the ritual. Despite the temptation to toss her over my shoulder and carry her out of there to hear my news.

Once she'd finished with Larry, she said, "I just need to check my email one last time and grab my bag, and we can head out."

Suppressing a groan, I dutifully followed her up to her office, an excited tension winding my shoulders tight. If I didn't tell her soon, I was at risk of coming apart at the seams. Absently, I touched the inside pocket of my suit jacket where the marked-up plat was neatly folded, waiting on the big reveal.

Everest shut down her computer and reached into her bottom drawer for the utilitarian leather bag she carried. "Ready?" she asked as she rummaged for her keys.

"Actually, there's something I wanted to talk to you about," I said, no longer able to keep the proverbial cat from clawing its way out of the bag.

Her eyes raised from the inside of her bag to meet mine with questions brimming. "I hope it's what I want you to fix for dinner," she said with a wink.

I rounded the corner of her desk and carefully shifted a stack of papers from the center of her desk to the side. Withdrawing the plat from its hiding place, I unfolded it onto her desk blotter and smoothed out the creases. I secured the corners of the paper with her Dolly Parton bobble head and a horseshoe tape dispenser. "It's a little more than dinner," I said.

Everest put her bag on the credenza behind her desk and came to stand next to me. Peering down at her desk, she studied the plat for a few minutes. "What am I looking at, Gideon?"

Suddenly nervous, I cleared my throat. *Why had I just decided to dive into this?* "Well, I know things haven't been going that well in your search for alternates to the Collier property."

With a groan, Everest rubbed a hand over her face. "That's the understatement of the year." She looked up at me with a teasingly menacing glare. "So you decided to do what? Show me what I can't have? Not cool, West."

"Actually," I said, tapping the paper with my finger, "I'm showing you what you *can* have."

Her eyes tracked back to where I was pointing, and she bent down for a closer look. The moment of comprehension reverberated through her posture, like she'd taken a punch. For a long moment, Everest said nothing. She just stared down at her desk. If I'd been tightly wound before, I was now a stringed instrument right before the opening number.

Finally, she straightened to look at me. "Gideon," she said, her voice a little strained, "what *exactly* am I looking at here?"

It wasn't the effusion of excitement I'd expected, but maybe she was just holding back hope until I laid it all out for her. "Well," I said, gesturing to the hatched red lines on the boundary of Second Chance. "I know this was your vision for expansion and that but for Standard buying the property, you would've achieved that vision. Eventually."

I looked over at her, but her expression was inscrutable. Swallowing was difficult, but I managed it. "Once you came up with the suggestion of shifting our focus from new construction to rehabilitation, we no longer needed as much of the Collier property. But we're already committed to its acquisition, which left us trying to figure out what to do with it."

"Uh-huh," Everest said—again, not the reaction I was looking for.

"Well, you see . . ." I smoothed down my tie and smiled, trying to will some of my excitement into her while being thoroughly flummoxed by her lack of reaction. "In the past when we have excess property, or property that isn't usable for our original purpose, we look to donate it. For parks, or greenways, or anything similar. We use the donation to offset the taxable income aspect of the development."

I touched her shoulder. "Only here, we've got this wonderful charity right next door that needs a way to expand its footprint." My palm curved over the slope of her shoulder. "It's a way to solve *both* problems."

chapter thirty

EVEREST

There was a static buzzing sound in my ears, like someone turned off the cable in my brain. This man, this unexpectedly wonderful man was presenting me with precisely what I wanted but couldn't accept. I looked up into his face, which practically radiated with excitement, and a cold, hard lump formed in my stomach. The weight of his hand on my shoulder became leaden, and I shrugged it off. He blinked in surprise as I turned away from him.

"Gideon, I didn't ask you to solve this problem for me," I said to the window. I felt him move behind me and saw the reflection of his hand reaching for me then falling to his side.

He cleared his throat. "Maybe not in so many words. But we've talked about how hard it's been for you to find something else that will work. And now, you don't have to."

"Just like that, huh?"

"Okay, I'm going to admit this conversation isn't going the way I thought it would," Gideon said. "What am I missing here?"

"Last year my dad offered to bankroll my acquisition of the Collier property." I laughed softly. "*Not* of course at the price Standard offered, but enough that it probably would've gotten them to the table to talk seriously about selling."

I turned to face him, leaning against the credenza behind my desk. "I turned him down."

Open-mouthed, Gideon stepped backward and bumped into my desk. "Why on earth would you have done that?"

I couldn't stop the half-smile from lifting one corner of my mouth. "It's almost cute how confused you are right now," I said. "But it just underscores the sad fact that it would never occur to you *why* I couldn't take his money any more than I can let Standard just hand over a portion of the property. No matter how much I'd love to accept it."

"Of course I don't understand it, because it doesn't make any sense, Everest," he said, a hint of irritation in his tone. "Second Chance is a charity, for God's sake. Charities run on donations. Donations like the one *I'm* trying to make."

I tamped down my own frustration because in simple black-and-white terms, what he said made sense. But unfortunately, the world didn't operate in black-and-white but shades of gray colored lighter or darker by people's perceptions. "It doesn't make any sense to you, Gideon, because when you walk into a room, people automatically take you seriously. You don't have to worry about the people—most of whom are men—in that room questioning your right to even be there or judging you based on what color lipstick you're wearing, the hemline of your skirt, or the height of your heels. When you walk into a room, you're walking onto a level playing field. Hell, at this point, you're probably walking onto one skewed in your favor. You've never experienced what it's like for that field to tilt so precariously that you have to fight to simply stay upright."

Gideon ran a hand through his hair and sank heavily onto my desk, resting his hands on his knees. "I'll be honest," he said, voice now devoid of the excited uptick it had when he'd first mentioned the donation. "I don't understand how that has anything to do with what we're talking about."

"Because I'm the one on that tilted field, struggling to hold on to the footing I've gained. When I started Second Chance, I was just Jack Kennedy's daughter with this little passion project. I've had to work hard to change people's view of me and of what I'm doing here with Second Chance. To take me and my organization seriously. Accepting some giant donation from my dad would undercut all that because it wouldn't be seen as a donation from Kennedy Acres to Second Chance but a handout from Jack Kennedy to his little girl. I can't afford to lose the credibility I've built over the last few years."

"What does that have to do with this?" Gideon jabbed at the plat beside him on the desk, sending it sliding to the edge.

"Everything," I said, rising to my feet. "It's a different chapter in the same story. Only instead of my dad giving the handout, it's the man I'm sleeping with."

He flinched at my characterization of what we'd been doing. "I'd like to think by now, Everest, that you can admit there's more here than just sex."

"Whatever you call this thing between us, Gideon, doesn't change the reality of the situation. And that's what this is about. Not what we want the reality to be, or wish it could be, or hope one day it will be. But what it is right now. And right now, if I accept this from you, it torpedoes my integrity as the director of Second Chance, because certain people will say I slept with you to get it," I said.

"That's nonsense, and you know it," Gideon said, crossing his arms over his chest. "What I'm talking about is a legitimate donation from

Standard to Second Chance, not a pile of bills on the nightstand, for God's sake." His brows lowered. "And I've not known you to be a woman who gives a damn what other people think, so I find it hard to believe you're suddenly worried. What's the real reason behind you turning down something we both know you want?"

"My reputation isn't a good enough reason?" I asked, temper rising.

"It would be if it were at real risk from you accepting the donation. Which it isn't," Gideon said. "You know as well as I do that to the extent this donation generates any interest, it's going to be met with glowing reviews. As will you for securing it. This is a win-win for Second Chance and Standard. You know it, I know it, and when it's made public, the whole community will know it." My desk creaked as he shifted his weight, eyes narrowing on me. "Why are you stonewalling me, Everest?"

"I'm not," I insisted, forcing myself to meet his gaze.

Gideon frowned. "You are, but for the life of me, I can't figure out why."

"You seem to have everything else figured out for me," I snapped.

His brows rose. "Care to elaborate on that?"

"There's nothing to elaborate on," I said. "There's really nothing further to discuss, since I've turned down your offer."

"I beg to differ," Gideon said, pushing off my desk and coming to stand in front of me. "You mentioned being on a playing field and how hard it was for you to stay on that field, Everest. What I didn't hear was the mention of any teammates out there with you. You see the game as one you have to play alone without help from anyone. Regardless of how many people are standing on the sidelines eager for you to put them in the field of play. *That's* what this is really about, isn't it? You being forced to let someone join your team and offer a solution to a problem."

The buzzing noise was back with a vengeance, along with a clenching sensation in my chest. "That's ridiculous," I said, pushing the words past the tightness in my throat. "I have a whole staff here that is a part of my team."

"A team that wants to do so much more for you than you'll let them." Gideon smiled down at me, but his eyes were sad. "Just like I do, Everest. You don't have to do this alone. Let me help you. Let me be a part of this with you. Trust in me the same way I trusted your suggestions for Mimosa Grove."

His words, although similar to ones I'd heard countless times from Leroy, hit home in an entirely different way. *Funny how that works when they're said by someone with whom you're in love.* It sounded so easy when he said it. To just let down my guard and trust someone. A partner who could spell me for long enough to let me catch my breath. But that required someone who would be with me. Not occasionally, not on alternating weekends or over video chats. A partner was, as I'd told Cammie and Elektra, someone who was in your life full-time. Which meant that no matter how badly I wanted him to be right about being in this with me, he couldn't be.

"Gideon, I . . ." I couldn't bring myself to say it out loud. I didn't have to, though, because the look in his eyes told me he already knew what I was going to say. But, of course, he didn't let that stop him.

"Just think about it. And once you have, once you're one hundred percent certain of the answer, then you can tell me. Okay?"

"Want me to kill him?"

I looked up from the saddle I'd been mindlessly cleaning for the better part of an hour to find Leroy standing in the doorway of the tack room. I wrinkled my brow in confusion at the greeting. "What?"

He came into the small room and leaned against the roughhewn wood wall. "Gideon. Want me to kill him?"

I dropped the sponge into the bucket at my feet. "Why would I want you to kill Gideon?"

Leroy lifted one shoulder in a careless shrug. "Figure he's got to be the reason you've been moping around this place for the last week like a whipped puppy. Which brings me back to my question. Want me to kill him?"

I laughed for what felt like the first time all week. "I appreciate the offer, but that's wholly unnecessary. And even if it were, I'm afraid I can't afford to lose you for twenty-five to life, Leroy. You're too important around here."

His lips turned down in a deep frown. "Hmph. If he hurt you, it'd be a justifiable homicide."

"He didn't, I promise," I said. Remembering the look in his eyes when he'd left made my shoulders slump. If anyone had been hurt, it had been him. By me.

"Then what's got you looking like someone canceled Christmas?"

I sighed wearily. "It's complicated."

He laughed. "What isn't these days?"

"True," I agreed. "But this is a little different."

"Why is that?"

I leaned a hip against the now shining saddle. "You really want to hear this?"

"You wanna tell me?"

Surprisingly, I did. Only I wasn't sure where to start. "I'd love to tell you," I said. "But I'm sort of at a loss on how to do it so it makes sense."

Leroy pursed his lips and then grinned. "How about I start?"

I couldn't help but laugh. "You start to tell me what's wrong . . . with me?"

At his nod, I thought, *why not?* "Who am I to question your wisdom, Leroy? Let's give it a shot."

He picked up a farrier's file and began turning it over in his hands. "Well, for starters, the boy is in love with you." With a shrewd glance in my direction, he went on, "And you've got it just as bad as he does."

When I started to object, Leroy waved a hand to cut me off. "Please, Evie. It's written all over his face when he looks at you. Hell, when he hears your name, little cartoon hearts start circling above his head." Replacing the file, he crossed his arms and smirked. "Don't think you're any better though. I haven't seen you moon over anything like that since you were five and your daddy gave you your first pony." He put his hands under his chin and batted his eyelashes dramatically with a wistful sigh.

"Maybe I *don't* want to hear this," I said, making him chuckle.

"That's what I know," he said. "What I don't know is what happened last week when he came by here to see you. And left with his tail between his legs about ten minutes before you came down red-eyed and miserable. *Something* happened. I just don't know what."

I blew out a breath, sagging with defeat. "He had this grand plan for Standard to donate some of the Collier acreage to Second Chance as a tax write-off."

Leroy's eyebrows rose, the wrinkles in his forehead resembling freshly tilled earth. "Did he now?"

I nodded. "Had a little survey drawn up and everything."

"Let me guess," Leroy put a hand to his chin, his thumb and forefinger tugging at the corners of his mouth. "You turned him down." I nodded and he frowned. "Why?"

I shifted uncomfortably, unsure how to answer, then settled on dodging the question. "When my dad made that offer to buy it, you supported me telling him no."

"That's an entirely different situation, Evie. That was Jack wanting to give his baby girl something she wanted without thinking about the repercussions of it. How it would set you back if people found out about it. You'd be pulled right back into his shadow when you'd just started to shine on your own."

"Is this really that different?" I asked, hoping he'd say no and I didn't have to continue with the soul-searching I'd been doing since Gideon left.

"You know it is, Evie. Without you and your suggestions about his development, Gideon wouldn't have that acreage to donate in the first place. *You* made that happen, Evie. Your ingenuity is going to make that development something more than it would've been without you."

Almost like you'd partnered with him on it, my conscience annoyingly pointed out. I ignored it.

"I hope you're right, Leroy," I said. "But what does that have to do with him turning around and giving it to me? Doesn't it undermine me as the director to accept something from someone I . . . uh, well, that is, someone who . . ."

"Someone who loves you?" Leroy saved me from further rambling. "Why would that matter when you did the same for him? There is no difference here, Evie. People are allowed to offer to help each other." His brows drew down. "And *you* are allowed to accept it when they do."

He was right. I knew it, he knew it, hell, even the horses knew it. But I still couldn't let go of the fear. That accepting not just what Gideon was offering for Second Chance, but for me as well, would leave me open to so much more heartache once he left. He'd be a part of everything, and yet he wouldn't be here. "Even if he leaves me behind?" I asked.

Leroy's brows were working overdrive, winging up from his stern frown into a surprised arch. "Who says he's going to do that?"

"Geography dictates that, Leroy, since Gideon lives in Boston, not Mimosa."

"Ask him to move," Leroy said, as though it were as simple as asking Gideon to grab the mail on his way into the house.

"I can't do that," I said.

"Yeah, you can. You just open up that mouth and say, 'Gideon, what if you moved to Mimosa?'"

"I *can't* ask him to do that."

Again, Leroy asked, "Why not?"

"I can't ask him to leave his whole life behind for me. That's a change you don't make for someone else. It has to be for yourself."

"How do you know it wouldn't be for him?"

I shook my head, resolute in my belief that I couldn't ask that of Gideon. "There's no way, Leroy. He's built something up there. Something amazing."

"Seems like he's trying to do the same down here," Leroy observed. "Why wouldn't he want to stick around and enjoy it?"

"That's crazy," I said, refusing to even glance at the tiny light of hope Leroy's words had lit within me. "Sure, he might like it in the beginning, but who's to say that will last? I'm not going to be the one he blames for missing opening day at Fenway or some other heralded event because he chose me over Boston. I won't be the reason he upends his entire life." I paused, still thinking of reasons why what Leroy proposed was completely unacceptable. "And anyway, what would he *do* here in Mimosa?"

Leroy regarded me placidly. "What's he doing here now?"

"That's different! There's a project here. Once that's through . . ."

"Once that's through, then what? Isn't one of his reasons for being here because it's such a . . ." He tapped a finger to his lips. "What were the words he used? 'Burgeoning area of development'? If that's true, then why couldn't he continue doing what he does from here?"

"Because . . ." I shook my head, dodging the question. "That's not the real point anyway. The real point is that it's unfair for me to ask him to do that."

"Why?"

My heart twisted guiltily. "Because I couldn't do the same for him." As I'd said to Cammie, I couldn't ask Gideon to do something for me I couldn't do for him. It wasn't fair.

"Hmph," Leroy said dismissively. "Love isn't about tradeoffs, Everest. It's not a tit-for-tat or quid-pro-quo situation. There's no tally sheet keeping score of who did what for whom. It's about giving what you can when you can to make the other person happy."

His brown eyes warmed when he smiled. "And that boy wants to make you happy. All you've got to do is let him."

chapter thirty—one

GIDEON

Where are the reports on the Waterville project?" I snarled through my open door without looking up from the spreadsheets taking up the majority of my desk.

"In your email where they have been since yesterday afternoon," Davidson said.

My head snapped up to see him lounging in my doorway, holding what appeared to be a rolled-up set of plans. I returned my gaze to the papers on my desk. "What are you doing here?"

Davidson came all the way into the room, closing the door behind him and dropping into the chair across from me. "I'm trying to figure out how to remove whatever has crawled all the way up your ass so you'll stop acting like a petulant toddler."

Without looking up, I said, "I don't have time for your bullshit, Davidson. I've got work to do."

He didn't move, just sat there tapping the papers against his knee in an annoying rat-a-tat-tat. The sound grated along my eardrums until

I couldn't take it any longer. I yanked off my reading glasses and threw them onto my desk. "What?" I bit out.

Davidson didn't even flinch, just reached down to flick an imaginary piece of lint from his immaculate trousers. "This partnership works, Gideon, because the three of us have assigned personality roles."

"What the fuc—"

"Those roles," Davidson continued over my outburst, "have been established since grad school and were honed while we were junior executives making other people lots of money. Now that we are captains of our own destiny, making ourselves pots of money, those roles are set in stone and are not to be changed."

There was a knock on my door, and before I could answer, Davidson said, "Come in."

Jamie opened the door and took the seat next to Davidson. "Am I late?"

What was happening? "Late for what?" I asked.

Ignoring me, Davidson answered Jamie. "No, as usual, your timing is impeccable. I was just telling Gideon here that the role of 'brutish asshat who yells without thinking' has already been taken. By you."

Jamie shrugged good-naturedly. "If the tailored suit fits."

"As though it were made just for you," Davidson said. Turning back to me, he said, "Which means, Gideon, that it's not open for you to step into. No matter how badly you've seemed to want to this last week."

My shoulders rounded into a guilty hunch over my behavior since flying back last Friday. I knew I'd been a dick but couldn't bring myself to care. Because I'd heard zip from Everest. Not a text, not a call, nothing. Granted, I was in a sorrow stew of my own making, since I'd told her to consider my offer and reach out when she was ready. But that didn't make it suck any less to check my phone every five minutes or scramble to pick it up anytime it vibrated. An ESPN alert had almost given me a heart attack.

I shook off the guilt and glowered at Davidson. "What's your point?"

Jamie and Davidson heaved matching sighs, then Davidson said, "My point, you jackass, is that you need to get your head out of your ass and fix your fuck up with Everest so we can all get back to normal around here." He pointed a finger at me. "*You're* not the asshole in this trio. You're the charmer, the salesman, the schmoozer. You're the one we send in to seal the deal, man. Start acting like it."

Unable to help myself, I asked, "What does that make you?"

Davidson tapped the plans on my desk and rose to his feet. "I'm glad you asked that, because it leads nicely into what I've brought to show you."

"Show me?"

With a flourish, Davidson unfurled the plans over the paperwork strewn across the surface of the desk. "Davidson, I'm not in the moo—"

"You haven't been in the mood to do anything but bitch and moan since you got back here. That stops now. Based on the minimal details you shared, somehow you found a way to screw things up." He glanced across my desk at Jamie. "We're here to help unscrew this to the extent possible. Starting with this," he stabbed a finger into the center of the plan.

Rolling my chair forward, I peered down. Then blinked. Then blinked again. Still uncertain of what I was seeing, I grabbed my reading glasses and adjusted them down on my nose. I recognized it as one of my favorite buildings in downtown Mimosa, the one with the blue door and broad front windows—although to my knowledge, there wasn't a Standard Development crest anywhere on those windows like there was in this drawing. After scanning over the sketch once again, I sat back and looked at Davidson. "When did you put this together?"

He grinned down at me. "Over the last few weeks, after you started raving rapturously about 'bones' of the buildings. These came in this morning. Hot off the presses."

"What do you think, Gids?" Jamie asked.

"I . . ." I swallowed hard. "I'm not sure what to think. It's . . . I'm . . ." I couldn't string words together to form a sentence, because I was so taken off guard by what they'd put together in my absence. My head couldn't wrap around what I was seeing, even though it was all there in black-and-white.

"Obviously, it's not a done deal," said Davidson. "But given how well we think Mimosa is going to do, it makes sense to have a satellite location. It gives us more accessibility to that development and a foothold in the area. The growth potential down there is massive, and we need to get in on it while we can. We'd have to take it to a vote, and this one, as you know, would have to be unanimous. Meaning, if you're not on board, it dies a quick death."

Again, the two of them shared a knowing look. "But," Davidson continued, "we had a pretty high degree of confidence you'd be supportive of this plan."

"What better way to show your girl you're in this for the long haul than by showing up with a moving truck?" Jamie asked with a laugh.

"Talk about grand gestures," Davidson said.

"How did you . . ." I couldn't finish the question, still overwhelmed by the proposition that I'd be in Mimosa full-time.

Taking in my dumbfounded expression, Davidson rested a hand on my shoulder. "Gids, c'mon, man. This project is practically on autopilot at this point. There's no need for you to be down there on a regular basis until we start construction. And yet"—he grinned at me—"you're there more than you are here. And when you're here, it's obvious you'd rather be there. Plus, you wanted her to see you as a real partner, right? Someone by her side in the trenches?" He arched a brow. "By her side doesn't mean over Zoom, man. It means right next to her every single day."

The concept of it felt very . . . *right*. How had I not considered this option? I'd been agonizing over how to make Everest see I was absolutely serious about making things work between us long-term. There was nothing that would convince her more quickly than packing my bags and putting down roots in her town.

"Gideon's the last one to know, yet again," Jamie said with a laugh.

"Always," Davidson said, joining his laughter. "Take whatever time you need to consider it, Gids. No rush. But seriously, get back into your lane, man. No need for Jamie to start acting like even more of an asshole to reclaim his territory."

I laughed. "I'll do my best."

Rapping his knuckles on my desk, Davidson started to walk to the door with Jamie following.

"Davidson?" I called out. He turned, raising a brow at me. "You never said what your role was."

He scoffed, tugging at his lapel. "How you don't know the answer to that is beyond me." One finger tapped his temple, and he winked. "Obviously, I'm the brains of this operation. The mastermind of our little domain, if you will. The wisest man in all the—"

I waved a hand, laughing, "Okay, okay, I get it. You're brilliant."

With a finger gun in my direction, he said, "Precisely."

"Hey, guys," I called, and they both stopped and looked at me.

"Thanks," I said, knowing the simple word didn't convey everything it should.

At the look on my face, Jamie shoved Davidson ahead of him, "Run, man, before he suggests a group hug." But he shot me a wink and a thumbs-up on their way out the door.

chapter thirty-two

EVEREST

There was a line four deep at the counter when I walked into Mean Muggin'. Elektra gave me the quickest of head jerks to let me know she'd seen me and would get my order when she broke free of the rush. I settled into the wing chair by the window to wait.

It had been a long two weeks since Gideon asked me to think about his offer. I'd reached for the phone at least a thousand times, even pulled up his number. But until I knew what to say to him, there was no reason to call just to say hi. And, despite thinking about it constantly, I remained at a loss.

"Evie," Aunt Betsy called, and I looked up. She was waving to me from a nearby table. I waved back and walked over to give her a hug.

"Hey," I said, giving into her warm embrace.

"Hey yourself," she said with one final squeeze. "Haven't seen you in a while."

"Yeah, I know," I said with a remorseful smile. "You know how it is." I took the chair across from her, keeping an eye on Elektra. She was still swamped, so I knew it would be a bit before my order was up.

"If you'd come around and see me more often, I would," she teased. With a surreptitious glance at Mrs. Hazelton's table, she added, "I've got to hear about your love life from the gossip mongers instead of from you."

My heart wrenched at the thought of Gideon. "Don't believe everything you hear," I said.

She frowned and stirred her coffee, pinning me with "the look," one honed by years of mothering her unruly boys—and me, to some extent. It was one that brooked no argument and required nothing less than the truth. I squirmed under it.

"I should think," she said, tapping her spoon against the rim of her cup and setting it to the side, "that you would've told me how serious things have gotten between the two of you." Her head tilted and she smiled, "Especially given this latest development."

Ignoring the reprimand, I squinted in confusion at her. "Latest development?"

Betsy blinked at me in surprise. "Well, yes. Gideon called me about it the other day, and I was so excited! His idea to revise the plans to include a . . ." At the stunned look on my face, her voice tapered off, and she looked perplexed. "Gideon didn't tell you?"

My heart lurched in my chest. He hadn't told me because I hadn't called him. What was the change? Was he going ahead with the donation to Second Chance, or had he changed his mind and not told me? The uncertainty—and that it resulted from my own stubbornness—made my lungs seize in panic. The reality of what I'd done crystalized in that moment. I was a complete and utter moron. *I* was the one failing to reach back for him, not the other way around. He'd been reaching for me the whole time, only to have his hand batted away. And yet he continued to reach. At least, he had, until I'd gone radio silent. *Shit!*

I forced down the crazy and took in a breath to say, "I'm sorry, Aunt Betsy. I have no idea what you're talking about."

Her eyes went wide, and her mouth fell into a tiny 'O.' "You don't?"

I shook my head, pulse thundering in my ears. "No, ma'am. Afraid I don't."

Betsy fidgeted with her coffee cup, turning it to and fro in the saucer without saying anything.

I wanted to shake her until her teeth rattled and the secret poured out of her. I was at once dying to know and terrified to hear. "Want to fill me in?"

"Evie, I don't know that I sh—"

"Everest!" Elektra called from the counter, "Order's up!"

I glanced over and then back at Betsy, dying for my caffeine fix but also freaking out over whatever it was Betsy knew that I didn't.

When I didn't move, Betsy said, "Go get your coffee, honey. Don't want it to get cold."

Grudgingly, I left the table and walked to the counter. I'd just picked up my latte when my phone dinged in my back pocket. Pulling it free, I made a little "eep" at the sight of a text from Gideon.

Hastily, I swiped to read it.

Gideon: Time's up, sweetheart. I'm back in town and this time I'm not leaving until you give me an answer. Today.

With nervous fingers, I responded.

Everest: When and where?

Bubbles appeared, and I chewed my lip watching them.

Gideon: Know the building with the blue door and bay window on Main Street?

A vacant building? I dithered for a millisecond then gave myself a mental slap to the face. Delay and vacillation had gotten me absolutely nothing.

Everest: Yeah.

Bubbles again.

Gideon: I'll be there at noon. Don't be late.

I typed in *"Sounds good"* and debated for a full minute whether to say anything more. Anything like "Can't wait" or "Missed you" or what I really wanted to say: "Love you." Deciding to leave well enough alone, I said nothing and hit send, tucking my phone back into my pocket.

Remembering Aunt Betsy, I looked back over to her table, but she was already gone.

At 11:59, I pulled into the parking space in front of the blue door. Gideon's rental car was already there. Nerves danced through me like a hive of bees as I got out of the car. Heart in my throat, I pushed open the blue door. "Gideon?" I called into the empty space.

"Back here, Everest," he replied, and I ventured further inside until I found him around the corner.

Standing behind a piece of plywood balanced between two sawhorses, he was the most handsome thing I'd ever seen. Wearing jeans and a T-shirt instead of his normal suit, he sported another unusual feature: a beard. Or at least a few days' worth of stubble. I'd never seen him anything other than clean-shaven, so the shadow of hair along his sharp jawline was a surprise. A surprise that did unexpected things to my lady bits. He looked *good* with some scruff.

"Hi," I said, my voice coming out in a squeak. I coughed. "Sorry, not sure what that was." *Yes, you do,* my ovaries said in a naughty whisper. Ignoring them, I focused on Gideon, who was smiling at me.

"Hey, sweetheart," he said, and I loved the sound of it. The way it rolled off his lips and hit me right in the chest. It did wonders to calm the raging sea of emotions currently occupying my insides.

Tearing my eyes away from him, I looked down at the makeshift table. The space was littered with paperwork. Papers and plats and sketches covered the surface. "What's all this?" I asked.

"This," he said, sweeping a hand over the table, "is unashamedly designed to influence your answer. I'll let you choose where to start."

"Gideon, about that," I said, hating the nervous tremor in my voice. "I don't think I need . . ."

"To answer any question," he interrupted, "you need to see all the facts." He tapped the table. "Here are the facts, Everest. Ready and waiting for your review. But"—he grinned at me—"since I know you like to have a say in things, I'll let you choose where to start."

The nerves were back, tingling up my spine and down my arms. "Okay, so how do I choose?"

"Left side or right side," he answered, and I shook my head, failing to grasp what he meant. With his left hand, he touched the left side of the table. "Left side." He repeated the movement with his right hand. "Right side."

It was then that I noticed the documents spread out before me were loosely arranged in two groups on either side of the table. They all looked the same to me, so I said, "Uh, right side?"

"Is that your final answer?" Gideon asked in a game show voice.

Laughing, I nodded, which made him grin in return. "I was hoping you'd say that. Come join me over here, if you will."

I walked over to his side of the table and stood next to him, looking down at the papers.

Gideon pinned a large drawing with one finger. "Start here," he said, and I leaned closer, looking at what he was pointing to.

My eyes came back to his. "Is this"—I pointed to the drawing then extended my arms to indicate the space we were standing in—"this?"

"One in the same," he confirmed.

"Why are we looking at plans for this space?"

"Look closer," he instructed, and I obeyed, reading over the various blocks, legends, and markings on the plat until I came to one in particular. My eyes locked in on it, and my blood turned heavy in my veins until I could hear the thud of my pulse in my ears. I stared until my vision blurred then blinked and looked some more.

"Is this . . ." My voice shook, so I stopped, swallowed, then tried again. "Am I reading this right?"

"If by 'right,' you mean are you reading the part where it identifies this building as the future southeastern headquarters of Standard Development, then yes, Everest, you certainly are reading this right."

The thud in my ears grew louder, and I gripped the table, unable to look at Gideon. "You're opening an office here? In Mimosa?"

"We are."

I risked a look at him and found him smiling down at me, excitement glittering in his blue eyes. I swallowed again, the exercise requiring more effort this time. "If there's an office here, that means there has to be someone to run that office, right?"

"It does," he said and put a hand on my lower back, his touch warm and gentle.

"And that someone would be . . ."

The hand at my back slid to my hip, pulling me to Gideon's side. "Who do you want it to be, Everest?"

Leroy's words played through my head: *Ask him to stay.*

"That choice isn't mine to make, Gideon." I forced out the words in a tight voice.

His fingers tightened on my hip. "Isn't it?"

Slowly, I turned to look at him, meeting his deep blue gaze. "It's your choice, not mine, Gideon."

Hurt flashed in his eyes. "You don't want me to stay?"

More than anything in the entire world. "I can't ask you to make that kind of sacrifice fo—"

"Sacrifice?" he interrupted. "What in the hell are you talking about, Everest?" His vehemence ricocheted around us.

I licked my lips then said, "Gideon, I've seen where you live. The life you have in Boston. What you'd be giving up to move here. There's no way I could expect you to choose me over any of that. It's not a fair trade-off."

He blinked down at me in disbelief. "Trade-off? Everest, I . . ." Gideon sank onto the makeshift table, papers crinkling underneath him. "You really don't get it, do you?"

"Get what?"

When he looked at me, his eyes blazed with an intensity that could've melted steel. He scraped a hand over his jaw and laughed.

"What's funny?" I asked.

His arm snaked around me and pulled me between his knees. My hands flew to his chest automatically. With both hands at my waist, his fingers splayed out over my hips. On a deep inhale, he closed his eyes, opening them with the release of breath.

"What's funny, Everest, is the idea that anyone in their right mind would consider the opportunity of a life with you as any sort of sacrifice. That anything I have in Boston compares even in the slightest with what I have here with you."

A kaleidoscope of butterflies released inside my chest at his words. "But don't you want—"

His fingers tightened their hold on me. "What I *want*, Everest, is you. For today, tomorrow, next week, next year, the entire next millennium. I. Want. You. For as long as you'll have me, wherever you'll have me. You're what I want, Everest. You."

The butterflies took flight and soared. "You do?"

"Yes, you maddening woman," he said on a laugh. "Now, *tell me* who you think should run this office."

Unable to resist temptation, I tapped a finger to my lips. "You know, I really think Jamie and I had something in Boston. Maybe he should . . ." At Gideon's growl, I laughed and threw my arms around his neck, planting a kiss on his mouth that answered his question in every possible way.

But when we broke apart, just to make sure there was nothing left unsaid, I confirmed, "You, Gideon West. I want you to stay with me here in Mimosa. For as long as you'll have me, I want you with me."

He growled again and pulled me in for another kiss, long and leisurely, deep and thorough until I could no longer feel my legs. When he lifted his head, I sighed with pleasure.

"Don't make that noise," he said, his voice deep and rough.

"Why not?"

His hands moved downward over my ass and squeezed. "Because then you'll miss what's on the left side of the table, since I'll toss you over my shoulder and take you back to my house so you can make that noise again and again and again."

My body pulsed in response to his threat. "Must be one helluva thing on the left side to top what's happened so far *and* interrupt your plans to ravage me."

With effort, he spun me away from him and over to the left side of the table. "See for yourself."

I stood at the edge of the table, and Gideon came up behind me, resting his hands at my hips. There was less on this side, just a smaller stack of papers and another plat. The plat drew my attention first, because it looked familiar. Tugging it closer, I stared down at it. Sure enough, it was the same one he'd shown me two weeks ago. Except . . . the boundary line for Second Chance was different once again. In the earlier version it extended farther over to the . . .

"Turns out we decided not to give *all* of the land to charity," he said. "The director of the one we chose is a real hard-ass, so the terms of that donation are going to take a little more work." Moving to my side, he looked at me, blue eyes warm and earnest. "But I'll be here to negotiate terms with her for as long as it takes."

I laughed. "That sounds more appealing than you'd think."

He smiled, the dimple winking on with full power. "But since she *did* dally around with the whole thing, we decided to carve out a piece of the acreage to do something for the town of Mimosa too. Especially since *someone* showed me how special this place is. But"—he tapped the plat in my hand—"I think you'll approve of the change we made."

My eyes moved to the newly surveyed area. In its center were block letters spelling out "Moira Kennedy Memorial Park."

There was no holding back tears any longer. Fat, wet drops hit the paper, blurring the words. I couldn't speak, couldn't find the words to tell him what this meant to me. What *he* meant to me for doing it. As it turned out, I didn't have to, because he did it for me.

"It's the best thing for that property, for the town, for you . . ." He turned me to face him, cupping my jaw in his hands and wiping the tears from my cheeks. "It's the best thing for us, for our home."

I hiccupped on a happy sob, sniffling and burying my face against his chest. On a ragged breath, I blinked up at him. "She would've loved you. You know?"

He waggled his brows at me. "What's not to love?"

And when he dipped his head to kiss me, I couldn't think of a single thing not to love about the man who would give up so much to give me everything I wanted.

GIDEON

C'mon, Smoky," I pleaded with the little gray terror. The diminutive horse cocked its head to the side and snorted, stamping its front hooves.

I knew what that meant. Loosely translated, it was, "Uh-uh, no way, no how, ain't gonna happen."

"Smoky, little buddy," I said, stepping a little closer, "I need this. You've got to come through for me. Don't you want to make our Everest happy?"

More snorting and head tossing let me know that Smoky Joe, the skinny little runt I'd helped Everest rescue last spring, did not give one single solitary crap about making *anyone* happy. One day before I died, I would learn that grand gestures are best left to the movies. They do not belong in real life, because without fail, something in real life will intervene, interfere, or more likely downright ruin your grand gesture. *Because real life isn't scripted, nor are there multiple takes to get everything just right.*

Case in point. I'd thought it would be a fantastic idea to propose to Everest in the field where we first met. After six months of work, that field was now in the process of becoming the park I'd promised her. Perfect backdrop, right? Well, not if you factor in the gigantic concrete pipes we'd had to haul in for drainage issues and the even larger grading equipment that had been brought in to level out portions of the land. So, not romantic. Not romantic at all.

Choice two had been to pop the question on a swan boat in Boston. Yes, yes, I know it's cliché and has been done to death, but that's what we did on our first trip together. So, again, *romance*! Well, between starting the new office and supervising construction at Mimosa Grove, and Everest getting twelve new rescues from a hoarding situation in Tennessee, the chances of us finding a free weekend to fly up to Boston was between slim and none, and slim was in the bathroom.

Which left me with choice three. Why not employ the baby horse I'd helped rescue? We'd saved him from starvation, nursed him to health, and given him the best life he could have. C'mon, it doesn't get more romantic than that, right? Unless the useless little cretin had gone from a cute little baby to demon spawn. Spoiler alert—Smoky Joe was demon spawn. Worse than that, he was currently demon spawn with a four-carat diamond set in a platinum band clipped loosely to his halter. And did I mention he'd managed to slip from the lead rope and was now loose in the largest pasture at Second Chance?

Let me back up and set the scene for you a little more clearly. I've wanted to marry this girl since the first derisive flip of her ponytail in my direction. Okay, that might be a little bit of a stretch. But in all seriousness, I can't remember not wanting her in my life, so that's probably why it's difficult for me to pinpoint the precise moment in time I knew I wanted to marry her. That being said, our proposal story needed to be epic. I'm talking McDreamy and Meredith level shit here. What? It's a good show. Shonda Rhimes is a freaking genius.

Which is how I came up with the idea to showcase both my developing equine skills and Smoky's budding ability to take direction. I'd been working in secret with the little bugger in the evenings on getting him used to wearing a halter, being groomed, understanding the purpose of a lead rope wasn't to drag someone halfway around the farm . . . you know, simple stuff. I figured we were both starting from the ground up, so she would be equally impressed with each of us. I'd lead him around, show off everything he'd learned that *I'd* taught, and then, when I passed him off to her—clip on the diamond ring and be on one knee when she turned around shocked, awed, and completely besotted with her devoted and newly minted fiancé. I mean, c'mon! How awesome would that be?

And it would've been. Except that I'd jumped the gun a bit on Smoky Joe's preparedness to participate in the life-altering event. If we're being honest here, I'd grossly overestimated his abilities. Things had been fine at first. He'd docilely allowed me to slide the halter over his nose and had followed me out of the barn without complaint. Not so much as a whicker of displeasure. We'd made a few wide rounds in the pasture, changing direction, testing out a little trot and coming to a full stop.

So, like a moron, I decided to give it a go with the diamond attached. Seemed reasonable enough to me to do a run through to make sure the ring would fasten onto the halter. Why I hadn't thought to check that when the halter was *hanging in the tack room*, I couldn't tell you. It had been fine until Smoky Joe spotted an opening. Specifically, when I was sliding the ring box back into my pocket and not giving him my full attention. The little bastard juked to the left then wheeled to the right, jerking the lead from my hand and almost skipping with joy at my astonished expression. I could almost hear him singing, "Free, free, free at last!" as he sidestepped and shimmied away from me.

Sheer, unadulterated panic gripped me at the prospect of the perfect engagement ring clinging tenuously to the halter of a deranged equine psychopath who was currently trying to escape to live the life of a free-range mustang. Knowing that the more terrified I sounded, the more hyped up he would get, I did my best to keep my voice level and calm.

"Easy, there, you little jerk," I said softly. "Steady boy, steady," I purred as I sidled closer to him. Each step I took, he parried, and I swear he smiled when he did it. I held out a tentative hand. "C'mon, boy," I begged, "there's a good fellow. Just let me get the diamond, and then you can wreak all the havoc you want."

Smoky Joe paused in his prancing and looked at me curiously, nostrils quivering and eyes bright with mischief. I edged closer and he didn't move. Inch by inch, I slid my feet through the grass, crooning to him to hold still. The sparkly bauble clipped to the buckle of his halter was almost in my grasp. One more step and I could grab the clip *and* the ring and end this whole nightmare.

"Good boy," I praised right as we locked eyes. In that instant, I knew I'd been played. You may disagree, but I'm telling you, the little shit smirked at me. As in, "I've got you now, sucker!" Before I could even blink, with the grace of Misty Copeland and the speed of a Triple Crown winner, Smoky Joe pivoted sharply and raced through the gap I'd unwittingly created between myself and the fence.

Temporarily stunned, I stood there and watched him canter away without looking back, secure in his triumph over my dumb ass. My legs recovered before the rest of me, and I gave chase, for all the good it did. I was no match for his speed and soon lost sight of him as he crested a hill. The saving grace was he was headed toward the barn, which gave me a better chance of catching him than if he'd headed into the woods in the other direction. I prayed the ring would still be attached if and when I finally caught up to him.

After what felt like an eternity, with legs pumping, arms churning, and lungs burning, I stumble-ran into the paddock at the back of the barn. I spotted Smoky at the rail . . . with Everest holding his halter.

EVEREST

God, what I wouldn't give for an hour-long soak in my clawfoot tub with a huge glass of wine. I stretched and rolled my shoulders, trying to dislodge the tension that had crept up as the day wore on. Leroy and I had spent the day with Doc Barnes and the new herd of rescues that had arrived a few weeks ago. None of them were accustomed to the human touch, so it had been a struggle to get them all checked out. But we'd managed it, and the last of them had just been let out to graze in the waning twilight.

I hung up the last of the lead ropes and clicked off the light in the tack room. Walking out the back of the barn, I inhaled a deep breath of crisp air. Sawdust mixed with freshly turned earth and the ever-present scent of horses greeted my nose. I leaned against the fence and marveled at how much things had changed in a year, the biggest being Gideon West's arrival and subsequent permanence in Mimosa . . . and in my heart. The thought of him brought a smile to my lips. Maybe I could convince him to join me in the tub. That thought had other places smiling in anticipation.

The sound of rapid hoofbeats brought me out of my dirty daydream. Looking out past the gate, I saw Smoky Joe come over the hill at top speed. Startled by his being in this pasture instead of in the barn with his mama, I hurried to open the gate and intercept him. As he got closer, I realized he was wearing a halter, and a lead rope alternated between flapping behind him and bouncing off the ground next to him.

Terrified it would get snagged and send him tumbling, I fought the urge to rush toward him, knowing that would only send him careening in the other direction. Thankfully, I had a few peppermint treats in a baggie that were left over from that afternoon's vet visit. Knowing the little gray's love for the treats, I kept my steps slow and measured, holding the bag out to the side and giving it a gentle shake. As expected, Smoky zeroed in on the bag and came straight toward it.

When he was close enough, I grabbed the lead rope with my free hand. While he munched on the crunchy treats, I gave him a quick once-over. He didn't look hurt or any worse for wear. I led him over to the fence, a little surprised by how easily he came with me. While we'd been working with him off and on, Smoky Joe wasn't the easiest of students when it came to simple tasks or commands. In all honesty, he was a gigantic pain in the ass. His docile compliance with a slight tug on the lead was unexpected.

As was what happened next. His ears swiveled back toward the direction he'd come then he twisted his head to look behind him. He whinnied slightly, then louder, as if to say, "Hey, there you are!" I followed the direction of Smoky's gaze, and my mouth fell open. Coming toward us at a full but pained sprint was Gideon. Smoky chuffled again at the sight of him, adding to the bizarre scene. What was going on?

Keeping a tight hold on Smoky's lead, I circled him around, and together we waited for Gideon to reach us. To his credit, at the sight of Smoky, he slowed down to a fast shuffle instead of a dead run. His jeans were filthy, and one of his sleeves had a tear in it.

"Gideon, what . . ." My voice trailed off because I wasn't sure what to ask. I had zero idea why he would've been in the back pasture . . . with Smoky Joe. At least, I assumed he'd been back there. It was the only explanation, no matter how illogical it seemed.

Gideon stopped a few feet away from us, resting his hands on his knees and drawing in heaving gulps of air.

I walked a little closer to him. "Are you all right?" I asked.

He nodded and stood up, hands going to his hips. "I'm fine," he wheezed. Nodding to Smoky, he asked, "Is he okay?"

I stroked the little horse's soft muzzle. "He seems to be."

"Good, good," he said and came toward us, dropping a kiss on my cheek then going around to the other side of Smoky.

"What is going on?" I asked, thoroughly perplexed.

Gideon made some adjustment to Smoky's halter and muttered under his breath. It sounded something like, "Oh, sweet Christ, thank God it's still here."

If I'd been confused before, now I was positively baffled. "Gideon?" I prompted, and he looked sheepishly over at me.

"I know this looks . . . odd," he said.

"To say the least," I replied. "What were you doing? And why was Smoky with you?"

He rubbed the back of his neck and nervously toed the dirt in front of him.

Smoky nuzzled Gideon's chest, and he absently ruffled his forelock. "You just couldn't keep it together, could you?" Gideon muttered, presumably to the horse.

"Keep what together?" I asked. "Gideon, what in the world is—"

A flash, or really a sparkle, from Gideon's pinky finger distracted me. I looked closer at his hand resting on Smoky's head. There was something on his finger.

"*What* is that?" I asked and pointed at his hand.

He looked at where I was pointing and swore under his breath. "Guess that makes two of us who can't keep our shit together," he said to Smoky, who whickered softly in what sounded like agreement.

Using the hand I hadn't pointed at, he took Smoky's lead from me and looped it over the top rail of the fence, securing it in a loose knot.

Turning back to face me, he looked positively miserable, which made me incredibly uneasy. Gideon miserable was reserved for rare occasions, like if the Patriots lost in the playoffs or some other travesty struck.

"What's wrong?" I asked, frightened of the answer.

"This," he said and held out what had to be the most gorgeous diamond ring I'd ever seen. Not just in real life, I mean *ever*. It was a cushion cut stone in a platinum setting and was big enough to have its own zip code. Hell, maybe even its own gravitational pull. If the moon had crashed down to earth because of the size of the thing, I wouldn't have been surprised. I couldn't speak, couldn't move, couldn't *swallow* as I stared at it. How that ring could be the source of anything bad, I had no clue.

Finally, I found a semblance of my voice and squeaked out, "What is that?"

"It's your engagement ring," he said disgustedly.

"My what?" My voice was so high, bats should've dipped down following the sonar signals.

"Your engagement ring," Gideon said again.

"I didn't know I had an engagement ring," I said dumbly.

"Well, you don't," he said. "I mean, you didn't . . . at least you wouldn't have until I gave it to you. Which I was practicing for with Smoky Joe."

I think the size and sparkle of the diamond mesmerized me, or the light reflecting off it lasered my brain to mush, because I couldn't stop staring at it. And, I was having a hard time following what in the hell Gideon was talking about. So, I asked, "Practicing?"

Gideon nodded, somehow in full control of his faculties and able to carry on a normal conversation despite the fact he was holding a piece of compressed carbon that could've sent the planet into a different orbit. "Yes," he said morosely. "I've had it for a few months and was planning the perfect proposal. One we could have written about in the *Times* and that our kids would tell their kids about. Only . . . I didn't account for my accomplice in the whole thing fucking it up quite so royally."

I started to hyperventilate but only slightly. "Kids?" I asked in a voice that sounded like mine but also sounded really far away.

Unaware of my fading consciousness, Gideon nodded, "Yeah, our kids. Their parents would've had the most romantic of proposal stories. And they could've regaled their friends with it."

That snapped me out of my ring-induced hyperventilation. "Uh, Gideon, I don't think that's really a thing," I said slowly.

His blue eyes snapped to mine. "Sure, it is!"

I shook my head. "No, I'm pretty sure it's not a thing." He drew back, ready to argue his point, so I changed tactics. "But let's say that it is," I said soothingly. "What would it have been? Just so I know."

Gideon looked positively deflated when he said, "I was going to attach it to Smoky's halter and impress you with all the training I've given him and—"

"Wait," I interrupted. "What do you mean *training?*"

He pouted adorably and said, "I've been working with him every night for the past month or so. On grooming and obeying a lead rope, stuff like that."

"You have?" I asked, my heart expanding at the idea of Gideon "training" Smoky "Pain in the Ass" Joe in secret. "When?"

"You know how I've been working late a few nights here and there?" he asked.

"Yeah," I said.

"Well, I have been, just not at the office. I've been here, working with Smoky."

Something cracked open in my chest, came loose, and spilled out a torrent of feelings. This man had come into my life and turned it upside down, sideways, and backward, and I couldn't love him more for it.

"You have?" I asked, fighting to hold back tears.

Gideon nodded. "Yeah, and it was going to be perfect, you know? The best way to show you how much you mean to me. How lucky I am you chose me to be your man. That you've shown me the best version of myself. That because of you, I'm finally the man that I want to be. And now, thanks to this little turd"—he gave Smoky a begrudgingly affectionate pat—"it's all been ruined."

Dear God, I loved this idiotic man. "Gideon," I said. "Do you really think there's a better way to show me all of that than by leaving your life completely behind, uprooting your entire existence, *creating a whole new arm of your company*, and moving here just so I could continue to pursue my dream?"

He tilted his chin as though that thought hadn't really occurred to him. I couldn't stifle the laugh that bubbled up. "Gideon, why on God's green earth would you think you needed to do anything more than you've already done?"

Gideon looked bemused by my question. "Well, I . . . I just thought that you . . . that I . . . that we . . ."

I held up a hand before he brought in the rest of the population of Mimosa. "I take it back," I said. "There is one thing that you haven't managed to do yet."

"There is?" he asked.

I nodded. "You haven't actually asked me anything."

The grin that stretched over his handsome face was almost as breathtaking as the ring. And trust me . . . that ring was *freaking amazing*! "I suppose that's true," he said while dropping down to one knee right there in the dirt of the barnyard.

"May I ask you a personal question?" he asked in a decent impression of Cary Grant.

Channeling my inner Grace Kelly, I said, "I've been hoping you would."

When he reached for my hand, I couldn't hold back the tears that spilled onto my cheeks. My hand trembled in his as he slid the ring onto the tip of my ring finger.

"Everest Alexandra Kennedy, will you do me the honor and make me the happiest man on the face of this entire planet and be my wife?"

"The entire planet, huh?" I asked with a watery smile.

"Well, it just seemed blasé to only include the contiguous forty-eight states," he teased as he slid the ring farther down my finger.

"We're not telling the children you used the word contiguous in the proposal," I said as the ring bumped over my knuckle.

"Funny," he said. "I definitely thought you'd excerpt the word 'turd.'"

As the ring reached the spot it would stay for the rest of my life—and after, because this thing was going to the freaking grave with me—I knew there was no snippet, portion, part, or element of our story that I would ever omit.

www.ingramcontent.com/pod-product-compliance
Lightning Source LLC
Chambersburg PA
CBHW051502150726
47997CB00001B/85